PENGUIN BOOKS

THE PORTABLE SWIFT

Each volume in The Viking Portable Library either presents a representative selection from the works of a single outstanding writer or offers a comprehensive anthology on a special subject. Averaging 700 pages in length and designed for compactness and readability, these books fill a need not met by other compilations. All are edited by distinguished authorities, who have written introductory essays and included much other helpful material.

"The Viking Portables have done more for good reading and good writers than anything that has come along since I can remember."

—Arthur Mizener

Some Volumes in
THE VIKING PORTABLE LIBRARY

THE PORTABLE
SWIFT

Edited, and with
an *Introduction*,
by CARL VAN DOREN

PENGUIN BOOKS

Penguin Books Ltd, Harmondsworth,
Middlesex, England
Penguin Books, 625 Madison Avenue,
New York, New York 10022, U.S.A.
Penguin Books Australia Ltd, Ringwood,
Victoria, Australia
Penguin Books Canada Limited, 2801 John Street,
Markham, Ontario, Canada L3R 1B4
Penguin Books (N.Z.) Ltd. 182–190 Wairau Road,
Auckland 10, New Zealand

First published in the United States of America by The Viking Press 1948
Paperbound edition published 1956
Reprinted 1959, 1960, 1961, 1963 (twice), 1964, 1966, 1967, 1968,
1969, 1973, 1974, 1975
Published in Penguin Books 1977
Reprinted 1978

LIBRARY OF CONGRESS CATALOGING IN PUBLICATION DATA
Swift, Jonathan, 1667–1745.
The portable Swift.
Bibliography: p. 49
I. Title.
[PR3722.V3 1977]   828'.5'08   77-7644
ISBN 0 14 015.037 4

Printed in the United States of America by
Kingsport Press, Inc., Kingsport, Tennessee
Set in Linotype Caledonia

Contents

v

Editor's Introduction

JONATHAN SWIFT, for most of his readers round the earth, survives as the author of one book. But that is one of the three most widely known English books, all of them written in the half-century when English literature began to use the prose still used in the present age. They are so familiar that none of them is commonly called by its correct title. John Bunyan's *The Pilgrim's Progress from this World to that which is to come* (1678) has become *Pilgrim's Progress* in customary speech. Daniel Defoe's *The Life and Strange Surprizing Adventures of Robinson Crusoe, of York, Mariner* (1719) is now merely *Robinson Crusoe*. Few readers are even aware that what they call *Gulliver's Travels* is properly *Travels into Several Remote Nations of the World . . . By Captain Lemuel Gulliver* (1726). All three of these books are thought of as primarily books for children, and are so often read in abridged versions in childhood that many older readers do not even know they have read only the simple plots within the total works. Each of the books is both a story and a commentary on human life: the story for everybody, the commentary for anybody who reflects on the plight and fate of men.

If the story in each of these books is only the core of the whole, so each book is only the core of the whole work of the author, each of whom wrote many books besides his most renowned masterpiece. As *Gulliver's Travels* is more than the bare story, so is Swift more than

Gulliver's Travels alone. The book is the essence of his mind and art, but it cannot be fully understood without some knowledge of his activities as clergyman, politician, lover, friend, satirist, wit, and poet, and of the dominating, pervading qualities of his powerful, troubled, restless spirit. Gulliver among the pygmies, the giants, the pedants, or the horses was hardly more extraordinary than Swift among the people of Ireland and England in his day.

An extraordinary man, with a boundless appetite for power, must master or please ordinary men, or else go hungry. Swift was born without the rank or fortune which are such a man's natural advantages. Worse, Swift was born without the hide of brass and bowels of iron which would have been nearly as good for him as rank and fortune. He could not climb without caring what he set his feet on. He could not take snubs and kicks and stabs as incidental, but had quick, ungovernable impulses to strike back. No man is so extraordinary that he can, starting below his fellows, scramble past all of them without a stubborn, insolent devotion to the main path. Swift was not single-minded enough to master his world.[1]

Nor would Swift rise, as some men do, by pleasing. To wriggle far, he would have had to be more supple than he was. Even in an age when it was still barely a disgrace to court a lord, Swift could not court one long. He was more ready to bully than to flatter. He used a winter speech in the most comfortable summers. Above all, he had no zeal to please, and was half ashamed when he pleased, as if he were a tragedian who had raised a laugh. This was not his part. This was for mountebanks.

---

[1] This Introduction draws freely on Carl Van Doren's *Swift* (Viking, 1930); included also in *The Portable Carl Van Doren* (Viking, 1945).

Nothing about Swift was more extraordinary than his blindness to the part which he played so well while he was failing in the one on which he had fixed his desire. Still in his twenties, or just out of them, he raged because he had no chance to command. Yet in those same years he flung off prose satire such as no Englishman had ever written before, and such as no Englishman but Swift ever wrote again. In London, scheming to rule among the Whigs or Tories, half winning, and then disappointed after his spell of power, Swift, almost without effort or concern, ruled the wits. In Ireland, where he thought of himself as a despairing exile, he wrote pamphlets that are monuments, poems that added to poetry what was almost a new species. He wrote his *Travels* in a vain fury of revenge, and entertained the world. On the other side of every failure was a triumph.

On the other side of all his hatreds were loves. Swift was a misanthropist, but he is famous for his friendships. He shrank from women, but he made two women famous. He detested Ireland, but he has the eternal affection of the Irish. He loathed the human race, but he has been a delight to it for two centuries. It was his extraordinary fortune to draw an interest of love from a principal of hate.

No doubt Swift should have measured his gifts more exactly and should have put himself into fitting roles, like any ordinary man of talent. But Swift was outside the shrewd discipline of talent. He could not sit down and write prose and verse as if they were sufficient ends. Prose and verse were the weapons he found in his fists, scarcely realizing how they came there. He used them in his tragic role, in the war of his ambition, not because he valued them, but because they were the only weapons he had. After he had lost his war and had given it up as hopeless when he was only forty-five, Swift would never again allow himself to be consoled. He would not see that he had been winning, and still was winning, a great war while he was losing a small one. His pride blinded him.

A few years reverse many verdicts. While Swift was still alive, king of Ireland but pretending to be king of triflers, he had good reasons for foreseeing the true verdict upon him. In the long run, he might have guessed, he would be remembered for what he had written before he even tried the world, or for what he had written and done in Ireland, after he had bitterly renounced his expectations. What he had thought his glorious episode, the years with Oxford and Bolingbroke, would look a little shabby. In time Swift would seem to have been most splendid when he had been most himself, and not the satellite of politicians.

Still, Swift might also have understood—if he had been without his blindness—that simple formulas would not explain him. To do what he had done he had needed the blind obsession of his will. What had raised Swift, scattered and random as most of his writing was, to the first rank among writers, was the high reach of his pride, the magnificence of his scorn. He had won the war in which he hardly noticed he was fighting because he had fought with so much passion in a war which was not worth it. It was his passion that mattered, and not his long illusion. Nature cares no more whether prose or verse is produced in illusion than it cares whether children are begotten in moods of unreason.

Unsurpassed in directness, Swift is one of the most personal of writers. There is autobiography in almost every line he wrote: not too often the facts of his life, but always the pulse and color of his temper. This is apparent in his later recollections of his restless youth in Ireland, at Kilkenny School and at Trinity College;

it is unmistakable in the letters and poems and satires
he wrote during his years from twenty-two to thirty-two,
of which he spent seven as half dependent, half secretary in the household of Sir William Temple, retired
English diplomat, at Moor Park in Surrey. Having written some conventional Pindaric odes which pleased no
one, Swift at twenty-four angrily renounced the "visionary power" of his Muse:

> And since thy essence on thy breath depends,
> Thus with a puff the whole delusion ends.

Instead he turned to satire, in another poem, and put his
trust in

> My hate, whose lash just heaven had long decreed
> Shall on a day make sin and folly bleed.

The character of his first satires was determined by
his circumstances. Living a little out of the world, in
Temple's suave realm, Swift had come to despise the
buzzing wits and upstart scientists who, he thought, infested the moral and intellectual life of the times.
Though Dryden was one of the wits and Newton one of
the scientists, Swift did not particularly distinguish
among them. His hate was no more disposed to scrupulous justice than another man's love. Temple, involved
in a current dispute over the relative merits of the
Ancients and Moderns, decided, like a gentleman, for
the past and dismissed the present. Swift, superficially
like Temple but fundamentally like himself, agreed. He
took the superiority of the Ancients for granted, with
nothing but contempt for any Modern who doubted it.
The contemporary world of learning Swift assumed to
be made up almost altogether of mean, starved, envious,
strident, stingless fools and fops, ignorant and arrogant,
who swarmed about their betters with a fly's equal in-

clination to dung or honey. But whereas Temple surveyed the contest in a smooth, stately exposition, Swift
turned it into burlesque comedy. The Ancients and Moderns of his *Battle of the Books* were personified as actual
warriors, brawling "on Friday last" in the King's library.
The spokesman of the Moderns was a venomous spider,
of the Ancients a bee praising sweetness and light.

In *A Tale of a Tub* Swift actively declared a war. This
satire was like a tub thrown by seamen to a whale to
keep it off the ship. Let the yelping wits and empty
scholars butt and tumble the satire instead of harming
the commonwealth. The *Tale* did not trouble to complete the allegory of Peter (St. Peter) and Martin
(Luther) and Jack (John Calvin), the three brothers who
stood for the Church of Rome, the Church of England,
and the Dissenting Churches. The allegory, satirizing the
abuses of religion, made up no more than a third of the
satire. The digressions were the larger and more varied
part. It was Swift's duty, as a clergyman, to defend his
Church by cutting down its enemies. He was ruthless
with the quibbles of theology, fanaticism, superstition,
priestly greed and imposture. But he felt a more seasoned malice when he turned aside to prune and lop
among the charlatans of wit whom he regarded as his
own enemies, and whom he ridiculed by the contemptuous device of praising them. Yet they were for him, at
most, annoying creatures that he studied briefly before
he trod on them. They roused only his irritation. His
hate, which after preliminary years of brooding had
found a language natural to it, was for human life at
large. Happiness was only "a perpetual possession of
being well deceived." Credulity, he satirically argued,
is better than curiosity, and it is better to accept the
surfaces of life with the senses than to inquire deeper
with the reason. "Last week I saw a woman flayed, and

you will hardly believe how much it altered her person for the worse." The "sublime and refined point of felicity" was the "serene, peaceful state of being a fool among knaves."

The two satires were probably written in 1696–97. When they were published in 1704, mankind did not mind. Fools did not read Swift. Wise men were only confirmed in their wisdom. The wits were delighted. But the *Tale* offended powerful prelates. Though it was published with guarded anonymity, and Swift never publicly acknowledged it, after a scuffle of ascriptions it settled down at his door. From that time on he was suspected, within his Church, of irreverence—or, as he phrased it, "the sin of wit."

This was certain to affect Swift's career, since the Church was his profession and his support. "I look upon myself, in the capacity of a clergyman," he wrote in his *Reflections on Religion*, "to be one appointed by Providence for defending a post assigned to me, and for gaining over as many enemies as I can. Although I think my cause is just, yet one great motive is my submitting to the pleasure of Providence, and to the laws of my country." This was the attitude not of a saint but of a soldier. Swift was always militant in his defense of the rights of the Church, and he never forgot, among the statesmen with whom he worked or among the wits with whom he played, that he was a clergyman; and he never let them forget it.

For eleven years after Temple's death in 1699 Swift lived in Ireland, sometimes in his rural parsonage at Laracor, more often in lodgings in Dublin, with visits to London where he watched the course of politics or relaxed with a few friends. Something in him kept him from more than brief satisfactions. Content to be a clergyman, he could not wait to become a bishop. Untroubled by debts, he longed for a fortune. A scholar, a clergyman, and a wit, he cared little for the company of his fellows. He could be at ease only among the great, and even there he did not lend himself wholly to their purposes. He stood solitary on the peak of his nature, his scornful eyes raking mankind.

So far as he was ever happy, it was with Joseph Addison, who was five years younger than Swift, but more precocious, and already established in the favor of the Whig ministers. The two wits became acquainted in February 1708, and were immediately friends. Addison called Swift "the most agreeable companion, the truest friend, and the greatest genius of his age." Swift thought that Addison had wit, charm, learning, virtue, "worth enough to give reputation to an age." Swift contributed to the *Tatler* and *Spectator*, and Addison persuaded Swift to revise his poem *Baucis and Philemon*. Too proud to be stubborn about his verses, Swift, as he loosely said, let Addison "blot out fourscore, add fourscore, and alter fourscore" of the lines. The poem suffered, but Swift did not. He would, and did, write more smoothly if it was pleasing to Addison, who was Swift's first equal friend. When Addison went to Ireland as chief secretary, with a salary of two thousand pounds a year, Swift, still without promotion or much hope, felt no envy, and was delighted for Ireland as well as for Addison.

So far as Swift was ever at peace during those waiting years, it was with Esther Johnson, whom he made famous by the name of Stella. She also had been a member of Temple's household at Moor Park, the daughter of a former steward whose widow was companion to Temple's sister. Stella was eight when Swift first met her. He took an early interest in directing the books she read, taught her to write, and came to depend upon comforts which only she could give him in those restive years: admiration without analysis, affection without exigence, a child's obedience, a child's worship. The attachment between them increased and deepened. After Swift left Moor Park for Ireland Stella soon followed him, on his advice. The reasons he gave for this were that living was cheaper in Ireland, and Stella's fortune, a legacy from Temple, was small. Stella never gave any reasons. She was barely twenty when she went to Ireland, in the company of another Temple dependent, an older woman named Rebecca Dingley. At first the venture looked, as Swift said, "like a frolic," and there was some talk, but this was soon quieted by the unwaveringly circumspect behavior of the two friends. Stella and Mrs. (that is, Miss) Dingley lived ordinarily in lodgings with their own servants. When Swift was at Laracor they lived in a cottage not far away. When he was in lodgings in Dublin they lodged elsewhere in the town. Only, it seems, during his absences did they economize by living in the vicarage at Laracor or in his Dublin lodgings. No one knew that Swift made Stella an allowance of fifty pounds a year. He almost never saw her in the morning, and never, it is said, in the afternoon or evening without at least a third person present.

If Stella and Swift were ever married, as gossip long ago asserted and some recent investigators believe, it was only privately, without license or record, when Swift was Dean of St. Patrick's. It was a marriage in name only, and it was without a name in public. Of the innumerable conjectures why Swift and Stella were never avowedly married, not one is better than a guess. "If my fortunes and humour served me to think of that state," Swift wrote in April 1704, he would have chosen Stella "among all persons on earth" for a wife, "because I never saw that person whose conversation I absolutely valued but hers." He preferred friendship with her to marriage. She preferred friendship with him to marriage with anybody else. Not a surviving syllable from Stella tells whether she knew of any barrier between her and Swift except the cold sword of his will, or whether she struggled against fitting herself to the place he made for her, or whether she felt bitterness or regret. She knew that Swift's devotion was partly his pride admiring itself in her as in its glass. He trusted her judgment, which was a bright reflection of his own. He took her advice, which was colored by what she deftly guessed to be his inclination. But she was no such replica in dough as might have bored him. She was witty and lively, talked back to him, was charmingly perverse when he convinced her of her errors, and would not permit him to have a maid or housekeeper "with a tolerable face."

Because Swift, after Stella's death, destroyed all her letters to him, and all his to her except one he apparently missed and those of the famous *Journal to Stella,* she hardly lives except in his words about her. But in the *Journal,* written from September 2, 1710, to June 6, 1713, many revealing as well as tantalizing lights fall incidentally on her character and tastes. Stella was the person in whom Swift chose to confide most in his days of power. She was the kind of person to whom Swift could write such letters, so candid, so vigorous, so unforgettable.

Swift went to London in September 1710 on a special mission for what was called the First Fruits. Queen Anne, devoted to the Church, had given up her right to any clergyman's first year's profit from an ecclesiastical benefice in England. The Irish Church hoped she would extend the same bounty to Ireland. The *Journal to Stella* speaks often of Swift's lobbying for this cause. But it was soon lost in the larger issues which absorbed him. The Whig ministers Swift had formerly looked to were falling out of power. The Tory Henry St. John (later Viscount Bolingbroke) had become Secretary of State. The Tory Robert Harley (later Earl of Oxford) had become first minister, as Chancellor of the Exchequer. "Every Whig in great office," Swift exultantly wrote to Stella on September 9, "will, to a man, be infallibly put out; and we shall have such a winter as has not been seen in England." Swift had never been entirely a Whig, as he was not now entirely a Tory. He was a churchman, and the Tories promptly won from the Queen the grant of the Irish First Fruits. Swift, now courted by Harley, began to think *A Tale of a Tub* would no longer be held against its author, and that at last he might have a place among the masters of the kingdom.

Harley, in fact no more concerned about the bounty of the First Fruits than about the orthodoxy of the *Tub,* had set out to seduce the most lively and deadly wit in England. At the price of a thousand pounds a year, cut out of the Queen's income, Swift would be a bargain for her minister. Nor would Swift be required to argue for principles he did not believe in. The Tories were, it was easy for Swift to think, more truly than the Whigs the party of order in Church and State. The Whigs had accused him of being a Tory. Then he would be a Tory. It was enough for Swift, as it had been enough when he took holy orders, that he was assigned a post in a cause which he thought good. He gave to the cause all his passion, intensity, genius.

When Swift closed with Harley there commenced a chapter singular in English history. No other man of affairs has ever made such use of a man of letters. At the outset Harley so misgauged his pamphleteer that after three months he could send him a banknote for fifty pounds. It was as if the squire had tipped the bishop.

Swift was furious at "both the thing and the manner."
He returned the money, refused to dine with Harley the
next day, and demanded satisfaction. "If we let these
great ministers pretend too much," he wrote to Stella,
"there will be no governing them." A week later, still un-
reconciled, he went to the lobby of the House of Commons, found Harley, and sent him into the House to call
St. John, "to let him know I would not dine with him if
he dined late." The Chancellor of the Exchequer, soon
to be Lord Treasurer, ran the errand to the Secretary
of State for the vicar of Laracor. The next day Swift told
Stella he had "taken Mr. Harley into favour again."

On Saturday of that week Swift was asked to dine
with Harley along with St. John and Simon Harcourt,
now Lord Keeper, and he became a member of the
group which, meeting every Saturday except when the
Queen was at Windsor, informally concerted the government. Together they planned the steps that were to be
taken to oust the Whigs, to get rid of the Duke of Marlborough, to bring about the peace. The ministers de-
vised the necessary intrigues. It was left to Swift to
master and direct public opinion with the *Examiner* and
with the pamphlets and lampoons with which he entertained, infuriated, aroused, and reassured the public.

The political situation was intricate in detail but simple in outline. King William, Prince of Orange, had involved his adoptive England with his native Holland
in the Grand Alliance with Austria against France. There
had for years been a war and there was still a war, of
which some of the English were very tired. The victories
of Marlborough abroad, though gratifying, were hardly
as regular as the taxes at home. The landowners, generally Tories, had begun to wonder whether they were
not paying taxes to help the bankers and jobbers, generally Whigs, reap enviable profits. Glory was something,

but it cost money. Men muttered in country houses that the Duke had been riding his whirlwind a long time. They had noted that Godolphin, who as Lord Treasurer had furnished the war chest, was father to one of Marlborough's sons-in-law; and that Sunderland, Secretary of State, was a son-in-law himself. They had noted, also, that the Duchess of Marlborough, Mistress of the Robes, and, it was said, mistress of Godolphin, did more than anybody else to make up the Queen's mind for her. Civil affairs, hardly less than military, were in the hands of Marlborough, who notoriously wanted to be Captain-General for life. A little more, and England would be mortgaged to the Marlboroughs.

Such a prospect ruffled and alarmed the Tories. Marlborough, veering like Godolphin with the parliamentary wind, had formerly called himself a Tory, but now called himself a Whig. The Whigs must share the blame for the prolongation of the war, for the increase in taxes and prices. All that was insular in England resisted this burden laid upon it for the possible benefit of the Continent. The Whigs had been kind to the Dissenters to gain their support in Marlborough's enterprises. All that was orthodox in England resented this comfort given to the sects which threatened the unity and authority of the Church. Finding itself on the dizzy brink of altruism and liberalism, England shrank back in a passion for its good old virtues, its stout old order.

The change had not come of itself or from the disinterested conclusions of philosophers, but had been contrived and forwarded by Harley and St. John. Both of them had owed much to Marlborough, who in 1704 had approved of Harley for Secretary of State and of St. John for Secretary at War. Under the wings of that eagle they had plotted against his feathers. St. John had gifts of eloquence and manipulation which made him incompa-

rable in the House of Commons. Harley, enough duller
than his colleague to be more widely trusted, was adroit
on the backstairs. Through his cousin Abigail Hill (Mrs.
Masham), for whom the Duchess of Marlborough, also a
cousin to the lady, had obtained a post in the Queen's
bedchamber, his whispers reached his sovereign. Marlborough and Godolphin, becoming aware of a secret influence against them, had in 1708 traced it to Harley
and had forced him out of the cabinet, along with St.
John. Harley had continued to whisper. The Queen, re-
senting the constant pressure from the Duke and Duchess, observing the popular unrest, and still listening to
the whispers, had been convinced that the Whigs threatened the peace of the State and the safety of the Church.
From this had come the overthrow of the Godolphin
ministry and the sudden rise to power of the Tories under the whispering Harley and the glittering St. John.
It was policy to win to their side the wit whom they
most desired to have with them and most feared to have
against them.

The arguments put forth may have been suggested
by any of the three men. Of the three, however, only
Swift can be credited with the high scorn, the grave
ingenuity of their polemic. It was he who, though he
thought Marlborough "as covetous as hell and ambitious
as the prince of it," kept his friends from pressing the
Duke too hard. Swift had the tact to be content with
pointing out how much it was to the interest of the com-
mander-in-chief to have the war go on. Public cynicism
might be trusted to do the rest.

Nor did Swift use only arguments. He hit upon the
most insidious illustrations, such as his contrast between
the rewards of a Roman conqueror and those of the
Duke. British ingratitude, Swift figured out, had already
been worth something over half a million pounds to the

British general. Roman gratitude, "which a victorious
general received after his return from the most glorious
expedition, conquered some great kingdom, brought the
king himself, his family and nobles to adorn the triumph
in chains, and made the kingdom either a Roman province, or at best a poor depending state, in humble alliance
to that empire," would have amounted to less than a
thousand pounds: incense, a sacrificial bull, an embroidered garment, a statue, a trophy, copper medals, a triumphal arch and car, and a laurel crown worth twopence.

Ingenious and insistent, Swift continued to pluck the
same string until the public could hear no other note
when it heard of Marlborough. After a year Marlborough
fell, and the Duke of Ormond, whom Swift ranked next
to Oxford (lately Harley) and Bolingbroke (lately St.
John) among his friends, was put in command of the
armies.

Toward the Whigs at large Swift turned an attention
which was no less masterly. They were, for him, only a
brawling faction, hungry for profits, and not more than
a tenth of England. The Whigs, having made their
fortunes at the expense of the majority, meant to go on
making other fortunes, and would stop at no lying, no
plotting, no uprising, no overthrowing which might
serve their factious ends. At the same time, Swift would
not admit that he was partisan. "We are unhappily
divided into two parties," he said, "both which pretend
a mighty zeal for our religion and government, only they
disagree about the means. The evils we must fence
against are, on one side, fanaticism and infidelity in religion, and anarchy, under the name of a commonwealth,
in government; on the other side, popery, slavery, and
the Pretender from France." Between these two extremes of Whig and Tory, Swift seemed to take his stand.

Or rather, again, above both. He was still a clergyman, who put religion first among his concerns. He was not a politician, but the conscience of politicians. He was the conscience of England, tight in its island, deep in its prejudices, contemptuous of ideals and metaphysics, plain, sturdy, obstinate.

No position was so natural for Swift to take, as no position was so effective with the voters. Oxford and Bolingbroke might work out of sight with their intrigues. Swift never ceased to keep the eyes of the world upon their main purposes. British purposes, for the sake of British interests, through the exercise of British virtues. The Revolution was achieved. The Succession was established. It was time now to make peace with the Continent and to settle down to a British destiny. The change must not be too precipitate. Swift wrote as firmly against the ferocious Tories, demanding all places instantly for their party, as against the ousted Whigs. His variety was in his art, not in his argument. He could abuse, ridicule, hoax, lampoon, in grim prose or easy verse. He could parade the accomplishments of the Ministry in sober pamphlets or could raise clouds of bright dust to hoodwink the Opposition. But always he was Swift, looking down from his peak at the whole race of mankind, only incidentally and temporarily supporting Oxford and Bolingbroke.

Throughout the Oxford administration Swift was loyal, less out of need than out of love. When his associates, disregarding the Grand Alliance, made a stealthy treaty of peace with France; when, insecure in the House of Lords, Oxford got the Queen to create a dozen Tory peers who would know why they were peers; when England, at the Treaty of Utrecht, took the largest share of the spoils though she had tricked and abandoned the allies: even then Swift loved his friends. Passionately loyal, he could be affectionately blind.

In Oxford's thick skin Swift saw a stoic dignity, and in Oxford's procrastination something not too far from a noble patience. "Regular in life," Swift described the Lord Treasurer to the Archbishop of Dublin, "with a true sense of religion, an excellent scholar and a good divine, of a very mild and affable disposition, intrepid in his notions and indefatigable in business, an utter despiser of money for himself yet frugal, perhaps to an extremity, for the public." Nor about Bolingbroke, libertine in thought and habit, would Swift be squeamish. He admired that "graceful, amiable person" and that mind "which was adorned with the choicest gifts that God hath yet thought fit to bestow upon the children of men." It was true that the Secretary had been "too great and criminal a pursuer" of pleasures which could "by no means be reconciled to religion or morals." But, Swift explained, "he was fond of mixing pleasure with business, and of being esteemed excellent at both; upon which account he had a great respect for the characters of Alcibiades and Petronius." Could Socrates resist the charm of Alcibiades, or Seneca the charm of Petronius?

Swift, moralist that he was, was little less susceptible to the dissolute Secretary than to the decorous Treasurer. His affection covered them with its flood. Bolingbroke hated Oxford, and Oxford suspected Bolingbroke. There was harmony between them only for a few months, if so long as that. Yet Swift, by nature so misanthropic, by experience so wary, set out with them in what he thought was a fellowship of love.

Though he learned better, he remained, to the end of his great episode, somewhat at the mercy of his love. It was, of course, the corollary of his hate. Hitherto alone

with his pride in what seemed to him a prison, he had
been able to hate all those whose neglect had kept him
there. Such companions as Stella and Addison had been
only alleviating visitors. But now half the circle of his
enemies had turned friends and had entreated him to
help them. They had taken him, apparently, to their
hearts. They had let him, apparently, into their minds.
They had given him a tiger's share not only in the battle
but in the command. Swift was so exultant at being delivered from his prison that he did not notice that he had
been brought out to be harnessed.

Oxford and Bolingbroke must have smiled at his generous tribute to their virtues. They did not trouble themselves over the excess of Swift's affection any more than
they minded his arrogance. They were men of the stormy
world, determined to get places and keep them. They
worked for profit. If Swift worked for love or hate, that
was his business. He was not, perhaps, as indispensable
as the backstairs Mrs. Masham, but he could hurt the
Whigs. They gave him all the room they could spare and
applauded his blows.

Loving too much, Swift hated too much, as in his attack on the Earl of Wharton. "He is," Swift said, "without the sense of shame or glory as some men are without
the sense of smelling; and therefore a good name to him
is no more than a precious ointment would be to those."
There was, Swift insisted, nothing personal in his remarks. "Whoever were to describe the nature of a ser-
pent, a wolf, a crocodile, or a fox must be understood
to do it for the sake of others, without any personal love
or hatred of the animals themselves." Nor would Wharton take it personally. "When these papers are public 'tis
odds but he will tell me, as he once did upon a like occasion, that 'he is damnably mauled,' and then with the
easiest transition in the world ask about the weather or

time of the day." And in fact, when Swift encountered Wharton at White's chocolate house after the character was published, "Lord Wharton saw me at the door, and I saw him but took no notice and was going away, but he came through the crowd, called after me, and asked me how I did."

This was, as Swift said, "not a humour put on to serve a turn or keep a countenance, not arising from the consciousness of his innocence or any grandeur of mind, but the mere unaffected bent of his nature." Yet few moralists could have carried themselves more justly under such abuse. Wharton needed no philosophy in the circumstances. Experience was enough to tell him that Swift, accusing him of so finished, so universal a villainy, had blamed him for what was remarkably near a virtue. The victim himself looked brilliant in this glare of wrath. Swift's hate, in its white-hot excess, had grown creative and had shaped a monster which had an insolent animal beauty along with its human vices.

But not all of Swift's victims had Wharton's whistling unconcern. There was the Duchess of Somerset, the red-haired Mistress of the Robes after the Marlboroughs had gone from Court. She had disliked Swift before he joined the Tories, and decided that he was "a man of no principle, either of honour or religion." Swift, knowing this, perversely circulated a lampoon in which he called her "Carrots" and brought up the old charge that she had connived in the assassination of her second husband. The Duchess, who though she had reached a third husband at fifteen had had no other for nearly thirty years, never forgave Swift. More than any of his enemies, more than the Archbishop of York, John Sharpe, who inflexibly held the *Tale of a Tub* against Swift, she stood between him and the favor of the Queen. He might serve the ministers as only he could, but he could not become a bishop without the Queen's approval. That, while the angry Duchess lived, he could not get. And the Duchess outlived the Queen.

More love than he needed, more hate than he needed: these were what hampered Swift in politics. He was impatient of craft, of what he called "refinements." "Whatever may be thought or practised by profound politicians, they will hardly be able to convince the reasonable part of mankind that the most plain, short, easy, safe, and lawful way to any good end is not more eligible than one directly contrary in some or all of these qualities. I have been frequently assured by great ministers that politics were nothing but common sense; which, as it was the only true thing they spoke, so it was the only thing they could have wished I should not believe." Swift did believe it. His whole instinct was to frame clear policies and go the straight way to work with them. In this he resembled statesmen of the first rank. But he lacked what statesmen of the first rank have, the touch of dispassion in his passion. He trusted his friends more than they deserved, because they were his friends. He worried and tore his enemies, even when nothing was to be gained by it, because they were his enemies. Zealous for order in the State, he could not keep order in himself. He had the excess and disproportion of genius.

Nor did his defects reduce him merely to the second rank of statesmen. They reduced him to the third. In the second were Oxford and Bolingbroke. They were neither clear in their policies nor straightforward in their methods, but they had the patience of guile, the persistence of selfishness, the pliability of talent. Moreover, they were men of rank and fortune, and they were in office. If at first they were afraid of Swift, and then came to treasure his virtues, they also found that they could, by dividing his love and hate, rule him. After his hate had sent him out against their enemies, his love brought him back to their leash. Let him hold himself to be their conscience. They knew how to deal with consciences.

Throughout 1711 and most of 1712 Swift worked too hard and too exultantly to have much time for hopes. He wrote often to Stella of his return to Ireland. Ormond might give him an addition to Laracor. He might get a Dublin parish. He said his highest ambition was "to live in England and with a competency to support me with honour." It was nearly enough to be able to advance his friends. The ministers declared that Swift never came to them without a Whig in his sleeve.

But by the third winter of his power he had begun to starve on his diet of promises. The rumor that he had been made Dean of Wells, when he had not, fretted him. The deaneries of Ely and Lichfield were vacant to no advantage of his. The Ministry must, he grumbled through the winter, do something for him or he would go back to Laracor. In January 1713 he wrote to Oxford: "I most humbly beg leave to inform your Lordship that the dean of Wells died this morning at one o'clock. I entirely submit my poor fortunes to your Lordship." And Bolingbroke wrote to Swift with a rhythmic unction: "Though I have not seen you I did not fail to write to Lord Treasurer. *Non tua res agitur,* dear Jonathan. It is the Treasurer's cause; it is my cause; it is every man's cause who is embarked in our bottom. Depend upon it that I never will neglect any opportunity of showing that true esteem, that sincere affection and honest friendship for you which fill the breast of your faithful servant."

It was a ministerial vow. That same month the bishopric of Hereford was filled, but not by Swift. In April, when the Treaty of Utrecht had at last been signed and Swift considered his work done, there were vacant preferments on every tree: in England the deaneries of

Wells, Ely, and Lichfield and the canonry of Windsor; in Ireland the bishoprics of Raphoe and Dromore. Not one of them fell to Swift. Oxford shuffled. Bolingbroke had Swift to dinner. The Archbishop of York shook his head. The Duchess of Somerset hissed. The Queen held out. She would not have Swift a dean or canon in England, or a bishop anywhere. Help came from the Duke of Ormond. If the present Dean of St. Patrick's in Dublin might be made Bishop of Dromore, Swift could have that deanery. The Queen consented.

Oxford suddenly became eager to keep Swift in England. Let him be Prebendary of Windsor. "Thus," wrote Swift, "he perplexes things. I expect neither. But I confess, as much as I love England, I am so angry at this treatment that if I had my choice I would rather have St. Patrick's." The appointment was patched up, and Swift became, as he was to be for the rest of his life, the Dean of St. Patrick's.

"All that the Court or Ministry did for me was to let me choose my station in the country where I am banished." He was not even allowed to become Historiographer, to chronicle the reign which he no longer influenced.

This was the career and this the climax of Swift's life among the great. After a summer in Ireland he was, it is true, called back to London for the fourth and last winter of the Ministry, but his own future was settled, and his time was chiefly taken up with keeping the peace between Oxford and Bolingbroke. They were, it seemed to Swift, "a ship's crew quarrelling in a storm, or while their enemies are within gunshot." The fellowship of love had ceased to exist even for Swift's loyal eyes.

The victors were wrangling over the spoils. What about their futures? The Queen would not live forever. The Elector of Hanover, upon whom the Succession had been fixed, was certain to be favourable to the Whigs. Both Oxford and Bolingbroke, both secretly, were dealing with the Pretender in France, willing to ruin the Succession if they could bring in a prince favorable to Tories. Meanwhile the mutinous Bolingbroke had determined to be first minister himself. Out-intriguing Oxford, he won Oxford's cousin, now Lady Masham, to another allegiance. London and Windsor buzzed and rumbled. All winter and all spring Swift struggled to divert or pacify the wranglers. Their war went on. Swift, despairing, took to a dull, angry retreat in Berkshire. In July 1714 Oxford was forced to break the white staff of his office. Bolingbroke, however, did not supplant him. In five days the Queen died. The Whiggish Elector was to become George I. Marlborough, returning from the Continent, entered London with two hundred men on horseback, drums, and fifty coaches.

Swift, in a letter to Oxford, said farewell to such power as he had had. "In your public capacity," he told him, "you have often angered me to the heart, but as a private man, never once. . . . Will you give me leave to say how I would desire to stand in your memory: as one who was truly sensible of the honour you did him, though he was too proud to be vain upon it; as one who was neither assuming, officious, nor teasing, who never wilfully misrepresented persons or facts to you, nor consulted his passions when he gave a character; and lastly, as one whose indiscretions proceeded altogether from a weak head, and not an ill heart? I will add one thing more, which is the highest compliment I can make: that I was never afraid of offending you, nor am I now in any pain for the manner I write to you in. I have said enough; and, like one at your levee, having made my bow, I shrink back into the crowd."

During his final winter in England, Swift turned from

his temporary friends, the men of politics and fashion, to his true and lasting friends, the men of wit. They were John Arbuthnot, the Queen's physician, and the rising young poets John Gay and Alexander Pope. All of them met Saturday evenings at Arbuthnot's rooms in St. James's Palace, where the Scriblerus Club, as they called themselves, plotted a burlesque biography which was to ridicule false learning.

Oxford had called Swift Dr. Martin, "because martin is a sort of a swallow, and so is a swift." From that had come the name of Martin Scriblerus, a phantom pedant whose career the Club was to trace through all his foolish blunders. The leader seems to have been Arbuthnot. "To talk of Martin in any hands but yours," Swift wrote to him, "is folly. You every day give better hints than all of us together could do in a twelvemonth." Arbuthnot wrote the history of Martin's youth and education so wittily that Sterne later pilfered from it for his history of Tristram Shandy. Pope, hunting among contemporary poets for examples of bathos, "the art of sinking in poetry," took the first step in his war upon the dunces in *The Dunciad*. Swift was to exhibit Martin on his bungling travels through the world. But the death of Queen Anne and the end of the Harley Ministry scattered the Scriblerus Club and put a stop to all work on Martin's travels. Swift in September 1714 went back to Ireland, beaten and bitter, to what for several years was a sullen if not desperate exile.

His early years in this Irish retreat were disturbed by another woman who loved him and whom he made famous by the name of Vanessa. Swift had met Esther Vanhomrigh in London in 1708 when she was twenty and he twice her age. She lived there with her widowed mother and a sister. At first she was merely a moody girl in a household he often visited, but after his return to

London two years later she fell in love with him and told him so. Though Swift seems never to have responded fully to her passion, he could not resist its flattering warmth. While he went on pouring out his heart, or most of it, to Stella in his *Journal,* he went on seeing Vanessa and letting her pour out her heart, all of it, to him. The course of their early history is told, with substantial accuracy, in Swift's fine poem *Cadenus and Vanessa,* written probably late in 1713. In the poem Cadenus (*Decanus,* dean) is Vanessa's tutor. When Vanessa declares her love, he replies with talk of friendship. She says that she has already learned from him about friendship, and now he can learn from her about love. Here the poem breaks off with deliberate inconclusiveness. What Swift had handled lightly, as in a comedy, was a tragedy for Vanessa. She spent the rest of her life trying to get out of the poem and nearer to the poet.

When Swift returned to Ireland in 1714, Vanessa, now orphaned, and her sister soon followed him and lived first in Dublin, then at Celbridge, a dozen miles away. It was no longer possible for Swift to see her so easily as in London. The Dean of St. Patrick's was a conspicuous man. He had in Stella a friend who was his frequent and expected companion. The situation was much as if Stella had been his wife and Vanessa his mistress. Vanessa reproached him for seeing her so little. He replied: "I ever feared the tattle of this nasty town, and told you so; and that I would see you seldom when you were in Ireland. . . . These are accidents in life that are necessary and must be submitted to; and tattle, by the help of discretion, will wear off." Here he discouraged her, and yet seemed to hold out hope for the future. He would neither take her nor let her go. This relation between them persisted for eight years. A kind word from him, and she was wild with joy. " 'Tis not in the power of art, time, or accident to lessen the unexpressible passion which I have for —— —— ——," she wrote in 1720, careful not to name him for fear her letter might fall into other hands. In the summer of 1722 he wrote her three letters (included in this collection) which sound cold enough, but which showed her how often he thought of her and remembered their past days together. With this the story breaks off. Vanessa died the following June, leaving *Cadenus and Vanessa* to be published under a cloud of gossip, which is all gossip.

Stella the extraordinary wife. Vanessa the extraordinary mistress. Swift the extraordinary husband and lover. No other terms will bound the extraordinary triangle. Gossip then and gossip since has wasted its strength in trying to find out whether Swift was technically lover or husband to either of his passionate friends. What if he was? What if he was not? The drama remains the same.

Stella was for nearly forty years, child and woman, "the truest, most virtuous and valuable friend that I," Swift said, "or perhaps any other person, ever was blessed with." Call Stella his wife or be pedantic. Vanessa was for fifteen years his occasional delight, his torment, to whom he wrote—in French—that there was no merit nor any proof of his good taste in finding in her all that nature had given any mortal in the way of honor, virtue, sense, wit, tenderness, agreeableness, and firmness of spirit. Call Vanessa his mistress or be pedantic. One side of Swift looked toward a wife, one toward a mistress. He maintained between them a singular course, but it was no more singular than his character in general. He was, after all, only the kind of man he was, and loved by two women.

Before Vanessa's death he had begun to take an interest in Irish affairs. The Whig government in England treated Ireland as if it were a conquered province, not a sister kingdom. The Irish Parliament had no power. The laws, all made in England, condemned Ireland to poverty. Cattle could not be shipped to England, woolen goods could not be shipped anywhere. Without a free hand in agriculture or trade, Ireland from being so long bound was numb or sodden.

Mortified by finding himself in exile among slaves, Swift first despised them and then hated their tyrants. The tyrants were the Whigs who had driven him out of power. He could not become a slave. He could not endure a tyrant. Everything in his nature urged him to rouse the slaves and resist the tyrants. And he had the advantage, when he turned his fury loose, of a long experience in hating the party to which his enemies belonged.

Where his whole cause was so good Swift did not need to be fastidious about his particular occasion for attack. William Wood, an English ironmonger, in 1722 obtained a patent from the King to coin halfpence and farthings for Ireland for fourteen years. The Irish were not agreed that they needed new copper coins, certainly not to the amount of a hundred thousand pounds. The Irish were not consulted, nor even the Lord Lieutenant. Higher interests were involved. The patent had really been granted to the Duchess of Kendal, the King's mistress, who sold it to Wood for ten thousand pounds. Walpole, Lord Treasurer, did not object. The Duchess had been loyal. The King was grateful. Through the method of the patent she could be rewarded, not by the King directly, but indirectly by his Irish subjects, who already, if they had known it, contributed three thousand annually in pensions to the loyal lady. Since there was some risk, Wood deserved a profit for his trouble. The necessary copper would cost him sixty thousand pounds. When he had satisfied the Duchess he would still have thirty thousand, of which perhaps one-fifth would pay for the coinage and about one-seventh go to fees required by the patent. As jobs went in the government of Ireland under Walpole, the profit was not unheard of.

But the failure to consult the Irish had angered them. Their Parliament protested to the Treasury. Lord Carteret, a friend of Swift and now Secretary of State, was at odds with Walpole. Walpole, persisting, got Carteret appointed Lord Lieutenant early in 1724, to get rid of him in London. By the time he reached Dublin the whole country was in a passion.

The passion was led and guided by Swift. Walpole's scheme, shabby, cynical, insulting, brought the satirist with a roar out of his long silence. He was as crafty as he was furious. Pretending to be a small tradesman named Drapier, he addressed, between April and November 1724, a series of letters to the shopkeepers, tradesmen, farmers, and common people, to his printer, to the nobility and gentry, to the whole people of Ireland. He was as furious as he was crafty. Wood was a "single, diminutive, insignificant mechanic." He and his agents, trying to force upon the Irish the coins which the patent did not oblige them to accept, were "enemies to God and this kingdom." "I will shoot Mr. Wood and his deputies through the head, like highwaymen or housebreakers, if they dare to force one farthing of their coin upon me in the payment of an hundred pounds. It is no loss of honour to submit to the lion, but who, with the figure of a man, can think with patience of being devoured alive by a rat." "I entreat you, my dear countrymen, not to be under the least concern upon these and the like rumours, which are no more than the last howls of a dog dissected alive, as I hope he hath sufficiently been."

Swift did not dare to accuse the King, and he only hinted at the honorarium to the Duchess. It was the ministers who had planned this contemptuous oppression. It was Wood who was to his own advantage carrying it out at the expense of Ireland. If Wood's copper became current every Irishman who received a coin, even in the smallest transaction, would get less than he gave, and every Irishman who paid out a coin would give less than he got. While Wood prospered "we should live together as merry and sociable as beggars, only with this one abatement, that we should have neither meat to feed nor manufactures to clothe us, unless we could be content to prance about in coats of mail or eat brass as ostriches do iron."

Swift must have known that his arguments were false, must have known that the intrinsic value of such small coins did not matter and that they would be as good as any if they were used. He who gave and he who got could not be equally losers. But Swift did not boggle over economic niceties. Here was a principle. To accept the coins would be to surrender to tyrants and become slaves. As soon as he had stirred the public to a fear of losing money and had assured them they could lawfully refuse the new halfpence and farthings, he moved toward a general position.

"Were not the people of Ireland born as free as those of England? How have they forfeited their freedom? Is not their Parliament as fair a representative of the people as that of England? . . . Are they not subjects of the same king? Does not the same sun shine upon them? And have they not the same God for their protector? Am I a freeman in England, and do I become a slave in six hours by crossing the channel?" "I have looked over all the English and Irish statutes without finding any law that makes Ireland depend upon England any more than England does upon Ireland. We have indeed obliged ourselves to have the same king with them, and consequently they are obliged to have the same king with us. For the law was made by our ancestors, and our ancestors then were not such fools (whatever they were in the preceding reign) to bring themselves under I know not what dependence which is now talked of without any ground of law, reason, or common sense." "All government without the consent of the governed is the very definition of slavery." "The remedy is wholly in your own hands. . . . By the laws of God, of Nature, of nations, and of your own country you are and ought to be as free a people as your brethren in England."

No voice like this had ever been raised by an Englishman in Ireland. All the Irish heard it. Never again were its echoes to be long silent in that country. "Money," Swift said, "the great divider of the world, hath by a strange revolution been the great uniter of a most divided people."

On the day Carteret landed in October, the fourth and most thoroughgoing of the Drapier letters was issued. Hawkers crying it through the streets met the Lord Lieutenant when he arrived in Dublin. Much as Carteret admired "that genius which has outshone most of this age and when you will display it again can convince us that its lustre and strength are still the same," he could not, in his station, overlook the Drapier. He offered a reward of three hundred pounds for information leading to the discovery of the author within six months. All Dublin, including the Lord Lieutenant, knew that Swift had written the dangerous letters. But there was no legal proof, even if there was anywhere an informer. During the six months Swift dined at the Castle and entertained Lady Carteret at a party in his garden. When Carteret heard that Swift had "some thoughts of declaring himself" he advised against it. Their friendship, however, was not tested to the utmost. Walpole, seeing that the

case was hopeless in such a tumult, gave it up. The
patent was withdrawn in 1725 as an instance of royal
favor and condescension. Wood was compensated with
a pension of three thousand pounds a year for twelve
years. Carteret later summed up his administration:
"The people ask me how I governed Ireland. I say that I
pleased Dr. Swift."

Something legendary began to enlarge Swift's fame.
Irishmen who could barely spell out his arguments and
knew only by hearsay that he was a man of learning who
had been great in London were roused to veneration.
They had thought of him as one of their rulers sent from
England, yet he had joined their cause against the English. He was not a tyrant but a patriot. Standing superbly
against the dread, incalculable ministers, he had defended men and women to whom halfpence and farthings were important. They stood uncovered when he
passed in the streets.

The success and effect of *The Drapier's Letters* in
1724, ten years after Swift retired to Ireland, roused him
from his apparent, or pretended, lethargy. He had come
out of his tent like Achilles. Not that Swift had ever been
quite so depressed and lonely as he sounded in his letters to his English friends. He had as many warm, devoted Irish friends as he chose to see at the Deanery or
at their houses, in Dublin or in the country, and he
traveled a good deal from one end of the island to the
other. His tongue was as rough as a cat's, but his friends
heard his rough words as the natural language of his
comic spirit. And his greatest work, which the world
knows as *Gulliver's Travels*, was outwardly a comedy
which countless readers have taken for merely that.

Yet Gulliver's travels were Swift's travels, disguised
with Swift's wit, loaded with Swift's hate. He gave years
to them as to nothing else he ever wrote about, five or

six years thinking of them as Martin Scriblerus's travels, nearly as long thinking of them as Gulliver's. "I am now writing a History of my Travels," Swift wrote to Charles Ford in April 1721, "which will be a large volume, and gives account of countries hitherto unknown." In June 1722 Vanessa had heard something about the giants. In January 1724 Swift had left "the Country of Horses" and was "in the Flying Island." In August 1725 he said he had finished his Travels and was transcribing them. Thereafter all Swift's friends waited to see how he would, as he said, "vex the world rather than divert it."

In the days of the Scriblerus Club it had been assumed that the bungling Martin would be a traveler. But later, at some uncertain date, Swift seems to have felt that Martin would no longer serve. If he were to be the traveler, much of the folly of the narrative would have to appear as his misadventures. Better to let the traveler be a plain, reasonable, unimaginative man, like Captain Lemuel Gulliver, who would report what he had seen in the language of common sense.

Swift's nature had included such a Gulliver. It was the best role he ever found. Without once taking ship to the far corners of the earth as Gulliver did, Swift had moved about at home too large for the pygmies, too small for the giants, too sensible for the philosophers, too human for the animals. He had never been able quite to adjust himself to the scale of life as other men lived it. Other men, even when they had the pride of distinction, could submit. Swift could not. As if he were really an alien to the race, he had been obliged, whether he chose or not, to feel and act alien. He had compromised so far as to have friends, but he was always conscious of the exceptions he was making. "I have ever hated all nations, professions, and communities, and all my love is towards individuals. . . . But principally I hate and detest that animal called man, although I heartily love John, Peter, Thomas, and so forth. This is the system upon which I have governed myself many years. . . . Upon this great foundation of misanthropy . . . the whole building of my Travels is erected; and I will never have peace of mind till all honest men are of my opinion."

If he had been fully alien he would not have troubled himself to be a missionary. He was a man to the extent that he was a moralist as well as a misanthrope. He would cure if he could. If not, he would punish. "Drown the world! I am not content with despising it, but I would anger it if I could with safety." Here was the flaw in his misanthropy. Here was the strain of humanity through which he could be fretted and hurt. But he was alien enough to feel, dramatically, that he was only a traveler in strange lands.

Yet Swift's misanthropy was in his constitution, not in his disposition. His friends spoke always of his sweetness, his charm, his delightful temper, his hearty affections, his honest generosity. He had about him a magic almost like beauty's magic. Nor did they think of him as morose and surly, whatever he said about himself. "Gulliver is a happy man," said the experienced Arbuthnot, "that at his age can write such a merry work." Swift on his travels could no more help the wit on his tongue than he could help the detestation in his heart.

He was as ingenious as he was grave. He took pains, with a few slips, to draw his pygmies and giants to scale, the pygmies an inch to a human foot, the giants a foot to a human inch. He deftly commandeered the inventions of earlier writers: Philostratus, Lucian, Rabelais, Cyrano de Bergerac, Perrot d'Ablancourt, Tom Browne. The nautical terms paraded in the voyage to Brobdingnag were copied almost word for word from a mariner's handbook. Swift did not disdain to parody contemporary travelers. Whereas a mere misanthrope would have clamored, a mere moralist scolded, Swift, being a wit, was satisfied to tell a story, pretending that he was a spectator who had no share in what he told. There were the characters, there were the incidents. They could be understood by anybody who had an understaning.

Consider the insectile people of Lilliput. Swift, in the guise of Gulliver, was at first received with dread, then with wonder, then with hospitality. Though they kept him a prisoner, they let him into the secrets of the Court and of the government, which were preposterously like England's. The Lilliputian ministers to commend themselves to the king capered before him on a tightrope. Gulliver, whose mind was part of Swift's, remembered larger ministers. Flimnap, who could caper an inch higher than any other lord in the empire, seemed remarkably like Walpole. The great men of Lilliput who sought honors from their king competed, by jumping over a stick held in his hand, for silken threads six inches long, one blue, one red, one green, which reminded Gulliver of the Order of the Garter, of the Bath, and of the Thistle.

Lilliput and the neighbouring Blefuscu had long been at war. A Lilliputian schism was the cause. Formerly all the people had broken their eggs at the larger end. One of their kings, having cut his finger on the larger end of one of his eggs, had by royal edict made the smaller end orthodox. There had been a civil war. Some of the defeated conservatives had fled to Blefuscu and had there found refuge and favour at the Court. England, Gulliver reflected, had been entirely Catholic before Henry VIII. The Catholic Pretender had fled to France, and France had long been at war with England.

Grateful for the kindness shown him, Gulliver aided Lilliput in its war by capturing the Blefuscudian fleet and bringing it as a gift to his royal host. But the Lilliputians were no more grateful in return than the English had been to the Oxford Ministry for ending the war with France. One party among the pygmies insisted that Blefuscu be subjugated to a province with a viceroy, as some of the Whigs had insisted France might be. The sourest of the tiny ministers became Gulliver's enemy, as the dismal Earl of Nottingham had become Swift's.

Gulliver's chief offence was that, when a fire broke out in the Queen's apartment at the palace, he extinguished it in a manner more natural to him than agreeable to the Queen. Had not Queen Anne implacably resented the spattering ridicule which Swift had let fall upon what he thought was menacing the Church and State? Thereafter the position of Gulliver in Lilliput was hopeless. The cabinet decided he must die. The friendly minister Reldresal, who may have stood for Carteret, thought it would be enough to blind Gulliver and allow him to starve to death.

From that compromise Gulliver escaped to Blefuscu, and back to England, knowing that the smallest people in the world had all the familiar follies and vices of mankind in general.

Next Swift, as Gulliver, was blown to the giants of Brobdingnag, that humane people. It was his turn to be insectile. He was exhibited as a toy freak by the kind, greedy farmer who had found him. Scientists wondered what species he could belong to. The King, being a philosopher, supposed that such creatures as Gulliver "have their titles and distinctions of honour; they contrive little nests and burrows that they call houses and cities; they make a figure in dress and equipage; they love, they fight, they dispute, they cheat, they betray." And when Gulliver had defended his species by an account of their government and politics, their wars and luxuries, the King, being a humane philosopher, concluded "your natives to be the most pernicious race of little odious vermin that nature ever suffered to crawl upon the surface of the earth."

He himself abominated mystery, refinement, and intrigue in governors. He limited government "to common sense and reason, to justice and lenity, to the speedy determination of civil and criminal causes." He held that "whoever could make two ears of corn or two blades of grass grow upon a spot of ground where only one grew before would deserve better of mankind . . . than the whole race of politicians put together." Gulliver, or Swift, sardonically despaired of such a monarch. His people were no better. Their learning was only in morality, history, poetry, and useful mathematics. They were unable to form conceptions of what Gulliver meant by "entities, abstractions, and transcendentals." They were dull with virtue and peace.

Gulliver found in their habits less to remind him of England than he had found in Lilliput. His story was taken up with the ingenious shifts by which he got along among them. But after the giants he could not so easily return to the old scale of life as he could after the pygmies. His own people seemed contemptible by their smallness. He was twice as far from mankind as he had been before.

Swift's, Gulliver's, third voyage seems to have been to the Country of Horses, but when he told the story he saved that for the venomous conclusion and in the third place put the account of the Flying Island and the continent which was topsy-turvy with philosophers.

Once more, as in Lilliput, he was often reminded of Europe. The name of Laputa was like the Spanish for harlot. The island, when its rulers wished, could hover over stubborn cities and shut out the sun, as England shut out the sun from Ireland. Whether aloft or on land the people were rapt in abstruse speculations or abandoned to fantastic projects. Among the islanders nobody spoke sense except, possibly, the tradesmen, women, and children. The others were so many pedants exaggerated from the breed that Swift had detested in his earliest satires. The Academy of Lagado was a Bedlam of Science, where men wore out their lives trying to extract sunbeams from cucumbers, to build houses downward from the roofs in the fashion of the bees and spiders, to plow fields only with the snouts of hogs, to make silk from spider webs, to cure colic with a pair of bellows, to soften marble for pincushions, to propagate naked sheep, to write books by a mechanical device, to discover painless methods of taxation.

Gulliver grew dizzy. He lacked the head, as Swift did, for this whirling universe. It did not steady him when, on the neighbouring island of Glubbdubdrib, he was allowed to call up the spirits of the famous dead and found how falsely they had been presented in history. It did not steady him when in Luggnagg he learned of the immortal struldbrugs, for whom immortality was only human life prolonged to an infinity of horrible old age. "I . . . thought," said Gulliver, for Swift, "that no tyrant could invent a death into which I would not run with pleasure from such a life." When he was out of the mad lands of Laputa, Balnibarbi, Glubbdubdrib, and Luggnagg, he was nearly upside down, giddy, and three times as far from mankind.

Now for the antipodes of misanthropy. Among the Houyhnhnms Gulliver was almost undisguisedly Swift, on an imagined island where the horses were as much wiser and nobler as they were stronger than the men. Nothing could disgust a traveler, even wholesome Gulliver, more than to study the horrid antics of a debased

human tribe in the company of utopian horses who could
see little difference between him and those apish copies.
Gulliver had been disgusted among the giants when the
maids of honor laid him against their terrible breasts.
That had been only a shrinking of his senses. Now his
soul itself must shrink with an absolute antipathy from
which he could not recover. When he came back he
would prefer the horses of England to the men.

On his icy, fiery travels among the Houyhnhnms Swift
(why call him Gulliver?) did not bother to observe such
stinging likenesses to particular English persons and
episodes as he observed among the pygmies and the
philosophers. The last of his adventures was the simplest,
as it was the most deadly. All actual fantasy, all apparent fact.

He came upon his first Yahoos without realizing that
they were inferior men and upon his first Houyhnhnms
without realizing that they were superior horses. When
he found himself taken for a Yahoo he hurried to tell
his Houyhnhnm master about Europe. He told him of
wars, their causes, means, and ends; of litigation and
the arts of lawyers; of money, and of poverty and riches;
of luxury and dissipation; of diseases and their remedies;
of ministers of state and noblemen. The reasonable
Houyhnhnm said he had noticed the rudiments of all
these human ways of life among the Yahoos.

They had their tribal and civil wars. They hoarded
shining stones which they could not use, fought over
them, and sometimes lost them to bystanders who
snatched them away as expertly as any lawyer. They
gorged themselves with food and sucked a root that
made them drunk. They had the only diseases in the
country, because of their gluttony and filth. They had
in most herds a sort of ruling Yahoo, always deformed
in body and mischievous in disposition, who continued

in office till a worse could be found. They were lewd and promiscuous. They were invariably dirty and sometimes splenetic. They had, it appeared, all the human vices except unnatural appetites, these "politer pleasures" not having occurred to them. They were unteachable because they were perverse and restive, but they had the brains to be cunning, malicious, treacherous, revengeful, insolent, abject, and cruel. It was plain to the Houyhnhnm who talked with Swift that the visitor was a Yahoo after all. That "small pittance of reason" which by some accident had been given to the European Yahoos they used only to multiply their natural corruptions and to acquire new ones not supplied by nature.

To be fully reasonable was to be like the Houyhnhnms. They did not know what lying was. They affirmed or denied only when they were certain. Their two principal virtues were friendship and benevolence, felt toward the whole species without partiality except where there were special virtues to attract them. In marriage they were without jealousy, fondness, quarreling, or discontent. The young of both sexes were brought up in moderation, industry, exercise, and cleanliness. Their only government was an annual council of the entire nation. They had no literature except poems composed, not written down, in praise of virtue. They were skillful workmen in the necessary arts, but wasted no time on superfluity or show. Reasonably born and bred, they lived reasonably without passions and died reasonably without sickness or fear.

"At first, indeed, I did not feel that natural awe which the Yahoos and all other animals bear towards them; but it grew upon me by degrees, much sooner than I imagined, and was mingled with a respectful love and gratitude that they would condescend to distinguish me from the rest of my species. When I thought of my

family, my friends, my countrymen, or the human race in
general, I considered them as they really were, Yahoos
in shape and disposition." Swift would have remained
with the Houyhnhnms forever if they had not sent him
away. The beasts could not tolerate a man. Nor could a
man who had lived among the beasts ever again live
among men without disgust.

The fourth voyage marked the peak of Swift's fury
and of his art. Great as that art was, it could not quite
conceal that fury. The narrative might seem, however
fantastic, to be the very mathematics of misanthropy,
never looser than a syllogism. But the cold tread of intellect was repeatedly broken by the rush of nerves. The
most reasonable sentence might suddenly throb with
words of a shuddering hate. "Imagine twenty thousand
of them breaking into the midst of an European army,
confounding the ranks, overturning the carriages, battering the warriors' faces into mummy by terrible yerks
from their hinder hoofs." Intellect would have been satisfied with beating the European Yahoos down; nerves,
furious and yet frightened at their own desperation,
must imagine battering the noisome faces into mummy.
Nothing less than an agonized antipathy could have
made Swift remark that the female Yahoo who embraced Gulliver was not red-haired, "which might have
been some excuse for an appetite a little irregular," but
"black as a sloe"—or as Stella. Hate possessed him as
love possesses some other men.

If he had been a lover of his kind he might have been
hot with praises for the lofty merits which he found in
them, and might have seen the world smirk at his tribute. Instead, he was a hater. Was there not as good an
excuse for hating as for loving? Was it any less accurate
to perceive ugliness, deformity, vice, stupidity, loath-
someness in the human race than to perceive beauty,

grace, virtue, wit, charm? Swift would have known that these were absurd questions, asked to no purpose. Mankind would always answer them for its own comfort, which demands that love must be, in moral arguments, preferred to hate. The crowded tribes of the earth lived too precariously to welcome the hate, however instinctive, which might come among them to separate man from man, tribe from tribe, man from tribe. Only in the warmth of love could they live together. If the Swifts of the world must hate they must live alone, even if what they hated, as with Swift, was hate itself, along with cruelty, avarice, oppression, filth, intemperance, presumption.

All this Swift had learned. But he had no choice. His nature insisted upon taking its revenge as a coiled spring insists upon uncoiling as soon as it is free. He had traveled through the world. He would tell the whole truth about his travels.

In March 1726 Swift finally returned to England, carrying with him the completed manuscript of *Travels into Several Remote Nations of the World . . . By Lemuel Gulliver.* Oxford was dead, and Bolingbroke, excluded from the House of Lords, was in forced retirement. The Whigs were in power, but they were new Whigs, not Swift's former friends, several of whom, including Addison, had died. But Pope and Gay and Arbuthnot were all that they had been before, and Swift was as happy during a few months as he probably ever was in his life. He was, Pope said, "the joy of all here who know him, as he was eleven years ago." Pope was working on *The Dunciad,* Gay on his *Fables.* They read and discussed Swift's *Travels.* Pope and Swift thought of means of publishing the book so stealthily that there would be no danger of prosecution. Pope made Swift demand two hundred pounds in payment within six months, the only money Swift ever got for anything he wrote. Only after he had left England in August did the printer receive the manuscript, "he knew not whence, nor from whom, dropped at his house in the dark from a hackney coach," in which it is likely that the mystifying Pope enjoyed his subterfuge. Of course it was only a subterfuge employed so the authorities could not prove by the printer that Swift was the writer. No doubt the printer knew, just as anybody could be sure that Swift alone of all living men could have written the *Travels*.

The book, published October 28 to vex the world rather than divert it, diverted it. Whether or not it was because the printer had made several cautious changes in the text, nobody spoke or apparently even thought of prosecution. "The politicians to a man agree," Pope and Gay wrote to Swift, "that it is free from particular reflections, but that the satire on general societies of men is too severe." Politicians were no more disposed than they were obliged to defend the human race against a libel. Mankind, invincibly abstract, invulnerably obtuse to general assaults, laughed. "From the highest to the lowest" the book was read, "from the cabinet council to the nursery." The Princess of Wales did not care, if she knew, that she was supposed to have sat for the Queen of Brobdingnag. She was delighted. The Duchess of Marlborough was "in raptures" and willing to forgive her old enemy. Arbuthnot saw that the book was to be a classic and forecast for it "as great a run as John Bunyan." The first impression was sold within a week. There were Dublin editions and translations into French and Dutch within a year.

Swift, accusing mankind of every vice and folly, had thought of it as more sensitive or less frivolous than it was. He let drive with all his pitiless force, and the world applauded his witty marksmanship.

Pleasant as his visit to England in 1726, and another the year following, had been, Swift lived thereafter in Ireland with fewer complaints than formerly. Ireland was now his home, and in the hearts of its people he was Ireland's hero, if not its king. Overwhelmed by Stella's death in January 1728, he nevertheless survived. In October 1729 he published *A Modest Proposal*, the most savage of all his pamphlets, the most terrible outcry of his misanthropy. Few of his readers seem to have shuddered at his scheme for eating the children of the Irish poor. Lord Bathurst wrote from England that he had almost brought his wife round to the opinion that the youngest of their children should help provide for the eldest. After all, any sensible reader knew that the Irish children would not actually be eaten, at least not in this forthright, economical way, just as he knew that there were no Houyhnhnms and no Yahoos. Swift, sensible readers said, was only joking, as an Irish bishop had said that Gulliver was only lying. Once more the misanthrope had run against mankind in the abstract. Except for a few hints, a few urgings, a few arguments, a few accusations, all scattered and occasional, Swift after the *Modest Proposal* wrote no more prose about Ireland. "Looking upon this kingdom as absolutely desperate," he said in 1731, "I would not prescribe a dose to the dead."

During his later years Swift amused himself with the study of contemporary clichés, which he brought together in 1738 as *A Complete Collection of Genteel and Ingenious Conversation*, in three illustrative dialogues and a brilliant introduction. His *Directions to Servants*, ironically advising them to do all the most objectionable things he had observed or thought of, was left unfinished.

But his most memorable writings of these final years were in verse: *On Poetry: A Rhapsody* (1733) and *Verses on the Death of Dr. Swift* (1739).

His rhapsody on poetry was all abuse, in the dry, crisp, easy, lethal lines of which he was a perfect master. To be a poet, he said, was as insane as to be a lover. There was no market and no use for poetry. Yet Swift,

> an old experienced sinner
> Instructing thus a young beginner,

went on to tell anyone who was fool enough to wish to be a poet how to go about it. If he did not succeed at poetry, then let him try writing for a political party. That might pay. Or he could turn critic. There were all kinds of "jobbers in the poet's art." And always the worst poets could write about the royal family. The King could stomach any praise. Swift mauled George and his Court with nearly a hundred lines of irony, then broke off. He would not give himself the bother of finishing his satire.

But he did take pains with the verses on his own death. When he wrote the poem he did not intend to let it be published while he was alive. He would keep it by him and enjoy the secret. He read it to some of his friends, and then to others. It became a little legend. He went to the length of writing another version, between an abridgment and a burlesque, dating it All Fools' Day, 1733, and contriving to have it come out in London. Then, to perfect the hoax, he claimed that somebody had partly memorized his original and played a trick on him. "But even this trick," he declared, "shall not provoke me to print the true one, which indeed is not proper to be seen till I can be seen no more." Then he changed his mind, after he had become tired of what he called his trifles, and published the most remarkable of them all.

Swift's representation of his character in the *Verses* was not entirely accurate. He had suffered from disappointments. He had taken revenges. He had aimed to hurt as well as to mend. But accuracy was not his purpose. This was the last and greatest of his hoaxes. Swift could not keep such a hoax to himself. It was too good to be left for any man's survivors. Swift had put all his cynicism and all his intensity into his lines on his death. But he could not miss the chance, by publishing them, to amuse himself, in his extraordinary way, at his own funeral.

Ever since his youth he had suffered from some obscure malady, probably affecting the inner ear, which troubled him at frequent intervals with giddiness and nausea. Now it became a torment, the thunder of oceans and the beating of insensate drums in his head. In March 1742 guardians were assigned to him by the Court of Chancery, and in August a commission found him to be of unsound mind. After weeks of agony he suffered paralysis and lived three years longer without pain but in almost silent apathy. He was buried in his St. Patrick's at midnight, in accordance with his own instructions in his will made five years before.

In that will he left his fortune, about eleven thousand pounds, to build a hospital for idiots and lunatics in Dublin. In the same document with this and other bequests, he left the world his aching epitaph. It was to say to any traveler who came to see it that the body of Jonathan Swift, Dean of this Cathedral, was buried here in a place where his furious indignation could no longer lacerate his heart. It was to tell the traveler to go and imitate, if he could, this strenuous defender of manly liberty. The inscription was to be on black marble, "in large letters, deeply cut and strongly gilded," and in the stately language of the Church and of the ancient Romans.

HIC DEPOSITUM EST CORPUS

JONATHAN SWIFT S.T.P.

HUJUS ECCLESIAE CATHEDRALIS

DECANI

UBI SAEVA INDIGNATIO

ULTERIUS COR LACERARE NEQUIT

ABI VIATOR

ET IMITARE SI POTERIS

STRENUUM PRO VIRILI LIBERTATIS VINDICEM

CARL VAN DOREN

Chronology

1667   Swift born at Dublin, November 30.

1673[?]–1681   At Kilkenny Grammar School.

1682–1686   At Trinity College, Dublin.

1689   Joins Sir William Temple's household in June.

1690   Returns to Ireland in May.

1691   Again with Temple, at Moor Park, in August.

1692   M.A., Hart Hall, Oxford, July 5.

1694   Returns to Ireland.

1695   Ordained and settles at Kilroot in January.

1696   Returns to Moor Park in May.

1696–1697   Writes *Tale of a Tub, Battle of the Books.*

1699   To Dublin Castle, as chaplain, in summer.

1700   Living of Laracor in February; prebend of St. Patrick's Cathedral, Dublin, in October.

1701   D.D. of Dublin in February; to London with Earl of Berkeley, April–September.

1702–1704   In England, April–November 1702, November 1703–May 1704; *Tale of a Tub* published, 1704.

1707–1709   In England with petition concerning the Irish First Fruits, November 1707–May 1709; makes friends with Addison and Steele; writes Partridge papers, 1708-1709; and contributes to *Tatler,* 1709; publishes *Baucis and Philemon,* 1709.

1710–1714   In England, September 1710–June 1713, September 1713–September 1714; main period of political activity, recorded in *Journal to Stella;* contributes to *Examiner,* 1710–1711, *Spectator* 1711; publishes *Miscellanies in Prose and Verse,* 1711; writes and publishes *The Conduct of the Allies,* 1711; *A Proposal for Correcting, Improving, and*

47

Ascertaining the English Tongue, 1711; to Ireland in summer of 1713, installed Dean of St. Patrick's, June 13; writes *Cadenus and Vanessa*, probably in fall of 1713; *The Public Spirit of the Whigs*, 1714; after death of Queen Anne in August 1714 returns to Ireland for a dozen years.

1720   *A Proposal for the Universal Use of Irish Manufactures.*

1721   *A Letter to a Young Gentleman, Lately enter'd into Holy Orders; A Letter of Advice to a Young Poet.*

1723   Death of Vanessa, June 2.

1724   *The Drapier's Letters* written and published.

1726   Visits London, March–August; *Cadenus and Vanessa* published without Swift's permission; *Travels into Several Remote Nations of the World*, October 28.

1727   Another visit to London, April–October; *Miscellanies in Prose and Verse*, three volumes, containing pieces also by Pope, Gay, and Arbuthnot.

1728   Death of Stella, January 28; *A Short View of the State of Ireland;* contributes to *Intelligencer* in Dublin.

1729   *A Modest Proposal;* Swift given Freedom of the City of Dublin.

1732   Fourth volume of *Miscellanies.*

1733   *On Poetry: A Rhapsody.*

1735   First collected edition of Swift, Dublin, four volumes; fifth volume of *Miscellanies.*

1738   *A Complete Collection of Genteel and Ingenious Conversation.*

1739   *Verses on the Death of Dr. Swift*, published in incomplete text in London and correctly in Dublin.

1740   Makes will, May 3, "being at this present of sound mind, although weak in body."

1742   Guardians appointed for Swift by Court of Chancery in March; commission finds him to be "of unsound mind and memory" in August; crisis of his illness in September.

1745   Dies in the Deanery, October 19, and buried in St.

Patrick's three days later; *Directions to Servants,* left incomplete but published posthumously.

1758   *The History of the Four Last Years of the Queen,* written in 1713 but left unpublished apparently for political reasons.

BIBLIOGRAPHICAL NOTE

The best collected editions of Swift are those of Sir Walter Scott (2nd ed. 1824) and Temple Scott (1897–1908), but neither is entirely satisfactory; nor is W. E. Browning's edition of the *Poems* (1910) uniform with the Temple Scott edition of the prose. Very valuable editions of particular works have recently been published by the Oxford University Press, which proposes to continue the series to make what promises to be an almost ideal collected edition. The volumes so far issued are *A Tale of a Tub,* etc. (1920), *The Drapier's Letters* (1935), *Letters to Charles Ford* (1935), *Poems* (3 vols., 1937), *Gulliver's Travels* (1941). The edition of Swift's *Correspondence* (6 vols., 1910-1914) by F. E. Ball is admirable and indispensable. The most substantial biography is still that of H. Craik (2 vols., 1882).

THE PORTABLE
SWIFT

Sweetness and Light

From *An Account of a Battel between the Antient and Modern Books in St. James's Library,* written in 1696–97, first published with *A Tale of a Tub* in 1704. Just before the burlesque hostilities in the *Account* begin, there is the famous episode of the Spider and the Bee, here given.   C.V.D.

THINGS were at this crisis when a material accident fell out. For, upon the highest corner of a large window, there dwelt a certain spider, swollen up to the first magnitude by the destruction of infinite numbers of flies, whose spoils lay scattered before the gates of his palace, like human bones before the cave of some giant. The avenues to his castle were guarded with turnpikes and palisadoes, all after the modern way of fortification. After you had passed several courts, you came to the centre, wherein you might behold the constable himself in his own lodgings, which had windows fronting to each avenue, and ports to sally out, upon all occasions of prey or defence. In this mansion he had for some time dwelt in peace and plenty, without danger to his person by swallows from above, or to his palace, by brooms from below; when it was the pleasure of fortune to conduct thither a wandering bee, to whose curiosity a broken pane in the glass had discovered itself, and in he went; where, expatiating a while, he at last happened to alight upon one of the outward walls of the spider's citadel; which, yielding to the unequal weight, sunk down to the very foundation. Thrice he endeavoured to force his passage, and thrice the centre shook. The spider within, feeling the terrible convulsion, supposed at first that nature was approaching to her final dissolution; or else, that Beelzebub, with all his legions, was come to revenge the death of many thousands of his subjects, whom his enemy had slain and devoured. However, he at length valiantly resolved to issue forth, and meet his fate. Meanwhile the bee had acquitted himself of his toils, and, posted securely at some distance, was employed in cleansing his wings, and disengaging them from the ragged remnants of the cobweb. By this time the spider was adventured out, when, beholding the chasms, the ruins, and dilapidations of his fortress, he was very near at his wit's end; he stormed and swore like a madman, and swelled till he was ready to burst. At length, casting his eye upon the bee, and wisely gathering causes from events (for they knew each other by sight): "A plague split you," said he, "for a giddy son of a whore. Is it you, with a vengeance, that have made this litter here? Could not you look before you, and be d—d? Do you think I have nothing else to do (in the devil's name) but to mend and repair after your arse?" —"Good words, friend," said the bee (having now pruned himself, and being disposed to droll), "I'll give you my hand and word to come near your kennel no more; I was never in such a confounded pickle since I was born."—"Sirrah," replied the spider, "if it were not for breaking an old custom in our family, never to stir abroad against an enemy, I should come and teach you better manners."—"I pray have patience," said the bee, "or you'll spend your substance, and, for aught I see, you may stand in need of it all, toward the repair of your house."—"Rogue, rogue," replied the spider, "yet, methinks you should have more respect to a person, whom all the world allows to be so much your betters."—"By

my troth," said the bee, "the comparison will amount
to a very good jest, and you will do me a favour to let
me know the reasons that all the world is pleased to use
in so hopeful a dispute." At this the spider, having
swelled himself into the size and posture of a disputant,
began his argument in the true spirit of controversy, with
resolution to be heartily scurrilous and angry, to urge
on his own reasons, without the least regard to the answers or objections of his opposite, and fully predeter-
mined in his mind against all conviction.

"Not to disparage myself," said he, "by the comparison with such a rascal, what art thou but a vagabond
without house or home, without stock or inheritance?
Born to no possession of your own, but a pair of wings
and a drone-pipe. Your livelihood is a universal plunder
upon nature; a freebooter over fields and gardens; and,
for the sake of stealing, will rob a nettle as easily as a
violet. Whereas I am a domestic animal, furnished with
a native stock within myself. This large castle (to shew
my improvements in the mathematics) is all built with
my own hands, and the materials extracted altogether
out of my own person."

"I am glad," answered the bee, "to hear you grant at
least that I am come honestly by my wings and my
voice; for then, it seems, I am obliged to Heaven alone
for my flights and my music; and Providence would
never have bestowed on me two such gifts, without designing them for the noblest ends. I visit indeed all the
flowers and blossoms of the field and garden; but whatever I collect thence enriches myself, without the least
injury to their beauty, their smell, or their taste. Now, for
you and your skill in architecture, and other mathematics, I have little to say. In that building of yours there
might, for aught I know, have been labour and method
enough; but, by woful experience for us both, it is plain,

the materials are naught, and I hope you will henceforth take warning, and consider duration and matter, as well as method and art. You boast, indeed, of being obliged to no other creature, but of drawing and spinning out all from yourself; that is to say, if we may judge of the liquor in the vessel by what issues out, you possess a good plentiful store of dirt and poison in your breast; and, though I would by no means lessen or disparage your genuine stock of either, yet, I doubt you are somewhat obliged, for an increase of both, to a little foreign assistance. Your inherent portion of dirt does not fail of acquisitions, by sweepings exhaled from below; and one insect furnishes you with a share of poison to destroy another. So that, in short, the question comes all to this —Whether is the nobler being of the two, that which, by a lazy contemplation of four inches round, by an overweening pride, feeding and engendering on itself, turns all into excrement and venom, producing nothing at all, but flybane and a cobweb; or that which, by a universal range, with long search, much study, true judgment, and distinction of things, brings home honey and wax."

This dispute was managed with such eagerness, clamour, and warmth, that the two parties of books, in arms below, stood silent a while, waiting in suspense what would be the issue, which was not long undetermined. For the bee, grown impatient at so much loss of time, fled straight away to a bed of roses, without looking for a reply, and left the spider, like an orator, collected in himself, and just prepared to burst out.

It happened upon this emergency, that Æsop broke silence first. He had been of late most barbarously treated by a strange effect of the regent's humanity, who had tore off his title-page, sorely defaced one half of his leaves, and chained them fast among a shelf of Moderns.

Where, soon discovering how high the quarrel was likely to proceed, he tried all his arts, and turned himself to a thousand forms. At length, in the borrowed shape of an ass, the regent mistook him for a Modern; by which means he had time and opportunity to escape to the Ancients, just when the spider and the bee were entering into their contest, to which he gave his attention with a world of pleasure; and when it was ended, swore in the loudest key, that in all his life he had never known two cases so parallel and adapt to each other, as that in the window, and this upon the shelves. "The disputants," said he, "have admirably managed the dispute between them, have taken in the full strength of all that is to be said on both sides, and exhausted the substance of every argument *pro* and *con*. It is but to adjust the reasonings of both to the present quarrel, then to compare and apply the labours and fruits of each, as the bee has learnedly deduced them, and we shall find the conclusion fall plain and close upon the Moderns and us. For, pray, gentlemen, was ever anything so modern as the spider in his air, his turns, and his paradoxes? He argues in the behalf of you his brethren and himself, with many boastings of his native stock and great genius, that he spins and spits wholly from himself, and scorns to own any obligation or assistance from without. Then he displays to you his great skill in architecture, and improvement in the mathematics. To all this the bee, as an advocate, retained by us the Ancients, thinks fit to answer —that, if one may judge of the great genius or inventions of the Moderns by what they have produced, you will hardly have countenance to bear you out, in boasting of either. Erect your schemes with as much method and skill as you please; yet if the materials be nothing but dirt, spun out of your own entrails (the guts of modern brains), the edifice will conclude at last in a cobweb, the duration of which, like that of other spiders' webs, may be imputed to their being forgotten, or neg- lected, or hid in a corner. For anything else of genuine that the Moderns may pretend to, I cannot recollect; unless it be a large vein of wrangling and satire, much of a nature and substance with the spider's poison; which, however they pretend to spit wholly out of them- selves, is improved by the same arts, by feeding upon the insects and vermin of the age. As for us the Ancients, we are content, with the bee, to pretend to nothing of our own, beyond our wings and our voice, that is to say, our flights and our language. For the rest, whatever we have got, has been by infinite labour and search, and ranging through every corner of nature; the difference is, that, instead of dirt and poison, we have rather chosen to fill our hives with honey and wax, thus furnishing mankind with the two noblest of things, which are sweetness and light."

A Digression Concerning Madness

From Section IX of *A Tale of a Tub,* written probably
in 1697 and first published in 1704. The full title of
Section IX is *A Digression concerning the Original, the
Use, and Improvement of Madness, in a Commonwealth.*

C.V.D.

IF WE take a survey of the greatest actions that have
been performed in the world, under the influence of
single men, which are, the establishment of new empires
by conquest, the advance and progress of new schemes
in philosophy, and the contriving, as well as the propagating, of new religions; we shall find the authors of them all
to have been persons, whose natural reason had admitted
great revolutions, from their diet, their education, the
prevalency of some certain temper, together with the particular influence of air and climate. Besides, there is something individual in human minds, that easily kindles, at
the accidental approach and collision of certain circumstances, which, though of paltry and mean appearance,
do often flame out into the greatest emergencies of life.
For great turns are not always given by strong hands,
but by lucky adaption, and at proper seasons; and it is
of no import where the fire was kindled, if the vapour
has once got up into the brain. For the upper region of
man is furnished like the middle region of the air; the
materials are formed from causes of the widest difference, yet produce at last the same substance and effect.
Mists arise from the earth, steams from dung hills, ex-

59

halations from the sea, and smoke from fire; yet all
clouds are the same in composition as well as consequences, and the fumes issuing from a jakes will furnish
as comely and useful a vapour as incense from an altar.
Thus far, I suppose, will easily be granted me; and then
it will follow, that, as the face of nature never produces
rain, but when it is overcast and disturbed, so human
understanding, seated in the brain, must be troubled
and overspread by vapours, ascending from the lower
faculties to water the invention, and render it fruitful.
Now, although these vapours (as it hath been already
said) are of as various original as those of the skies, yet
the crops they produce differ both in kind and degree,
merely according to the soil. I will produce two instances
to prove and explain what I am now advancing.

A certain great prince[1] raised a mighty army, filled his
coffers with infinite treasures, provided an invincible
fleet, and all this without giving the least part of his
design to his greatest ministers, or his nearest favourites.
Immediately the whole world was alarmed; the neighbouring crowns in trembling expectations, towards what
point the storm would burst; the small politicians every-
where forming profound conjectures. Some believed he
had laid a scheme for universal monarchy; others, after
much insight, determined the matter to be a project for
pulling down the pope, and setting up the reformed religion, which had once been his own. Some, again, of a
deeper sagacity, sent him into Asia to subdue the Turk,
and recover Palestine. In the midst of all these projects
and preparations, a certain state-surgeon,[2] gathering the
nature of the disease by these symptoms, attempted the
cure, at one blow performed the operation, broke the
bag, and out flew the vapour; nor did anything want to

---

[1] This was Harry the Great of France.
[2] Ravillac, who stabbed Henry the Great in his coach.

render it a complete remedy, only that the prince unfortunately happened to die in the performance. Now, is
the reader exceeding curious to learn whence this vapour took its rise, which had so long set the nations at
a gaze? What secret wheel, what hidden spring, could
put into motion so wonderful an engine? It was afterwards discovered, that the movement of this whole machine had been directed by an absent female, whose
eyes had raised a protuberancy, and, before emission,
she was removed into an enemy's country. What should
an unhappy prince do in such ticklish circumstances as
these? He tried in vain the poet's never-failing receipt
of *corpora quæque;* for

> *Idque petit corpus mens unde est saucia amore:*
> *Unde feritur, eo tendit, gestique coire.*—Lucr.

Having to no purpose used all peaceable endeavours,
the collected part of the semen, raised and inflamed, became a dust, converted to choler, turned head upon the
spinal duct, and ascended to the brain. The very same
principle that influences a bully to break the windows of
a whore who has jilted him, naturally stirs up a great
prince to raise mighty armies, and dream of nothing but
sieges, battles, and victories.

> ——*Teterrima belli*
> *Causa*——

The other instance[3] is what I have read somewhere in
a very ancient author, of a mighty king, who, for the
space of above thirty years, amused himself to take and
lose towns, beat armies, and be beaten, drive princes out
of their dominions; fright children from their bread and
butter; burn, lay waste, plunder, dragoon, massacre subject and stranger, friend and foe, male and female. 'Tis
recorded, that the philosophers of each country were in

---

[3] This is meant of the present French king.

grave dispute upon causes natural, moral, and political, to find out where they should assign an original solution of this phenomenon. At last, the vapour or spirit, which animated the hero's brain, being in perpetual circulation, seized upon that region of the human body, so renowned for furnishing the zibeta occidentalis,[4] and, gathering there into a tumour, left the rest of the world for that time in peace. Of such mighty consequence it is where those exhalations fix, and of so little from whence they proceed. The same spirits, which, in their superior progress, would conquer a kingdom, descending upon the anus, conclude in a fistula.

Let us next examine the great introducers of new schemes in philosophy, and search till we can find from what faculty of the soul the disposition arises in mortal man, of taking it into his head to advance new systems, with such an eager zeal, in things agreed on all hands impossible to be known; from what seeds this disposition springs, and to what quality of human nature these grand innovators have been indebted for their number of disciples. Because it is plain, that several of the chief among them, both ancient and modern, were usually mistaken by their adversaries, and indeed by all, except their own followers, to have been persons crazed, or out of their wits; having generally proceeded, in the common course of their words and actions, by a method very different from the vulgar dictates of unrefined reason; agreeing for the most part in their several models, with their present undoubted successors in the academy of modern Bedlam (whose merits and principles I shall farther examine in due place). Of this kind were *Epi-*

---

[4] Paracelsus, who was so famous for chemistry, tried an experiment upon human excrement, to make a perfume of it; which, when he had brought to perfection, he called *zibeta occidentalis*, or western civet; the back parts of man . . . being the west.

*curus, Diogenes, Apollonius, Lucretius, Paracelsus, Des
Cartes,* and others, who, if they were now in the world,
tied fast, and separate from their followers, would, in
this our undistinguishing age, incur manifest danger of
phlebotomy, and whips, and chains, and dark chambers,
and straw. For what man, in the natural state or course
of thinking, did ever conceive it in his power to reduce
the notions of all mankind exactly to the same length,
and breadth, and height of his own? Yet this is the first
humble and civil design of all innovators in the empire
of reason. Epicurus modestly hoped, that, one time or
other, a certain fortuitous concourse of all men's opinions, after perpetual justlings, the sharp with the smooth,
the light and the heavy, the round and the square,
would, by certain clinamina, unite in the notions of
atoms and void, as these did in the originals of all things.
Cartesius reckoned to see, before he died, the sentiments
of all philosophers, like so many lesser stars in his romantic system, wrapped and drawn within his own vor-
tex. Now, I would gladly be informed, how it is possible
to account for such imaginations as these in particular
men, without recourse to my phenomenon of vapours,
ascending from the lower faculties to overshadow the
brain, and there distilling into conceptions, for which
the narrowness of our mother-tongue has not yet assigned any other name beside that of madness or phrenzy.
Let us therefore now conjecture how it comes to pass,
that none of these great prescribers do ever fail providing themselves and their notions with a number of
implicit disciples. And, I think, the reason is easy to be
assigned: for there is a peculiar string in the harmony of
human understanding, which, in several individuals, is
exactly of the same tuning. This, if you can dexterously
screw up to its right key, and then strike gently upon it,
whenever you have the good fortune to light among

those of the same pitch, they will, by a secret necessary sympathy, strike exactly at the same time. And in this one circumstance lies all the skill or luck of the matter; for, if you chance to jar the string among those who are either above or below your own height, instead of subscribing to your doctrine, they will tie you fast, call you mad, and feed you with bread and water. It is therefore a point of the nicest conduct, to distinguish and adapt this noble talent, with respect to the differences of persons and times. Cicero understood this very well, when writing to a friend in England, with a caution, among other matters, to beware of being cheated by our hackney-coachmen (who, it seems, in those days were as arrant rascals as they are now), has these remarkable words: *Est quod gaudeas te in ista loca venisse, ubi aliquid sapere viderere.*[5] For, to speak a bold truth, it is a fatal miscarriage so ill to order affairs, as to pass for a fool in one company, when, in another, you might be treated as a philosopher. Which I desire some certain gentlemen of my acquaintance to lay up in their hearts, as a very seasonable *innuendo*.

This, indeed, was the fatal mistake of that worthy gentleman, my most ingenious friend, Mr. Wotton: a person, in appearance, ordained for great designs, as well as performances; whether you will consider his notions or his looks. Surely no man ever advanced into the public with fitter qualifications of body and mind, for the propagation of a new religion. Oh, had those happy talents, misapplied to vain philosophy, been turned into their proper channels of dreams and visions, where distortion of mind and countenance are of such sovereign use, the base detracting world would not then have dared to report, that something is amiss, that his brain has undergone an unlucky shake; which even his brother

---

[5] Epist. ad Fam. Trebatio.

modernists themselves, like ungrates, do whisper so loud,
that it reaches up to the very garret I am now writing in.

Lastly, whosoever pleases to look into the fountains
of enthusiasm, from whence, in all ages, have eternally
proceeded such fattening streams, will find the spring-
head to have been as troubled and muddy as the current; of such great emolument is a tincture of this vapour, which the world calls madness, that without its
help, the world would not only be deprived of those two
great blessings, conquests and systems, but even all
mankind would unhappily be reduced to the same belief
in things invisible. Now, the former *postulatum* being
held, that it is of no import from what originals this
vapour proceeds, but either in what angles it strikes and
spreads over the understanding, or upon what species of
brain it ascends; it will be a very delicate point to cut
the feather, and divide the several reasons to a nice and
curious reader, how this numerical difference in the
brain can produce effects of so vast a difference from
the same vapour, as to be the sole point of individuation
between Alexander the Great, Jack of Leyden, and Mon-
sieur Des Cartes. The present argument is the most abstracted that ever I engaged in; it strains my faculties to
their highest stretch; and I desire the reader to attend
with the utmost perpensity, for I now proceed to un-
ravel the knotty point.

There is in mankind a certain[6]   .   .   .

.   .   .   .

   Hic multa   .   .   .   .   .   .
desiderantur.   .

.   .   .   And this I take to be a clear solution of the matter.

---

   [6] Here is another defect in the manuscript; but I think the author
did wisely, and that the matter, which thus strained faculties, was
not worth a solution; and it were well if all metaphysical cobweb
problems were no otherwise answered.

Having therefore so narrowly passed through this intricate difficulty, the reader will, I am sure, agree with me in the conclusion, that if the moderns mean by madness, only a disturbance or transposition of the brain, by force of certain vapours issuing up from the lower faculties, then has this madness been the parent of all those mighty revolutions that have happened in empire, philosophy, and in religion. For the brain, in its natural position and state of serenity, disposeth its owner to pass his life in the common forms, without any thoughts of subduing multitudes to his own power, his reasons, or his visions; and the more he shapes his understanding by the pattern of human learning, the less he is inclined to form parties, after his particular notions, because that instructs him in his private infirmities, as well as in the stubborn ignorance of the people. But when a man's fancy gets astride on his reason; when imagination is at cuffs with the senses, and common understanding, as well as common sense, is kicked out of doors; the first proselyte he makes is himself; and when that is once compassed, the difficulty is not so great in bringing over others; a strong delusion always operating from without as vigorously as from within. For cant and vision are to the ear and the eye, the same that tickling is to the touch. Those entertainments and pleasures we most value in life, are such as dupe and play the wag with the senses. For, if we take an examination of what is generally understood by happiness, as it has respect either to the understanding or the senses, we shall find all its properties and adjuncts will herd under this short definition, that it is a perpetual possession of being well deceived. And, first, with relation to the mind or understanding, 'tis manifest what mighty advantages fiction has over truth; and the reason is just at our elbow, because imagination can build nobler scenes, and produce

more wonderful revolutions than fortune or nature will
be at expense to furnish. Nor is mankind so much to
blame in his choice thus determining him, if we consider
that the debate merely lies between things past and
things conceived; and so the question is only this:—
whether things, that have place in the imagination, may
not as properly be said to exist, as those that are seated
in the memory, which may be justly held in the affirmative, and very much to the advantage of the former,
since this is acknowledged to be the womb of things,
and the other allowed to be no more than the grave.
Again, if we take this definition of happiness, and examine it with reference to the senses, it will be acknowledged wonderfully adapt. How fading and insipid do
all objects accost us, that are not conveyed in the vehicle
of delusion! How shrunk is everything, as it appears in
the glass of nature! So that if it were not for the assistance of artificial mediums, false lights, refracted angles,
varnish and tinsel, there would be a mighty level in the
felicity and enjoyments of mortal men. If this were seriously considered by the world, as I have a certain reason
to suspect it hardly will, men would no longer reckon
among their high points of wisdom, the art of exposing
weak sides, and publishing infirmities; an employment,
in my opinion, neither better nor worse than that of un-
masking, which, I think, has never been allowed fair
usage, either in the world, or the play-house.

In the proportion that credulity is a more peaceful
possession of the mind than curiosity; so far preferable
is that wisdom, which converses about the surface, to
that pretended philosophy, which enters into the depth
of things, and then comes gravely back with the informations and discoveries, that in the inside they are good
for nothing. The two senses, to which all objects first
address themselves, are the sight and the touch; these

never examine farther than the colour, the shape, the
size, and whatever other qualities dwell, or are drawn
by art upon the outward of bodies; and then comes
reason officiously with tools 'for cutting, and opening,
and mangling, and piercing, offering to demonstrate,
that they are not of the same consistence quite through.
Now I take all this to be the last degree of perverting
nature; one of whose eternal laws it is, to put her best
furniture forward. And therefore, in order to save the
charges of all such expensive anatomy for the time to
come, I do here think fit to inform the reader, that in
such conclusions as these, reason is certainly in the right,
and that in most corporeal beings, which have fallen
under my cognizance, the outside has been infinitely
preferable to the in; whereof I have been farther convinced from some late experiments. Last week I saw a
woman flayed, and you will hardly believe how much
it altered her person for the worse. Yesterday I ordered
the carcass of a beau to be stripped in my presence,
when we were all amazed to find so many unsuspected
faults under one suit of clothes. Then I laid open his
brain, his heart, and his spleen; but I plainly perceived
at every operation, that the farther we proceeded, we
found the defects increase upon us in number and bulk;
from all which, I justly formed this conclusion to myself; that whatever philosopher or projector can find out
an art to sodder and patch up the flaws and imperfections of nature, will deserve much better of mankind,
and teach us a more useful science, than that so much
in present esteem, of widening and exposing them (like
him who held anatomy to be the ultimate end of physic).
And he, whose fortunes and dispositions have placed
him in a convenient station to enjoy the fruits of this
noble art; he that can, with Epicurus, content his ideas
with the films and images that fly off upon his senses

from the superficies of things; such a man, truly wise, creams off nature, leaving the sour and the dregs for philosophy and reason to lap up. This is the sublime and refined point of felicity, called the possession of being well deceived; the serene peaceful state, of being a fool among knaves.

But to return to madness. It is certain, that, according to the system I have above deduced, every species thereof proceeds from a redundancy of vapours; therefore, as some kinds of phrenzy give double strength to the sinews, so there are of other species, which add vigour, and life, and spirit to the brain. Now, it usually happens, that these active spirits, getting possession of the brain, resemble those that haunt other waste and empty dwellings, which, for want of business, either vanish, and carry away a piece of the house, or else stay at home, and fling it all out of the windows. By which, are mystically displayed the two principal branches of madness, and which some philosophers, not considering so well as I, have mistaken to be different in their causes, over hastily assigning the first to deficiency, and the other to redundance.

I think it therefore manifest, from what I have here advanced, that the main point of skill and address is, to furnish employment for this redundancy of vapour, and prudently to adjust the season of it; by which means, it may certainly become of cardinal and catholic emolument, in a commonwealth. Thus one man, choosing a proper juncture, leaps into a gulf, from whence proceeds a hero, and is called the saver of his country; another achieves the same enterprise, but, unluckily timing it, has left the brand of madness fixed as a reproach upon his memory; upon so nice a distinction, are we taught to repeat the name of Curtius with reverence and love, that of Empedocles with hatred and contempt. Thus also

it is usually conceived, that the elder Brutus only personated the fool and madman for the good of the public;
but this was nothing else than a redundancy of the same
vapour long misapplied, called by the Latins, *ingenitum
par negotiis;*[7] or (to translate it as nearly as I can) a sort
of phrenzy, never in its right element, till you take it up
in the business of the state.

Upon all which, and many other reasons of equal
weight, though not equally curious, I do here gladly embrace an opportunity I have long sought for, of recom-
mending it as a very noble undertaking to Sir Edward
Seymour, Sir Christopher Musgrave, Sir John Bowls,
John How, Esq., and other patriots concerned, that they
would move for leave to bring in a bill for appointing
commissioners to inspect into Bedlam, and the parts
adjacent; who shall be empowered to send for persons,
papers, and records, to examine into the merits and
qualifications of every student and professor, to observe
with utmost exactness their several dispositions and behaviour, by which means, duly distinguishing and adapt-
ing their talents, they might produce admirable instruments for the several offices in a state . . . civil, and
military, proceeding in such methods as I shall here
humbly propose. And I hope the gentle reader will give
some allowance to my great solicitudes in this important
affair, upon account of the high esteem I have borne that
honourable society, whereof I had some time the happiness to be an unworthy member.

Is my student tearing his straw in piece-meal, swearing and blaspheming, biting his grate, foaming at the
mouth, and emptying his piss-pot in the spectators'
faces? Let the right worshipful the commissioners of in-
spection give him a regiment of dragoons, and send him
into Flanders among the rest. Is another eternally talk-

---

[7] Tacit.

ing, sputtering, gaping, bawling in a sound without period or article? What wonderful talents are here mislaid!
Let him be furnished immediately with a green bag and
papers, and threepence in his pocket,[8] and away with
him to Westminster-Hall. You will find a third gravely
taking the dimensions of his kennel, a person of foresight and insight, though kept quite in the dark; for why,
like Moses, *ecce cornuta*[9] *erat ejus facies.* He walks duly
in one pace, entreats your penny with due gravity and
ceremony, talks much of hard times, and taxes, and the
whore of Babylon, bars up the wooden window of his
cell constantly at eight o'clock, dreams of fire, and shop-
lifters, and court-customers, and privileged places. Now,
what a figure would all these acquirements amount to,
if the owner were sent into the city among his brethren!
Behold a fourth, in much and deep conversation with
himself, biting his thumbs at proper junctures, his countenance checkered with business and design, sometimes
walking very fast, with his eyes nailed to a paper that
he holds in his hands; a great saver of time, somewhat
thick of hearing, very short of sight, but more of memory; a man ever in haste, a great hatcher and breeder of
business, and excellent at the famous art of whispering
nothing; a huge idolator of monosyllables and procrastination, so ready to give his word to everybody, that he
never keeps it; one that has forgot the common meaning
of words, but an admirable retainer of the sound; extremely subject to the looseness, for his occasions are
perpetually calling him away. If you approach his grate
in his familiar intervals; "Sir," says he, "give me a penny,
and I'll sing you a song; but give me the penny first"
(hence comes the common saying, and commoner prac-

---

[8] A lawyer's coach-hire.
[9] Cornutus is either horned or shining, and by this term Moses is
described in the vulgar Latin of the Bible.

tice, of parting with money for a song). What a complete system of court skill is here described in every branch of it, and all utterly lost with wrong application! Accost the hole of another kennel, first stopping your nose, you will behold a surly, gloomy, nasty, slovenly mortal, raking in his own dung, and dabbling in his urine. The best part of his diet is the reversion of his own ordure, which, expiring into steams, whirls perpetually about, and at last re-infunds. His complexion is of a dirty yellow, with a thin scattered beard, exactly agreeable to that of his diet upon its first declination, like other insects, who, having their birth and education in an excrement, from thence borrow their colour and their smell. The student of this apartment is very sparing of his words, but somewhat over-liberal of his breath. He holds his hand out ready to receive your penny, and immediately upon receipt withdraws to his former occupations. Now, is it not amazing to think, the society of Warwick-lane should have no more concern for the recovery of so useful a member; who, if one may judge from these appearances, would become the greatest ornament to that illustrious body? Another student struts up fiercely to your teeth, puffing with his lips, half squeezing out his eyes, and very graciously holds you out his hand to kiss. The keeper desires you not to be afraid of this professor, for he will do you no hurt; to him alone is allowed the liberty of the ante-chamber, and the orator of the place gives you to understand, that this solemn person is a tailor run mad with pride. This considerable student is adorned with many other qualities, upon which at present I shall not farther enlarge . . . . Hark in your ear[10] . . . . I am strangely mistaken, if all his ad-

---

[10] I cannot conjecture what the author means here, or how this chasm should be filled, though it is capable of more than one interpretation.

dress, his motions, and his airs, would not then be very natural, and in their proper element.

I shall not descend so minutely, as to insist upon the vast number of beaux, fiddlers, poets, and politicians, that the world might recover by such a reformation; but what is more material, beside the clear gain redounding to the commonwealth, by so large an acquisition of persons to employ, whose talents and acquirements, if I may be so bold as to affirm it, are now buried, or at least misapplied; it would be a mighty advantage accruing to the public from this enquiry, that all these would very much excel, and arrive at great perfection in their several kinds; which, I think, is manifest from what I have already shewn, and shall enforce by this one plain instance, that even I myself, the author of these momentous truths, am a person, whose imaginations are hardmouthed, and exceedingly disposed to run away with his reason, which I have observed, from long experience, to be a very light rider, and easily shook off; upon which account, my friends will never trust me alone, without a solemn promise to vent my speculations in this, or the like manner, for the universal benefit of human kind; which perhaps the gentle, courteous, and candid reader, brimful of that modern charity and tenderness usually annexed to his office, will be very hardly persuaded to believe.

When I Come to Be Old. 1699.

These grim resolutions for old age were written when Swift was thirty-two, and the manuscript was found among his papers after his death. The text is here transcribed literally from the original.   c.v.d.

Not to marry a young Woman.

Not to keep young Company unless they reely desire it.

Not to be peevish or morose, or suspicious.

Not to scorn present Ways, or Wits, or Fashions, or Men, or War, &c.

Not to be fond of Children, *or let them come near me hardly.*[1]

Not to tell the same story over and over to the same People.

Not to be covetous.

Not to neglect decency, or cleenlyness, for fear of falling into Nastyness.

Not to be over severe with young People, but give Allowances for their youthfull follyes, and weaknesses.

Not to be influenced by, or give ear to knavish tatling servants, or others.

Not to be too free of advise, nor trouble any but those that desire it.

To desire[2] some good Friends to inform me wch of these Resolutions I break, or neglect, and wherein; and reform accordingly.

---

[1] The words in italics were scratched out, possibly by another hand, certainly at a later date.

[2] Changed from "conjure" as first written.

Not to talk much, nor of my self.

Not to boast of my former beauty, or strength, or favour
with Ladyes, &c.

Not to hearken to Flatteryes, nor conceive I can be beloved by a young woman, et eos qui hereditatem
captant, odisse ac vitare.

Not to be positive or opiniative.

Not to sett up for observing all these Rules; for fear I
should observe none.

Thoughts on Various Subjects, Moral and Diverting

The earliest of these thoughts are supposed to have been
written in October 1706, and the rest at different times
later. Of the selection here reprinted, the first thirty-four
appeared in Swift's *Miscellanies* of 1711. Others were
added in the *Miscellanies* of Swift and Pope (1727);
and still others posthumously.   C.V.D.

WE HAVE just religion enough to make us hate,
but not enough to make us love one another.

Reflect on things past, as wars, negotiations, factions,
&c. We enter so little into those interests, that we wonder how men could possibly be so busy and concerned
for things so transitory; look on the present times, we
find the same humour, yet wonder not at all.

A wise man endeavours, by considering all circumstances, to make conjectures, and form conclusions; but
the smallest accident intervening (and in the course of
affairs it is impossible to foresee all) does often produce
such turns and changes, that at last he is just as much
in doubt of events, as the most ignorant and unexperi-
enced person.

Positiveness is a good quality for preachers and orators, because he that would obtrude his thoughts and
reasons upon a multitude, will convince others the more,
as he appears convinced himself.

How is it possible to expect that mankind will take
advice, when they will not so much as take warning?

I forget whether advice be among the lost things, which Ariosto says may be found in the moon; that, and time, ought to have been there.

No preacher is listened to but Time, which gives us the same train and turn of thought that elder people have in vain tried to put into our heads before.

When we desire or solicit any thing, our minds run wholly on the good side or circumstances of it; when it is obtained, our minds run wholly on the bad ones.

In a glass house, the workmen often fling in a small quantity of fresh coals, which seems to disturb the fire, but very much enlivens it. This may allude to a gentle stirring of the passions, that the mind may not languish.

Religion seems to have grown an infant with age, and requires miracles to nurse it, as it had in its infancy.

All fits of pleasure are balanced by an equal degree of pain or languor; 'tis like spending this year, part of the next year's revenue.

The latter part of a wise man's life is taken up in curing the follies, prejudices, and false opinions he had contracted in the former.

Would a writer know how to behave himself with relation to posterity, let him consider in old books what he finds that he is glad to know, and what omissions he most laments.

Whatever the poets pretend, it is plain they give immortality to none but themselves; 'tis Homer and Virgil we reverence and admire, not Achilles or Æneas. With historians it is quite the contrary; our thoughts are taken up with the actions, persons, and events we read, and we little regard the authors.

When a true genius appears in the world, you may know him by this sign, that the dunces are all in confederacy against him.

Men who possess all the advantages of life, are in a

state where there are many accidents to disorder and discompose, but few to please them.

'Tis unwise to punish cowards with ignominy; for if they had regarded that, they would not have been cowards: Death is their proper punishment, because they fear it most.

I am apt to think, that, in the day of judgment, there will be small allowance given to the wise for their want of morals, and to the ignorant for their want of faith, because both are without excuse. This renders the advantages equal of ignorance and knowledge. But some scruples in the wise, and some vices in the ignorant, will perhaps be forgiven, upon the strength of temptation to each.

'Tis grown a word of course for writers to say, This critical age, as divines say, This sinful age.

'Tis pleasant to observe how free the present age is in laying taxes on the next. Future ages shall talk of this; this shall be famous to all posterity; whereas their time and thoughts will be taken up about present things, as ours are now.

It is in disputes, as in armies, where the weaker side sets up false lights, and makes a great noise, to make the enemy believe them more numerous and strong than they really are.

Some men, under the notion of weeding out prejudices, eradicate virtue, honesty, and religion.

In all well-instituted commonwealths, care has been taken to limit men's possessions; which is done for many reasons, and, among the rest, for one which, perhaps, is not often considered; that when bounds are set to men's desires, after they have acquired as much as the laws will permit them, their private interest is at an end, and they have nothing to do but to take care of the public.

There are but three ways for a man to revenge himself

of the censure of the world; to despise it, to return the like, or to endeavour to live so as to avoid it. The first of these is usually pretended, the last is almost impossible, the universal practice is for the second.

I have known some men possessed of good qualities which were very serviceable to others, but useless to themselves; like a sun-dial on the front of a house, to inform the neighbours and passengers, but not the owner within.

What they do in heaven we are ignorant of; what they do *not* we are told expressly, that they neither marry, nor are given in marriage.

The stoical scheme of supplying our wants by lopping off our desires, is like cutting off our feet, when we want shoes.

Physicians ought not to give their judgment of religion, for the same reason that butchers are not admitted to be jurors upon life and death.

The reason why so few marriages are happy, is, because young ladies spend their time in making nets, not in making cages.

Nothing more unqualifies a man to act with prudence, than a misfortune that is attended with shame and guilt.

The power of fortune is confessed only by the miserable; for the happy impute all their success to prudence or merit.

Ambition often puts men upon doing the meanest offices; so climbing is performed in the same posture with creeping.

Ill company is like a dog, who dirts those most whom he loves best.

Censure is the tax a man pays to the public for being eminent.

Although men are accused for not knowing their own weakness, yet, perhaps, as few know their own strength.

It is in men as in soils, where sometimes there is a vein of gold, which the owner knows not of.

Satire is reckoned the easiest of all wit; but I take it to be otherwise in very bad times: for it is as hard to satirize well a man of distinguished vices, as to praise well a man of distinguished virtues. It is easy enough to do either to people of moderate characters.

Invention is the talent of youth, and judgment of age; so that our judgment grows harder to please, when we have fewer things to offer it: this goes through the whole commerce of life. When we are old, our friends find it difficult to please us, and are less concerned whether we be pleased or no.

No wise man ever wished to be younger.

An idle reason lessens the weight of the good ones you gave before.

The motives of the best actions will not bear too strict an enquiry. It is allowed, that the cause of most actions, good or bad, may be resolved into the love of ourselves; but the self-love of some men, inclines them to please others; and the self-love of others is wholly employed in pleasing themselves. This makes the great distinction between virtue and vice. Religion is the best motive of all actions, yet religion is allowed to be the highest instance of self-love.

When the world has once begun to use us ill, it afterwards continues the same treatment with less scruple or ceremony, as men do to a whore.

Complaint is the largest tribute Heaven receives, and the sincerest part of our devotion.

The common fluency of speech in many men, and most women, is owing to a scarcity of matter, and a scarcity of words; for whoever is a master of language, and has a mind full of ideas, will be apt, in speaking, to hesitate upon the choice of both; whereas common speakers have only one set of ideas, and one set of words to clothe them in; and these are always ready at the mouth; so people come faster out of a church when it is almost empty, than when a crowd is at the door.

To be vain, is rather a mark of humility than pride. Vain men delight in telling what honours have been done them, what great company they have kept, and the like, by which they plainly confess that these honours were more than their due, and such as their friends would not believe, if they had not been told: whereas a man truly proud, thinks the greatest honours below his merit, and consequently scorns to boast. I therefore deliver it as a maxim, that whoever desires the character of a proud man, ought to conceal his vanity.

Small causes are sufficient to make a man uneasy, when great ones are not in the way: for want of a block he will stumble at a straw.

Dignity, high station, or great riches, are in some sort necessary to old men, in order to keep the younger at a distance, who are otherwise too apt to insult them upon the score of their age.

Every man desires to live long; but no man would be old.

Love of flattery, in most men, proceeds from the mean opinion they have of themselves; in women, from the contrary.

A very little wit is valued in a woman, as we are pleased with a few words spoken plain by a parrot.

A nice man is a man of nasty ideas.

There is a story in Pausanias of a plot for betraying a city discovered by the braying of an ass: the cackling of geese saved the Capitol, and Cataline's conspiracy was discovered by a whore. These are the only three animals, as far as I remember, famous in history for evidences and informers.

Most sorts of diversion in men, children, and other animals, are an imitation of fighting.

If a man makes me keep my distance, the comfort is, he keeps his at the same time.

Who can deny that all men are violent lovers of truth, when we see them so positive in their errors; which they will maintain out of their zeal to truth, although they contradict themselves every day of their lives?

That was excellently observed, say I, when I read a passage in an author, where his opinion agrees with mine. When we differ, there I pronounce him to be mistaken.

Very few men, properly speaking, *live* at present, but are providing to *live* another time.

As universal a practice as lying is, and as easy a one as it seems, I do not remember to have heard three good lies in all my conversation, even from those who were most celebrated in that faculty.

Men are contented to be laughed at for their wit, but not for their folly.

If the men of wit and genius would resolve never to complain in their works of critics and detractors, the next age would not know that they ever had any.

A man would have but few spectators, if he offered to shew for threepence how he could thrust a redhot iron into a barrel of gunpowder, and it should not take fire.

Query, Whether churches are not dormitories of the living as well as of the dead?

Since the union of divinity and humanity is the great article of our religion, it is odd to see some clergymen, in their writings of divinity, wholly devoid of humanity.

Sometimes I read a book with pleasure, and detest the author.

When somebody was telling a certain great minister that people were discontented, "Pho," said he, "half a dozen fools are prating in a coffeehouse, and presently think their own noise about their ears is made by the world."

The death of a private man is generally of so little importance to the world, that it cannot be a thing of great importance in itself; and yet I do not observe, from the practice of mankind, that either philosophy or nature have sufficiently armed us against the fears which attend it. Neither do I find anything able to reconcile us to it, but extreme pain, shame, or despair; for poverty, imprisonment, ill fortune, grief, sickness, and old age, do generally fail.

I never wonder to see men wicked, but I often wonder to see them not ashamed.

Do not we see how easily we pardon our own actions and passions, and the very infirmities of our bodies; why should it be wonderful to find us pardon our own dulness?

There is no vice or folly that requires so much nicety and skill to manage, as vanity; nor any which, by ill management, makes so contemptible a figure.

Observation is an old man's memory.

Eloquence, smooth and cutting, is like a razor whetted with oil.

Imaginary evils soon become real ones by indulging our reflections on them; as he, who in a melancholy fancy sees something like a face on the wall or the wainscot, can, by two or three touches with a lead pencil, make it look visible, and agreeing with what he fancied.

Men of great parts are often unfortunate in the management of public business, because they are apt to go out of the common road by the quickness of their imagination. This I once said to my Lord Bolingbroke, and desired he would observe, that the clerks in his office used a sort of ivory knife with a blunt edge to divide a sheet of paper, which never failed to cut it even, only requiring a steady hand: whereas if they should make use of a sharp penknife, the sharpness would make it go often out of the crease and disfigure the paper.

When a man pretends love, but courts for money, he is like a juggler, who conjures away your shilling, and conveys something very indecent under the hat.

Vision is the art of seeing things invisible.

The two maxims of any great man at court are, always to keep his countenance, and never to keep his word.

I must complain the cards are ill shuffled, till I have a good hand.

When I am reading a book, whether wise or silly, it seems to me to be alive and talking to me.

Whoever live at a different end of the town from me, I look upon as persons out of the world, and only myself and the scene about me to be in it.

When I was young, I thought all the world, as well as myself, was wholly taken up in discoursing upon the last new play.

It is said of the horses in the vision, that "their power was in their mouths and in their tails." What is said of horses in the vision, in reality may be said of women.

Elephants are always drawn smaller than life, but a flea always larger.

No man will take counsel, but every man will take money: therefore money is better than counsel.

Thoughts on Religion

These thoughts sound as if they were written when
Swift was a young man, possibly about the time he entered into holy orders, but this is mere conjecture. They
were not published till twenty years after his death.

C.V.D.

I AM in all opinions to believe according to my own
impartial reason; which I am bound to inform and
improve, as far as my capacity and opportunities will
permit.

It may be prudent in me to act sometimes by other
men's reason, but I can think only by my own.

If another man's reason fully convinceth me, it be-
comes my own reason.

To say a man is bound to believe, is neither truth nor
sense.

You may force men, by interest or punishment, to say
or swear they believe, and to act as if they believed: You
can go no further.

Every man, as a member of the commonwealth, ought
to be content with the possession of his own opinion in
private, without perplexing his neighbour or disturbing
the public.

Violent zeal for truth hath an hundred to one odds to
be either petulancy, ambition, or pride.

There is a degree of corruption wherein some nations,
as bad as the world is, will proceed to an amendment;
till which time particular men should be quiet.

To remove opinions fundamental in religion is impossible, and the attempt wicked, whether those opinions be true or false; unless your avowed design be to abolish that religion altogether. So, for instance, in the famous doctrine of Christ's divinity, which hath been universally received by all bodies of Christians, since the condemnation of Arianism under Constantine and his successors: Wherefore the proceedings of the Socinians are both vain and unwarrantable; because they will be never able to advance their own opinion, or meet any other success than breeding doubts and disturbances in the world. *Qui ratione sua disturbant mœnia mundi.*

The want of belief is a defect that ought to be concealed when it cannot be overcome.

The Christian religion, in the most early times, was proposed to the Jews and heathens without the article of Christ's divinity; which, I remember, Erasmus accounts for, by its being too strong a meat for babes. Perhaps, if it were now softened by the Chinese missionaries, the conversion of those infidels would be less difficult: And we find by the Alcoran, it is the great stumbling-block of the Mahometans. But, in a country already Christian, to bring so fundamental a point of faith into debate, can have no consequences that are not pernicious to morals and public peace.

I have been often offended to find St. Paul's allegories, and other figures of Grecian eloquence, converted by divines into articles of faith.

God's mercy is over all His works, but divines of all sorts lessen that mercy too much.

I look upon myself, in the capacity of a clergyman, to be one appointed by Providence for defending a post assigned me, and for gaining over as many enemies as I can. Although I think my cause is just, yet one great motive is my submitting to the pleasure of Providence, and to the laws of my country.

I am not answerable to God for the doubts that arise
in my own breast, since they are the consequence of
that reason which He hath planted in me; if I take care
to conceal those doubts from others, if I use my best
endeavours to subdue them, and if they have no influence on the conduct of my life.

I believe that thousands of men would be orthodox
enough in certain points, if divines had not been too
curious, or too narrow, in reducing orthodoxy within the
compass of subtleties, niceties, and distinctions, with little warrant from Scripture and less from reason or good
policy.

I never saw, heard, nor read, that the clergy were
beloved in any nation where Christianity was the religion of the country. Nothing can render them popular
but some degree of persecution.

Those fine gentlemen who affect the humour of railing
at the clergy, are, I think, bound in honour to turn parsons themselves, and shew us better examples.

Miserable mortals! Can we contribute to the honour
and glory of God? I wish that expression were struck
out of our Prayer-books.

Liberty of conscience, properly speaking, is no more
than the liberty of possessing our own thoughts and
opinions, which every man enjoys without fear of the
magistrate: But how far he shall publicly act in pursu-
ance of those opinions, is to be regulated by the laws of
the country. Perhaps, in my own thoughts, I prefer a
well-instituted commonwealth before a monarchy; and
I know several others of the same opinion. Now, if, upon
this pretence, I should insist upon liberty of conscience,
form conventicles of republicans, and print books preferring that government and condemning what is established, the magistrate would, with great justice, hang
me and my disciples. It is the same case in religion, al-

though not so avowed, where liberty of conscience, under the present acceptation, equally produces revolutions, or at least convulsions and disturbances in a state; which politicians would see well enough, if their eyes were not blinded by faction, and of which these kingdoms, as well as France, Sweden, and other countries, are flaming instances. Cromwell's notion upon this article was natural and right; when, upon the surrender of a town in Ireland, the Popish governor insisted upon an article for liberty of conscience, Cromwell said, he meddled with no man's conscience; but, if by liberty of conscience, the governor meant the liberty of the mass, he had express orders from the Parliament of England against admitting any such liberty at all.

It is impossible that anything so natural, so necessary, and so universal as death, should ever have been designed by Providence as an evil to mankind.

Although reason were intended by Providence to govern our passions, yet it seems that, in two points of the greatest moment to the being and continuance of the world, God hath intended our passions to prevail over reason. The first is, the propagation of our species, since no wise man ever married from the dictates of reason. The other is, the love of life, which, from the dictates of reason, every man would despise, and wish it at an end, or that it never had a beginning.

Hints towards an Essay
on Conversation

Swift's brilliant later *Complete Collection of Genteel and Ingenious Conversation* (1738), too long to be included here, is a compilation of contemporary clichés with a satiric introduction full of advice on how to make use of them. But the clichés, though many of them are still current, belong primarily to the eighteenth century, and the introduction accommodates itself to them. In *Hints towards an Essay on Conversation,* a subject in which Swift took a lifelong interest, the comments are timeless and still have as much application as when they were written. The style of the *Hints* makes it seem early, but it was not printed until 1758. 　　　　　C.V.D.

I HAVE observed few obvious subjects to have been so seldom, or, at least, so slightly handled, as this; and, indeed, I know few so difficult to be treated as it ought, nor yet upon which there seemeth so much to be said.

Most things, pursued by men for the happiness of public or private life, our wit or folly have so refined, that they seldom subsist but in idea; a true friend, a good marriage, a perfect form of government, with some others, require so many ingredients, so good in their several kinds, and so much niceness in mixing them, that for some thousands of years men have despaired of reducing their schemes to perfection. But, in conversation, it is, or might be otherwise; for here we are only to avoid a multitude of errors, which, although a matter of some difficulty, may be in every man's power, for want of which it remaineth as mere an idea as the other. Therefore it seemeth to me, that the truest way to understand conversation, is to know the faults and errors to which it is subject, and from thence every man to form maxims to himself whereby it may be regulated, because it requireth few talents to which most men are not born, or at least may not acquire without any great genius or study. For nature hath left every man a capacity of being agreeable, though not of shining in company; and there are an hundred men sufficiently qualified for both, who, by a very few faults, that they might correct in half an hour, are not so much as tolerable.

I was prompted to write my thoughts upon this subject by mere indignation, to reflect that so useful and innocent a pleasure, so fitted for every period and condition of life, and so much in all men's power, should be so much neglected and abused.

And in this discourse it will be necessary to note those errors that are obvious, as well as others which are seldomer observed, since there are few so obvious, or acknowledged, into which most men, some time or other, are not apt to run.

For instance: Nothing is more generally exploded than the folly of talking too much; yet I rarely remember to have seen five people together, where some one among them hath not been predominant in that kind, to the great constraint and disgust of all the rest. But among such as deal in multitudes of words, none are comparable to the sober deliberate talker, who proceedeth with much thought and caution, maketh his preface, brancheth out into several digressions, findeth a hint that putteth him in mind of another story, which he promiseth to tell you when this is done; cometh back regularly to his subject, cannot readily call to mind some person's name, holding his head, complaineth of his memory; the whole company all this while in suspense; at length says, it is no matter, and so goes on. And, to crown the business, it perhaps proveth at last a story the company hath heard fifty times before; or, at best, some insipid adventure of the relater.

Another general fault in conversation is, that of those who affect to talk of themselves: Some, without any ceremony, will run over the history of their lives; will relate the annals of their diseases, with the several symptoms and circumstances of them; will enumerate the hardships and injustice they have suffered in court, in parliament, in love, or in law. Others are more dexterous, and with great art will lie on the watch to hook in their own praise: They will call a witness to remember, they always foretold what would happen in such a case, but none would believe them; they advised such a man from the beginning, and told him the consequences, just as they happened; but he would have his own way. Others make a vanity of telling their faults; they are the strangest men in the world; they cannot dissemble; they own it is a folly; they have lost abundance of advantages by it; but, if you would give them the world, they cannot help it; there is something in their nature that abhors insincerity and constraint; with many other insufferable topics of the same altitude.

Of such mighty importance every man is to himself, and ready to think he is so to others; without once making this easy and obvious reflection, that his affairs can have no more weight with other men, than theirs have with him; and how little that is, he is sensible enough.

Where company hath met, I often have observed two persons discover, by some accident, that they were bred together at the same school or university, after which the rest are condemned to silence, and to listen while these two are refreshing each other's memory with the arch tricks and passages of themselves and their comrades.

I know a great officer of the army, who will sit for some time with a supercilious and impatient silence, full of anger and contempt for those who are talking; at length of a sudden demand audience, decide the matter in a short dogmatical way; then withdraw within himself again, and vouchsafe to talk no more, until his spirits circulate again to the same point.

There are some faults in conversation, which none are so subject to as the men of wit, nor ever so much as when they are with each other. If they have opened their mouths, without endeavouring to say a witty thing, they think it is so many words lost: It is a torment to the hearers, as much as to themselves, to see them upon the rack for invention, and in perpetual constraint, with so little success. They must do something extraordinary, in order to acquit themselves, and answer their character, else the standers-by may be disappointed and be apt to think them only like the rest of mortals. I have known two men of wit industriously brought together, in order to entertain the company, where they have made a very ridiculous figure, and provided all the mirth at their own expense.

I know a man of wit, who is never easy but where he can be allowed to dictate and preside: he neither expecteth to be informed or entertained, but to display his own talents. His business is to be good company, and not good conversation; and, therefore, he chooseth to frequent those who are content to listen, and profess themselves his admirers. And, indeed, the worst conversation I ever remember to have heard in my life, was that of Will's coffeehouse, where the wits (as they were called) used formerly to assemble; that is to say, five or six men, who had writ plays, or at least prologues, or had share in a miscellany, came thither, and entertained one another with their trifling composures, in so important an air, as if they had been the noblest efforts of human nature, or that the fate of kingdoms depended on them; and they were usually attended with an humble audience of young students from the inns of court, or the universities, who, at due distance, listened to these oracles, and returned home with great contempt for their law and philosophy, their heads filled with trash, under the name of politeness, criticism and *belles lettres*.

By these means the poets, for many years past, were all overrun with pedantry. For, as I take it, the word is not properly used; because pedantry is the too frequent or unseasonable obtruding our own knowledge in common discourse, and placing too great a value upon it; by which definition, men of the court or the army may be as guilty of pedantry as a philosopher or a divine; and, it is the same vice in women, when they are over copious upon the subject of their petticoats, or their fans, or their china. For which reason, although it be a piece of prudence, as well as good manners, to put men upon talking on subjects they are best versed in, yet that is a liberty a wise man could hardly take; because, besides the imputation of pedantry, it is what he would never improve by.

The great town is usually provided with some player, mimic, or buffoon, who hath a general reception at the good tables; familiar and domestic with persons of the first quality, and usually sent for at every meeting to divert the company; against which I have no objection. You go there as to a farce or a puppetshow; your business is only to laugh in season, either out of inclination or civility, while this merry companion is acting his part. It is a business he hath undertaken, and we are to suppose he is paid for his day's work. I only quarrel, when in select and private meetings, where men of wit and learning are invited to pass an evening, this jester should be admitted to run over his circle of tricks, and make the whole company unfit for any other conversation, besides the indignity of confounding men's talents at so shameful a rate.

Raillery is the finest part of conversation; but, as it is our usual custom to counterfeit and adulterate whatever is too dear for us, so we have done with this, and turned it all into what is generally called repartee, or being smart; just as when an expensive fashion cometh up, those who are not able to reach it, content themselves with some paltry imitation. It now passeth for raillery to run a man down in discourse, to put him out of countenance, and make him ridiculous, sometimes to expose the defects of his person or understanding; on all which occasions he is obliged not to be angry, to avoid the imputation of not being able to take a jest. It is admirable to observe one who is dexterous at this art, singling out a weak adversary, getting the laugh on his side, and then carrying all before him. The French, from whence we borrow the word, have a quite different idea of the thing, and so had we in the politer age of our fathers. Raillery was to say something that at first appeared a reproach of reflection; but, by some turn of wit unexpected and surprising, ended always in a compliment, and to the advantage of the person it was addressed to. And surely one of the best rules in conversation is, never to say a thing which any of the company can reasonably wish we had rather left unsaid; nor can there anything be well more contrary to the ends for which people meet together, then to part unsatisfied with each other or themselves.

There are two faults in conversation, which appear

very different, yet arise from the same root, and are equally blameable; I mean, an impatience to interrupt others, and the uneasiness of being interrupted ourselves. The two chief ends of conversation are to entertain and improve those we are among, or to receive those benefits ourselves; which whoever will consider, cannot easily run into either of those two errors; because when any man speaketh in company, it is to be supposed he doth it for his hearers' sake, and not his own; so that common discretion will teach us not to force their attention, if they are not willing to lend it; nor on the other side, to interrupt him who is in possession, because that is in the grossest manner to give the preference to our own good sense.

There are some people, whose good manners will not suffer them to interrupt you; but, what is almost as bad, will discover abundance of impatience, and lie upon the watch until you have done, because they have started something in their own thoughts which they long to be delivered of. Meantime, they are so far from regarding what passes, that their imaginations are wholly turned upon what they have in reserve, for fear it should slip out of their memory; and thus they confine their invention, which might otherwise range over a hundred things full as good, and that might be much more naturally introduced.

There is a sort of rude familiarity, which some people, by practising among their intimates, have introduced into their general conversation, and would have it pass for innocent freedom or humour, which is a dangerous experiment in our northern climate, where all the little decorum and politeness we have are purely forced by art, and are so ready to lapse into barbarity. This, among the Romans, was the raillery of slaves, of which we have many instances in Plautus. It seemeth to have been intro-

duced among us by Cromwell, who, by preferring the
scum of the people, made it a court entertainment, of
which I have heard many particulars; and, considering
all things were turned upside down, it was reasonable
and judicious: Although it was a piece of policy found
out to ridicule a point of honour in the other extreme,
when the smallest word misplaced among gentlemen
ended in a duel.

There are some men excellent at telling a story, and
provided with a plentiful stock of them, which they can
draw out upon occasion in all companies; and, considering how low conversation runs now among us, it is not
altogether a contemptible talent; however, it is subject
to two unavoidable defects; frequent repetition, and being soon exhausted; so that whoever valueth this gift in
himself, hath need of a good memory, and ought frequently to shift his company, that he may not discover
the weakness of his fund; for those who are thus endowed, have seldom any other revenue, but live upon
the main stock.

Great speakers in public, are seldom agreeable in
private conversation, whether their faculty be natural,
or acquired by practice, and often venturing. Natural
elocution, although it may seem a paradox, usually
springeth from a barrenness of invention and of words,
by which men who have only one stock of notions upon
every subject, and one set of phrases to express them in,
they swim upon the superficies, and offer themselves on
every occasion; therefore, men of much learning, and
who know the compass of a language, are generally the
worst talkers on a sudden, until much practice hath
inured and emboldened them, because they are confounded with plenty of matter, variety of notions, and of
words, which they cannot readily choose, but are per-

plexed and entangled by too great a choice; which is no disadvantage in private conversation; where, on the other side, the talent of haranguing is, of all others, most insupportable.

Nothing hath spoiled men more for conversation, than the character of being wits, to support which, they never fail of encouraging a number of followers and admirers, who list themselves in their service, wherein they find their accounts on both sides, by pleasing their mutual vanity. This hath given the former such an air of superiority, and made the latter so pragmatical, that neither of them are well to be endured. I say nothing here of the itch to dispute and contradiction, telling of lies, or of those who are troubled with the disease called the wandering of the thoughts, that they are never present in mind at what passeth in discourse; for whoever labours under any of these possessions, is as unfit for conversation as a madman in Bedlam.

I think I have gone over most of the errors in conversation, that have fallen under my notice or memory, except some that are merely personal, and others too gross to need exploding; such as lewd or profane talk; but I pretend only to treat the errors of conversation in general, and not the several subjects of discourse, which would be infinite. Thus we see how human nature is most debased, by the abuse of that faculty, which is held the great distinction between men and brutes; and how little advantage we make of that which might be the greatest, the most lasting, and the most innocent, as well as useful pleasure of life. In default of which, we are forced to take up with those poor amusements of dress and visiting, or the more pernicious ones of play, drink, and vicious amours, whereby the nobility and gentry of both sexes are entirely corrupted both in body and mind, and have lost all notions of love, honour, friendship, generosity; which, under the name of fopperies, have been for some time laughed out of doors.

This degeneracy of conversation, with the pernicious consequences thereof upon our humours and dispositions, hath been owing, among other causes, to the custom arisen, for some time past, of excluding women from any share in our society, further than in parties at play, or dancing, or in the pursuit of an amour. I take the highest period of politeness in England (and it is of the same date in France) to have been the peaceable part of King Charles the First's reign; and from what we read of those times, as well as from the accounts I have formerly met with from some who lived in that court, the methods then used for raising and cultivating conversation, were altogether different from ours. Several ladies, whom we find celebrated by the poets of that age, had assemblies at their houses, where persons of the best understanding, and of both sexes, met to pass the evenings in discoursing upon whatever agreeable subjects were occasionally started; and although we are apt to ridicule the sublime platonic notions they had, or personated in love and friendship, I conceive their refinements were grounded upon reason, and that a little grain of the romance is no ill ingredient to preserve and exalt the dignity of human nature, without which it is apt to degenerate into everything that is sordid, vicious, and low. If there were no other use in the conversation of ladies, it is sufficient that it would lay a restraint upon those odious topics of immodesty and indecencies, into which the rudeness of our northern genius is so apt to fall. And, therefore, it is observable in those sprightly gentlemen about the town, who are so very dexterous at entertaining a vizard mask in the park or the playhouse, that, in the company of ladies of virtue and honour, they are silent and disconcerted, and out of their element.

There are some people who think they sufficiently acquit themselves and entertain their company with re-lating of facts of no consequence, nor at all out of the road of such common incidents as happen every day; and this I have observed more frequently among the Scots than any other nation, who are very careful not to omit the minutest circumstances of time or place; which kind of discourse, if it were not a little relieved by the uncouth terms and phrases, as well as accent and gesture, peculiar to that country, would be hardly toler-able. It is not a fault in company to talk much; but to continue it long is certainly one; for, if the majority of those who are got together be naturally silent or cau-tious, the conversation will flag, unless it be often re-newed by one among them, who can start new subjects, provided he doth not dwell upon them, but leaveth room for answers and replies.

From Journal to Stella

The *Journal* is simply the letters Swift wrote to Esther Johnson (his Stella) and her companion Rebecca Dingley in Ireland while he was in England from September 2, 1710, to June 6, 1713. Twenty-six out of the original sixty-five survive in Swift's manuscript. All of them were preserved by him and published posthumously. The "little language" (baby talk) which appears in them is supposed to be a teasing imitation of Stella's speech when she was a small child, still affectionately remembered by Swift. He refers to her often as "Ppt," which may mean "poppet" (doll or baby) or "poor pretty thing," and to himself as "Pdfr," which may mean "poor dear foolish rogue." The word "Presto" referring to Swift in letters here printed is an early editor's substitution for "Pdfr" in the original manuscript. "D," "DD," "MD" are supposed to mean respectively "Dingley," "Dear Dingley," "My Dear" or "My Dears." "FW" and "ME" have not been clearly explained. The frequent "lele, lele" may mean "there, there." It appears that Stella as an infant had confused or exchanged the letters *l* and *r*. Hence Swift's "nevle saw ze rike" for "never saw the like," and "deelest logues" for "dearest rogues," and so on.   C.V.D.

L ONDON, September 9, Saturday, 1710. I got here last Thursday, after five days travelling, weary the first, almost dead the second, tolerable the third, and well enough the rest; and am now glad of the fatigue, which has served for exercise; and I am at present well enough. The Whigs were ravished to see me, and would

lay hold on me as a twig while they are drowning, and
the great men making me their clumsy apologies, &c.
But my Lord-Treasurer received me with a great deal of
coldness, which has enraged me so, I am almost vowing
revenge. I have not yet gone half my circle; but I find all
my acquaintance just as I left them. I hear my Lady Giffard is much at court, and Lady Wharton was ridiculing
it t'other day; so I have lost a friend there. I have not
yet seen her, nor intend it; but I will contrive to see
Stella's mother some other way. I writ to the Bishop of
Clogher from Chester; and I now write to the Archbishop of Dublin. Every thing is turning upside down;
every Whig in great office will, to a man, be infallibly
put out; and we shall have such a winter as has not been
seen in England. Every body asks me, how I came to be
so long in Ireland, as naturally as if here were my being;
but no soul offers to make it so: and I protest I shall return to Dublin, and the canal at Laracor, with more satisfaction than I ever did in my life. The Tatler expects
every day to be turned out of his employment; and the
Duke of Ormond, they say, will be Lieutenant of Ireland. I hope you are now peaceably in Presto's lodgings:
but I resolve to turn you out by Christmas: in which
time I shall either do my business, or find it not to be
done. Pray be at Trim by the time this letter comes to
you, and ride little Johnson, who must needs be now in
good case. I have begun this letter unusually on the post
night, and have already written to the Archbishop, and
cannot lengthen this. Henceforth I will write something
every day to MD, and make it a sort of journal: and
when it is full, I will send it whether MD writes or no:
and so that will be pretty: and I shall always be in conversation with MD, and MD with Presto. Pray make
Parvisol pay you the ten pounds immediately; so I
ordered him. They tell me I am growing fatter, and look

better; and, on Monday, Jervas is to retouch my picture.
I thought I saw Jack Temple and his wife pass by me to-
day in their coach; but I took no notice of them. I am
glad I have wholly shaken off that family. Tell the Prov-
ost I have obeyed his commands to the Duke of Ormond; or let it alone, if you please. I saw Jemmy Leigh
just now at the coffeehouse, who asked after you with
great kindness: he talks of going in a fortnight to Ireland. My service to the Dean, and Mrs Walls, and her
Archdeacon. Will Frankland's wife is near bringing to
bed, and I have promised to christen the child. I fancy
you had my Chester letter the Tuesday after I writ. I presented Dr Raymond to Lord Wharton at Chester. Pray
let me know when Joe gets his money. It is near ten,
and I hate to send by the bellman. MD shall have a
longer letter in a week, but I send this only to tell I am
safe in London; and so farewell, &c.

10. To-day I dined with Lord Mountjoy at Kensington; saw my mistress, Ophy Butler's wife, who is grown
a little charmless. I sat till ten in the evening with Addison and Steele; Steele will certainly lose his Gazetteer's
place, all the world detesting his engaging in parties. At
ten I went to the coffeehouse, hoping to find Lord Rad-
nor, whom I had not seen. He was there; for an hour and
a half we talked treason heartily against the Whigs, their
baseness and ingratitude. And I am come home rolling
resentments in my mind, and framing schemes of revenge: full of which (having written down some hints),
I go to bed. I am afraid MD dined at home, because it
is Sunday; and there was the little half-pint of wine; for
God's sake be good girls, and all will be well. Ben Tooke
was with me this morning.

29. I wish MD a merry Michaelmas. I dined with Mr
Addison, and Jervas the painter, at Addison's country
place; and then came home, and writ more to my lam-

poon. I made a Tatler since I came; guess which it is, and whether the Bishop of Clogher smokes it. I saw Mr Sterne to-day; he will do as you order, and I will give him chocolate for Stella's health. He goes not these three weeks. I wish I could send it some other way. So now to your letter, brave boys. I don't like your way of saving shillings: nothing vexes me but that it does not make Stella a coward in a coach. I don't think any lady's advice about my ear signifies twopence; however, I will, in compliance to you, ask Dr. Cockburn. Radcliffe I know not, and Bernard I never see. Walls will certainly be stingier for seven years, upon pretence of his robbery. So Stella puns again; why, 'tis well enough; but I'll not second it, though I could make a dozen: I never thought of a pun since I left Ireland.—Bishop of Clogher's bill? why, he paid it me; do you think I was such a fool to go without it? As for the four shillings, I will give you a bill on Parvisol for it on t'other side this paper; and pray tear off the two letters I shall write to him and Joe, or let Dingley transcribe and send them; though that to Parvisol, I believe, he must have my hand for.—No, no, I'll eat no grapes; I eat about six the other day at Sir John Holland's; but would not give sixpence for a thousand, they are so bad this year. Yes, faith, I hope in God Presto and MD will be together this time twelvemonth; what then? Last year, I suppose, I was at Laracor; but next I hope to eat my Michaelmas goose at my little gooses' lodgings. I drink no *aile* (I suppose you mean *ale*), but yet good wine every day, of five and six shillings a bottle. O Lord, how much Stella writes; pray don't carry that too far, young women, but be temperate to hold out. To-morrow I go to Mr Harley. Why small hopes from the Duke of Ormond? he loves me very well, I believe, and would, in my turn, give me something to make me easy; and I have good interest among his best friends.

But I don't think of any thing further than the business I am upon: you see I writ to Manley before I had your letter, and I fear he will be out. Yes, Mrs Owl, Blighe's corpse came to Chester when I was there, and I told you so in my letter, or forgot it. I lodge in Bury Street, where I removed a week ago. I have the first floor, a dining-room and bed-chamber, at eight shillings a week; plaguy deep, but I spend nothing for eating, never go to a tavern, and very seldom in a coach; yet after all it will be expensive. Why do you trouble yourself, Mrs Stella, about my instrument? I have the same the Archbishop gave me; and it is as good now the bishops are away. The Dean friendly! The Dean be pox't: a great piece of friendship indeed, what you heard him tell the Bishop of Clogher; I wonder he had the face to talk so: but he lent me money, and that's enough. Faith I would not send this these four days, only for writing to Joe and Parvisol. Tell the Dean that when the bishops send me any packets, they must not write to me at Mr Steele's; but direct for Mr Steele, at his office at the Cockpit; and let the enclosed be directed for me; that mistake cost me eighteenpence t'other day.

Oct. 2. Lord Halifax was at Hampton Court at his lodgings, and I dined with him there with Methuen and Delaval, and the late Attorney General. I went to the drawing-room before dinner (for the Queen was at Hampton Court), and expected to see nobody; but I met acquaintance enough. I walked in the gardens, saw the cartoons of Raphael, and other things, and with great difficulty got from Lord Halifax, who would have kept me to-morrow to show me his house and park, and improvements. We left Hampton Court at sunset, and got here in a chariot and two horses time enough by starlight. That's something charms me mightily about London; that you go dine a dozen miles off in October, stay all day, and return so quickly; you cannot do anything like this in Dublin. I writ a second penny-post letter to your mother, and hear nothing of her. Did I tell you that Earl Berkeley died last Sunday was se'nnight, at Berkeley Castle, of a dropsy? Lord Halifax began a health to me to-day: it was the resurrection of the Whigs, which I refused, unless he would add their reformation too: and I told him he was the only Whig in England I loved, or had any good opinion of.

4. After I had put out my candle last night, my landlady came into my room, with a servant of Lord Halifax, to desire I would go dine with him at his house near Hampton Court; but I sent him word I had business of great importance that hindered me, &c. And, to-day, I was brought privately to Mr Harley, who received me with the greatest respect and kindness imaginable: he has appointed me an hour on Saturday at four, afternoon, when I will open my business to him; which expression I would not use if I were a woman. I know you smoked it; but I did not till I writ it. I dined to-day at Mr Delaval's, the envoy of Portugal, with Nic. Rowe the poet, and other friends; and I gave my lampoon to be printed. I have more mischief in my heart; and I think it shall go round with them all, as this hits, and I can find hints. I am certain I answered your 2d letter, and yet I do not find it here. I suppose it was in my 4th; and why N. 2d, 3d; is it not enough to say, as I do, 1, 2, 3? &c. I am going to work at another Tatler: I will be far enough but I say the same thing over two or three times, just as I do when I am talking to little MD; but what care I? they can read it as easily as I can write it: I think I have brought these lines pretty straight again. I fear it will be long before I finish two sides at this rate. Pray, dear MD, when I occasionally give you a little commission mixed with my letters, don't forget it, as that to

Morgan and Joe, &c., for I write just as I can remember, otherwise I would put them all together. I was to visit Mr Sterne to-day, and gave him your commission about handkerchiefs: that of chocolate I will do myself, and send it him when he goes, and you will pay me when *the giver's bread*, &c. To-night I will read a pamphlet, to amuse myself. God preserve your dear healths.

7. I wonder when this letter will be finished: it must go by Tuesday, that is certain; and if I have one from MD before, I will not answer it, that's as certain too! 'Tis now morning, and I did not finish my papers for Mr Harley last night; for you must understand Presto was sleepy, and made blunders and blots. Very pretty that I must be writing to young women in a morning fresh and fasting, faith. Well, good morrow to you: and so I go to business, and lay aside this paper till night, sirrahs.—At night. Jack How told Harley, that if there were a lower place in hell than another, it was reserved for his porter, who tells lies so gravely, and with so civil a manner. This porter I have had to deal with, going this evening at four to visit Mr Harley, by his own appointment. But the fellow told me no lie, though I suspected every word he said. He told me his master was just gone to dinner, with much company, and desired I would come an hour hence, which I did, expecting to hear Mr Harley was gone out; but they had just done dinner. Mr Harley came out to me, brought me in, and presented me his son-in-law, Lord Doblane [Dupplin], or some such name, and his own son, and among others, Will Penn the Quaker: we sat two hours, drinking as good wine as you do; and two hours more he and I alone; where he heard me tell my business: entered into it with all kindness; asked for my powers, and read them; and read likewise a memorial I had drawn up, and put it in his pocket to show the Queen; told me the measures he would take;

and, in short, said every thing I could wish; told me he must bring Mr St John (Secretary of State) and me acquainted; and spoke so many things of personal kindness and esteem for me, that I am inclined half to believe what some friends have told me, that he would do every thing to bring me over. He has desired to dine with me (what a comical mistake that was), I mean, he has desired me to dine with him on Tuesday; and after four hours being with him, set me down at St James's Coffeehouse, in a hackney coach. All this is odd and comical if you consider him and me. He knew my christian name very well. I could not forbear saying thus much upon this matter, although you will think it tedious. But I will tell you; you must know, 'tis fatal to me to be a scoundrel and a prince the same day: for being to see him at four, I could not engage myself to dine at my friend's; so I went to Tooke, to give him a ballad and dine with him; but he was not at home; so I was forced to go to a blind chophouse, and dine for tenpence upon gill ale, bad broth, and three chops of mutton; and then go reeking from thence to the first minister of state. And now I am going in charity to send Steele a Tatler, who is very low of late. I think I am civiller than I used to be; and have not used the expression of *"you in* Ireland" and *"we in* England," as I did when I was here before, to your great indignation.—They may talk of the *you know what;*[1] but, gad, if it had not been for that, I should never have been able to get the access I have had; and if that helps me to succeed, then that *same thing* will be serviceable to the church. But how far we must depend upon new friends, I have learnt by long practice, though I think, among great ministers, they are just as good as old ones. And so I think this important day has made a great hole in this side of the paper; and the fiddle faddles of to-

---

[1] *A Tale of a Tub.*

morrow and Monday will make up the rest; and, besides, I shall see Harley on Tuesday before this letter goes.

15. I will write plainer, if I can remember it; for Stella must not spoil her eyes, and Dingley can't read my hand very well; and I am afraid my letters are too long: then you must suppose one to be two, and read them at twice. I dined to-day with Mr Harley: Mr Prior dined with us. He has left my memorial with the Queen, who has consented to give the First-Fruits and Twentieth parts, and will, we hope, declare it to-morrow in the cabinet. But I beg you to tell it to no person alive; for so I am ordered, till in public; and I hope to get something of greater value. After dinner came in Lord Peterborow: we renewed our acquaintance, and he grew mightily fond of me. They began to talk of a paper of verses called Sid Hamet. Mr Harley repeated part, and then pulled them out, and gave them to a gentleman at the table to read, though they had all read them often: Lord Peterborow would let nobody read them but himself: so he did; and Mr Harley bobbed me at every line to take notice of the beauties. Prior rallied Lord Peterborow for author of them; and Lord Peterborow said, he knew them to be his; and Prior then turned it upon me, and I on him. I am not guessed at all in town to be the author; yet so it is: but that is a secret only to you. Ten to one whether you see them in Ireland; yet here they run prodigiously. Harley presented me to Lord President of Scotland, and Mr. Benson, Lord of the Treasury. Prior and I came away at nine, and sat at the Smyrna till eleven, receiving acquaintance.

Nov. 8. Here's ado and a clutter! I must now answer MD's fifth; but first you must know I dined at the Portugal envoy's to-day, with Addison, Vanbrugh, Admiral Wager, Sir Richard Temple, Methuen, &c. I was weary of their company, and stole away at five, and came home

like a good boy, and studied till ten, and had a fire; O
ho! and now am in bed. I have no fire-place in my bed-
chamber; but 'tis very warm weather when one's in bed.
Your fine cap, Madam Dingley, is too little, and too hot:
I'll have that fur taken off; I wish it were far enough;
and my old velvet cap is good for nothing. Is it velvet
under the fur? I was feeling, but cannot find: if it be,
'twill do without it, else I will face it; but then I must
buy new velvet: but may be I may beg a piece. What
shall I do? well, now to rogue MD's letter. God be
thanked for Stella's eyes mending; and God send it bolds;
but faith you write too much at a time; better write less,
or write it at ten times. Yes, faith, a long letter in a
morning from a dear friend is a dear thing. I smoke a
compliment, little mischievous girls, I do so. But who are
those *wiggs* that think I am turned Tory? Do you mean
Whigs? Which *wiggs*, and *wat* do you mean? I know
nothing of Raymond, and only had one letter from him a
little after I came here. (Pray remember Morgan.) Raymond is indeed like to have much influence over me in
London, and to share much of my conversation. I shall
no doubt introduce him to Harley, and Lord Keeper,
and the Secretary of State. The Tatler upon Ithuriel's
spear is not mine, madam. What a puzzle there is between you and your judgment? In general you may be
sometimes sure of things as that about *style*, because it is
what I have frequently spoken of; but guessing is mine
a—; and I defy mankind if I please. Why, I writ a
pamphlet when I was last in London, that you and a
thousand have seen, and never guessed it to be mine.
Could you have guessed the Shower in Town to be
mine? How chance you did not see that before your last
letter went? But I suppose you in Ireland did not think
it worth mentioning. Nor am I suspected for the lampoon: only Harley said he smoked me (have I told you

so before?), and some others knew it. 'Tis called the Rod of Sid Hamet. And I have written several other things that I hear commended, and nobody suspects me for them; nor you should not know till I see you again. What do you mean "That boards near me, that I dine with now and then?" I know no such person: I do not dine with boarders. What the pox! You know whom I have dined with every day since I left you, better than I do. What do you mean, sirrah? Slids, my ailment has been over these two months almost. Impudence, if you vex me, I will give ten shillings a-week for my lodging; for I am almost st—k out of this with the sink, and it helps me to verses in my Shower. Well, Madam Dingley, what say you to the world to come? What ballad? Why go look, it was not good for much: have patience till I come back; patience is a gay thing as, &c. I hear nothing of Lord Mountjoy's coming for Ireland. When is Stella's birthday? in March? Lord bless me, my turn at Christ Church; it is so natural to hear you write about that, I believe you have done it a hundred times; it is as fresh in my mind, the verger coming to you; and why to you? would he have you preach for me? O, pox on your spelling of Latin. *Jonsonibus atque*, that's the way. How did the Dean get that name by the end? 'Twas you betrayed me: not I, faith; I'll not break his head. Your mother is still in the country, I suppose, for she promised to see me when she came to town. I writ to her four days ago, to desire her to break it to Lady Giffard, to put some money for you in the Bank, which was then fallen thirty *per cent*. Would to God mine had been here, I should have gained one hundred pounds, and got as good interest as in Ireland, and much securer. I would fain have borrowed three hundred pounds; but money is so scarce here, there is no borrowing by this fall of stocks. 'Tis rising now, and I knew it would: it fell from one

hundred and twenty-nine to ninety-six. I have not heard
since from your mother. Do you think I would be so
unkind not to see her, that you desire me in a style
so melancholy? Mrs Raymond you say is with child:
I am sorry for it, and so is, I believe, her husband. Mr
Harley speaks all the kind things to me in the world;
and I believe, would serve me, if I were to stay here; but
I reckon in time the Duke of Ormond may give me some
addition to Laracor. Why should the Whigs think I
came to England to leave them? Sure my journey was no
secret? I protest sincerely, I did all I could to hinder it, as
the Dean can tell you, although now I do not repent it.
But who the devil cares what they think? Am I under obligations in the least to any of them all? Rot 'em, for ungrateful dogs; I will make them repent their usage before
I leave this place. They say here the same thing of my
leaving the Whigs; but they own they cannot blame me,
considering the treatment I have had. I will take care of
your spectacles, as I told you before, and of the Bishop
of Killala's; but I will not write to him, I han't time.
What do you mean by my fourth, Madam *Dinglibus*?
Does not Stella say you have had my fifth, Goody
Blunder? you frighted me till I looked back. Well, this is
enough for one night. Pray give my humble service to
Mrs Stoyte and her sister, Kate it is or Sarah? I have
forgot her name, faith. I think I will even (and to Mrs
Walls and the archdeacon) send this to-morrow: no,
faith, that will be in ten days from the last. I will keep it
till Saturday, though I write no more. But what if a letter
from MD should come in the mean time? why then I
would only say, madam, I have received your sixth letter; your most humble servant to command, Presto; and
so conclude. Well, now I will write and think a little, and
so to bed, and dream of MD.

Dec. 1. Morning. I wish Smyth were hanged. I was

dreaming the most melancholy things in the world of
poor Stella, and was grieving and crying all night.—
Pshah, it is foolish: I will rise and divert myself; so good-
morrow, and God of his infinite mercy keep and protect
you. The Bishop of Clogher's letter is dated Nov. 21. He
says, you thought of going with him to Clogher. I am
heartily glad of it, and wish you would ride there, and
Dingley go in a coach. I have had no fit since my first, although sometimes my head is not quite in good order.—
At night. I was this morning to visit Mr Pratt, who is
come over with poor sick Lord Shelburn; they made me
dine with them, and there I staid like a booby, till eight,
looking over them at ombre, and then came home. Lord
Shelburn's giddiness is turned into a colic, and he looks
miserably.

3. Pshaw, I must be writing to those dear saucy brats
every night, whether I will or no, let me have what business I will, or come home ever so late, or be ever so
sleepy; but an old saying and a true one,

> Be you lords, or be you earls,
> You must write to naughty girls.

I was to-day at court, and saw Raymond among the
beef-eaters, staying to see the Queen; so I put him in a
better station, made two or three dozen of bows, and
went to church, and then to court again to pick up a dinner, as I did with Sir John Stanley, and then we went to
visit Lord Mountjoy, and just now left him, and 'tis near
eleven at night, young women, and methinks this letter
comes pretty near to the bottom, and 'tis but eight days
since the date, and don't think I'll write on the other side,
I thank you for nothing. Faith, if I would use you to letters on sheets as broad as this room, you would always
expect them from me. O, faith, I know you well enough;
but an old saying, &c.

Two sides in a sheet,
And one in a street.

I think that's but a silly old saying, and so I'll go to sleep, and do you so too.

13. Morning. I am to go trapesing with Lady Kerry and Mrs Pratt to see sights all this day: they engaged me yesterday morning at tea. You hear the havock making in the army: Meredyth, Macartney, and Colonel Honeywood, are obliged to sell their commands at half value, and leave the army, for drinking destruction to the present ministry, and dressing up a hat on a stick, and calling it Harley; then drinking a glass with one hand, and discharging a pistol with the other at the maukin, wishing it were Harley himself; and a hundred other such pretty tricks, as inflaming their soldiers and foreign ministers against the late changes at court. Cadogan has had a little paring; his mother told me yesterday he had lost the place of envoy: but I hope they will go no farther with him, for he was not at those mutinous meetings. Well, these saucy jades take up so much of my time, with writing to them in a morning; but faith I am glad to see you whenever I can: a little snap and away; and so hold your tongue, for I must rise: not a word your life. How nowww? so very well; stay till I come home, and then perhaps you may hear farther from me. And where will you go to-day, for I can't be with you for these ladies? It is a rainy ugly day. I'd have you send for Walls, and go to Dean's; but don't play small games when you lose. You'll be ruined by manilio, basto, the queen, and two small trumps in red. I confess 'tis a good hand against the player; but then there are spadilio, punto, the king, strong trumps against you, which, with one trump more, are three tricks ten ace: for, suppose you play your manilio—O, silly, how I prate and can't

get away from this MD in a morning. Go, get you gone,
dear naughty girls, and let me rise. There, Patrick locked
up my ink again the third time last night: the rogue gets
the better of me; but I will rise in spite of you, sirrahs.—
At night. Lady Kerry, Mrs Pratt, Mrs Cadogan, and I,
in one coach; Lady Kerry's son and his governor, and
two gentlemen, in another; maids and misses, and little
master (Lord Shelburn's children) in a third, all hack-
neys, set out at ten o'clock this morning from Lord Shelburn's home in Piccadilly to the Tower, and saw all the
sights, lions, etc., then to Bedlam; then dined at the
chophouse behind the Exchange; then to Gresham College (but the keeper was not at home), and concluded
the night at the puppet-show, whence we came home
safe at eight, and I left them. The ladies were all in
mobs; how do you call it? undressed; and it was the rain-
iest day that ever dripped; and I'm weary, and 'tis now
past eleven.

31. Morning. It is now seven, and I have got a fire,
but am writing abed in my bed-chamber. 'Tis not shaving day, so I shall be ready early to go before church to
Mr St John, and to-morrow I will answer our MD's letter.

> Would you answer MD's letter,
> On New-year's-day you'll do it better:
> For when the year with MD 'gins,
> It without MD never lins.

These proverbs have always old words in them; *lins* is
leave off.

> But if on New-year you write nones,
> MD then will bang your bones.—

But Patrick says I must rise.—Night. I was early this
morning with Secretary St John, and gave him a memorial to get the Queen's letter for the First-Fruits, who has
promised to do it in a very few days. He told me he had

been with the Duke of Marlborough, who was lamenting
his former wrong steps in joining with the Whigs, and
said he was worn out with age, fatigues, and misfortunes. I swear it pitied me; and I really think they will
not do well in too much mortifying that man, although
indeed it is his own fault. He is covetous as Hell, and
ambitious as the prince of it: he would fain have been
General for life, and has broken all endeavours for peace,
to keep his greatness and get money. He told the queen
he was neither covetous nor ambitious. She said, if she
could have conveniently turned about, she would have
laughed, and could hardly forbear it in his face. He fell
in with all the abominable measures of the late ministry,
because they gratified him for their own designs. Yet he
has been a successful general, and I hope he will continue his command. O Lord, smoke the politics to MD.
Well; but if you like them, I will scatter a little now and
then, and mine are all fresh from the chief hands. Well,
I dined with Mr Harley, and came away at six: there was
much company, and I was not merry at all. Mr Harley
made me read a paper of verses of Prior's. I read them
plain without any fine manner, and Prior swore I should
never read any of his again; but he would be revenged,
and read some of mine as bad. I excused myself, and
said, I was famous for reading verses the worst in the
world, and that every body snatched them from me
when I offered to begin. So we laughed.—Sir Andrew
Fountaine still continues ill. He is plagued with some
sort of bile.

Jan. 7, 1711. Morning. Your new Lord-Chancellor sets
out to-morrow for Ireland: I never saw him. He carries
over one Trapp, a parson, as his chaplain, a sort of pretender to wit, a second-rate pamphleteer for the cause,
whom they pay by sending him to Ireland. I never saw
Trapp neither. I met Tighe, and your Smyth, of Lovet's,

yesterday by the Exchange. Tighe and I took no notice
of each other: but I stopped Smyth, and told him of the
box that lies for you at Chester, because he says he goes
very soon to Ireland, I think this week: and I will send
this morning to Sterne, to take measures with Smyth; so
good morrow, sirrahs, and let me rise, pray. I took up
this paper when I came in at evening, I mean this minute, and then, said I, No, no, indeed, MD, you must
stay, and then was laying it aside, but could not for my
heart, though I am very busy, till I just ask you how you
do since morning; by and by we shall talk more, so let
me leave you softly down, little paper, till then; so there
—now to business; there, I say, get you gone: no, I won't
push you neither, but hand you on one side—So—Now
I am got into bed, I'll talk with you. Mr Secretary St
John sent for me this morning in all haste; but I would
not lose my shaving for fear of missing church. I went to
court, which is of late always very full, and young Manley and I dined at Sir Matthew Dudley's. I must talk
politics. I protest I am afraid we shall all be embroiled
with parties. The Whigs, now they are fallen, are the
most malicious toads in the world. We have had now a
second misfortune, the loss of several Virginia ships. I
fear people will begin to think that nothing thrives under
this ministry: and if the ministry can once be rendered
odious to the people, the Parliament may be chosen
Whig or Tory, as the Queen pleases. Then I think our
friends press a little too hard on the Duke of Marlborough. The country members are violent to have past faults
inquired into, and they have reason; but I do not observe
the ministry to be very fond of it. In my opinion, we
have nothing to save us but a peace, and I am sure we
cannot have such a one as we hoped, and then the Whigs
will bawl what they would have done had they continued
in power. I tell the ministry this as much as I dare, and

shall venture to say a little more to them, especially
about the Duke of Marlborough, who, as the Whigs give
out, will lay down his command; and I question whether
ever any wise state laid aside a general who had been
successful nine years together, whom the enemy so much
dread, and his own soldiers cannot but believe must always conquer; and you know that in war opinion is nine
parts in ten. The ministry hear me always with appearance of regard, and much kindness; but I doubt they let
personal quarrels mingle too much with their proceedings. Meantime, they seem to value all this as nothing,
and are as easy and merry as if they had nothing in their
hearts, or upon their shoulders; like physicians, who endeavour to cure, but feel no grief, whatever the patient
suffers. Pshaw, what's all this? Do you know one thing,
that I find I can write politics to you much easier than to
any body alive? But I swear my head is full, and I wish I
were at Laracor, with dear charming MD, &c.

21. Morning. It has snowed terribly all night, and is
vengeance cold. I am not yet up, but cannot write long;
my hands will freeze. Is there a good fire, Patrick? Yes,
sir, then I'll rise; come take away the candle. You must
know I write on the dark side of my bed-chamber, and
am forced to have a candle till I rise, for the bed stands
between me and the window, and I keep the curtains
shut this cold weather. So pray let me rise, and, Patrick,
here take away the candle.—At night. We are now here
in high frost and snow, the largest fire can hardly keep
us warm. It is very ugly walking; a baker's boy broke his
thigh yesterday. I walk slow, make short steps, and never
tread on my heel. 'Tis a good proverb the Devonshire
people have:

> Walk fast in snow,
> In frost walk slow,
> And still as you go,

Tread on your toe:
When frost and snow are both together,
Sit by the fire and spare shoe leather.

I dined to-day with Dr Cockburn, but will not do so
again in haste, he has generally such a parcel of Scots
with him.

22. Morning. Starving, starving, uth, uth, uth, uth,
uth.—Don't you remember I used to come into your
chamber, and turn Stella out of her chair, and rake up
the fire in a cold morning, and cry uth, uth, uth? &c. O
faith I must rise, my hand is so cold I can write no more.
So good morrow, sirrahs.—At night. I went this morning
to Lady Giffard's house, and saw your mother, and made
her give me a pint bottle of palsy water, which I brought
home in my pocket; and sealed and tied up in a paper,
and sent it to Mr Smyth, who goes to-morrow for Ireland, and sent a letter to him to desire his care of it, and
that he would inquire at Chester about the box. He was
not within, so the bottle and letter were left for him at
his lodgings, with strict orders to give them to him; and
I will send Patrick in a day or two, to know whether it
was given, &c. Dr Stratford and I dined to-day with Mr
Stratford in the city, by appointment: but I chose to
walk there for exercise in the frost. But the weather had
given a little, as you women call it, so it was something
slobbery. I did not get home till nine, and now I am in
bed to break your head.

Feb. 5. Morning. I am going this morning to see Prior,
who dines with me at Mr Harley's; so I can't stay fiddling
and talking with dear little brats in a morning, and 'tis
still terribly cold. I wish my cold hand was in the warm-
est place about you, young women, I'd give ten guineas
upon that account with all my heart, faith; oh, it starves
my thigh; so I'll rise, and bid you good morrow, my
ladies both, good morrow. Come stand away, let me

rise: Patrick, take away the candle. Is there a good fire?
—So—up adazy.—At night. Mr Harley did not sit down
till six, and I staid till eleven; henceforth, I will choose
to visit him in the evenings, and dine with him no more,
if I can help it. It breaks all my measures, and hurts my
health; my head is disorderly, but not ill, and I hope it
will mend.

7. I was this morning early with Mr Lewis of the
Secretary's office, and saw a letter Mr Harley had sent to
him, desiring to be reconciled; but I was deaf to all entreaties, and have desired Lewis to go to him, and let
him know I expect farther satisfaction. If we let these
great ministers pretend too much, there will be no governing them. He promises to make me easy, if I will but
come and see him; but I won't, and he shall do it by
message, or I will cast him off. I'll tell you the cause of
our quarrel when I see you, and refer it to yourselves. In
that he did something,[1] which he intended for a favour,
and I have taken it quite otherwise, disliking both the
thing and the manner, and it has heartily vexed me, and
all I have said is truth, though it looks like jest: and I
absolutely refused to submit to his intended favour, and
expect farther satisfaction. Mr Ford and I dined with Mr
Lewis. We have a monstrous deal of snow, and it has cost
me two shillings to-day in chair and coach, and walked
till I was dirty besides. I know not what it is now to
read or write after I am in bed. The last thing I do up is
to write something to our MD, and then get into bed,
and put out my candle, and so go sleep as fast as ever I
can. But in the mornings I do write sometimes in bed, as
you know.

17. I took some good walks in the Park to-day, and
then went to Mr Harley. Lord Rivers was got there before me, and I chid him for presuming to come on a day

---

[1] Harley sent Swift a bank note for £50, which Swift returned.

when only Lord-Keeper, the Secretary, and I were to be there; but he regarded me not; so we all dined together, and sat down at four; and the secretary has invited me to dine with him to-morrow. I told them, I had no hopes they could ever keep in, but that I saw they loved one another so well, as indeed they seem to do. They call me nothing but Jonathan; and I said, I believed they would leave me Jonathan, as they found me; and that I never knew a ministry do any thing for those whom they make companions of their pleasures; and I believe you will find it so; but I care not. I am upon a project of getting five hundred pounds, without being obliged to any body; but that is a secret, till I see my dearest MD; and so hold your tongue, and do not talk, sirrahs, for I am now about it.

Chelsea, May 2. A fine day, but begins to grow a little warm; and that makes your little fat Presto sweat in the forehead. Pray, are not the fine buns sold here in our town; was it not *Rrrrrrrrrrare Chelsea Buns?* I bought one to-day in my walk; it cost me a penny; it was stale, and I did not like it, as the man said, &c. Sir Andrew Fountaine and I dined at Mrs Vanhomrigh's; and had a flask of my Florence, which lies in their cellar; and so I came home gravely, and saw nobody of consequence to-day. I am very easy here, nobody plaguing me in a morning; and Patrick saves many a score lies. I sent over to Mrs. Atterbury, to know whether I might wait on her? but she is gone a visiting: we have exchanged some compliments, but I have not seen her yet. We have no news in our town.

4. I dined to-day at Lord Shelburn's, where Lady Kerry made me a present of four India handkerchiefs, which I have a mind to keep for little MD, only that I had rather, &c. I have been a mighty handkerchiefmonger, and have bought abundance of snuff ones since I

have left off taking snuff. And I am resolved, when I come over, MD shall be acquainted with Lady Kerry: we have struck up a mighty friendship: and she has much better sense than any other lady of your country. We are almost in love with one another: but she is most egregiously ugly; but perfectly well bred, and governable as I please. I am resolved, when I come, to keep no company but MD; you know I kept my resolution last time; and, except Mr Addison, conversed with none but you and your club of Deans and Stoytes. 'Tis three weeks, young women, since I had a letter from you; and yet, methinks, I would not have another for five pound till this is gone; and yet I send every day to the coffee-house, and I would fain have a letter, and not have a letter: and I don't know what, nor I don't know how; and this goes on very slow; 'tis a week to-morrow since I began it. I am a poor country gentleman, and don't know how the world passes. Do you know that every syllable I write I hold my lips just for all the world as if I were talking in our own little language to MD. Faith, I am very silly; but I can't help it for my life. I got home early to-night. My solicitors, that used to ply me every morning, knew not where to find me; and I am so happy not to hear Patrick, Patrick, called a hundred times every morning. But I looked backward, and find I have said this before. What care I? go to the Dean, and roast the oranges.

May 15. My walk to town to-day was after ten, and prodigiously hot: I dined with Lord Shelburn, and have desired Mrs Pratt, who lodges there, to carry over Mrs Wall's tea; I hope she will do it, and they talk of going in a fortnight. My way is this: I leave my best gown and periwig at Mrs Vanhomrigh's, then walk up the Pall Mall, through the Park, out at Buckingham House, and so to Chelsea a little beyond the church: I

set out about sunset, and get here in something less
than an hour: it is two good miles, and just five thousand
seven hundred and forty-eight steps; so there is four
miles a day walking, without reckoning what I walk
while I stay in town. When I pass the Mall in the evening it is prodigious to see the number of ladies walking
there; and I always cry shame at the ladies of Ireland,
who never walk at all, as if their legs were of no use,
but to be laid aside. I have been now almost three weeks
here, and I thank God, am much better in my head, if it
does but continue. I tell you what, if I was with you,
when we went to Stoyte at Donnybrook, we would only
take a coach to the hither end of Stephen's Green, and
from thence go every step on foot, yes faith, every step;
it would do: DD goes as well as Presto. Every body tells
me I look better already; for faith I looked sadly, that's
certain. My breakfast is milk porridge: I don't love it,
faith I hate it, but 'tis cheap and wholesome; and I hate
to be obliged to either of those qualities for any thing.

19. Do you know that about our town we are mowing
already and making hay, and it smells so sweet as we
walk through the flowery meads; but the hay-making
nymphs are perfect drabs, nothing so clean and pretty as
farther in the country. There is a mighty increase of dirty
wenches in straw hats since I knew London. I staid at
home till five o'clock, and dined with Dean Atterbury:
then went by water to Mr Harley's, where the Saturday
club was met, with the addition of the Duke of Shrewsbury. I whispered Lord Rivers, that I did not like to see
a stranger among us: and the rogue told it aloud: but Mr
Secretary said, the Duke writ to have leave: so I appeared satisfied, and so we laughed. Mr Secretary told
me the Duke of Buckingham had been talking to him
much about me, and desired my acquaintance. I answered, it could not be: for he had not made sufficient

advances. Then the Duke of Shrewsbury said, he
thought that Duke was not used to make advances. I
said I could not help that; for I always expected advances in proportion to men's quality, and more from a
Duke than other men. The Duke replied, that he did not
mean anything of his quality; which was handsomely
said enough; for he meant his pride: and I have invented
a notion to believe that nobody is proud. At ten all the
company went away; and from ten till twelve Mr Harley
and I sat together, where we talked through a great deal
of matters I had a mind to settle with him, and then
walked, in a fine moonshine night, to Chelsea, where I
got by one. Lord Rivers conjured me not to walk so late;
but I would, because I had no other way; but I had no
money to lose.

20. By what Lord-Keeper told me last night, I find
he will not be made a peer so soon: but Mr Harley's
patent for Earl of Oxford is now drawing, and will be
done in three days. We made him own it, which he did
scurvily, and then talked of it like the rest. Mr Secretary
had too much company with him to-day; so I came away
soon after dinner. I give no man liberty to swear or talk
b—dy, and I found some of them were in constraint, so
I left them to themselves. I wish you a merry Whitsun-
tide, and pray tell me how you pass away your time: but
faith, you are going to Wexford, and I fear this letter is
too late; it shall go on Thursday, and sooner it cannot, I
have so much business to hinder me answering yours.
Where must I direct in your absence? Do you quit your
lodgings?

23. Morning. I sat up late last night, and waked late
to-day; but will now answer your letter in bed before I
go to town, and I will send it to-morrow; for perhaps
you mayn't go so soon to Wexford.—No, you are not
out in your number: the last was November 14, and so I

told you twice or thrice; will you never be satisfied? What shall we do for poor Stella? Go to Wexford, for God's sake: I wish you were to walk there by three miles a-day, with a good lodging at every mile's end. Walking has done me so much good, that I cannot but prescribe it often to poor Stella. Parvisol has sent me a bill for fifty pounds, which I am sorry for, having not written to him for it, only mentioned it two months ago; but I hope he will be able to pay you what I have drawn upon him for; he never sent me any sum before but one bill of twenty pounds, half a year ago. You are welcome as my blood to every farthing I have in the world: and all that grieves me is, I am not richer, for MD's sake, as [I] hope [to be] saved. I suppose you give up your lodgings when you go to Wexford; yet that will be inconvenient too: yet I wish again you were under the necessity of rambling the country till Michaelmas, faith. No, let them keep the shelves, with a pox; yet they are exacting people about those four weeks, or Mrs. Brent may have the shelves, if she please. I am obliged to your Dean for his kind offer of lending me money. Will that be enough to say? A hundred people would lend me money, or to any man who has not the reputation of a squanderer. O faith, I should be glad to be in the same kingdom with MD, however, although you were at Wexford. But I am kept here by a most capricious fate, which I would break through, if I could do it with decency or honour.—To return without some mark of distinction, would look extremely little: and I would likewise gladly be somewhat richer than I am. I will say no more, but beg you to be easy, till Fortune take her course, and to believe that MD's felicity is the great end I aim at in my pursuits. And so let us talk no more on this subject, which makes me melancholy, and that I would fain divert. Believe me, no man breathing at present has less share of happiness in life

than I: I do not say I am unhappy at all, but that every
thing here is tasteless to me for want of being as I would
be. And so a short sigh, and no more of this. Well, come
and let's see what's next, young women. Pox take Mrs
Edgeworth and Sterne: I will take some methods about
that box. What orders would you have me give about the
picture? Can't you do with it as if it were your own? No,
I hope Manley will keep his place; for I hear nothing of
Sir Thomas Frankland's losing his. Send nothing under
cover to Mr Addison, but to Erasmus Lewis, Esq., at my
Lord Dartmouth's office at Whitehall. Direct your outside so.—Poor dear Stella, don't write in the dark, nor in
the light neither, but dictate to Dingley; she is a naughty
healthy girl, and may drudge for both. Are you good
company together? and don't you quarrel too often?
Pray, love one another, and kiss one another just now, as
Dingley is reading this; for you quarreled this morning
just after Mrs Marget had poured water on Stella's head:
I heard the little bird say so. Well, I have answered
every thing in your letter that required it, and yet the
second side is not full. I'll come home at night, and say
more; and to-morrow this goes for certain. Go, get you
gone to your own chambers, and let Presto rise like a
modest gentleman, and walk to town. I fancy I begin to
sweat less in the forehead by constant walking than I
used to do; but then I shall be so sunburnt, the ladies
won't like me. Come, let me rise, sirrahs, Morrow.—At
night. I dined with Ford to-day at his lodgings, and I
found wine out of my own cellar, some of my own chest
of the great Duke's wine: it begins to turn. They say
wine with you in Ireland is half-a-crown a bottle. 'Tis as
Stella says, nothing that once grows dear in Ireland ever
grows cheap again, except corn, with a pox, to ruin the
parson. I had a letter to-day from the Archbishop of
Dublin, giving me farther thanks about vindicating him

to Mr Harley and Mr St John, and telling me a long
story about your Mayor's election, wherein I find he has
had a finger, and given way to farther talk about him;
but we know nothing of it here yet. This walking to and
fro, and dressing myself, takes up so much of my time,
that I cannot go among company so much as formerly;
yet what must a body do? I thank God I yet continue
much better since I left the town; I know not how long it
may last. I am sure it has done me some good for the
present. I do not totter as I did, but walk as firm as a
cock, only once or twice for a minute, I dont know how;
but it went off, and I never followed it. Does Dingley
read my hand as well as ever? Do you, sirrah? Poor Stella
must not read Presto's ugly small hand. Preserve your
eyes, if you be wise. Your friend Walls's tea will go in a
day or two toward Chester by one parson Richardson.
My humble service to her, and to good Mrs Stoyte, and
Catherine; and pray walk while you continue in Dublin.
I expect your next but one will be from Wexford. God
bless dearest MD.

June 6. Morning. This letter shall go to-morrow; so
I will answer yours when I come home to-night. I feel
no hurt from last night's swimming. I lie with nothing
but the sheet over me, and my feet quite bare. I must
rise and go to town before the tide is against me. Morrow, sirrahs; dear sirrahs, morrows.—At night. I never
felt so hot a day as this since I was born. I dined with
Lady Betty Germain, and there was the young Earl of
Berkeley and his fine lady. I never saw her before, nor
think her near so handsome as she passes for.—After
dinner Mr Bertue would not let me put ice in my wine;
but said my Lord Dorchester got the bloody flux with
it, and that it was the worst thing in the world. Thus are
we plagued, thus are we plagued; yet I have done it five
or six times this summer, and was but the drier and the

hotter for it. Nothing makes me so excessively peevish
as hot weather. Lady Berkeley after dinner clapped my
hat on another lady's head, and she in roguery put it
upon the rails. I minded them not, but in two minutes
they called me to the window, and Lady Carteret
showed me my hat out of her window five doors off,
where I was forced to walk to it, and pay her and old
Lady Weymouth a visit, with some more beldames, then
I went and drank coffee, and made one or two puns with
Lord Pembroke, and designed to go to Lord-Treasurer;
but it was too late, and besides I was half broiled, and
broiled without butter; for I never sweat after dinner, if
I drink any wine. Then I sat an hour with Lady Betty
Butler at tea, and every thing made me hotter and drier.
Then I walked home, and was here by ten, so miserably
hot, that I was in as perfect a passion as ever I was in
my life at the greatest affront of provocation. Then I sat
an hour till I was quite dry and cool enough to go
swim; which I did, but with so much vexation, that I
think I have given it over: for I was every moment disturbed by boats, rot them; and that puppy Patrick,
standing ashore, would let them come within a yard or
two, and then call sneakingly to them. The only comfort
I proposed here in hot weather is gone; for there is no
jesting with those boats after 'tis dark: I had none last
night. I dived to dip my head, and held my cap on with
both hands, for fear of losing it.—Pox take the boats!
Amen. 'Tis near twelve, and so I'll answer your letter (it
strikes twelve now) to-morrow morning.

21. I went at noon to see Mr Secretary at his office,
and there was Lord-Treasurer: so I killed two birds, &c.
and we were glad to see one another, and so forth. And
the secretary and I dined at Sir William Wyndham's,
who married Lady Catherine Seymour, your acquaintance, I suppose. There were ten of us at dinner. It

seems in my absence they had erected a club, and made me one; and we made some laws to-day, which I am to digest, and add to, against next meeting. Our meetings are to be every Thursday: we are yet but twelve: Lord-Keeper and Lord-Treasurer were proposed; but I was against them, and so was Mr Secretary, though their sons are of it, and so they are excluded; but we design to admit the Duke of Shrewsbury. The end of our club is to advance conversation and friendship, and to reward deserving persons with our interest and recommendation. We take in none but men of wit or men of interest; and if we go on as we begin, no other club in this town will be worth talking of. The Solicitor-General, Sir Robert Raymond, is one of our club; and I ordered him immediately to write to your Lord-Chancellor in favour of Dr Raymond; so tell Raymond, if you see him; but I believe this will find you at Wexford. This letter will come three weeks after the last; so there is a week lost; but that is owing to my being out of town; yet I think it is right, because it goes enclosed to Mr Reading: and why should he know how often Presto writes to MD, pray?—I sat this evening with Lady Butler and Lady Ashburnham, and then came home by eleven, and had a good cool walk; for we have had no extreme hot weather this fortnight, but a great deal of rain at times, and a body can live and breathe. I hope it will hold so. We had peaches to-day.

22. I went late to-day to town, and dined with my friend Lewis. I saw Will. Congreve attending at the Treasury, by order, with his brethren, the commissioners of the wine licenses. I had often mentioned him with kindness to Lord-Treasurer; and Congreve told me, that after they had answered to what they were sent for, my lord called him privately, and spoke to him with great kindness, promising his protection, &c. The poor man

said, he had been used so ill of late years, that he was quite astonished at my lord's goodness, &c. and desired me to tell my lord so; which I did this evening, and recommended him heartily. My lord assured me he esteemed him very much, and would be always kind to him; that what he said was to make Congreve easy, because he knew people talked as if his lordship designed to turn every body out, and particularly Congreve; which indeed was true, for the poor man told me he apprehended it. As I left my Lord-Treasurer I called on Congreve (knowing where he dined), and told him what had passed between my lord and me: so I have made a worthy man easy, and that is a good day's work. I am proposing to my lord to erect a society or academy for correcting and settling our language, that we may not perpetually be changing as we do. He enters mightily into it, so does the Dean of Carlisle; and I design to write a letter to Lord-Treasurer with the proposals of it, and publish it; and so I told my lord, and he approves of it. Yesterday's was a sad Examiner, and last week was very indifferent, though some little scraps of the old spirit, as if he had given some hints; but yesterday's is all trash. It is plain the hand is changed.

London, July 25. I was this afternoon with Mr Secretary at his office, and helped to hinder a man of his pardon, who is condemned for a rape. The Under Secretary was willing to save him, upon an old notion that a woman cannot be ravished: but I told the Secretary he could not pardon him without a favourable report from the judge; besides he was a fiddler, and consequently a rogue, and deserved hanging for something else; and so he shall swing. What: I must stand up for the honour of the fair sex? 'Tis true, the fellow had lain with her a hundred times before; but what care I for that? what! must a woman be ravished because she is a whore?—The

Secretary and I go on Saturday to Windsor for a week. I
dined with Lord-Treasurer, and staid with him till past
ten. I was to-day at his levee, where I went against my
custom, because I had a mind to do a good office for a
gentleman: so I talked with him before my lord, that he
might see me, and then found occasion to recommend
him this afternoon. I was forced to excuse my coming to
the levee, that I did it to see the sight; for he was going
to chide me away: I had never been there before but
once, and that was long before he was treasurer. The
rooms were all full, and as many Whigs as Tories. He
whispered me a jest or two, and bid me come to dinner.
I left him just now, and 'tis late.

Windsor, Sept. 19. The Queen designs to have cards
and dancing here next week, which makes us think she
will stay here longer than we believed. Mrs Masham is
not well after her lying-in: I doubt she got some cold:
she is lame in one of her legs with a rheumatic pain. Dr
Arbuthnot and Mrs Hill go to-morrow to Kensington to
see her, and return the same night. Mrs Hill and I dined
with the Doctor to-day. I rode out this morning with the
Doctor to see Cranburn, a house of Lord Ranelagh's,
and the Duchess of Marlborough's lodge, and the Park;
the finest places they are for nature, and plantations, that
ever I saw; and the finest riding upon artificial roads,
made on purpose for the Queen. Arbuthnot made me
draw up a sham subscription for a book, called a History
of the Maids of Honour since Harry the Eighth, showing they make the best wives, with a list of all the Maids
of Honour since, &c. to pay a crown in hand, and t'other
crown upon delivery of the book; and all in the common
forms of those things. We got a gentleman to write it
fair, because my hand is known, and we sent it to the
maids of honour when they came to supper. If they bite

at it, 'twill be a very good court jest; and the queen will certainly have it; we did not tell Mrs Hill.

Oct. 4. It was the finest day in the world, and we got out before eleven, a noble caravan of us. The Duchess of Shrewsbury in her own chaise with one horse, and Miss Touchet with her; Mrs Masham and Mrs Scarborow, one of the dressers, in one of the queen's chaises: Miss Forester and Miss Scarborow, two maids of honour, and Mrs Hill on horseback. The Duke of Shrewsbury, Mr Masham, George Fielding, Arbuthnot, and I, on horseback too. Mrs Hill's horse was hired for Miss Scarborow, but she took it in civility, her own horse was galled and could not be rid, but kicked and winced: the hired horse was not worth eighteenpence. I borrowed coat, boots, and horse, and in short we had all the difficulties, and more than we used to have in making a party from Trim to Longfield's. My coat was light camlet, faced with red velvet, and silver buttons. We rode in the great park and the forest about a dozen miles, and the Duchess and I had much conversation; we got home by two, and Mr Masham, his lady, Arbuthnot and I, dined with Mrs Hill. Arbuthnot made us all melancholy, by some symptoms of bloody ur—e: he expects a cruel fit of the stone in twelve hours; he says he is never mistaken, and he appears like a man that was to be racked to-morrow. I cannot but hope it will not be so bad; he is a perfectly honest man, and one I have much obligation to. It rained a little this afternoon, and grew fair again. Lady Oglethorp sent to speak to me, and it was to let me know that Lady Rochester desires she and I may be better acquainted. 'Tis a little too late; for I am not now in love with Lady Rochester: they shame me out of her, because she is old. Arbuthnot says, he hopes my strained thumb is not the gout; for he has often found people so mistaken. I do not remember the particular thing that gave it me, only I had it just after beating Patrick, and now it is better: so I believe he is mistaken.

London, Oct. 23. This goes to-day, and shall be sealed by and by. Lord-Treasurer takes physic again to-day; I believe I shall dine with Lord Dupplin. Mr Tooke brought me a letter directed for me at Morphew's the bookseller. I suppose, by the postage, it came from Ireland; it is a woman's hand, and seems false spelt on purpose; it is in such sort of verse as Harris's petition; rallies me for writing merry things, and not upon divinity; and is like the subject of the Archbishop's last letter, as I told you. Can you guess whom it came from? it is not ill written; pray find it out; there is a Latin verse at the end of it all rightly spelt; yet the English, as I think, affectedly wrong in many places. My plaguing time is coming. A young fellow brought me a letter from Judge Coote, with recommendation to be lieutenant of a man of war. He is the son of one Echlin, who was minister of Belfast before Tisdall, and I have got some other new customers; but I shall trouble my friends as little as possible. Saucy Stella used to jeer me for meddling with other folks affairs; but now I am punished for it.—Patrick has brought the candle, and I have no more room. Farewell, &c. &c.

Here is a full and true account of Stella's new spelling.

Plaguely, . .	Plaguily.[1]	A bout, . .	About.
Dineing, . .	Dining.	Intellegence, .	Intelligence.
Straingers, .	Strangers.	Aboundance, .	Abundance.
Chais, . .	Chase.	Merrit, . .	Merit.
Waist, . .	Wast.	Secreet, . .	Secret.
Houer, . .	Hour.	Phamphlets, .	Pamphlets.
Immagin, . .	Imagine.	Bussiness, . .	Business.

---

[1] The corrected spellings are in Stella's hand.

Tell me truly, sirrah, how many of these are mistakes of the pen, and how many are you to answer for as real ill spelling? There are but fourteen; I said twenty by guess. You must not be angry, for I will have you spell right, let the world go how it will. Though, after all, there is but a mistake of one letter in any of these words. I allow you henceforth but six false spellings in every letter you send me.

London, Nov. 3. A fine day this, and I walked a pretty deal: I stuffed the Secretary's pockets with papers, which he must read and settle at Hampton Court, where he went to-day, and stays some time. They have no lodgings for me there, so I can't go, for the town is small, chargeable, and inconvenient. Lord-Treasurer had a very ill night last night, with much pain in his knee and foot, but is easier to-day.—And so I went to visit Prior about some business, and so he was not within, and so Sir Andrew Fountaine made me dine to-day again with Mrs. Van, and I came home soon, remembering this must go to-night, and that I had a letter of MD's to answer. O Lord, where is it? let me see; so, so, here it is. You grudge writing so soon. Pox on that bill; the woman would have me manage that money for her. I do not know what to do with it now I have it: I am like the un- profitable steward in the Gospel: I laid it up in a napkin; there thou hast what is thine own, &c. Well, well, I know of your new mayor. (I'll tell you a pun; a fishmonger owed a man two crowns; so he sent him a piece of bad ling and a tench, and then said he was paid: how is that now? find it out; for I won't tell it you: which of you finds it out?) Well, but as I was saying, what care I for your mayor? I fancy Ford may tell Forbes right about my returning to Ireland before Christmas, or soon after. I'm sorry you did not go on with your story about Pray God you be John; I never heard it in my life, and won-

der what it can be.—Ah, Stella, faith you leaned upon
your Bible to think what to say when you writ that. Yes,
that story of the Secretary's making me an example is
true; "never heard it before;" why how could you hear
it? is it possible to tell you the hundredth part of what
passes in our companies here? the Secretary is as easy
with me as Mr Addison was. I have often thought what
a splutter Sir William Temple makes [made] about being Secretary of State; I think Mr St John the greatest
young man I ever knew; wit, capacity, beauty, quickness of apprehension, good learning, and an excellent
taste; the best orator in the House of Commons, admirable conversation, good nature, and good manners; generous, and a despiser of money. His only fault is talking
to his friends in way of complaint of too great a load of
business, which looks a little like affectation; and he
endeavours too much to mix the fine gentleman, and
man of pleasure, with the man of business. What truth
and sincerity he may have I know not: he is now but
thirty-two, and has been Secretary above a year. Is not
all this extraordinary? how he stands with the Queen and
Lord-Treasurer I have told you before. This is his character; and I believe you will be diverted by knowing it.
I writ to the Archbishop of Dublin, Bishop of Cloyne
and of Clogher together, five weeks ago from Windsor:
I hope they had my letters; pray know if Clogher had
his.—Fig for your physician and his advice, Madam
Dingley; if I grow worse, I will; otherwise I will trust
to temperance and exercise: your fall of the leaf; what
care I when the leaves fall? I am sorry to see them fall
with all my heart; but why should I take physic because leaves fall off from trees? that won't hinder
them from falling. If a man falls from a horse, must I
take physic for that?—This arguing makes you mad; but
it is true right reason, not to be disproved.—I am glad

at heart to hear poor Stella is better; use exercise and walk, spend pattens and spare potions, wear out clogs and waste claret. Have you found out my pun of the fishmonger? don't read a word more till you have got it. And Stella is handsome again you say? and is she fat? I have sent to Leigh the set of Examiners; the first thirteen were written by several hands, some good, some bad; the next three-and-thirty were all by one hand, that makes forty-six: then that author, whoever he was, laid it down on purpose to confound guessers; and the last six were written by a woman. Then there is an account of Guiscard by the same woman, but the facts sent by Presto. Then an answer to the letter to the lords about Gregg by Presto; Prior's Journey by Presto; Vindication of the Duke of Marlborough entirely by the same woman; Comment on Hare's Sermon by the same woman, only hints sent to the printer from Presto to give her. Then there's the Miscellany, an apron for Stella, a pound of chocolate, without sugar, for Stella, a fine snuff-rasp of ivory, given me by Mrs St John for Dingley, and a large roll of tobacco, which she must hide or cut shorter out of modesty, and four pair of spectacles for the Lord knows who. There's the cargo, I hope it will come safe. O, Mrs Masham and I are very well; we write to one another, but it is upon business; I believe I told you so before: pray pardon my forgetfulness in these cases; poor Presto can't help it. MD shall have the money as soon as Tooke gets it. And so I think I have answered all, and the paper is out, and now I have fetched up my week, and will send you another this day fortnight.— Why, you rogues, two crowns make *tench-ill-ling:* you are so dull you could never have found it out. Farewell, &c. &c.

Dec. 5. They are now printing the fourth edition,[1]

---

[1] Of Swift's pamphlet "The Conduct of the Allies."

which is reckoned very extraordinary, considering 'tis
a dear twelvepenny book, and not bought up in numbers by the party to give away, as the Whigs do, but
purely upon its own strength. I have got an under spur-
leather to write an Examiner again, and the Secretary
and I will now and then send hints; but we would have
it a little upon the Grub Street, to be a match for their
writers. I dined with Lord-Treasurer to-day at five: he
dined by himself after his family, and drinks no claret
yet, for fear of his rheumatism, of which he is almost
well. He was very pleasant, as he is always: yet I fancied
he was a little touched with the present posture of affairs.
The Elector of Hanover's minister here has given in a
violent memorial against the peace, and caused it to be
printed. The Whig lords are doing their utmost for a
majority against Friday, and design, if they can, to address the Queen against the peace. Lord Nottingham,
a famous Tory and speechmaker, is gone over to the
Whig side: they toast him daily, and Lord Wharton says,
It is Dismal (so they call him from his looks) will save
England at last. Lord-Treasurer was hinting as if he
wished a ballad was made on him, and I will get up one
against to-morrow. He gave me a scurrilous printed
paper of bad verses on himself, under the name of the
English Catiline, and made me read them to the company. It was his birth-day, which he would not tell us,
but Lord Harley whispered it to me.

6. I was this morning making the ballad, two degrees
above Grub Street; at noon I paid a visit to Mrs Masham,
and then went to dine with our Society. Poor Lord-
Keeper dined below stairs, I suppose, on a bit of mutton.
We chose two members; we were eleven met, the greatest meeting we ever had: I am next week to introduce
Lord Orrery. The printer came before we parted, and
brought the ballad, which made them laugh very heart-

ily a dozen times. He is going to print the pamphlet in small, a fifth edition, to be taken off by friends, and sent into the country. A sixpenny answer is come out, good for nothing, but guessing me, among others, for the author. To-morrow is the fatal day for the Parliament meeting, and we are full of hopes and fears. We reckon we have a majority of ten on our side in the House of Lords; yet I observed Mrs Masham a little uneasy; she assures me the Queen is stout. The Duke of Marlborough has not seen the Queen for some days past; Mrs Masham is glad of it, because she says he tells a hundred lies to his friends of what she says to him: he is one day humble, and the next day on the high ropes. The Duke of Ormond, they say, will be in town to-night by twelve.

25. I wish MD a merry Christmas, and many a one; but mine is melancholy: I durst not go to church to-day, finding myself a little out of order, and it snowing prodigiously, and freezing. At noon I went to Mrs Van, who had this week engaged me to dine there to-day: and there I received the news, that poor Mrs Long died at Lynn in Norfolk on Saturday last, at four in the morning; she was sick but four hours. We suppose it was the asthma, which she was subject to as well as the dropsy, as she sent me word in her last letter, written about five weeks ago; but then said she was recovered. I never was more afflicted at any death. The poor creature had retired to Lynn two years ago, to live cheap, and pay her debts. In her last letter she told me she hoped to be easy by Christmas; and she kept her word, although she meant it otherwise. She had all sorts of amiable qualities, and no ill ones, but the indiscretion of too much neglecting her own affairs. She had two thousand pounds left her by an old grandmother, with which she intended to pay her debts, and live on an annuity she had of one hundred pounds a-year, and Newburg House, which

would be about sixty pounds more. That odious grandmother living so long, forced her to retire; for the two
thousand pounds was settled on her after the old
woman's death, yet her brute of a brother, Sir James
Long, would not advance it for her; else she might have
paid her debts, and continued here, and lived still: I believe melancholy helped her on to her grave. I have
ordered a paragraph to be put in the Post-Boy, giving an
account of her death, and making honourable mention
of her; which is all I can do to serve her memory: but
one reason was spite; for her brother would fain have her
death a secret, to save the charge of bringing her up
here to bury her, or going into mourning. Pardon all this,
for the sake of a poor creature I had so much friendship
for.

27. I entertained our Society at the Thatched House
Tavern to-day at dinner; but brother Bathurst sent for
wine, the house affording none. The printer had not received my letter, and so he brought up dozens a-piece of
the Prophecy; but I ordered him to part with no more.
'Tis an admirable good one, and people are mad for it.
The frost still continues violently cold. Mrs Masham invited me to come to-night and play at cards; but our society did not part till nine. But I supped with Mrs Hill,
her sister, and there was Mrs Masham and Lord-Treasurer, and we staid till twelve. He is endeavouring to get
a majority against next Wednesday, when the House of
Lords is to meet, and the Whigs intend to make some
violent addresses against a peace, if not prevented. God
knows what will become of us.—It is still prodigiously
cold; but so I told you already. We have eggs on the
spit, I wish they may not be addled. When I came home
to-night I found, forsooth, a letter from MD, N. 24, 24,
24, 24; there, do you know the numbers now? and at the
same time one from Joe, full of thanks: let him know I

have received it, and am glad of his success, but won't put him to the charge of a letter. I had a letter some time ago from Mr Warburton, and I beg one of you will copy out what I shall tell you, and send it by some opportunity to Warburton. 'Tis as follows: The doctor has received Mr Warburton's letter, and desires he will let the doctor know, where [?whether] that accident he mentions is like soon to happen, and he will do what he can in it.—And pray, madam, let them know, that I do this to save myself the trouble, and them the expence of a letter. And I think that this is enough for one that comes home at twelve from a Lord-Treasurer and Mrs Masham. Oh, I could tell you ten thousand things of our mad politics, upon what small circumstances great affairs have turned. But I will go rest my busy head.

Jan. 9, 1712. I could not go sleep last night till past two, and was waked before three by a noise of people endeavouring to break open my window. For a while I would not stir, thinking it might be my imagination; but hearing the noise continued, I rose and went to the window, and then it ceased. I went to bed again, and heard it repeated more violently; then I rose and called up the house, and got a candle: the rogues had lifted up the sash a yard; there are great sheds before my windows, although my lodgings be a storey high; and if they get upon the sheds they are almost even with my window. We observed their track, and panes of glass fresh broken. The watchmen told us today they saw them, but could not catch them. They attacked others in the neighbourhood about the same time, and actually robbed a house in Suffolk Street, which is the next street but one to us. It is said they are seamen discharged from service. I went up to call my man, and found his bed empty; it seems he often lies abroad. I challenged him this morning as one of the robbers. He is a sad dog; and the minute I come to Ireland I will discard him. I have this day got double iron bars to every window in my dining-room and bed-chamber; and I hide my purse in my thread stocking between the bed's head and the wainscoat. Lewis and I dined with an old Scotch friend, who brought the Duke of Douglas, and three or four more Scots upon us.

Mar. 5. I wish you a merry Lent. I hate Lent; I hate different diets, and furmity and butter, and herb por-ridge; and sour devout faces of people who only put on religion for seven weeks. I was at the Secretary's office this morning; and there a gentleman brought me two letters, dated last October; one from the Bishop of Clogher, t'other from Walls. The gentleman is called Colonel Newburgh. I think you mentioned him to me some time ago; he has business in the House of Lords. I will do him what service I can. The Representation of the House of Commons is printed; I have not seen it yet; it is plaguy severe, they say. I dined with Dr Arbuthnot, and had a true Lenten dinner, not in point of victuals, but spleen; for his wife and a child or two were sick in the house, and that was full as mortifying as fish. We have had fine mighty cold frosty weather for some days past. I hope you take the advantage of it, and walk now and then. You never answer that part of my letters, where I desire you to walk. I must keep my breath to cool my Lenten porridge. Tell Jemmy Leigh that his boy that robbed him now appears about the town: Patrick has seen him once or twice. I knew nothing of his being robbed till Patrick told me he had seen the boy. I wish it had been Sterne that had been robbed, to be revenged for the box that he lost, and be poxed to him. Nite, MD.

Windsor, Sept. 15. I never was so long without writing to MD as now, since I left them, nor ever will again

while I am able to write. I have expected from one week
to another that something would be done in my own
affairs; but nothing at all is, nor I don't know when any
thing will, or whether, ever at all, so slow are people at
doing favours. I have been much out of order of late
with the old giddiness in my head. I took a vomit for
it two days ago, and will take another about a day or
two hence. I have eat mighty little fruit; yet I impute
my disorder to that little, and shall henceforth wholly
forbear it. I am engaged in a long work, and have done
all I can of it, and wait for some papers from the ministry for materials for the rest; and they delay me, as if it
were a favour I asked of them; so that I have been idle
here this good while, and it happened in a right time,
when I was too much out of order to study. One is kept
constantly out of humour by a thousand unaccountable
things in public proceedings; and when I reason with
some friends, we cannot conceive how affairs can last
as they are. God only knows, but it is a very melancholy
subject for those who have any near concern in it. I am
again endeavouring, as I was last year, to keep people
from breaking to pieces upon a hundred misunderstand-
ings. One cannot withhold them from drawing different
ways, while the enemy is watching to destroy both. See
how my style is altered, by living and thinking and talking among these people, instead of my canal and river-
walk and willows. I lose all my money here among the
ladies; so that I never play when I can help it, being
sure to lose. I have lost five pounds the five weeks I have
been here. I hope Ppt is luckier at picquet with the
Dean and Mrs Walls. The Dean never answered my letter though. I have clearly forgot whether I sent a bill
for ME in any of my last letters. I think I did; pray
let me know, and always give me timely notice. I wait

here but to see what they will do for me; and whenever preferments are given from me, as hope saved, I will come over.

London, Oct. 30. The Duchess of Ormond found me out to-day, and made me dine with her. Lady Masham is still expecting. She has had a cruel cold. I could not finish my letter last post for the soul of me. Lord Bolingbroke has had my papers these six weeks, and done nothing to them. Is Tisdall yet in the world? I propose writing controversies, to get a name with posterity. The Duke of Ormond will not be over these three or four days. I design to make him join with me in settling all right among our people. I have ordered the Duchess to let me have an hour with the Duke at his first coming, to give him a true state of persons and things. I believe the Duke of Shrewsbury will hardly be declared your governor yet; at least, I think so now; but resolutions alter very often. The Duke of Hamilton gave me a pound of snuff to-day, admirable good. I wish DD had it, and Ppt too, if she likes it. It cost me a quarter of an hour of his politics, which I was forced to hear. Lady Orkney is making me a writing-table of her own contrivance, and a bed nightgown. She is perfectly kind, like a mother. I think the devil was in it the other day, that I should talk to her of an ugly squinting cousin of hers, and the poor lady herself, you know, squints like a dragon. The other day we had a long discourse with her about love; and she told us a saying of her sister Fitzharding, which I thought excellent, that *in men, desire begets love*, and *in women, love begets desire*. We have abundance of our old criers still hereabouts. I hear every morning your women with the old satin and taffata, &c., the fellow with old coats, suits or cloaks. Our weather is abominable of late. We have not two tolerable days in twenty. I have lost money again at ombre, with Lord Orkney and others; yet, after all, this year I have lost but three-and-twenty shillings; so that, considering card money, I am no loser.

Our Society hath not yet renewed their meetings. I hope we shall continue to do some good this winter; and Lord-Treasurer promises the academy for reforming our language shall soon go forward. I must now go hunt those dry letters for materials. You will see something very notable, I hope. So much for that. God Almighty bless you.

London, Jan. 3, 1713. I am just now told that poor dear Lady Ashburnham, the Duke of Ormond's daughter, died yesterday at her country house. The poor creature was with child. She was my greatest favourite, and I am in excessive concern for her loss. I hardly knew a more valuable person on all accounts. You must have heard me talk of her. I am afraid to see the Duke and Duchess. She was naturally very healthy; I am afraid she has been thrown away for want of care. Pray condole with me. 'Tis extremely moving. Her lord's a puppy; and I shall never think it worth my while to be troubled with him, now he has lost all that was valuable in his possession; yet I think he used her pretty well. I hate life when I think it exposed to such accidents; and to see so many thousand wretches burdening the earth, while such as her die, makes me think God did never intend life for a blessing. Farewell.

London, Jan. 8. Oo must understand that I am in my geers, and have got a chocolate-pot, a present from Mrs Ashe of Clogher, and some chocolate from my brother Ormond, and I treat folks sometimes. I dined with Lord-Treasurer at five o'clock to-day, and was by while he and Lord Bolingbroke were at business; for it is fit I should know all that passes now, because, &c. The Duke of Ormond employed me to speak to Lord-Treasurer to-day about an affair, and I did so; and the Duke had spoke himself two hours before, which vexed me, and I will chide the Duke about it. I'll tell you a good thing; there is not one of the ministry but what will employ me as gravely to speak for them to Lord-Treasurer, as if I were their brother or his; and I do it as gravely: though I know they do it only because them will not make themselves uneasy, or had rather I should be denied than they. I believe our peace will not be finished these two months; for I think we must have a return from Spain by a messenger, who will not go till Sunday next. Lord-Treasurer has invited me to dine with him again to-morrow. Your commissioner, Keatly, is to be there. Nite deelest MD.

9. Dr. Pratt drank chocolate with me this morning, and then we walked. I was yesterday with him to see Lady Betty Butler, grieving for her sister Ashburnham. The jade was in bed in form, and she did so cant, she made me sick. I meet Tom Leigh every day in the Park, to preserve his health. He is as ruddy as a rose, and tells me his Bishop of Dromore recovers very much. That Bishop has been very near dying. This day's Examiner talks of the play of what is it like? and you will think it to be mine, and be bit; for I have no hand in these papers at all. I dined with Lord-Treasurer, and shall again to-morrow, which is his day when all the ministers dine with him. He calls it whipping-day. It is always on Saturday, and we do indeed usually rally him about his faults on that day. I was of the original club, when only poor Lord Rivers, Lord-Keeper, and Lord Bolingbroke came; but now Ormond, Anglesey, Lord-Steward, Dartmouth, and other rabble intrude, and I scold at it; but now they pretend as good a title as I; and, indeed, many Saturdays I am not there. The company being too many, I don't love it. Nite MD.

Feb. 12. I have reckoned days wrong all this while; for this is the twelfth. I do not know when I lost it. I dined to-day with our Society, the greatest dinner I have ever seen. It was at Jack Hill's, the governor of Dunkirk. I gave an account of sixty guineas I had collected, and am to give them away to two authors to-morrow; and Lord-Treasurer has promised us a hundred pounds to reward some others. I found a letter on my table last night, to tell me, that poor little Harrison, the Queen's secretary, that came lately from Utrecht with the Barrier Treaty, was ill, and desired to see me at night; but it was late, and I could not go till to-day. I have often mentioned him in my letters, you may remember. . . . I went in the morning, and found him mighty ill, and got thirty guineas for him from Lord Bolingbroke, and an order for a hundred pounds from the Treasury to be paid him to-morrow; and I have got him removed to Knightsbridge for air. He has a fever and inflammation on his lungs; but I hope will do well. Nite MD.

13. I was to see a poor poet, one Mr Diaper, in a nasty garret, very sick. I gave him twenty guineas from Lord Bolingbroke, and disposed the other sixty to two other authors, and desired a friend to receive the hundred pounds for poor Harrison, and will carry it to him to-morrow morning. I sent to see how he did, and he is extremely ill; and I very much afflicted for him, for he is my own creature, and in a very honourable post, and very worthy of it. I dined in the city. I am much concerned for this poor lad. His mother and sister attend him, and he wants nothing. Nite dee MD.

14. I took Parnell this morning, and we walked to see poor Harrison. I had the hundred pounds in my pocket. I told Parnell I was afraid to knock at the door; my mind misgave me. I knocked, and his man in tears told me his master was dead an hour before. Think what grief this is

to me! I went to his mother, and have been ordering
things for his funeral with as little cost as possible, to-
morrow at ten at night. Lord-Treasurer was much concerned when I told him. I could not dine with Lord-
Treasurer, nor any where else; but got a bit of meat
toward evening. No loss ever grieved me so much: poor
creature! Pray God Almighty bless poor MD. Adieu.

I send this away to-night, and am sorry it must go
while I am in so much grief.

18. The Earl of Abingdon has been teasing me these
three months to dine with him; and this day was appointed about a week ago, and I named my company;
Lord Stawell, Colonel Disney, and Dr. Arbuthnot; but
the two last slipped out their necks, and left Stawell and
me to dine there. We did not dine till seven, because it
is Ash Wednesday. We had nothing but fish, which Lord
Stawell could not eat, and got a broiled leg of a turkey.
Our wine was poison; yet the puppy has twelve thousand pound a year. His carps were raw, and his candles
tallow. I [He] shall not catch me in haste again, and
every body has laughed at me for dining with him. I was
to-day to let Harrison's mother know I could not pay till
she administers; which she will do. I believe she is an
old bitch, and her daughter a ——. There were more
Whigs to-day at court than Tories. I believe they think
the peace must be made, and so come to please the
Queen. She is still lame with the gout. Nite MD.

Apr. 6. I was this morning at ten at the rehearsal of
Mr Addison's play, called Cato, which is to be acted on
Friday. There were not above half-a-score of us to see it.
We stood on the stage, and it was foolish enough to see
the actors prompted every moment, and the poet direct-
ing them; and the drab that acts Cato's daughter, out in
the midst of a passionate part, and then calling out,
"What's next?" The Bishop of Clogher was there too;

but he stood privately in a gallery. I went to dine with
Lord-Treasurer, but he was gone to Wimbleton, his
daughter Caermarthen's country seat, seven miles off.
So I went back, and dined privately with Mr Addison,
whom I had left to go to Lord-Treasurer. I keep fires yet;
I am very extravagant. I sate this evening with Sir
Andrew Fountaine, and we amused ourselves with making *ifs* for Dilly. It is rainy weather again; nevle saw ze
rike. This letter shall go to-morrow; remember, ung
oomens, it is seven weeks since your last, and I allow oo
but five weeks; but oo have been galloping in the country to Swanton's. O pray tell Swanton I had his letter
but cannot contrive how to serve him. If a governor
were to go over, I would recommend him as far as lay
in my power, but I can do no more: and you know all
employments in Ireland, at least almost all, are engaged
in reversions. If I were on the spot, and had credit with
a Lord-Lieutenant, I would very heartily recommend
him; but employments here are no more in my power
than the monarchy itself. Nite, dee MD.

13. This morning, my friend, Mr Lewis, came to me,
and showed me an order for a warrant for the three
vacant deaneries; but none of them to me. This was what
I always foresaw, and received the notice of it better, I
believe, than he expected. I bid Mr Lewis tell Lord-
Treasurer, that I take nothing ill of him, but his not
giving me timely notice, as he promised to do, if he found
the Queen would do nothing for me. At noon, Lord-
Treasurer hearing I was in Mr Lewis's office, came to
me, and said many things too long to repeat. I told him
I had nothing to do but go to Ireland immediately; for
I could not, with any reputation, stay longer here, unless
I had something honourable immediately given to me.
We dined together at the Duke of Ormond's. He there
told me, he had stopped the warrants for the deans,

that what was done for me might be at the same time,
and he hoped to compass it to-night; but I believe him
not. I told the Duke of Ormond my intentions. He is
content Sterne should be a bishop, and I have St
Patrick's; but I believe nothing will come of it, for stay
I will not; and so I believe for all oo . . . . oo may
see me in Dublin before April ends. I am less out of
humour than you would imagine: and if it were not, that
impertinent people will condole with me, as they used
to give me joy, I would value it less. But I will avoid
company, and muster up my baggage, and send them
next Monday by the carrier to Chester, and come and
see my willows, against the expectation of all the world.
—Hat care I? Nite deelest logues, MD.

14. I dined in the city to-day, and ordered a lodging
to be got ready for me against I came to pack up my
things; for I will leave this end of the town as soon as
ever the warrants for the deaneries are out, which are yet
stopped. Lord-Treasurer told Mr Lewis, that it should be
determined to-night: and so he will see [say] a hundred
nights. So he said yesterday, but I value it not. My daily
journals shall be but short till I get into the city, and
then I will send away this, and follow it myself; and
design to walk it all the way to Chester, my man and I,
by ten miles a-day. It will do my health a great deal of
good. I shall do it in fourteen days. Nite dee MD.

15. Lord Bolingbroke made me dine with him to-day,
I was as good company as ever: and told me the Queen
would determine something for me to-night. The dispute
is, Windsor or St Patrick's. I told him I would not stay
for their disputes, and he thought I was in the right.
Lord Masham told me, that Lady Masham is angry I
have not been to see her since this business, and desires
I will come to-morrow. Nite deelest MD.

16. I was this noon at Lady Masham's who was just

come from Kensington, where her eldest son is sick. She
said much to me of what she had talked to the Queen
and Lord-Treasurer. The poor lady fell a shedding tears
openly. She could not bear to think of my having St
Patrick's, &c. I was never more moved than to see so
much friendship. I would not stay with her, but went
and dined with Dr Arbuthnot, with Mr. Berkeley, one
of your fellows, whom I have recommended to the doctor, and to Lord Berkeley of Stratton. Mr Lewis tells me,
that the Duke of Ormond has been to-day with the
Queen; and she was content, that Dr Sterne should be
Bishop of Dromore, and I Dean of St Patrick's; but then
out came Lord-Treasurer, and said, he would not be
satisfied, but that I must be Prebend[ary] of Windsor.
Thus he perplexes things. I expect neither; but I confess,
as much as I love England, I am so angry at this treatment, that, if I had my choice, I would rather have St
Patrick's. Lady Masham says, she will speak to purpose
to the Queen to-morrow. Nite, dee MD.

17. I went to dine at Lady Masham's to-day, and she
was taken ill of a sore throat, and aguish. She spoke to
the Queen last night, but had not much time. The Queen
says she will determine to-morrow with Lord-Treasurer.
The warrants for the deaneries are still stopped, for fear
I should be gone. Do you think any thing will be done?
I don't care whether it is or no. In the mean time, I
prepare for my journey, and see no great people, nor
will see Lord-Treasurer any more, if I go. Lord-Treasurer
told Mr Lewis it should be done to-night; so he said five
nights ago. Nite MD.

18. This morning Mr Lewis sent me word, that Lord-
Treasurer told him the Queen would determine at noon.
At three Lord-Treasurer sent to me to come to his lodgings at St James's, and told me the Queen was at last
resolved, that Dr Sterne should be Bishop of Dromore,

and I Dean of St Patrick's; and that Sterne's warrant
should be drawn immediately. You know the deanery
is in the Duke of Ormond's gift; but this is concerted
between the Queen, Lord-Treasurer, and the Duke of
Ormond, to make room for me. I do not know whether
it will yet be done; some unlucky accident may yet
come. Neither can I feel joy at passing my days in Ireland; and I confess, I thought the ministry would not let
me go; but perhaps they can't help it. Nite MD.

   Chester, June 6. I am come here after six days. I set
out on Monday last, and got here to-day about eleven
in the morning. A noble rider, fais! and all the ships
and people went off yesterday with a rare wind. This
was told me, to my comfort, upon my arrival. Having not
used riding these three years, made me terrible weary;
yet I resolve on Monday to set out for Holyhead, as
weary as I am. 'Tis good for my health, mun. When I
came here, I found MD's letter of the 26th of May, sent
down to me. Had you written a post sooner, I might
have brought some pins: but you were lazy, and would
not write your orders immediately, as I desired you. I
will come, when God pleases; perhaps I may be with
you in a week. I will be three days going to Holyhead;
I cannot ride faster, say hat oo will. I am upon Stay-
behind's mare. I have the whole inn to myself. I would
fain 'scape this Holyhead journey; but I have no prospect of ships, and it will be almost necessary I should be
in Dublin before the 25th instant, to take the others
[oaths]; otherwise I must wait to a quarter sessions. I
will lodge as I can; therefore take no lodgings for me, to
pay in my absence. The poor Dean can't afford it. I
spoke again to the Duke of Ormond about Moimed for
Raymond, and hope he may yet have it, for I laid it
strongly to the Duke, and gave him the Bishop of
Meath's memorial. I am sorry for Raymond's fistula; tell

him so. I will speak to Lord-Treasurer about Mrs Smith
to-morrow.—Odso! I forgot; I thought I had been in
London. Mrs Tisdall is very big, ready to lie down. Her
husband is a puppy. Do his feet stink still? The letters to
Ireland go at so uncertain an hour, that I am forced to
conclude. Farewell, MD, MD MD FW FW FW ME
ME ME ME

> Lele lele
> lele logues and
> Ladies bose fair
> and slender.

[*On flyleaf.*]

I mightily approve Ppt's project of hanging the blind
parson. When I read that passage upon Chester walls, as
I was coming into town, and just received your letter,
I said aloud—Agreeable B—tch.

The Earl of Wharton

Swift's sketch in vitriol of the Earl of Wharton was apparently written in August 1710 and printed in December. The pamphlet from which this extract is taken is *A Short Character of his Ex[cellency] T[homas] E[arl] of W[harton] L[ord-] L[ieutenant] of I[reland]*. It did not print Wharton's name in full, but of course nobody could doubt that Wharton was the subject.   C.V.D.

T[HOMAS] E[arl] of W[harton] L[ord-]L[ieutenant] of I[reland,] by the force of a wonderful constitution, hath some years passed his grand climacteric, without any visible effects of old age, either on his body or his mind, and in spite of a continual prostitution to those vices which usually wear out both. His behaviour is in all the forms of a young man at five-and-twenty. Whether he walks, or whistles, or swears, or talks bawdy, or calls names, he acquits himself in each beyond a templar of three years standing. With the same grace and in the same style, he will rattle his coachman in the midst of the street, where he is governor of the kingdom: and all this is without consequence, because it is in his character, and what every body expects. He seems to be but an ill dissembler and an ill liar, though they are the two talents he most practices, and most values himself upon. The ends he has gained by lying, appear to be more owing to the frequency than the art of them; his lies being sometimes detected in an hour, often in a day, and always in a week: He tells them freely in mixed companies, though he knows half of

those that hear him to be his enemies, and is sure they
will discover them the moment they leave him. He
swears solemnly he loves and will serve you, and your
back is no sooner turned, but he tells those about him, you
are a dog and a rascal. He goes constantly to prayers in
the forms of his place, and will talk bawdy and blas-
phemy at the chapel door. He is a Presbyterian in politics, and an atheist in religion; but he chooses at present
to whore with a Papist. In his commerce with mankind,
his general rule is to endeavour imposing on their
understandings, for which he has but one receipt, a composition of lies and oaths; and this he applies indifferently to a freeholder of forty shillings, and a privy-coun-
cillor, by which the easy and the honest are often either
deceived or amused; and either way he gains his point.
He will openly take away your employment to-day, because you are not of his party; to-morrow he will meet
or send for you, as if nothing at all had passed, lay his
hands with much friendliness on your shoulders, and
with the greatest ease and familiarity in the world, tell
you that the faction are driving at something in the
House; that you must be sure to attend, and to speak
to all your friends to be there, though he knows at the
same time that you and your friends are against him in
that very point he mentions: And however absurd, ridiculous, and gross, this may appear, he has often found it
successful; some men having such an awkward bashfulness they know not how to refuse upon a sudden, and
every man having something to fear or to hope, which
often hinders them from driving things to extremes with
persons of power, whatever provocations they may have
received. He hath sunk his fortunes by endeavouring to
ruin one kingdom, and hath raised them by going far in
the ruin of another. With a good natural understanding,
a great fluency in speaking, and no ill taste of wit, he is

generally the worst companion in the world; his thoughts
being wholly taken up between vice and politics, so that
bawdy, prophaneness, and business fill up his whole conversation. To gratify himself in the two first, he makes
choice of suitable favourites, whose talent reaches no
higher than to entertain him with all the lewdness that
passes in town. As for business, he is said to be very
dexterous at that part of it which turns upon intrigue,
and he seems to have transferred the talents of his youth
for intriguing with women, into public affairs: For, as
some vain young fellows, to make a gallantry appear of
consequence, will choose to venture their necks by
climbing up a wall or window at midnight to a common
wench, where they might as freely have gone at the door
and at noonday; so his excellency, either to keep himself
in practice, or to advance the fame of his politics, affects
the most obscure, troublesome, and winding paths, even
in the commonest affairs, those which would as well be
brought about in the ordinary forms, or which would
proceed of course whether he intervened or no.

He bears the gallantries of his lady with the indifference of a Stoic, and thinks them well recompensed by
a return of children to support his family, without the
fatigues of being a father.

He has three predominant passions, which you will
seldom observe united in the same man, as arising from
different dispositions of mind, and naturally thwarting
each other; these are love of power, love of money, and
love of pleasure: They ride him sometimes by turns, and
sometimes all together: Since he went into that kingdom,
he seems most disposed to the second, and has met with
great success, having gained by his government of under
two years, five-and-forty thousand pounds, by the most
favourable computation, half in the regular way, and
half in the prudential.

He was never yet known to refuse or keep a promise; as I remember he told a lady, but with an exception to the promise he then made (which was to get her a pension), yet he broke even that, and I confess, deceived us both. But here, I desire to distinguish between a promise and a bargain; for he will be sure to keep the latter, when he has had the fairest offer.

The Art of Political Lying

In No. 15 of *The Examiner*, dated November 2–9, 1710.

E quibus hi vacuas implent sermonibus aures,
Hi narrata ferunt alio: mensuraque ficti
Crescit, et auditis aliquid novus adjicit autor,
Illic Credulitas, illic temerarius Error,
Vanaque Laetitia est, consternatique Timores
Seditioque recens, dubioque autore susurri.

I AM prevailed on, through the importunity of friends, to interrupt the scheme I had begun in my last paper, by an Essay upon the Art of Political Lying. We are told, "the Devil is the father of lies, and was a liar from the beginning"; so that beyond contradiction, the invention is old: And which is more, his first essay of it was purely political, employed in undermining the authority of his Prince, and seducing a third part of the subjects from their obedience. For which he was driven down from Heaven, where (as Milton expresseth it) he had been viceroy of a great western province; and forced to exercise his talent in inferior regions among other fallen spirits, or poor deluded men, whom he still daily tempts to his own sin, and will ever do so till he is chained in the bottomless pit.

But though the Devil be the father of lies, he seems, like other great inventors, to have lost much of his reputation, by the continual improvements that have been made upon him.

156

Who first reduced lying into an art, and adapted it to politics, is not so clear from history, though I have made some diligent enquiries: I shall therefore consider it only according to the modern system, as it has been cultivated these twenty years past in the southern part of our own island.

The poets tell us, that after the giants were overthrown by the gods, the earth in revenge produced her last offspring, which was Fame. And the fable is thus interpreted; that when tumults and seditions are quieted, rumours and false reports are plentifully spread through a nation. So that by this account, *lying* is the last relief of a routed, earth-born, rebellious party in a state. But here, the moderns have made great additions, applying this art to the gaining of power, and preserving it, as well as revenging themselves after they have lost it: as the same instruments are made use of by animals to feed themselves when they are hungry, and bite those that tread upon them.

But the same genealogy cannot always be admitted for *political lying;* I shall therefore desire to refine upon it, by adding some circumstances of its birth and parents. A political lie is sometimes born out of a discarded statesman's head, and thence delivered to be nursed and dandled by the mob. Sometimes it is produced a monster, and *licked* into shape; at other times it comes into the world completely formed, and is spoiled in the licking. It is often born an infant in the regular way, and requires time to mature it: and often it sees the light in its full growth, but dwindles away by degrees. Sometimes it is of noble birth; and sometimes the spawn of a stock-jobber. *Here,* it screams aloud at the opening of the womb; and *there,* it is delivered with a whisper. I know a lie that now disturbs half the kingdom with its noise, which though too proud and great at present to own its parents, I can remember in its whisper-hood. To conclude the nativity of this monster; when it comes into the world without a *sting*, it is still-born; and whenever it loses its sting, it dies.

No wonder, if an infant so miraculous in its birth, should be destined for great adventures: and accordingly we see it has been the guardian spirit of a prevailing party for almost twenty years. It can conquer kingdoms without fighting, and sometimes with the loss of a battle: It gives and resumes employments; can sink a mountain to a mole-hill, and raise a mole-hill to a mountain; has presided for many years at committees of elections; can wash a blackamoor white; make a saint of an atheist, and a patriot of a profligate; can furnish foreign ministers with intelligence, and raise or let fall the credit of the nation. This goddess flies with a huge looking-glass in her hands, to dazzle the crowd, and make them see, according as she turns it, their ruin in their interest, and their interest in their ruin. In this glass you will behold your best friends clad in coats powdered with *flower-de-luces* and triple crowns; their girdles hung round with chains, and beads, and wooden shoes: and your worst enemies adorned with the ensigns of liberty, property, indulgence, and moderation, and a cornucopia in their hands. Her large wings, like those of a flying-fish, are of no use but while they are moist; she therefore dips them in mud, and soaring aloft scatters it in the eyes of the multitude, flying with great swiftness; but at every turn is forced to stoop in dirty way for new supplies.

I have been sometimes thinking, if a man had the art of the second sight for seeing lies, as they have in Scotland for seeing spirits, how admirably he might entertain himself in this town; to observe the different shapes, sizes, and colours, of those swarms of lies which buzz about the heads of some people, like flies about a horse's ears in summer: or those legions hovering every afternoon in Popes-head Alley, enough to darken the air; or over a club of discontented grandees, and thence sent down in cargoes to be scattered at elections.

There is one essential point wherein a political liar differs from others of the faculty; that he ought to have but a short memory, which is necessary according to the various occasions he meets with every hour, of differing from himself, and swearing to both sides of a contradiction, as he finds the persons disposed, with whom he has to deal. In describing the virtues and vices of mankind, it is convenient upon every article, to have some eminent person in our eye, from whence we copy our description. I have strictly observed this rule; and my imagination this minute represents before me a certain great man famous for this talent, to the constant practice of which he owes his twenty years' reputation of the most skilful head in England, for the management of nice affairs. The superiority of his genius consists in nothing else but an inexhaustible fund of political lies, which he plentifully distributes every minute he speaks, and by an unparalleled generosity forgets, and consequently contradicts the next half-hour. He never yet considered whether any proposition were true or false, but whether it were convenient for the present minute or company to affirm or deny it; so that if you think to refine upon him, by interpreting every thing he says, as we do dreams by the contrary, you are still to seek, and will find yourself equally deceived, whether you believe him or no: the only remedy is to suppose that you have heard some inarticulate sounds, without any meaning at all. And besides, that will take off the horror you might be apt to conceive at the oaths wherewith he perpetually tags both ends of every proposition: though at the same time I think he cannot with any justice be taxed for perjury, when he invokes God and Christ, because he has often fairly given public notice to the world, that he believes in neither.

Some people may think that such an accomplishment as this, can be of no great use to the owner or his party, after it has been often practised, and is become notorious; but they are widely mistaken: Few lies carry the inventor's mark; and the most prostitute enemy to truth may spread a thousand without being known for the author. Besides, as the vilest writer has his readers, so the greatest liar has his believers; and it often happens, that if a lie be believed only for an hour, it has done its work, and there is no farther occasion for it. Falsehood flies, and Truth comes limping after it; so that when men come to be undeceived, it is too late, the jest is over, and the tale has had its effect: like a man who has thought of a good repartee, when the discourse is changed, or the company parted: or, like a physician who has found out an infallible medicine, after the patient is dead.

Considering that natural disposition in many men to lie, and in multitudes to believe, I have been perplexed what to do with that maxim, so frequent in every body's mouth, that "Truth will at last prevail." Here has this island of ours, for the greatest part of twenty years, lain under the influence of such counsels and persons, whose principle and interest it was to corrupt our manners, blind our understandings, drain our wealth, and in time destroy our constitution both in Church and State; and we at last were brought to the very brink of ruin; yet by the means of perpetual misrepresentations, have never been able to distinguish between our enemies and friends. We have seen a great part of the nation's money got into the hands of those who by their birth, education and merit, could pretend no higher than to wear our liveries; while others, who by their credit, quality and fortune, were only able to give reputation and success to the Revolution, were not only laid aside, as dangerous and useless; but loaden with the scandal of Jacobites, men of arbitrary principles, and pensioners to France; while Truth, who is said to lie in a well, seemed now to be buried there under a heap of stones. But I remember, it was a usual complaint among the Whigs, that the bulk of landed men was not in their interests, which some of the wisest looked on as an ill omen; and we saw it was with the utmost difficulty that they could preserve a majority, while the court and ministry were on their side; till they had learned those admirable expedients for deciding elections, and influencing distant boroughs by *powerful motives* from the city. But all this was mere force and constraint, however upheld by most dexterous artifice and management: till the people began to apprehend their properties, their religion, and the monarchy itself in danger; then we saw them greedily laying hold on the first occasion to interpose. But of this mighty change in the dispositions of the people, I shall discourse more at large in some following paper; wherein I shall endeavour to undeceive those deluded or deluding persons, who hope or pretend, it is only a short madness in the vulgar, from which they may soon recover. Whereas I believe it will appear to be very different in its causes, its symptoms, and its consequences; and prove a great example to illustrate the maxim I lately mentioned, that "Truth" (however sometimes late) "will at last prevail."

The Rewards of Marlborough

In No. 17 of *The Examiner*, dated November 16–23, 1710.

Qui sunt boni cives? Qui belli, qui domi de patria bene
merentes, nisi qui patriae beneficia meminerunt?

I WILL employ this present paper upon a subject,
which of late hath very much affected me, which I
have considered with a good deal of application, and
made several enquiries about, among those persons who
I thought were best able to inform me; and if I deliver
my sentiments with some freedom, I hope it will be forgiven, while I accompany it with that tenderness which
so nice a point requires.

I said in a former paper (Numb. 14) that one spe-
cious objection to the late removals at court, was the fear
of giving uneasiness to a general, who has been long
successful abroad: and accordingly, the common clamour of tongues and pens for some months past, has run
against the baseness, the inconstancy and ingratitude of
the whole kingdom to the Duke of M[arlborough], in
return of the most eminent services that ever were performed by a subject to his country; not to be equalled
in history. And then to be sure some bitter stroke of detraction against Alexander and Cæsar, who never did
us the least injury. Besides, the people that read Plutarch
come upon us with parallels drawn from the Greeks and
Romans, who ungratefully dealt with I know not how

many of their most deserving generals: while the profounder politicians, have seen pamphlets, where Tacitus and Machiavel have been quoted to shew the danger of too resplendent a merit. Should a stranger hear these furious outcries of ingratitude against our general, without knowing the particulars, he would be apt to enquire where was his tomb, or whether he were allowed Christian burial? not doubting but we had put him to some ignominious death. Or, has he been tried for his life, and very narrowly escaped? has he been accused of high crimes and misdemeanours? has the prince seized on his estate, and left him to starve? has he been hooted at as he passed the streets, by an ungrateful mob? have neither honours, offices, nor grants, been conferred on him or his family? have not he and they been barbarously stripped of them all? have not he and his forces been ill paid abroad? and does not the prince by a scanty, limited commission, hinder him from pursuing his own methods in the conduct of the war? has he no power at all of disposing commissions as he pleases? is he not severely used by the ministry or Parliament, who yearly call him to a strict account? has the senate ever thanked him for good success, and have they not always publicly censured him for the least miscarriage? Will the accusers of the nation join issue upon any of these particulars, or tell us in what point, our damnable sin of ingratitude lies? Why, it is plain and clear; for while he is commanding abroad, the Queen dissolves her Parliament, and changes her ministry at home: in which universal calamity, no less than two persons allied by marriage to the general, have lost their places. Whence came this wonderful sympathy between the civil and military powers? Will the troops in Flanders refuse to fight, unless they can have their own lord keeper, their own lord president of the council, their own chief Governor of

Ireland, and their own Parliament? In a kingdom where
the people are free, how came they to be so fond of having their councils under the influence of their army, or
those that lead it? who in all well instituted states, had
no commerce with the civil power, further than to receive their orders, and obey them without reserve.

When a general is not so popular, either in his army
or at home, as one might expect from a long course of
success; it may perhaps be ascribed to his wisdom, or
perhaps to his complexion. The possession of some one
quality, or a defect in some other, will extremely damp
the people's favour, as well as the love of the soldiers.
Besides, this is not an age to produce favourites of the
people, while we live under a Queen who engrosses all
our love, and all our veneration; and where the only way
for a great general or minister to acquire any degree of
subordinate affection from the public, must be by all
marks of the most entire submission and respect, to her
sacred person and commands; otherwise, no pretence of
great services, either in the field or the cabinet, will be
able to screen them from universal hatred.

But the late ministry was closely joined to the general,
by friendship, interest, alliance, inclination, and opinion,
which cannot be affirmed of the present; and the ingratitude of the nation, lies in the people's joining as one
man, to wish that such a ministry should be changed. Is
it not at the same time notorious to the whole kingdom,
that nothing but a tender regard to the general was able
to preserve that ministry so long, till neither God nor
man could suffer their continuance? Yet in the highest
ferment of things, we heard few or no reflections upon
this great commander, but all seemed unanimous in
wishing he might still be at the head of the confederate
forces; only at the same time, in case he were resolved
to resign, they chose rather to turn their thoughts some-

where else than throw up all in despair. And this I cannot but add, in defence of the people, with regard to the person we are speaking of, that in the high station he has been for many years past, his real defects (as nothing human is without them) have in a detracting age been very sparingly mentioned, either in libels or conversation, and all his successes very freely and universally applauded.

There is an active and a passive ingratitude; applying both to this occasion, we may say, the first is, when a prince or people returns good services with cruelty or ill usage: the other is, when good services are not at all, or very meanly rewarded. We have already spoke of the former; let us therefore in the second place, examine how the services of our general have been rewarded; and whether upon that article, either prince or people have been guilty of ingratitude.

Those are the most valuable rewards, which are given to us from the certain knowledge of the donor, that they *fit our temper best:* I shall therefore say nothing of the title of Duke, or the Garter, which the Queen bestowed [on] the general in the beginning of her reign; but I shall come to more substantial instances, and mention nothing which has not been given in the face of the world. The lands of Woodstock, may, I believe, be reckoned with 40,000*l.* On the building of Blenheim Castle 200,000*l.* have been already expended, though it be not yet near finished. The grant of 5,000*l. per ann.* on the post-office is richly worth 100,000*l.* His principality in Germany may be computed at 30,000*l.* Pictures, jewels, and other gifts from foreign princes, 60,000*l.* The grant at the Pall-Mall, the rangership, &c. for want of more certain knowledge, may be called 10,000*l.* His own, and his duchess's employments at five years' value, reckoning only the known and avowed salaries, are very low rated at 100,000*l.* Here is a good deal above half a million of money, and I dare say, those who are loudest with the clamour of ingratitude will readily own that all this is but a trifle in comparison of what is untold.

The reason of my stating this account is only to convince the world, that we are not quite so ungrateful either as the Greeks or the Romans. And in order to adjust this matter with all fairness, I shall confine myself to the latter, who were much the more generous of the two. A victorious general of Rome in the height of that empire, having entirely subdued his enemy, was rewarded with the larger triumph; and perhaps a statue in the Forum, a bull for a sacrifice, an embroidered garment to appear in: a crown of laurel, a monumental trophy with inscriptions; sometimes five hundred or a thousand copper coins were struck on occasion of the victory, which doing honour to the general, we will place to his account; and lastly, sometimes, though not very frequently, a triumphal arch. These are all the rewards that I can call to mind, which a victorious general received after his return from the most glorious expedition, conquered some great kingdom, brought the king himself, his family and nobles to adorn the triumph in chains, and made the kingdom either a Roman province, or at best a poor depending state, in humble alliance to that empire. Now of all these rewards, I find but two which were of real profit to the general; the laurel crown, made and sent him at the charge of the public, and the embroidered garment; but I cannot find whether this last were paid for by the senate or the general: however, we will take the more favourable opinion, and in all the rest, admit the whole expense, as if it were ready money in the general's pocket. Now according to these computations on both sides, we will draw up two fair accounts, the one of Roman gratitude, and the other of British in-gratitude, and set them together in balance.

A BILL OF ROMAN GRATITUDE.

	l.	s.	d.
Imprimis for frankincense and earthen pots to burn it in	4	10	0
A bull for sacrifice	8	0	0
An embroidered garment	50	0	0
A crown of laurel	0	0	2
A statue	100	0	0
A trophy	80	0	0
A thousand copper medals value half pence a piece	2	1	8
A triumphal arch	500	0	0
A triumphal car, valued as a modern coach	100	0	0
Casual charges at the triumph . . .	150	0	0
Sum total . . .	994	11	10

A BILL OF BRITISH INGRATITUDE.

	l.	s.	d.
Imprimis Woodstock	40,000	0	0
Blenheim	200,000	0	0
Post-office grant	100,000	0	0
Mildenheim	30,000	0	0
Pictures, jewels, &c.	60,000	0	0
Pall-Mall grant, &c.	10,000	0	0
Employments	100,000	0	0
Sum total . . .	540,000	0	0

This is an account of the visible profits on both sides; and if the Roman general had any private perquisites, they may be easily discounted, and by more probable computation, and differ yet more upon the balance; if we consider, that all the gold and silver for safeguards and contributions, also all valuable prizes taken in the war were openly exposed in the triumph, and then lodged in the Capitol for the public service.

So that upon the whole, we are not yet quite so bad at *worst*, as the Romans were at *best*. And I doubt those who raise this hideous cry of ingratitude, may be mightily mistaken in the consequence they propose from such complaints. I remember a saying of Seneca, *Multos ingratos invenimus, plures facimus;* "We find many ungrateful persons in the world, but we *make* more," by setting too high a rate upon our pretensions, and undervaluing the rewards we receive. When unreasonable bills are brought in, they ought to be taxed, or cut off in the middle. Where there have been long accounts between two persons, I have known one of them perpetually making large demands and pressing for payments, who when the accounts were cast up on both sides, was found to be creditor for some hundreds. I am thinking if a proclamation were issued out for every man to send in his *bill of merits,* and the lowest price he set them at, what a pretty sum it would amount to, and how many such islands as this must be sold to pay them. I form my judgment from the practice of those who sometimes happen to pay themselves, and I dare affirm, would not be so unjust to take a farthing more than they think is due to their deserts. I will instance only in one article. A lady of my acquaintance, appropriated twenty-six pounds a year out of her allowance, for certain uses, which her woman received, and was to pay to the lady or her order, as it was called for. But after eight years, it appeared upon the strictest calculation, that the woman had paid but four pound a year, and sunk two-and-twenty for her own pocket. It is but supposing instead of twenty-six pound, twenty-six thousand, and by that you may judge what the pretensions of *modern merit* are, where it happens to be its own paymaster.

To Alexander Pope

Dublin, June 28, 1715.

MY LORD BISHOP of Clogher gave me your kind letter full of reproaches for my not writing. I am naturally no very exact correspondent, and when I leave a country without a probability of returning, I think as seldom as I can of what I loved or esteemed in it, to avoid the *desiderium* which of all things makes life most uneasy. But you must give me leave to add one thing, that you talk at your ease, being wholly unconcerned in public events: for if your friends the Whigs continue, you may hope for some favour; if the Tories return, you are at least sure of quiet. You know how well I loved both Lord Oxford and Bolingbroke, and how dear the Duke of Ormond is to me. Do you imagine I can be easy while their enemies are endeavouring to take off their heads. *I nunc, et versus tecum meditare canoros.* Do you imagine I can be easy, when I think of the probable consequences of these proceedings, perhaps upon the very peace of the nation, but certainly of the minds of so many hundred thousand good subjects? Upon the whole, you may truly attribute my silence to the eclipse, but it was that eclipse which happened on the first of August.

I borrowed your Homer from the Bishop—mine is not yet landed—and read it out in two evenings. If it pleases others as well as me, you have got your end in profit and reputation: yet I am angry at some bad rhymes and triplets, and pray in your next do not let me have so

many unjustifiable rhymes to *war* and *gods*. I tell you all
the faults I know, only in one or two places you are a
little obscure: but I expected you to be so in one or two
and twenty. I have heard no soul talk of it here, for indeed it is not come over; nor do we very much abound
in judges—at least I have not the honour to be acquainted with them. Your notes are perfectly good, and
so are your preface and essay. You were pretty bold
in mentioning Lord Bolingbroke in that preface. I saw
the Key to the Lock but yesterday: I think you have
changed it a good deal, to adapt it to the present times.

God be thanked I have yet no parliamentary business,
and if they have none with me, I shall never seek their
acquaintance. I have not been very fond of them for
some years past, not when I thought them tolerably
good; and therefore if I can get leave to be absent, I
shall be much inclined to be on that side when there is
a Parliament on this: but truly I must be a little easy in
my mind before I can think of Scriblerus.

You are to understand that I live in the corner of a
vast unfurnished house. My family consists of a steward,
a groom, a helper in the stable, a footman, and an old
maid, who are all at board wages, and when I do not
dine abroad, or make an entertainment, which last is
very rare, I eat a mutton-pie, and drink half a pint of
wine. My amusements are defending my small dominions against the Archbishop, and endeavouring to reduce
my rebellious choir. *Perditur haec inter misero lux.* I
desire you will present my humble service to Mr. Addison, Mr. Congreve, and Mr. Rowe, and Gay. I am, and
will be always,

                                   Extremely yours, etc.

To Esther Vanhomrigh [Vanessa]

In these last three letters to Vanessa, as in all Swift wrote to her, he took care to say as little as possible that might identify either of them if the letters should be read by other persons. But what sounds mystifying now was only exciting to her, who clearly recognized all his allusions to their past history. The coffee and coffee-drinking to which he so often refers has been sometimes taken to mean love and love-making, but may mean only that she preferred coffee to tea and that he drank it when with her.   C.V.D.

> Clogher, June 1, 1722.

THIS is the first time I have set pen to paper since I left Dublin, having not been in any settled place till ten days ago, and I missed one post by ignorance, and that has stopped me five days. Before that time I was much out of order, by the usual consequences of wet weather and change of drink, neither am I yet established, though much better than I was. The weather has been so constantly bad, that I have wanted all the healthy advantages of the country, and it seems likely to continue so. It would have been infinitely better once a week to have met Kendall and so forth, where one might pass three or four hours in drinking coffee in the morning, or dining *tête-à-tête*, and drinking coffee again till seven. I answer all the questions you can ask me in the affirmative. I remember your detesting and despising the conversation of the world. I have been so mortified with a man and his lady here two days, that it has made

171

me as peevish as—I want a comparison. I hope you are gone or going to your country-seat, though I think you have a term upon your hands. I shall be here long enough to receive your answer, and perhaps to write to you again; but then I shall go farther off, if my health continues, and shall let you know my stages. I have been for some days as spleenatic as ever you was in your life, which is a bold word.

Remember I still enjoin you reading and exercise for the improvement of your mind, and health of your body, and grow less romantic, and talk and act like a man of this world. It is the saying of the world, and I believe you often say, I love myself, but I am so low, I cannot say it, though your new acquaintance were with you, which I heartily wish for the sake of you and myself. God send you through your law and your reference; and remember that riches are nine parts in ten of all that is good in life, and health is the tenth—drinking coffee comes long after, and yet it is the eleventh, but without the two former you cannot drink it right; and remember the china in the old house, and Ryder Street, and the Colonel's journey to France, and the London wedding, and the sick lady at Kensington, and the indisposition at Windsor, and the strain by the box of books at London. Last year I writ you civilities, and you were angry; this year I will write you none, and you will be angry; yet my thoughts were still the same, and I give you leave to be [carver?], and will be answerable for them. I hope you will let me have some of your money, when I see you, which I will pay honestly you again. *Répondez moy si vous entendez bien tout cela, et croyez que je seray toujours tout ce que vous désirez.* Adieu.

Loughgall, County of Armagh, July 13, 1722. I have received yours, and have changed places so often since, that I could not assign a place where I might expect an answer from ——; and if you be now in the country, and this letter does not reach you in the due time after the date, I shall not expect to hear from you, because I leave this place the beginning of August. I am well pleased with the account of your visit, and the behaviour of the ladies. I see every day as silly things among both sexes, and yet endure them for the sake of amusement. The worst thing in you and me is, that we are too hard to please, and, whether we have not made ourselves so, is the question; at least I believe we have the same reason. One thing that I differ from you in, is that I do not quarrel with my best friends. I believe you have ten angry passages in your letter, and every one of them enough to spoil two days apiece of riding and walking. We differ prodigiously in one point: I fly from the spleen to the world's end, you run out of your way to meet it. I doubt the bad weather has hindered you much from the diversions of your country-house, and put you upon thinking in your chamber.

The use I have made of it was to read I know not how many diverting books of history and travels. I wish you would get yourself a horse, and have always two servants to attend you, and visit your neighbours—the worse the better. There is a pleasure in being reverenced, and that is always in your power, by your superiority of sense, and an easy fortune. The best maxim I know in life is, to drink your coffee when you can, and when you cannot, to be easy without it; while you continue to be spleenatic, count upon it, I will always preach. Thus much I sympathize with you, that I am not cheerful enough to write, for, I believe, coffee once a week is necessary to that. I can sincerely answer all your questions, as I used to do, but then I give all possible way to amusements, because they preserve my

temper, as exercise does my health; and without health
and good humour I had rather be a dog. I have shifted
scenes oftener than I ever did in my life, and I believe
have lain in thirty beds since I left the town; I always
drew up the clothes with my left hand, which is a superstition I have learnt these ten years. These country posts
are always so capricious, that we are forced to send out
letters at a call on a sudden, and mine is now demanded,
though it goes not out till to-morrow. Be cheerful, and
read, and ride, and laugh, as Cad—— used to advise
you long ago. I hope your affairs are in some better settlement. I long to see you in figure and equipage; pray
do not lose that taste. Farewell.

Loughgall, County of Armagh, August 7th, 1722.
I am this hour leaving my present residence, and if I
fix anywhere, shall let you know it; for I would fain wait
till I get a little good weather for riding and walking,
there never having been such a season as this remembered, though I doubt you know nothing of it, but what
you learn by sometimes looking out at your back window to call your people. I had your last, with a spleenatic account of your law affairs. You were once a better
solicitor, when you could contrive to make others desire
your consent to an Act of Parliament against their own
interest to advance yours. Yet at present you neither
want power nor skill, but disdain to exercise either.
When you are melancholy, read diverting or amusing
books; it is my receipt, and seldom fails. Health, good
humour, and fortune, are all that is valuable in this life,
and the last contributes to the two former. I have not
rode in all above four hundred miles since I saw you,
nor do I believe I shall ride above two hundred more
till I see you again; but I desire you will not venture to
shake me by the hand, for I am in mortal fear of the

itch, and have no hope left, but that some ugly vermin
called ticks have got into my skin, of which I have
pulled out some, and must scratch out the rest. Is not
this enough to give me the spleen? For I doubt no Christian family will receive me, and this is all a man gets by
a northern journey. It would be unhappy for me to be
as nice in my conversation and company as you are,
which is the only thing wherein you agree with Glass-
heel, who declares there is not a conversable creature in
Ireland except Cad. What would you do in these parts,
where politeness is as much a stranger as cleanliness? I
am stopped and this letter is intended to travel with me;
so adieu till the next stage.

August 8th.

Yesterday I rode twenty-nine miles without being
weary, and I wish little Heskinage could do as much.
Here I leave this letter to travel one way while I go
another, but where I do not know, nor what cabins or
bogs are in my way. I see you this moment as you are
visible at ten in the morning, and now you are asking
your questions round, and I am answering them with a
great deal of affected delays, and the same scene has
passed forty times as well as the other, from two till
seven, longer than the first by two hours, yet each its
ses agremens particuliers. A long vacation, law lies
asleep, and bad weather; how do you wear away the
time? Is it among the fields and groves of your country-
seat, or among your cousins in town, or thinking in a
train that will be sure to vex you, and then reasoning
and forming teasing conclusions from mistaken thoughts?
The best companion for you is a philosopher, whom you
would regard as much as a sermon. I have read more
trash since I left you than would fill all your shelves, and
am abundantly the better for it, though I scarce remember a syllable. Go over the scenes of Windsor, Cleve-

land Row, Ryder Street, St James's Street, Kensington, the Sluttery, the Colonel in France, etc. Cad thinks often of these, especially on horseback, as I am assured. What a foolish thing is time, and how foolish is man, who would be as angry if time stopped as if it passed. But I will not proceed at this rate; for I am writing and thinking myself fast into a spleen, which is the only thing that I would not compliment you by imitating. So adieu till the next place I fix in, if I fix at all till I return, and that I leave to fortune and the weather.

To John Gay

Dublin, January 8, 1722–3.

COMING home after a short Christmas ramble, I
found a letter upon my table, and little expected
when I opened it to read your name at the bottom. The
best and greatest part of my life, until these last eight
years, I spent in England: there I made my friendships,
and there I left my desires. I am condemned for ever to
another country; what is in prudence to be done? I think
to be *oblitusque meorum, obliviscendus et illis.* What
can be the design of your letter but malice, to wake me
out of a scurvy sleep, which however is better than
none? I am towards nine years older since I left you, yet
that is the least of my alterations; my business, my diversions, my conversations, are all entirely changed for
the worse, and so are my studies and my amusements in
writing. Yet, after all, this humdrum way of life might
be passable enough, if you would let me alone. I shall
not be able to relish my wine, my parsons, my horses,
nor my garden, for three months, until the spirit you
have raised shall be dispossessed. I have sometimes wondered that I have not visited you, but I have been
stopped by too many reasons, besides years and laziness,
and yet these are very good ones. Upon my return after
half a year amongst you, there would be to me, *De-
siderio nec pudor nec modus.* I was three years recon-
ciling myself to the scene, and the business, to which
fortune has condemned me, and stupidity was what I had
recourse to. Besides, what a figure should I make in

London, while my friends are in poverty, exile, distress, or imprisonment, and my enemies with rods of iron? Yet I often threaten myself with the journey, and am every summer practising to ride and get health to bear it; the only inconvenience is, that I grow old in the experiment.

Although I care not to talk to you as a divine, yet I hope you have not been author of your colic. Do you drink bad wine, or keep bad company? Are you not as many years older as I? It will not be always: *Et tibi quos mihi dempserit apponet annos.* I am heartily sorry you have any dealings with that ugly distemper, and I believe our friend Arbuthnot will recommend you to temperance and exercise. I wish they would have as good an effect upon the giddiness I am subject to, and which this moment I am not free from. I should have been glad if you had lengthened your letter by telling me the present condition of many of my old acquaintance—Congreve, Arbuthnot, Lewis, etc., but you mention only Mr. Pope, who, I believe, is lazy, or else he might have added three lines of his own. I am extremely glad he is not in your case of needing great men's favour, and could heartily wish that you were in his.

I have been considering why poets have such ill success in making their court, since they are allowed to be the greatest and best of all flatterers. The defect is, that they flatter only in print or in writing, but not by word of mouth: they will give things under their hand which they make a conscience of speaking. Besides, they are too libertine to haunt ante-chambers, too poor to bribe porters and footmen, and too proud to cringe to second-hand favourites in a great family. Tell me, are you not under original sin by the dedication of your Eclogues to Lord Bolingbroke? I am an ill judge at this distance; and besides, am, for my ease, utterly ignorant of the commonest things that pass in the world; but if all Courts have a sameness in them, as the parsons' phrase is, things may be as they were in my time, when all employments went to Parliament-men's friends, who had been useful in elections, and there was always a huge list of names in arrears at the Treasury, which would take up at least your seven years' expedient to discharge even one half.

I am of opinion, if you will not be offended, that the surest course would be to get your friend who lodges in your house, to recommend you to the next chief governor who comes over here, for a good civil employment, or to be one of his secretaries, which your Parliament-men are fond enough of, when there is no room at home. The wine is good and reasonable; you may dine twice a week at the Deanery House; there is a set of company in this town sufficient for one man; folks will admire you, because they have read you, and read of you; and a good employment will make you live tolerably in London, or sumptuously here; or if you divide between both places, it will be for your health. The Duke of Wharton settled a pension on Dr. Young. Your landlord is much richer. These are my best thoughts after three days' reflections. Mr. Budgell got a very good office here, and lost it by a great want of common politics. If a [Whig] recommendation be hearty, and the governor who comes here be already inclined to favour you, nothing but *fortuna Trojanae* can hinder the success.

If I write to you once a quarter, will you promise to send me an answer in a week, and then I will leave you at rest till the next quarter-day; and I desire you will leave part of a blank side for Mr. Pope. Has he some *quelque chose* of his own upon the anvil? I expect it from him since poor Homer helped to make him rich. Why have not I your works, and with a civil inscription

before it, as Mr. Pope ought to have done to his, for so
I had from your predecessors of the two last reigns. I
hear yours were sent to Ben Tooke, but I never had
them. You see I wanted nothing but provocation to send
you a long letter, which I am not weary of writing, because I do not hear myself talk, and yet I have the
pleasure of talking to you, and if you are not good at
reading ill hands, it will cost you as much time as it has
done me. I wish I could do more than say I love you. I
left you in a good way both for the late Court, and the
successors; and by the force of too much honesty or too
little sublunary wisdom, you fell between two stools.
Take care of your health and money; be less modest and
more active; or else turn parson and get a bishopric here.
Would to God they would send us as good ones from
your side! I am ever, with all friendship and esteem,

                                        Yours.

Mr. Ford presents his service to Mr. Pope and you.
We keep him here as long as we can.

From The Drapier's Letters

Letter IV. *A Letter to the Whole People of Ireland,* published October 1724.

MY DEAR COUNTRYMEN,
 Having already written three letters upon so disagreeable a subject as Mr. Wood and his halfpence; I conceived my task was at an end: But I find that cordials must be frequently applied to weak constitutions, political as well as natural. A people long used to hardships lose by degrees the very notions of liberty; they look upon themselves as creatures at mercy, and that all impositions laid on them by a stronger hand are, in the phrase of the Report, legal and obligatory. Hence proceeds that poverty and lowness of spirit to which a kingdom may be subject as well as a particular person. And when Esau came fainting from the field at the point to die, it is no wonder that he sold his birthright for a mess of pottage.

 I thought I had sufficiently shewn to all who could want instruction, by what methods they might safely proceed, whenever this coin should be offered to them; and I believe there hath not been for many ages an example of any kingdom so firmly united in a point of great importance as this of ours is at present, against that detestable fraud. But however, it so happens that some weak people begin to be alarmed anew, by rumours industriously spread. Wood prescribes to the newsmongers in London what they are to write. In one of their papers

published here by some obscure printer (and probably
with no good design) we are told that "the Papists in
Ireland have entered into an association against his
coin," although it be notoriously known that they never
once offered to stir in the matter; so that the two Houses
of Parliament, the Privy-Council, the great number of
corporations, the lord mayor and aldermen of Dublin,
the ‚grand juries, and principal gentlemen of several
counties are stigmatized in a lump under the name of
"Papists."

This impostor and his crew do likewise give out that,
by refusing to receive his dross for sterling, we "dispute
the King's prerogative, are grown ripe for rebellion, and
ready to shake off the dependency of Ireland upon the
crown of England." To countenance which reports he
hath published a paragraph in another newspaper, to
let us know that "the Lord Lieutenant is ordered to come
over immediately to settle his halfpence."

I entreat you, my dear countrymen, not to be under
the least concern upon these and the like rumours, which
are no more than the last howls of a dog dissected alive,
as I hope he hath sufficiently been. These calumnies are
the only reserve that is left him. For surely our continued and (almost) unexampled loyalty will never be
called in question for not suffering ourselves to be
robbed of all that we have, by one obscure ironmonger.

As to disputing the King's prerogative, give me leave
to explain to those who are ignorant, what the meaning
of that word *prerogative* is.

The Kings of these realms enjoy several powers
wherein the laws have not interposed: So they can make
war and peace without the consent of Parliament; and
this is a very great prerogative. But if the Parliament
doth not approve of the war, the King must bear the
charge of it out of his own purse, and this is as great a

check on the crown. So the King hath a prerogative to coin money without consent of Parliament. But he cannot compel the subject to take that money except it be sterling, gold or silver; because herein he is limited by law. Some princes have indeed extended their prerogative further than the law allowed them; wherein however, the lawyers of succeeding ages, as fond as they are of precedents, have never dared to justify them. But to say the truth, it is only of late times that prerogative hath been fixed and ascertained. For whoever reads the histories of England, will find that some former Kings, and these none of the worst, have upon several occasions ventured to control the laws with very little ceremony or scruple, even later than the days of Queen Elizabeth. In her reign that pernicious counsel of sending base money hither very narrowly failed of losing the kingdom, being complained of by the lord-deputy, the council, and the whole body of the English here: So that soon after her death it was recalled by her successor, and lawful money paid in exchange.

Having thus given you some notion of what is meant by the King's "prerogative," as far as a tradesman can be thought capable of explaining it, I will only add the opinion of the great Lord Bacon: That "as God governs the world by the settled laws of nature, which he hath made, and never transcends those laws but upon high important occasions; so among earthly princes, those are the wisest and the best, who govern by the known laws of the country, and seldomest make use of their prerogative."

Now, here you may see that the vile accusation of Wood and his accomplices, charging us with "disputing. the King's prerogative" by refusing his brass, can have no place, because compelling the subject to take any coin which is not sterling is no part of the King's pre-

rogative, and I am very confident if it were so, we should
be the last of his people to dispute it, as well from that
inviolable loyalty we have always paid to His Majesty,
as from the treatment we might in such a case justly
expect from some who seem to think we have neither
common sense nor common senses. But God be thanked,
the best of them are only our fellow-subjects, and not
our masters. One great merit I am sure we have, which
those of English birth can have no pretence to, that our
ancestors reduced this kingdom to the obedience of
England, for which we have been rewarded with a worse
climate, the privilege of being governed by laws to
which we do not consent, a ruined trade, a House of
Peers without jurisdiction, almost an incapacity for all
employments; and the dread of Wood's halfpence.

But we are so far from disputing the King's prerogative in coining, that we own he has power to give a
patent to any man for setting his royal image and super-
scription upon whatever materials he pleases, and liberty
to the patentee to offer them in any country from England to Japan, only attended with one small limitation,
That nobody alive is obliged to take them.

Upon these considerations I was ever against all recourse to England for a remedy against the present impending evil, especially when I observed that the addresses of both Houses, after long expectance, produced
nothing but a REPORT altogether in favour of Wood,
upon which I made some observations in a former letter,
and might at least have made as many more: For it is a
paper of as singular a nature as I ever beheld.

But I mistake; for before this Report was made, His
Majesty's most gracious answer to the House of Lords
was sent over and printed, wherein there are these
words, "granting the patent for coining halfpence and

farthings AGREEABLE TO THE PRACTICE OF HIS ROYAL
PREDECESSORS, &c." That King Charles 2d. and King
James 2d. (AND THEY ONLY) did grant patents for this
purpose is indisputable, and I have shewn it at large.
Their patents were passed under the great seal of Ireland
by references to Ireland, the copper to be coined in Ireland, the patentee was bound on demand to receive his
coin back in Ireland, and pay silver and gold in return.
Wood's patent was made under the great seal of England, the brass coined in England, not the least reference made to Ireland, the sum immense, and the patentee under no obligation to receive it again and give
good money for it: This I only mention, because in
my private thoughts I have sometimes made a query,
whether the penner of those words in His Majesty's
most gracious answer, "agreeable to the practice of his
royal predecessors," had maturely considered the several
circumstances, which, in my poor opinion seem to make
a difference.

Let me now say something concerning the other great
cause of some people's fear, as Wood has taught the
London newswriter to express it. That "his Excellency
the Lord Lieutenant is coming over to settle Wood's
halfpence."

We know very well that the Lords Lieutenants for
several years past have not thought this kingdom worthy
the honour of their residence, longer than was absolutely
necessary for the King's business, which consequently
wanted no speed in the dispatch; and therefore it naturally fell into most men's thoughts, that a new governor
coming at an unusual time must portend some unusual
business to be done, especially if the common report be
true, that the Parliament prorogued to I know not when,
is by a new summons (revoking that prorogation) to as-

semble soon after his arrival: For which extraordinary proceeding the lawyers on t'other side the water have by great good fortune found two precedents.

All this being granted, it can never enter into my head that so little a creature as Wood could find credit enough with the King and his ministers to have the Lord Lieutenant of Ireland sent hither in a hurry upon his errand.

For let us take the whole matter nakedly as it lies before us, without the refinements of some people, with which we have nothing to do. Here is a patent granted under the great seal of England, upon false suggestions, to one William Wood for coining copper halfpence for Ireland: The Parliament here, upon apprehensions of the worst consequences from the said patent, address the King to have it recalled; this is refused, and a committee of the Privy-council report to His Majesty, that Wood has performed the conditions of his patent. He then is left to do the best he can with his halfpence; no man being obliged to receive them; the people here, being likewise left to themselves, unite as one man, resolving they will have nothing to do with his ware. By this plain account of the fact it is manifest that the King and his ministry are wholly out of the case, and the matter is left to be disputed between him and us. Will any man therefore attempt to persuade me that a Lord Lieutenant is to be dispatched over in great haste before the ordinary time, and a Parliament summoned by anticipating a prorogation, merely to put an hundred thousand pounds into the pocket of a sharper, by the ruin of a most loyal kingdom.

But supposing all this to be true. By what arguments could a Lord Lieutenant prevail on the same Parliament which addressed with so much zeal and earnestness against this evil, to pass it into a law? I am sure their opinion of Wood and his project is not mended since the last prorogation; and supposing those methods should be used which detractors tell us have been sometimes put in practice for gaining votes. It is well known that in this kingdom there are few employments to be given, and if there were more, it is as well known to whose share they must fall.

But because great numbers of you are altogether ignorant in the affairs of your country, I will tell you some reasons why there are so few employments to be disposed of in this kingdom. All considerable offices for life here are possessed by those to whom the reversions were granted, and these have been generally followers of the chief governors, or persons who had interest in the Court of England. So the Lord Berkeley of Stratton holds that great office of master of the rolls, the Lord Palmerstown is first remembrancer worth near 2000*l. per ann.* One Dodington, secretary to the Earl of Pembroke, begged the reversion of clerk of the pells worth 2500*l.* a year, which he now enjoys by the death of the Lord Newton. Mr. Southwell is secretary of state, and the Earl of Burlington lord high treasurer of Ireland by inheritance. These are only a few among many others which I have been told of, but cannot remember. Nay, the reversion of several employments during pleasure are granted the same way. This among many others is a circumstance whereby the kingdom of Ireland is distinguished from all other nations upon earth, and makes it so difficult an affair to get into a civil employ, that Mr. Addison was forced to purchase an old obscure place, called keeper of the records of Bermingham's Tower of ten pounds a year, and to get a salary of 400*l.* annexed to it, though all the records there are not worth half-a-crown, either for curiosity or use. And we lately saw a favourite secretary descend to be master of the revels, which by his credit and extortion he hath made pretty considerable. I say nothing of the under-treasurership worth about 8000*l.* a year, nor the commissioners of the revenue, four of whom generally live in England; For I think none of these are granted in reversion. But the test is, that I have known upon occasion some of these absent officers as keen against the interest of Ireland as if they had never been indebted to her for a single groat.

I confess, I have been sometimes tempted to wish that this project of Wood might succeed, because I reflected with some pleasure what a jolly crew it would bring over among us of lords and squires, and pensioners of both sexes, and officers civil and military, where we should live together as merry and sociable as beggars, only with this one abatement, that we should neither have meat to feed, nor manufactures to clothe us, unless we could be content to prance about in coats of mail, or eat brass as ostriches do iron.

I return from this digression to that which gave me the occasion of making it: And I believe you are now convinced that if the Parliament of Ireland were as temptable as any other assembly within a mile of Christendom (which God forbid), yet the managers must of necessity fail for want of tools to work with. But I will yet go one step further, by supposing that a hundred new employments were erected on purpose to gratify compliers; yet still an insuperable difficulty would remain; for it happens, I know not how, that money is neither Whig nor Tory, neither of town nor country party, and it is not improbable that a gentleman would rather choose to live upon his own estate which brings him gold and silver, than with the addition of an employment, when his rents and salary must both be paid in Wood's brass, at above eighty *per cent.* discount.

For these and many other reasons, I am confident you

need not be under the least apprehensions from the sudden expectation of the Lord Lieutenant, while we continue in our present hearty disposition; to alter which there is no suitable temptation can possibly be offered: And if, as I have often asserted from the best authority, the law hath not left a power in the crown to force any money except sterling upon the subject, much less can the crown devolve such a power upon another.

This I speak with the utmost respect to the person and dignity of his Excellency the Lord Carteret, whose character hath been given me by a gentleman that hath known him from his first appearance in the world: That gentleman describes him as a young nobleman of great accomplishments, excellent learning, regular in his life, and of much spirit and vivacity. He hath since, as I have heard, been employed abroad, was principal secretary of state, and is now about the 37th year of his age appointed Lord Lieutenant of Ireland. From such a governor this kingdom may reasonably hope for as much prosperity as, under so many discouragements, it can be capable of receiving.

It is true indeed, that within the memory of man, there have been governors of so much dexterity as to carry points of terrible consequence to this kingdom, by their power with *those who were in office,* and by their arts in managing or deluding others with oaths, affability, and even with dinners. If Wood's brass had in those times been upon the anvil, it is obvious enough to conceive what methods would have been taken. Depending persons would have been told in plain terms that it was a "service expected from them, under pain of the public business being put into more complying hands." Others would be allured by promises. To the country gentleman, besides good words, burgundy and closeting. It would perhaps have been hinted how "kindly it would be taken to comply with a royal patent, though it were not compulsory," that if any inconveniences ensued, it might be made up with other "graces or favours hereafter." That "gentlemen ought to consider whether it were prudent or safe to disgust England": They would be desired to "think of some good bills for encouraging of trade, and setting the poor to work, some further acts against Popery and for uniting Protestants." There would be solemn engagements that we should "never be troubled with above forty thousand pounds in his coin, and all of the best and weightiest sort, for which we should only give our manufactures in exchange, and keep our gold and silver at home." Perhaps a "seasonable report of some invasion would have been spread in the most proper juncture," which is a great smoother of rubs in public proceedings; and we should have been told that "this was no time to create differences when the kingdom was in danger."

These, I say, and the like methods would in corrupt times have been taken to let in this deluge of brass among us; and I am confident would even then have not succeeded, much less under the administration of so excellent a person as the Lord Carteret, and in a country where the people of all ranks, parties and denominations are convinced to a man, that the utter undoing of themselves and their posterity for ever will be dated from the admission of that execrable coin; that if it once enters, it can be no more confined to a small or moderate quantity, than the plague can be confined to a few families, and that no equivalent can be given by any earthly power, any more than a dead carcass can be recovered to life by a cordial.

There is one comfortable circumstance in this universal opposition to Mr. Wood, that the people sent over hither from England to fill up our vacancies ecclesias-

tical, civil, and military, are all on our side: Money, the
great divider of the world, hath by a strange revolution,
been the great uniter of a most divided people. Who
would leave a hundred pounds a year in England (a
country of freedom) to be paid a thousand in Ireland out
of Wood's exchequer. The gentleman they have lately
made primate would never quit his seat in an English
House of Lords, and his preferments at Oxford and
Bristol, worth twelve hundred pounds a year, for four
times the denomination here, but not half the value;
therefore I expect to hear he will be as good an Irishman, upon this article, as any of his brethren, or even
of us who have had the misfortune to be born in this
island. For those, who, in the common phrase, do not
"come hither to learn the language," would never change
a better country for a worse, to receive brass instead of
gold.

Another slander spread by Wood and his emissaries is,
that by opposing him we discover an inclination to
"shake off our dependence upon the crown of England."
Pray observe how important a person is this same William Wood, and how the public weal of two kingdoms
is involved in his private interest. First, all those who refuse to take his coin are Papists; for he tells us that
"none but Papists are associated against him"; Secondly,
they "dispute the King's prerogative"; Thirdly, "they are
ripe for rebellion"; and Fourthly, they are going to
"shake off their dependence upon the crown of England"; That is to say, "they are going to choose another
king"; For there can be no other meaning in this expression, however some may pretend to strain it.

And this gives me an opportunity of explaining, to
those who are ignorant, another point, which hath often
swelled in my breast. Those who come over hither to us
from England, and some weak people among ourselves,

whenever in discourse we make mention of liberty and property, shake their heads, and tell us that Ireland is a "depending kingdom," as if they would seem, by this phrase, to intend that the people of Ireland is in some state of slavery or dependence different from those of England; Whereas a "depending kingdom" is a modern term of art, unknown, as I have heard, to all ancient civilians, and writers upon government; and Ireland is on the contrary called in some statutes an "imperial crown," as held only from God; which is as high a style as any kingdom is capable of receiving. Therefore by this expression a "depending kingdom," there is no more understood than that by a statute made here in the 33d year of Henry 8th, "The King and his successors are to be kings imperial of this realm as united and knit to the imperial crown of England." I have looked over all the English and Irish statutes without finding any law that makes Ireland depend upon England, any more than England does upon Ireland. We have indeed obliged ourselves to have the same king with them, and consequently they are obliged to have the same king with us. For the law was made by our own Parliament, and our ancestors then were not such fools (whatever they were in the preceding reign) to bring themselves under I know not what dependence, which is now talked of without any ground of law, reason, or common sense.

Let whoever think otherwise, I, M. B. Drapier, desire to be excepted, for I declare, next under God, I *depend* only on the King my sovereign, and on the laws of my own country; and I am so far from *depending* upon the people of England, that if they should ever rebel against my sovereign (which God forbid) I would be ready at the first command from His Majesty to take arms against them, as some of *my* countrymen did against *theirs* at Preston. And if such a rebellion should prove so success-

ful as to fix the Pretender on the throne of England, I
would venture to transgress that statute so far as to lose
every drop of my blood to hinder him from being King
of Ireland.

'Tis true indeed, that within the memory of man the
Parliaments of England have sometimes assumed the
power of binding this kingdom by laws enacted there,
wherein they were at first openly opposed (as far as
truth, reason, and justice are capable of opposing) by
the famous Mr. Molineux, an English gentleman born
here, as well as by several of the greatest patriots, and
best Whigs in England; but the love and torrent of
power prevailed. Indeed the arguments on both sides
were invincible. For in reason, all government without
the consent of the governed is the very definition of
slavery: But in fact, eleven men well armed will certainly subdue one single man in his shirt. But I have
done. For those who have used power to cramp liberty
have gone so far as to resent even the liberty of complaining, although a man upon the rack was never
known to be refused the liberty of roaring as loud as he
thought fit.

And as we are apt to sink too much under unreasonable fears, so we are too soon inclined to be raised by
groundless hopes (according to the nature of all con-
sumptive bodies like ours); thus it hath been given
about for several days past that somebody in England
empowered a second somebody to write to a third somebody here to assure us that we "should no more be troubled with those halfpence." And this is reported to have
been done by the same person who was said to have
sworn some months ago that he would "ram them down
our throats" (though I doubt they would stick in our
stomachs), but whichever of these reports is true or
false, it is no concern of ours. For in this point we have

nothing to do with English ministers, and I should be sorry it lay in their power to redress this grievance or to enforce it: For the "Report of the Committee" hath given me a surfeit. The remedy is wholly in your own hands, and therefore I have digressed a little in order to refresh and continue that spirit so seasonably raised amongst you, and to let you see that by the laws of GOD, of NATURE, of NATIONS, and of your own COUNTRY, you ARE and OUGHT to be as FREE a people as your brethren in England.

If the pamphlets published at London by Wood and his journeymen in defence of his cause, were reprinted here, and that our countrymen could be persuaded to read them, they would convince you of his wicked design more than all I shall ever be able to say. In short I make him a perfect saint in comparison of what he appears to be from the writings of those whom he hires to justify his project. But he is so far master of the field (let others guess the reason) that no London printer dare publish any paper written in favour of Ireland, and here nobody hath yet been so bold as to publish anything in favour of him.

There was a few days ago a pamphlet sent me of near 50 pages written in favour of Mr. Wood and his coinage, printed in London; it is not worth answering, because probably it will never be published here: But it gave me an occasion to reflect upon an unhappiness we lie under, that the people of England are utterly ignorant of our case, which however is no wonder, since it is a point they do not in the least concern themselves about, farther than perhaps as a subject of discourse in a coffeehouse when they have nothing else to talk of. For I have reason to believe that no minister ever gave himself the trouble of reading any papers written in our defence, because I suppose their opinions are already determined, and are formed wholly upon the reports of Wood and his accomplices; else it would be impossible that any man could have the impudence to write such a pamphlet as I have mentioned.

Our neighbours whose understanding are just upon a level with ours (which perhaps are none of the brightest) have a strong contempt for most nations, but especially for Ireland: They look upon us as a sort of savage Irish, whom our ancestors conquered several hundred years ago, and if I should describe the Britons to you as they were in Cæsar's time, when they painted their bodies, or clothed themselves with the skins of beasts, I would act full as reasonably as they do: However they are so far to be excused in relation to the present subject, that, hearing only one side of the cause, and having neither opportunity nor curiosity to examine the other, they believe a lie merely for their ease, and conclude, because Mr. Wood pretends to have power, he hath also reason on his side.

Therefore to let you see how this case is represented in England by Wood and his adherents, I have thought it proper to extract out of that pamphlet a few of those notorious falsehoods in point of fact and reasoning contained therein; the knowledge whereof will confirm my countrymen in their own right sentiments, when they will see by comparing both, how much their enemies are in the wrong.

First, The writer positively asserts, "That Wood's halfpence were current among us for several months with the universal approbation of all people, without one single gainsayer, and we all to a man thought ourselves happy in having them."

Secondly, He affirms, "That we were drawn into a

dislike of them only by some cunning evil-designing men among us, who opposed this patent of Wood to get another for themselves."

Thirdly, That "those who most declared at first against Wood's patent were the very men who intended to get another for their own advantage."

Fourthly, That "our Parliament and Privy-council, the Lord Mayor and aldermen of Dublin, the grand juries and merchants, and in short the whole kingdom, nay the very dogs" (as he expresseth it) "were fond of those halfpence, till they were inflamed by those few designing persons aforesaid."

Fifthly, He says directly, That "all those who opposed the halfpence were Papists and enemies to King George."

Thus far I am confident the most ignorant among you can safely swear from your own knowledge that the author is a most notorious liar in every article; the direct contrary being so manifest to the whole kingdom, that if occasion required, we might get it confirmed under five hundred thousand hands.

Sixthly, He would persuade us, that "if we sell five shillings worth of our goods or manufactures for two shillings and fourpence worth of copper, although the copper were melted down, and that we could get five shillings in gold or silver for the said goods, yet to take the said two shillings and fourpence in copper would be greatly for our advantage."

And Lastly, He makes us a very fair offer, as empowered by Wood, that "if we will take off two hundred thousand pounds in his halfpence for our goods, and likewise pay him three *per cent.* interest for thirty years, for an hundred and twenty thousand pounds (at which he computes the coinage above the intrinsic value of the copper) for the loan of his coin, he will after that time give us good money for what halfpence will be then left."

Let me place this offer in as clear a light as I can to shew the unsupportable villainy and impudence of that incorrigible wretch. First (says he) "I will send two hundred thousand pounds of my coin into your country, the copper I compute to be in real value eighty thousand pounds, and I charge you with an hundred and twenty thousand pounds for the coinage; so that you see I lend you an hundred and twenty thousand pounds for thirty years, for which you shall pay me three *per cent*. That is to say three thousand six hundred pounds *per ann*. which in thirty years will amount to an hundred and eight thousand pounds. And when these thirty years are expired, return me my copper and I will give you good money for it."

This is the proposal made to us by Wood in that pamphlet written by one of his commissioners; and the author is supposed to be the same infamous Coleby one of his under-swearers at the committee of council, who was tried for robbing the treasury here, where he was an under-clerk.

By this proposal he will first receive two hundred thousand pounds, in goods or sterling for as much copper as he values at eighty thousand pounds, but in reality not worth thirty thousand pounds. Secondly, He will receive for interest an hundred and eight thousand pounds. And when our children come thirty years hence to return his halfpence upon his executors (for before that time he will be probably gone to his own place), those executors will very reasonably reject them as raps and counterfeits, which probably they will be, and millions of them of his own coinage.

Methinks I am fond of such a dealer as this who

mends every day upon our hands, like a Dutch reckoning, where if you dispute the unreasonableness and exorbitance of the bill, the landlord shall bring it up every time with new additions.

Although these and the like pamphlets published by Wood in London be altogether unknown here, where nobody could read them without as much indignation as contempt would allow, yet I thought it proper to give you a specimen how the man employs his time, where he rides alone without one creature to contradict him, while our FEW FRIENDS there wonder at our silence, and the English in general, if they think of this matter at all, impute our refusal to wilfulness or disaffection, just as Wood and his hirelings are pleased to represent.

But although our arguments are not suffered to be printed in England, yet the consequence will be of little moment. Let Wood endeavour to persuade the people there that we ought to receive his coin, and let me convince our people here that they ought to reject it under pain of our utter undoing. And then let him do his best and his worst.

Before I conclude, I must beg leave in all humility to tell Mr. Wood, that he is guilty of great indiscretion, by causing so honourable a name as that of Mr. Walpole to be mentioned so often, and in such a manner, upon this occasion: A short paper printed at Bristol and reprinted here reports Mr. Wood to say that he "wonders at the impudence and insolence of the Irish in refusing his coin, and what he will do when Mr. Walpole comes to town." Where, by the way, he is mistaken, for it is the true English people of Ireland who refuse it, although we take it for granted that the Irish will do so too whenever they are asked. He orders it to be printed in another paper that "Mr. Walpole will cram this brass down our throats." Sometimes it is given out that we must "either take these halfpence or eat our brogues," And, in another newsletter but of yesterday, we read that the same great man "hath sworn to make us swallow his coin in fire-balls."

This brings to my mind the known story of a Scotch-man, who receiving sentence of death, with all the circumstances of hanging, beheading, quartering, em-bowelling, and the like, cried out, "What need all this COOKERY?" And I think we have reason to ask the same question; for if we believe Wood, here is a dinner getting ready for us, and you see the bill of fare, and I am sorry the drink was forgot, which might easily be sup-plied with melted lead and flaming pitch.

What vile words are these to put into the mouth of a great councillor, in high trust with His Majesty, and looked upon as a prime-minister. If Mr. Wood hath no better a manner of representing his patrons, when I come to be a great man he shall never be suffered to at-tend at my levee. This is not the style of a great minister, it savours too much of the kettle and the furnace, and came entirely out of Mr. Wood's forge.

As for the threat of making us eat our brogues, we need not be in pain; for if his coin should pass, that unpolite covering for the feet would no longer be a national reproach; because then we should have neither shoe nor brogue left in the kingdom. But here the false-hood of Mr. Wood is fairly detected; for I am confident Mr. Walpole never heard of a brogue in his whole life.

As to "swallowing these halfpence in fire-balls," it is a story equally improbable. For to execute this operation the whole stock of Mr. Wood's coin and metal must be melted down and moulded into hollow balls with wild-fire, no bigger than a reasonable throat can be able to swallow. Now the metal he hath prepared, and already coined will amount at least fifty millions of halfpence to be swallowed by a million and a half of people; so that allowing two halfpence to each ball, there will be about seventeen balls of wild-fire a-piece to be swallowed by every person in this kingdom, and to administer this dose, there cannot be conveniently fewer than fifty thousand operators, allowing one operator to every thirty, which, considering the squeamishness of some stomachs and the peevishness of young children, is but reasonable. Now, under correction of better judgments, I think the trouble and charge of such an experiment would exceed the profit, and therefore I take this report to be spurious, or at least only a new scheme of Mr. Wood himself, which to make it pass the better in Ireland he would father upon a minister of state.

But I will now demonstrate beyond all contradiction that Mr. Walpole is against this project of Mr. Wood, and is an entire friend to Ireland, only by this one invincible argument, that he has the universal opinion of being a wise man, an able minister, and in all his proceedings pursuing the true interest of the King his master: And that as his integrity is above all corruption, so is his fortune above all temptation. I reckon therefore we are perfectly safe from that corner, and shall never be under the necessity of contending with so formidable a power, but be left to possess our brogues and potatoes in peace as remote from thunder as we are from Jupiter.

> I am,
> My dear countrymen,
> Your loving fellow-subject,
> fellow-sufferer and humble servant.
> M. B.

Oct. 13. 1724.

TRAVELS

INTO SEVERAL

Remote Nations

OF THE

WORLD.

In Four PARTS.

By *LEMUEL GULLIVER*,
First a Surgeon, and then a Captain of several SHIPS.

VOL. I.

LONDON

Printed for Benj. Motte, *at the*
Middle Temple-Gate *in* Fleet-street.
MDCCXXVI.

Travels into Several Remote Nations of the World

The text of the first edition (1726) of the *Travels* was cautiously altered by the London printer Benjamin Motte to avoid the risk of prosecution. The text here printed restores the lost original so far as possible on the basis of the corrections furnished by Swift to Charles Ford, and by Ford written into a large paper copy of the first edition, which is still preserved. These corrections were incorporated in the Dublin edition printed by George Faulkner in 1735, which has lately come to be spoken of as preferable to the Motte-Ford text. But since the Faulkner text includes a good many demonstrable errors due, it seems, to careless editing and printing, and omits one considerable passage in Part III apparently out of fear of further prosecution, the Motte-Ford text is here preferred.

C.V.D.

THE PUBLISHER TO THE READER

THE author of these Travels, Mr. Lemuel Gulliver, is my ancient and intimate friend; there is likewise some relation between us by the mother's side. About three years ago, Mr. Gulliver growing weary of the concourse of curious people coming to him at his house in Redriff, made a small purchase of land, with a convenient house, near Newark, in Nottinghamshire, his native country; where he now lives retired, yet in good esteem among his neighbours.

Although Mr. Gulliver was born in Nottinghamshire, where his father dwelt, yet I have heard him say his family came from Oxfordshire; to confirm which, I have observed in the churchyard at Banbury, in that county, several tombs and monuments of the Gullivers.

Before he quitted Redriff, he left the custody of the following papers in my hands, with the liberty to dispose of them as I should think fit. I have carefully perused them three times: the style is very plain and simple; and the only fault I find is, that the author, after the manner of travellers, is a little too circumstantial. There is an air of truth apparent through the whole; and indeed the author was so distinguished for his veracity, that it became a sort of proverb among his neighbours at Redriff, when any one affirmed a thing, to say it was as true as if Mr. Gulliver had spoke it.

By the advice of several worthy persons, to whom, with the author's permission, I communicated these papers, I now venture to send them into the world, hoping they may be at least, for some time, a better entertainment to our young noblemen, than the common scribbles of politics and party.

This volume would have been at least twice as large, if I had not made bold to strike out innumerable passages relating to the winds and tides, as well as to the variations and bearings in the several voyages; together with the minute descriptions of the management of the ship in storms, in the style of sailors: likewise the account of longitudes and latitudes; wherein I have reason to apprehend that Mr. Gulliver may be a little dissatisfied: but I was resolved to fit the work as much as possible to the general capacity of readers. However, if my own ignorance in sea-affairs shall have led me to commit some mistakes, I alone am answerable for them: and if any traveller hath a curiosity to see the whole work at large, as it came from the hand of the author, I will be ready to gratify him.

As for any further particulars relating to the author, the reader will receive satisfaction from the first pages of the book.

RICHARD SYMPSON.

A LETTER FROM CAPTAIN GULLIVER TO HIS COUSIN SYMPSON

I hope you will be ready to own publicly, whenever you shall be called to it, that by your great and frequent urgency you prevailed on me to publish a very loose and uncorrect account of my travels; with direction to hire some young gentlemen of either university to put them in order, and correct the style, as my cousin Dampier did by my advice, in his book called, *A Voyage round the World*. But I do not remember I gave you power to consent, that any thing should be omitted, and much less that any thing should be inserted: therefore, as to the latter, I do here renounce every thing of that kind; particularly a paragraph about her Majesty the late Queen Anne, of most pious and glorious memory; although I did reverence and esteem her more than any of human species. But you, or your interpolator, ought to have considered, that as it was not my inclination, so was it not decent to praise any animal of our composition before my master *Houyhnhnm:* and besides, the fact was altogether false; for to my knowledge, being in England during some part of her Majesty's reign, she did govern by a chief minister; nay, even by two successively; the first whereof was the Lord of Godolphin, and the second the Lord of Oxford; so that you have made me *say the thing that was not*. Likewise, in the account of the

Academy of Projectors, and several passages of my discourse to my master *Houyhnhnm,* you have either
omitted some material circumstances, or minced or
changed them in such a manner, that I do hardly know
my own work. When I formerly hinted to you something
of this in a letter, you were pleased to answer that you
were afraid of giving offence; that people in power were
very watchful over the press, and apt not only to interpret, but to punish every thing which looked like an
innuendo (as I think you called it). But pray, how could
that whtch I spoke so many years ago, and at about five
thousand leagues distance, in another reign, be applied
to any of the *Yahoos,* who now are said to govern the
herd; especially, at a time when I little thought on or
feared the unhappiness of living under them? Have not
I the most reason to complain, when I see these very
Yahoos carried by *Houyhnhnms* in a vehicle, as if these
were brutes, and those the rational creatures? And indeed, to avoid so monstrous and detestable a sight, was
one principal motive of my retirement hither.

Thus much I thought proper to tell you in relation to
yourself, and to the trust I reposed in you.

I do in the next place complain of my own great want
of judgment, in being prevailed upon by the entreaties
and false reasonings of you and some others, very much
against my own opinion, to suffer my travels to be published. Pray bring to your mind how often I desired you
to consider, when you insisted on the motive of public
good; that the *Yahoos* were a species of animals utterly
incapable of amendment by precepts or examples: and
so it hath proved; for instead of seeing a full stop put to
all abuses and corruptions, at least in this little island,
as I had reason to expect: behold, after above six months
warning, I cannot learn that my book hath produced
one single effect according to my intentions: I desired

you would let me know by a letter, when party and faction were extinguished; judges learned and upright; pleaders honest and modest, with some tincture of common sense; and Smithfield blazing with pyramids of law-books; the young nobility's education entirely changed; the physicians banished; the female *Yahoos* abounding in virtue, honour, truth and good sense; courts and levees of great ministers thoroughly weeded and swept; wit, merit and learning rewarded; all disgracers of the press in prose and verse, condemned to eat nothing but their own cotton, and quench their thirst with their own ink. These, and a thousand other reformations, I firmly counted upon by your encouragement; as indeed they were plainly deducible from the precepts delivered in my book. And, it must be owned, that seven months were a sufficient time to correct every vice and folly to which *Yahoos* are subject; if their natures had been capable of the least disposition to virtue or wisdom: yet so far have you been from answering my expectation in any of your letters; that on the contrary, you are loading our carrier every week with libels, and keys, and reflections, and memoirs, and second parts; wherein I see myself accused of reflecting upon great states-folk; of degrading human nature (for so they have still the confidence to style it), and of abusing the female sex. I find likewise that the writers of those bundles are not agreed among themselves; for some of them will not allow me to be author of my own travels; and others make me author of books to which I am wholly a stranger.

I find likewise, that your printer hath been so careless as to confound the times, and mistake the dates of my several voyages and returns; neither assigning the true year, or the true month, or day of the month: and I hear the original manuscript is all destroyed, since the publication of my book. Neither have I any copy left: however, I have sent you some corrections, which you may insert, if ever there should be a second edition: and yet I cannot stand to them, but shall leave that matter to my judicious and candid readers, to adjust it as they please.

I hear some of our sea-*Yahoos* find fault with my sea-language, as not proper in many parts, nor now in use. I cannot help it. In my first voyages, while I was young, I was instructed by the oldest mariners, and learned to speak as they did. But I have since found that the sea-*Yahoos* are apt, like the land ones, to become new-fangled in their words; which the latter change every year; insomuch, as I remember upon each return to my own country, their old dialect was so altered, that I could hardly understand the new. And I observe, when any *Yahoo* comes from London out of curiosity to visit me at my own house, we neither of us are able to deliver our conceptions in a manner intelligible to the other.

If the censure of *Yahoos* could any way affect me, I should have great reason to complain, that some of them are so bold as to think my book of travels a mere fiction out of my own brain; and have gone so far as to drop hints, that the *Houyhnhnms* and *Yahoos* have no more existence than the inhabitants of Utopia.

Indeed I must confess, that as to the people of *Lilliput*, *Brobdingrag* (for so the word should have been spelt, and not erroneously *Brobdingnag*), and *Laputa*; I have never yet heard of any *Yahoo* so presumptuous as to dispute their being, or the facts I have related concerning them; because the truth immediately strikes every reader with conviction. And is there less probability in my account of the *Houyhnhnms* or *Yahoos*, when it is manifest as to the latter, there are so many thousands even in this city, who only differ from their

brother brutes in *Houyhnhnm-land*, because they use a
sort of a jabber, and do not go naked? I wrote for their
amendment, and not their approbation. The united
praise of the whole race would be of less consequence to
me, than the neighing of those two degenerate *Houyhnhnms* I keep in my stable; because, from these, degenerate as they are, I still improve in some virtues, without any mixture of vice.

Do these miserable animals presume to think that I
am so far degenerated as to defend my veracity? *Yahoo*
as I am, it is well known through all *Houyhnhnm-land*,
that by the instructions and example of my illustrious
master, I was able in the compass of two years (although
I confess with the utmost difficulty) to remove that in-
fernal habit of lying, shuffling, deceiving, and equivo-
cating, so deeply rooted in the very souls of all my species; especially the Europeans.

I have other complaints to make upon this vexatious
occasion; but I forbear troubling myself or you any further. I must freely confess, that since my last return,
some corruptions of my *Yahoo* nature have revived in
me by conversing with a few of your species, and particularly those of my own family, by an unavoidable
necessity; else I should never have attempted so absurd
a project as that of reforming the *Yahoo* race in this kingdom; but I have now done with all such visionary
schemes for ever.

April 2, 1727.

PART I

A Voyage to Lilliput

CHAP. I

The Author gives some account of himself and family, his first inducements to travel. He is shipwrecked, and swims for his life, gets safe on shore in the country of Lilliput, is made a prisoner, and is carried up country.

MY FATHER had a small estate in Nottinghamshire; I was the third of five sons. He sent me to Emanuel College in Cambridge, at fourteen years old, where I resided three years, and applied myself close to my studies; but the charge of maintaining me (although I had a very scanty allowance) being too great for a narrow fortune, I was bound apprentice to Mr. James Bates, an eminent surgeon in London, with whom I continued four years; and my father now and then sending me small sums of money, I laid them out in learning navigation, and other parts of the mathematics, useful to those who intend to travel, as I always believed it would be some time or other my fortune to do. When I left Mr. Bates, I went down to my father; where, by the assistance of him and my uncle John, and some other relations, I got forty pounds, and a promise of thirty pounds a year to maintain me at Leyden: there I studied physic two years and seven months, knowing it would be useful in long voyages.

Soon after my return from Leyden, I was recommended by my good master, Mr. Bates, to be surgeon to the *Swallow*, Captain Abraham Pannell, commander; with whom I continued three years and a half, making a voyage or two into the Levant, and some other parts. When I came back, I resolved to settle in London, to which Mr. Bates, my master, encouraged me, and by him I was recommended to several patients. I took part of a small house in the Old Jury; and being advised to alter my condition, I married Mrs. Mary Burton, second daughter to Mr. Edmund Burton, hosier, in Newgate-street, with whom I received four hundred pounds for a portion.

But, my good master Bates dying in two years after, and I having few friends, my business began to fail; for my conscience would not suffer me to imitate the bad practice of too many among my brethren. Having therefore consulted with my wife, and some of my acquaintance, I determined to go again to sea. I was surgeon successively in two ships, and made several voyages, for six years, to the East and West-Indies, by which I got some addition to my fortune. My hours of leisure I spent in reading the best authors, ancient and modern, being always provided with a good number of books; and when I was ashore, in observing the manners and dispositions of the people, as well as learning their language, wherein I had a great facility by the strength of my memory.

The last of these voyages not proving very fortunate, I grew weary of the sea, and intended to stay at home with my wife and family. I removed from the Old Jury to Fetter-Lane, and from thence to Wapping, hoping to get business among the sailors; but it would not turn to account. After three years expectation that things would mend, I accepted an advantageous offer from Captain William Prichard, master of the *Antelope*, who

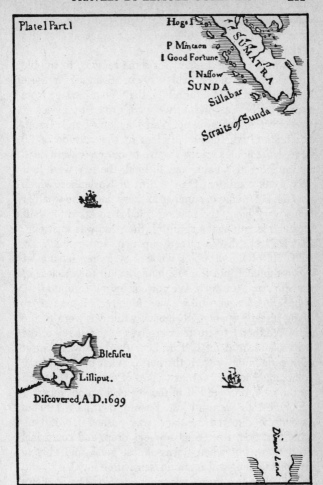

Plate 1 Part 1

Hog I.

SUMATRA

P Mintaon
I Good Fortune

I Naſſow

SUNDA

Sillabar

Straits of Sunda

Blefuſcu

Liſliput.

Diſcovered, A.D. 1699

Diment Land

was making a voyage to the South-Sea. We set sail
from Bristol, May 4, 1699, and our voyage at first was
very prosperous.

It would not be proper, for some reasons, to trouble
the reader with the particulars of our adventures in those
seas: let it suffice to inform him, that in our passage from
thence to the East-Indies, we were driven by a violent
storm to the north-west of Van Diemen's Land. By an
observation, we found ourselves in the latitude of 30
degrees 2 minutes south. Twelve of our crew were dead
by immoderate labour, and ill food, the rest were in a
very weak condition. On the fifth of November, which
was the beginning of summer in those parts, the weather
being very hazy, the seamen spied a rock, within half
a cable's length of the ship; but the wind was so strong,
that we were driven directly upon it, and immediately
split. Six of the crew, of whom I was one, having let
down the boat into the sea, made a shift to get clear of
the ship, and the rock. We rowed, by my computation,
about three leagues, till we were able to work no longer,
being already spent with labour while we were in the
ship. We therefore trusted ourselves to the mercy of the
waves, and in about half an hour the boat was overset
by a sudden flurry from the north. What became of my
companions in the boat, as well as of those who escaped
on the rock, or were left in the vessel, I cannot tell; but
conclude they were all lost. For my own part, I swam
as fortune directed me, and was pushed forward by
wind and tide. I often let my legs drop, and could feel
no bottom: but when I was almost gone, and able to
struggle no longer, I found myself within my depth; and
by this time the storm was much abated. The declivity
was so small, that I walked near a mile before I got to
the shore, which I conjectured was about eight a clock
in the evening. I then advanced forward near half a mile,

but could not discover any sign of houses or inhabitants; at least I was in so weak a condition, that I did not observe them. I was extremely tired, and with that, and the heat of the weather, and about half a pint of brandy that I drank as I left the ship, I found myself much inclined to sleep. I lay down on the grass, which was very short and soft, where I slept sounder than ever I remember to have done in my life, and, as I reckoned, about nine hours; for when I awaked, it was just day-light. I attempted to rise, but was not able to stir: for as I happened to lie on my back, I found my arms and legs were strongly fastened on each side to the ground; and my hair, which was long and thick, tied down in the same manner. I likewise felt several slender ligatures across my body, from my arm-pits to my thighs. I could only look upwards, the sun began to grow hot, and the light offended my eyes. I heard a confused noise about me, but in the posture I lay, could see nothing except the sky. In a little time I felt something alive moving on my left leg, which advancing gently forward over my breast, came almost up to my chin; when bending my eyes downwards as much as I could, I perceived it to be a human creature not six inches high, with a bow and arrow in his hands, and a quiver at his back. In the mean time, I felt at least forty more of the same kind (as I conjectured) following the first. I was in the utmost astonishment, and roared so loud, that they all ran back in a fright; and some of them, as I was afterwards told, were hurt with the falls they got by leaping from my sides upon the ground. However, they soon returned, and one of them, who ventured so far as to get a full sight of my face, lifting up his hands and eyes by way of admiration, cried out in a shrill, but distinct voice, *Hekinah degul:* the others repeated the same words several times, but then I knew not what they meant. I lay all this while, as the reader may believe, in great uneasiness: at length, struggling to get loose, I had the fortune to break the strings, and wrench out the pegs that fastened my left arm to the ground; for, by lifting it up to my face, I discovered the methods they had taken to bind me, and at the same time with a violent pull, which gave me excessive pain, I a little loosened the strings that tied down my hair on the left side, so that I was just able to turn my head about two inches. But the creatures ran off a second time, before I could seize them; whereupon there was a great shout in a very shrill accent, and after it ceased, I heard one of them cry aloud, *Tolgo phonac;* when in an instant I felt above an hundred arrows discharged on my left hand, which pricked me like so many needles; and besides, they shot another flight into the air, as we do bombs in Europe, whereof many, I suppose, fell on my body (though I felt them not), and some on my face, which I immediately covered with my left hand. When this shower of arrows was over, I fell a groaning with grief and pain, and then striving again to get loose, they discharged another volley larger than the first, and some of them attempted with spears to stick me in the sides; but, by good luck, I had on a buff jerkin, which they could not pierce. I thought it the most prudent method to lie still, and my design was to continue so till night, when, my left hand being already loose, I could easily free myself: and as for the inhabitants, I had reason to believe I might be a match for the greatest armies they could bring against me, if they were all of the same size with him that I saw. But fortune disposed otherwise of me. When the people observed I was quiet, they discharged no more arrows; but, by the noise I heard, I knew their numbers increased; and about four yards from me, over-against my right ear, I heard a knocking for above an

hour, like that of people at work; when turning my head
that way, as well as the pegs and strings would permit me, I saw a stage erected, about a foot and a half
from the ground, capable of holding four of the inhabitants, with two or three ladders to mount it: from
whence one of them, who seemed to be a person of
quality, made me a long speech, whereof I understood
not one syllable. But I should have mentioned, that before the principal person began his oration, he cried out
three times, *Langro dehul san:* (these words and the
former were afterwards repeated and explained to me).
Whereupon immediately about fifty of the inhabitants
came and cut the strings that fastened the left side
of my head, which gave me the liberty of turning it to
the right, and of observing the person and gesture of
him that was to speak. He appeared to be of a middle
age, and taller than any of the other three who attended
him, whereof one was a page that held up his train, and
seemed to be somewhat longer than my middle finger;
the other two stood one on each side to support him. He
acted every part of an orator, and I could observe many
periods of threatenings, and others of promises, pity, and
kindness. I answered in a few words, but in the most
submissive manner, lifting up my left hand, and both
my eyes to the sun, as calling him for a witness; and
being almost famished with hunger, having not eaten a
morsel for some hours before I left the ship, I found the
demands of nature so strong upon me, that I could not
forbear showing my impatience (perhaps against the
strict rules of decency) by putting my finger frequently
on my mouth, to signify that I wanted food. The *Hurgo*
(for so they call a great lord, as I afterwards learnt)
understood me very well. He descended from the stage,
and commanded that several ladders should be applied
to my sides, on which above an hundred of the inhabit-

ants mounted and walked towards my mouth, laden with baskets full of meat, which had been provided and sent thither by the King's orders, upon the first intelligence he received of me. I observed there was the flesh of several animals, but could not distinguish them by the taste. There were shoulders, legs, and loins, shaped like those of mutton, and very well dressed, but smaller than the wings of a lark. I eat them by two or three at a mouthful, and took three loaves at a time, about the bigness of musket bullets. They supplied me as fast as they could, showing a thousand marks of wonder and astonishment at my bulk and appetite. I then made another sign that I wanted drink. They found by my eating, that a small quantity would not suffice me; and being a most ingenious people, they slung up with great dexterity one of their largest hogsheads, then rolled it towards my hand, and beat out the top; I drank it off at a draught, which I might well do, for it did not hold half a pint, and tasted like a small wine of Burgundy, but much more delicious. They brought me a second hogshead, which I drank in the same manner, and made signs for more, but they had none to give me. When I had performed these wonders, they shouted for joy, and danced upon my breast, repeating several times as they did at first, *Hekinah degul.* They made me a sign that I should throw down the two hogsheads, but first warning the people below to stand out of the way, crying aloud, *Borach mivola,* and when they saw the vessels in the air, there was an universal shout of *Hekinah degul.* I confess I was often tempted, while they were passing backwards and forwards on my body, to seize forty or fifty of the first that came in my reach, and dash them against the ground. But the remembrance of what I had felt, which probably might not be the worst they could do, and the promise of honour I made them, for so I interpreted my submissive behaviour, soon drove out these imaginations. Besides, I now considered myself as bound by the laws of hospitality to a people who had treated me with so much expense and magnificence. However, in my thoughts, I could not sufficiently wonder at the intrepidity of these diminutive mortals, who durst venture to mount and walk upon my body, while one of my hands was at liberty, without trembling at the very sight of so prodigious a creature as I must appear to them. After some time, when they observed that I made no more demands for meat, there appeared before me a person of high rank from his Imperial Majesty. His Excellency, having mounted on the small of my right leg, advanced forwards up to my face, with about a dozen of his retinue. And producing his credentials under the Signet Royal, which he applied close to my eyes, spoke about ten minutes, without any signs of anger, but with a kind of determinate resolution; often pointing forwards, which, as I afterwards found, was towards the capital city, about half a mile distant, whither it was agreed by his Majesty in council that I must be conveyed. I answered in few words, but to no purpose, and made a sign with my hand that was loose, putting it to the other (but over his Excellency's head for fear of hurting him or his train) and then to my own head and body, to signify that I desired my liberty. It appeared that he understood me well enough, for he shook his head by way of disapprobation, and held his hand in a posture to show that I must be carried as a prisoner. However, he made other signs to let me understand that I should have meat and drink enough, and very good treatment. Whereupon I once more thought of attempting to break my bonds; but again, when I felt the smart of their arrows, upon my face and hands, which were all in blisters, and many of the darts still sticking in

them, and observing likewise that the number of my
enemies increased, I gave tokens to let them know that
they might do with me what they pleased. Upon this,
the *Hurgo* and his train withdrew, with much civility
and cheerful countenances. Soon after I heard a general
shout, with frequent repetitions of the words, *Peplom
selan,* and I felt great numbers of people on my left side
relaxing the cords to such a degree, that I was able to
turn upon my right, and to ease myself with making
water; which I very plentifully did, to the great astonishment of the people, who conjecturing by my motions
what I was going to do, immediately opened to the right
and left on that side, to avoid the torrent which fell
with such noise and violence from me. But before this,
they had daubed my face and both my hands with a
sort of ointment very pleasant to the smell, which in a
few minutes removed all the smart of their arrows. These
circumstances, added to the refreshment I had received
by their victuals and drink, which were very nourishing, disposed me to sleep. I slept about eight hours, as
I was afterwards assured; and it was no wonder, for the
physicians, by the Emperor's order, had mingled a
sleepy potion in the hogshead of wine.

It seems that upon the first moment I was discovered
sleeping on the ground after my landing, the Emperor
had early notice of it by an express; and determined in
council that I should be tied in the manner I have related (which was done in the night while I slept), that
plenty of meat and drink should be sent to me, and a
machine prepared to carry me to the capital city.

This resolution perhaps may appear very bold and
dangerous, and I am confident would not be imitated
by any prince in Europe on the like occasion; however,
in my opinion, it was extremely prudent, as well as generous: for supposing these people had endeavoured to

kill me with their spears and arrows while I was asleep, I should certainly have awaked with the first sense of smart, which might so far have roused my rage and strength, as to have enabled me to break the strings wherewith I was tied; after which, as they were not able to make resistance, so they could expect no mercy.

These people are most excellent mathematicians, and arrived to a great perfection in mechanics, by the countenance and encouragement of the Emperor, who is a renowned patron of learning. This prince hath several machines fixed on wheels, for the carriage of trees and other great weights. He often builds his largest men of war, whereof some are nine foot long, in the woods where the timber grows, and has them carried on these engines three or four hundred yards to the sea. Five hundred carpenters and engineers were immediately set at work to prepare the greatest engine they had. It was a frame of wood raised three inches from the ground, about seven foot long and four wide, moving upon twenty-two wheels. The shout I heard was upon the arrival of this engine, which it seems set out in four hours after my landing. It was brought parallel to me as I lay. But the principal difficulty was to raise and place me in this vehicle. Eighty poles, each of one foot high, were erected for this purpose, and very strong cords of the bigness of packthread were fastened by hooks to many bandages, which the workmen had girt round my neck, my hands, my body, and my legs. Nine hundred of the strongest men were employed to draw up these cords by many pulleys fastened on the poles, and thus, in less than three hours, I was raised and slung into the engine, and there tied fast. All this I was told, for, while the whole operation was performing, I lay in a profound sleep, by the force of that soporiferous medicine infused into my liquor. Fifteen hundred of the Emperor's largest horses, each about four inches and a half high, were employed to draw me towards the metropolis, which, as I said, was half a mile distant.

About four hours after we began our journey, I awaked by a very ridiculous accident; for the carriage being stopped a while to adjust something that was out of order, two or three of the young natives had the curiosity to see how I looked when I was asleep; they climbed up into the engine, and advancing very softly to my face, one of them, an officer in the guards, put the sharp end of his half-pike a good way up into my left nostril, which tickled my nose like a straw, and made me sneeze violently: whereupon they stole off unperceived, and it was three weeks before I knew the cause of my awaking so suddenly. We made a long march the remaining part of that day, and rested at night with five hundred guards on each side of me, half with torches, and half with bows and arrows, ready to shoot me if I should offer to stir. The next morning at sun-rise we continued our march, and arrived within two hundred yards of the city gates about noon. The Emperor, and all his court, came out to meet us; but his great officers would by no means suffer his Majesty to endanger his person by mounting on my body.

At the place where the carriage stopped, there stood an ancient temple, esteemed to be the largest in the whole kingdom; which, having been polluted some years before by an unnatural murder, was, according to the zeal of those people, looked upon as profane, and therefore had been applied to common uses, and all the ornaments and furniture carried away. In this edifice it was determined I should lodge. The great gate fronting to the north was about four foot high, and almost two foot wide, through which I could easily creep. On each side of the gate was a small window not above six inches from the ground: into that on the left side, the King's smiths conveyed fourscore and eleven chains, like those that hang to a lady's watch in Europe, and almost as large, which were locked to my left leg with six and thirty padlocks. Over against this temple, on t'other side of the great highway, at twenty foot distance, there was a turret at least five foot high. Here the Emperor ascended, with many principal lords of his court, to have an opportunity of viewing me, as I was told, for I could not see them. It was reckoned that above an hundred thousand inhabitants came out of the town upon the same errand; and, in spite of my guards, I believe there could not be fewer than ten thousand at several times, who mounted my body by the help of ladders. But a proclamation was soon issued to forbid it upon pain of death. When the workmen found it was impossible for me to break loose, they cut all the strings that bound me; whereupon I rose up, with as melancholy a disposition as ever I had in my life. But the noise and astonishment of the people at seeing me rise and walk, are not to be expressed. The chains that held my left leg were about two yards long, and gave me not only the liberty of walking backwards and forwards in a semicircle; but, being fixed within four inches of the gate, allowed me to creep in, and lie at my full length in the temple.

CHAP. II

The Emperor of Lilliput, *attended by several of the nobility, comes to see the Author in his confinement. The Emperor's person and habit described. Learned men appointed to teach the Author their language. He gains favour by his mild disposition. His pockets are searched, and his sword and pistols taken from him.*

When I found myself on my feet, I looked about me, and must confess I never beheld a more entertaining prospect. The country round appeared like a continued garden, and the inclosed fields, which were generally forty foot square, resembled so many beds of flowers. These fields were intermingled with woods of half a stang, and the tallest trees, as I could judge, appeared to be seven foot high. I viewed the town on my left hand, which looked like the painted scene of a city in a theatre.

I had been for some hours extremely pressed by the necessities of nature; which was no wonder, it being almost two days since I had last disburthened myself. I was under great difficulties between urgency and shame. The best expedient I could think on, was to creep into my house, which I accordingly did; and shutting the gate after me, I went as far as the length of my chain would suffer, and discharged my body of that uneasy load. But this was the only time I was ever guilty of so uncleanly an action; for which I cannot but hope the candid reader will give some allowance, after he hath maturely and impartially considered my case, and the distress I was in. From this time my constant practice was, as soon as I rose, to perform that business in open air, at the full extent of my chain, and due care was taken every morning before company came, that the offensive matter should be carried off in wheel-barrows, by two servants appointed for that purpose. I would not have dwelt so long upon a circumstance, that perhaps at first sight may appear not very momentous, if I had not thought it necessary to justify my character in point of cleanliness to the world; which I am told some of my maligners have been pleased, upon this and other occasions, to call in question.

When this adventure was at an end, I came back out of my house, having occasion for fresh air. The Emperor was already descended from the tower, and advancing on horseback towards me, which had like to have cost him dear; for the beast, though very well trained, yet wholly unused to such a sight, which appeared as if a mountain moved before him, reared up on his hinder feet: but that prince, who is an excellent horseman, kept his seat, till his attendants ran in, and held the bridle, while his Majesty had time to dismount. When he alighted, he surveyed me round with great admiration, but kept beyond the length of my chain. He ordered his cooks and butlers, who were already prepared, to give me victuals and drink, which they pushed forward in a sort of vehicles upon wheels, till I could reach them. I took these vehicles, and soon emptied them all; twenty of them were filled with meat, and ten with liquor; each of the former afforded me two or three good mouthfuls, and I emptied the liquor of ten vessels, which was contained in earthen vials, into one vehicle, drinking it off at a draught; and so I did with the rest. The Empress, and young Princes of the blood of both sexes, attended by many ladies, sat at some distance in their chairs; but upon the accident that happened to the Emperor's horse, they alighted, and came near his person, which I am now going to describe. He is taller by almost the breadth of my nail, than any of his court; which alone is enough

to strike an awe into the beholders. His features are
strong and masculine, with an Austrian lip and arched
nose, his complexion olive, his countenance erect, his
body and limbs well proportioned, all his motions graceful, and his deportment majestic. He was then past his
prime, being twenty-eight years and three quarters old,
of which he had reigned about seven, in great felicity,
and generally victorious. For the better convenience of
beholding him, I lay on my side, so that my face was
parallel to his, and he stood but three yards off: however,
I have had him since many times in my hand, and therefore cannot be deceived in the description. His dress was
very plain and simple, and the fashion of it between the
Asiatic and the European: but he had on his head a light
helmet of gold, adorned with jewels, and a plume on the
crest. He held his sword drawn in his hand, to defend
himself, if I should happen to break loose; it was almost
three inches long, the hilt and scabbard were gold en-
riched with diamonds. His voice was shrill, but very
clear and articulate, and I could distinctly hear it when
I stood up. The ladies and courtiers were all most mag-
nificently clad, so that the spot they stood upon seemed
to resemble a petticoat spread on the ground, embroidered with figures of gold and silver. His Imperial
Majesty spoke often to me, and I returned answers, but
neither of us could understand a syllable. There were
several of his priests and lawyers present (as I conjectured by their habits) who were commanded to address
themselves to me, and I spoke to them in as many languages as I had the least smattering of, which were High
and Low Dutch, Latin, French, Spanish, Italian, and
Lingua Franca; but all to no purpose. After about two
hours the court retired, and I was left with a strong
guard, to prevent the impertinence, and probably the
malice of the rabble, who were very impatient to crowd

about me as near as they durst, and some of them had the impudence to shoot their arrows at me as I sat on the ground by the door of my house, whereof one very narrowly missed my left eye. But the colonel ordered six of the ringleaders to be seized, and thought no punishment so proper as to deliver them bound into my hands, which some of his soldiers accordingly did, pushing them forwards with the butt-ends of their pikes into my reach; I took them all in my right hand, put five of them into my coat-pocket, and as to the sixth, I made a countenance as if I would eat him alive. The poor man squalled terribly, and the colonel and his officers were in much pain, especially when they saw me take out my penknife: but I soon put them out of fear: for, looking mildly, and immediately cutting the strings he was bound with, I set him gently on the ground, and away he ran. I treated the rest in the same manner, taking them one by one out of my pocket, and I observed both the soldiers and people were highly obliged at this mark of my clemency, which was represented very much to my advantage at court.

Towards night I got with some difficulty into my house, where I lay on the ground, and continued to do so about a fortnight; during which time the Emperor gave orders to have a bed prepared for me. Six hundred beds of the common measure were brought in carriages, and worked up in my house; an hundred and fifty of their beds sewn together made up the breadth and length, and these were four double, which, however, kept me but very indifferently from the hardness of the floor, that was of smooth stone. By the same computation they provided me with sheets, blankets, and coverlets, tolerable enough for one who had been so long inured to hardships as I.

As the news of my arrival spread through the kingdom, it brought prodigious numbers of rich, idle, and curious people to see me; so that the villages were almost emptied, and great neglect of tillage and household affairs must have ensued, if his Imperial Majesty had not provided, by several proclamations and orders of state, against this inconveniency. He directed that those who had already beheld me should return home, and not presume to come within fifty yards of my house without licence from court; whereby the secretaries of state got considerable fees.

In the mean time, the Emperor held frequent councils to debate what course should be taken with me; and I was afterwards assured by a particular friend, a person of great quality, who was looked upon to be as much in the secret as any, that the court was under many difficulties concerning me. They apprehended my breaking loose, that my diet would be very expensive, and might cause a famine. Sometimes they determined to starve me, or at least to shoot me in the face and hands with poisoned arrows, which would soon dispatch me; but again they considered, that the stench of so large a carcass might produce a plague in the metropolis, and probably spread through the whole kingdom. In the midst of these consultations, several officers of the army went to the door of the great council-chamber; and two of them being admitted, gave an account of my behaviour to the six criminals above-mentioned, which made so favourable an impression in the breast of his Majesty and the whole board, in my behalf, that an Imperial Commission was issued out, obliging all the villages nine hundred yards round the city, to deliver in every morning six beeves, forty sheep, and other victuals for my sustenance; together with a proportionable quantity of bread, and wine, and other liquors; for the due payment of which his Majesty gave assignments upon his treasury. For this prince lives chiefly upon his own demesnes, seldom, except upon great occasions, raising any subsidies upon his subjects, who are bound to attend him in his wars at their own expense. An establishment was also made of six hundred persons to be my domestics, who had board-wages allowed for their maintenance, and tents built for them very conveniently on each side of my door. It was likewise ordered, that three hundred tailors should make me a suit of clothes after the fashion of the country: that six of his Majesty's greatest scholars should be employed to instruct me in their language: and, lastly, that the Emperor's horses, and those of the nobility, and troops of guards, should be frequently exercised in my sight, to accustom themselves to me. All these orders were duly put in execution, and in about three weeks I made a great progress in learning their language; during which time, the Emperor frequently honoured me with his visits, and was pleased to assist my masters in teaching me. We began already to converse together in some sort; and the first words I learnt were to express my desire that he would please give me my liberty, which I every day repeated on my knees. His answer, as I could comprehend it, was, that this must be a work of time, not to be thought on without the advice of his council, and that first I must *Lumos kelmin pesso desmar lon Emposo;* that is, swear a peace with him and his kingdom. However, that I should be used with all kindness; and he advised me to acquire, by my patience and discreet behaviour, the good opinion of himself and his subjects. He desired I would not take it ill, if he gave orders to certain proper officers to search me; for probably I might carry about me several weapons, which must needs be dangerous things, if they answered the bulk of so prodigious a person. I said, his Majesty should be satisfied, for I was ready to strip myself, and turn up my pockets before him. This I delivered part in words, and part in signs. He replied, that by the laws of the kingdom I must be searched by two of his officers; that he knew this could not be done without my consent and assistance; that he had so good an opinion of my generosity and justice, as to trust their persons in my hands: that whatever they took from me should be returned when I left the country, or paid for at the rate which I would set upon them. I took up the two officers in my hands, put them first into my coat-pockets, and then into every other pocket about me, except my two fobs, and another secret pocket which I had no mind should be searched, wherein I had some little necessaries that were of no consequence to any but myself. In one of my fobs there was a silver watch, and in the other a small quantity of gold in a purse. These gentlemen, having pen, ink, and paper about them, made an exact inventory of every thing they saw; and when they had done, desired I would set them down, that they might deliver it to the Emperor. This inventory I afterwards translated into English, and is word for word as follows.

Imprimis, In the right coat-pocket of the Great Man-Mountain (for so I interpret the words *Quinbus Flestrin*), after the strictest search, we found only one great piece of coarse cloth, large enough to be a foot-cloth for your Majesty's chief room of state. In the left pocket we saw a huge silver chest, with a cover of the same metal, which we, the searchers, were not able to lift. We desired it should be opened, and one of us stepping into it, found himself up to the mid-leg in a sort of dust, some part whereof flying up to our faces, set us both a sneezing for several times together. In his right waistcoat-pocket we found a prodigious bundle of white thin substances, folded one over another, about the bigness of three men, tied with a strong cable, and marked with black figures; which we humbly conceive to be writings, every letter almost half as large as the palm of our hands. In the left there was a sort of engine, from the back of which were extended twenty long poles, resembling the pallisados before your Majesty's court; wherewith we conjecture the Man-Mountain combs his head; for we did not always trouble him with questions, because we found it a great difficulty to make him understand us. In the large pocket on the right side of his middle cover (so I translate the word *ranfu-lo*, by which they meant my breeches), we saw a hollow pillar of iron, about the length of a man, fastened to a strong piece of timber, larger than the pillar; and upon one side of the pillar were huge pieces of iron sticking out, cut into strange figures, which we know not what to make of. In the left pocket, another engine of the same kind. In the smaller pocket, on the right side, were several round flat pieces of white and red metal, of different bulk; some of the white, which seemed to be silver, were so large and heavy, that my comrade and I could hardly lift them. In the left pocket were two black pillars irregularly shaped: we could not, without difficulty, reach the top of them as we stood at the bottom of his pocket. One of them was covered, and seemed all of a piece: but at the upper end of the other, there appeared a white round substance, about twice the bigness of our heads. Within each of these was enclosed a prodigious plate of steel; which, by our orders, we obliged him to show us, because we apprehended they might be dangerous engines. He took them out of their cases, and told us, that in his own country his practice was to shave his beard with one of these, and cut his meat with the other. There were two pockets which we could not enter: these he called his fobs; they were two large slits cut into the top

230 THE PORTABLE SWIFT

of his middle cover, but squeezed close by the pressure
of his belly. Out of the right fob hung a great silver
chain, with a wonderful kind of engine at the bottom.
We directed him to draw out whatever was fastened to
that chain; which appeared to be a globe, half silver,
and half of some transparent metal; for, on the transparent side, we saw certain strange figures circularly
drawn, and thought we could touch them, till we found
our fingers stopped by that lucid substance. He put this
engine to our ears, which made an incessant noise like
that of a water-mill. And we conjecture it is either some
unknown animal, or the god that he worships; but we
are more inclined to the latter opinion, because he assured us (if we understood him right, for he expressed
himself very imperfectly), that he seldom did any thing
without consulting it. He called it his oracle, and said
it pointed out the time for every action of his life. From
the left fob he took out a net almost large enough for a
fisherman, but contrived to open and shut like a purse,
and served him for the same use: we found therein
several massy pieces of yellow metal, which, if they be
real gold, must be of immense value.

Having thus, in obedience to your Majesty's commands, diligently searched all his pockets, we observed
a girdle about his waist made of the hide of some prodigious animal; from which, on the left side, hung a sword
of the length of five men; and on the right, a bag or
pouch divided into two cells, each cell capable of holding three of your Majesty's subjects. In one of these cells
were several globes or balls of a most ponderous metal,
about the bigness of our heads, and requiring a strong
hand to lift them: the other cell contained a heap of certain black grains, but of no great bulk or weight, for we
could hold above fifty of them in the palms of our hands.
This is an exact inventory of what we found about

the body of the Man-Mountain, who used us with great
civility, and due respect to your Majesty's Commission.
Signed and sealed on the fourth day of the eighty-ninth
moon of your Majesty's auspicious reign.

CLEFRIN FRELOCK, MARSI FRELOCK.

When this inventory was read over to the Emperor,
he directed me, although in very gentle terms, to deliver
up the several particulars. He first called for my scimitar, which I took out, scabbard and all. In the mean time
he ordered three thousand of his choicest troops (who
then attended him) to surround me at a distance, with
their bows and arrows just ready to discharge: but I
did not observe it, for my eyes were wholly fixed upon
his Majesty. He then desired me to draw my scimitar,
which, although it had got some rust by the sea-water,
was in most parts exceeding bright. I did so, and immediately all the troops gave a shout between terror
and surprise; for the sun shone clear, and the reflection
dazzled their eyes, as I waved the scimitar to and fro in
my hand. His Majesty, who is a most magnanimous
prince, was less daunted than I could expect; he ordered
me to return it into the scabbard, and cast it on the
ground as gently as I could, about six foot from the end
of my chain. The next thing he demanded was one of
the hollow iron pillars, by which he meant my pocket-
pistols. I drew it out, and at his desire, as well as I could,
expressed to him the use of it; and charging it only with
powder, which, by the closeness of my pouch, happened to escape wetting in the sea (an inconvenience
against which all prudent mariners take special care to
provide), I first cautioned the Emperor not to be afraid,
and then I let it off in the air. The astonishment here
was much greater than at the sight of my scimitar. Hundreds fell down as if they had been struck dead; and

even the Emperor, although he stood his ground, could
not recover himself in some time. I delivered up both
my pistols in the same manner as I had done my scimitar, and then my pouch of powder and bullets; begging
him that the former might be kept from fire, for it would
kindle with the smallest spark, and blow up his imperial
palace into the air. I likewise delivered up my watch,
which the Emperor was very curious to see, and commanded two of his tallest yeomen of the guards to bear
it on a pole upon their shoulders, as draymen in England do a barrel of ale. He was amazed at the continual
noise it made, and the motion of the minute-hand, which
he could easily discern; for their sight is much more
acute than ours: and asked the opinions of his learned
men about him, which were various and remote, as the
reader may well imagine without my repeating; although, indeed, I could not very perfectly understand
them. I then gave up my silver and copper money, my
purse, with nine large pieces of gold, and some smaller
ones; my knife and razor, my comb and silver snuff-box,
my handkerchief and journal-book. My scimitar, pistols,
and pouch, were conveyed in carriages to his Majesty's
stores; but the rest of my goods were returned to me.

I had, as I before observed, one private pocket which
escaped their search, wherein there was a pair of spectacles (which I sometimes use for the weakness of my
eyes), a pocket perspective, and several other little conveniences; which being of no consequence to the Emperor, I did not think myself bound in honour to discover, and I apprehended they might be lost or spoiled
if I ventured them out of my possession.

CHAP. III

*The Author diverts the Emperor, and his nobility of both
sexes, in a very uncommon manner. The diversions of the
court of Lilliput described. The Author has his liberty
granted him upon certain conditions.*

My gentleness and good behaviour had gained so far
on the Emperor and his court, and indeed upon the
army and people in general, that I began to conceive
hopes of getting my liberty in a short time. I took all
possible methods to cultivate this favourable disposition. The natives came by degrees to be less apprehen-
sive of any danger from me. I would sometimes lie
down, and let five or six of them dance on my hand.
And at last the boys and girls would venture to come
and play at hide and seek in my hair. I had now made
a good progress in understanding and speaking their
language. The Emperor had a mind one day to entertain
me with several of the country shows, wherein they
exceed all nations I have known, both for dexterity and
magnificence. I was diverted with none so much as that
of the rope-dancers, performed upon a slender white
thread, extended about two foot, and twelve inches from
the ground. Upon which I shall desire liberty, with the
reader's patience, to enlarge a little.

This diversion is only practised by those persons who
are candidates for great employments, and high favour,
at court. They are trained in this art from their youth,
and are not always of noble birth, or liberal education.
When a great office is vacant, either by death or disgrace (which often happens), five or six of those candidates petition the Emperor to entertain his Majesty and
the court with a dance on the rope, and whoever jumps

the highest without falling, succeeds in the office. Very often the chief ministers themselves are commanded to show their skill, and to convince the Emperor that they have not lost their faculty. Flimnap, the Treasurer, is allowed to cut a caper on the straight rope, at least an inch higher than any other lord in the whole empire. I have seen him do the summerset several times together upon a trencher fixed on the rope, which is no thicker than a common pack-thread in England. My friend Reldresal, principal Secretary for private Affairs, is, in my opinion, if I am not partial, the second after the Treasurer; the rest of the great officers are much upon a par.

These diversions are often attended with fatal accidents, whereof great numbers are on record. I myself have seen two or three candidates break a limb. But the danger is much greater when the ministers themselves are commanded to show their dexterity; for, by contending to excel themselves and their fellows, they strain so far, that there is hardly one of them who hath not received a fall, and some of them two or three. I was assured that a year or two before my arrival, Flimnap would have infallibly broke his neck, if one of the King's cushions, that accidentally lay on the ground, had not weakened the force of his fall.

There is likewise another diversion, which is only shown before the Emperor and Empress, and first minister, upon particular occasions. The Emperor lays on the table three fine silken threads of six inches long. One is blue, the other red, and the third green. These threads are proposed as prizes for those persons whom the Emperor hath a mind to distinguish by a peculiar mark of his favour. The ceremony is performed in his Majesty's great chamber of state, where the candidates are to undergo a trial of dexterity very different from the

former, and such as I have not observed the least resemblance of in any other country of the old or the
new world. The Emperor holds a stick in his hands, both
ends parallel to the horizon, while the candidates advancing one by one, sometimes leap over the stick,
sometimes creep under it backwards and forwards several times, according as the stick is advanced or depressed. Sometimes the Emperor holds one end of the
stick, and his first minister the other; sometimes the
minister has it entirely to himself. Whoever performs
his part with most agility, and holds out the longest in
leaping and creeping, is rewarded with the blue-coloured
silk; the red is given to the next, and the green to the
third, which they all wear girt twice round about the
middle; and you see few great persons about this court,
who are not adorned with one of these girdles.

The horses of the army, and those of the royal stables,
having been daily led before me, were no longer shy,
but would come up to my very feet without starting.
The riders would leap them over my hand as I held it on
the ground, and one of the Emperor's huntsmen, upon
a large courser, took my foot, shoe and all; which was
indeed a prodigious leap. I had the good fortune to
divert the Emperor one day after a very extraordinary
manner. I desired he would order several sticks of two
foot high, and the thickness of an ordinary cane, to be
brought me; whereupon his Majesty commanded the
master of his woods to give directions accordingly; and
the next morning six woodmen arrived with as many
carriages, drawn by eight horses to each. I took nine of
these sticks, fixing them firmly in the ground in a quad-
rangular figure, two foot and a half square. I took four
other sticks, and tied them parallel at each corner, about
two foot from the ground; then I fastened my handkerchief to the nine sticks that stood erect, and extended it

on all sides, till it was tight as the top of a drum; and the four parallel sticks rising about five inches higher than the handkerchief, served as ledges on each side. When I had finished my work, I desired the Emperor to let a troop of his best horse, twenty-four in number, come and exercise upon this plain. His Majesty approved of the proposal, and I took them up, one by one, in my hands, ready mounted and armed, with the proper officers to exercise them. As soon as they got into order, they divided into two parties, performed mock skirmishes, discharged blunt arrows, drew their swords, fled and pursued, attacked and retired, and in short discovered the best military discipline I ever beheld. The parallel sticks secured them and their horses from falling over the stage; and the Emperor was so much delighted, that he ordered this entertainment to be repeated several days, and once was pleased to be lifted up and give the word of command; and, with great difficulty, persuaded even the Empress herself to let me hold her in her close chair within two yards of the stage, from whence she was able to take a full view of the whole performance. It was my good fortune that no ill accident happened in these entertainments, only once a fiery horse, that belonged to one of the captains, pawing with his hoof, struck a hole in my handkerchief, and his foot slipping, he overthrew his rider and himself; but I immediately relieved them both, and covering the hole with one hand, I set down the troop with the other, in the same manner as I took them up. The horse that fell was strained in the left shoulder, but the rider got no hurt, and I repaired my handkerchief as well as I could: however, I would not trust to the strength of it any more in such dangerous enterprises.

About two or three days before I was set at liberty, as I was entertaining the court with these kind of feats,

there arrived an express to inform his Majesty, that some
of his subjects riding near the place where I was first
taken up, had seen a great black substance lying on the
ground, very oddly shaped, extending its edges round
as wide as his Majesty's bedchamber, and rising up in
the middle as high as a man; that it was no living creature, as they at first apprehended, for it lay on the grass
without motion, and some of them had walked round it
several times: that by mounting upon each other's shoulders, they had got to the top, which was flat and even,
and stamping upon it they found it was hollow within;
that they humbly conceived it might be something belonging to the Man-Mountain; and if his Majesty pleased,
they would undertake to bring it with only five horses.
I presently knew what they meant, and was glad at
heart to receive this intelligence. It seems upon my first
reaching the shore after our shipwreck, I was in such
confusion, that before I came to the place where I went
to sleep, my hat, which I had fastened with a string to
my head while I was rowing, and had stuck on all the
time I was swimming, fell off after I came to land; the
string, as I conjecture, breaking by some accident which
I never observed, but thought my hat had been lost at
sea. I intreated his Imperial Majesty to give orders it
might be brought to me as soon as possible, describing
to him the use and the nature of it: and the next day
the waggoners arrived with it, but not in a very good
condition; they had bored two holes in the brim, within
an inch and half of the edge, and fastened two hooks in
the holes; these hooks were tied by a long cord to the
harness, and thus my hat was dragged along for above
half an English mile; but the ground in that country
being extremely smooth and level, it received less damage than I expected.

Two days after this adventure, the Emperor having

ordered that part of his army which quarters in and
about his metropolis to be in readiness, took a fancy of
diverting himself in a very singular manner. He desired
I would stand like a Colossus, with my legs as far
asunder as I conveniently could. He then commanded
his General (who was an old experienced leader, and
a great patron of mine) to draw up the troops in close
order, and march them under me; the foot by twenty-
four in a breast, and the horse by sixteen, with drums
beating, colours flying, and pikes advanced. This body
consisted of three thousand foot, and a thousand horse.
His Majesty gave orders, upon pain of death, that every
soldier in his march should observe the strictest decency
with regard to my person; which, however, could not
prevent some of the younger officers from turning up
their eyes as they passed under me. And, to confess the
truth, my breeches were at that time in so ill a condition,
that they afforded some opportunities for laughter and
admiration.

I had sent so many memorials and petitions for my
liberty, that his Majesty at length mentioned the matter,
first in the cabinet, and then in a full council; where it
was opposed by none, except Skyresh Bolgolam, who
was pleased, without any provocation, to be my mortal
enemy. But it was carried against him by the whole
board, and confirmed by the Emperor. That minister
was *Galbet,* or Admiral of the Realm, very much in his
master's confidence, and a person well versed in affairs,
but of a morose and sour complexion. However, he was
at length persuaded to comply; but prevailed that the
articles and conditions upon which I should be set free,
and to which I must swear, should be drawn up by himself. These articles were brought to me by Skyresh Bolgolam in person, attended by two under-secretaries,

and several persons of distinction. After they were read, I was demanded to swear to the performance of them; first in the manner of my own country, and afterwards in the method prescribed by their laws; which was to hold my right foot in my left hand, to place the middle finger of my right hand on the crown of my head, and my thumb on the tip of my right ear. But because the reader may be curious to have some idea of the style and manner of expression peculiar to that people, as well as to know the articles upon which I recovered my liberty, I have made a translation of the whole instrument word for word, as near as I was able, which I here offer to the public.

GOLBASTO MOMAREM EVLAME GURDILO SHEFIN MULLY ULLY GUE, most mighty Emperor of Lilliput, delight and terror of the universe, whose dominions extend five thousand *blustrugs* (about twelve miles in circumference) to the extremities of the globe; monarch of all monarchs, taller than the sons of men; whose feet press down to the centre, and whose head strikes against the sun; at whose nod the princes of the earth shake their knees; pleasant as the spring, comfortable as the summer, fruitful as autumn, dreadful as winter. His most sublime Majesty proposeth to the Man-Mountain, lately arrived to our celestial dominions, the following articles, which by a solemn oath he shall be obliged to perform.

First, The Man-Mountain shall not depart from our dominions, without our licence under our great seal.

2d, He shall not presume to come into our metropolis, without our express order; at which time, the inhabitants shall have two hours warning to keep within their doors.

3d, The said Man-Mountain shall confine his walks to our principal high roads, and not offer to walk or lie down in a meadow or field of corn.

4th, As he walks the said roads, he shall take the utmost care not to trample upon the bodies of any of our loving subjects, their horses, or carriages, nor take any of our subjects into his hands, without their own consent.

5th, If an express requires extraordinary dispatch, the Man-Mountain shall be obliged to carry in his pocket the messenger and horse a six days' journey once in every moon, and return the said messenger back (if so required) safe to our Imperial Presence.

6th, He shall be our ally against our enemies in the Island of Blefuscu, and do his utmost to destroy their fleet, which is now preparing to invade us.

7th, That the said Man-Mountain shall, at his times of leisure, be aiding and assisting to our workmen, in helping to raise certain great stones, towards covering the wall of the principal park, and other our royal buildings.

8th, That the said Man-Mountain shall, in two moons time, deliver in an exact survey of the circumference of our dominions by a computation of his own paces round the coast.

Lastly, That upon his solemn oath to observe all the above articles, the said Man-Mountain shall have a daily allowance of meat and drink sufficient for the support of 1728 of our subjects, with free access to our Royal Person, and other marks of our favour. Given at our Palace at Belfaborac the twelfth day of the ninety-first moon of our reign.

I swore and subscribed to these articles with great cheerfulness and content, although some of them were

not so honourable as I could have wished; which proceeded wholly from the malice of Skyresh Bolgolam, the
High-Admiral: whereupon my chains were immediately
unlocked, and I was at full liberty; the Emperor himself
in person did me the honour to be by at the whole ceremony. I made my acknowledgments by prostrating myself at his Majesty's feet: but he commanded me to rise;
and after many gracious expressions, which, to avoid
the censure of vanity, I shall not repeat, he added, that
he hoped I should prove a useful servant, and well deserve all the favours he had already conferred upon
me, or might do for the future.

The reader may please to observe, that in the last
article for the recovery of my liberty, the Emperor
stipulates to allow me a quantity of meat and drink
sufficient for the support of 1728 Lilliputians. Some
time after, asking a friend at court how they came to
fix on that determinate number, he told me that his
Majesty's mathematicians, having taken the height of
my body by the help of a quadrant, and finding it to
exceed theirs in the proportion of twelve to one, they
concluded from the similarity of their bodies, that mine
must contain at least 1728 of theirs, and consequently
would require as much food as was necessary to support
that number of Lilliputians. By which, the reader may
conceive an idea of the ingenuity of that people, as well
as the prudent and exact economy of so great a prince.

CHAP. IV

Mildendo, *the metropolis of* Lilliput, *described, together with
the Emperor's palace. A conversation between the Author
and a principal Secretary, concerning the affairs of that
empire. The Author's offers to serve the Emperor in his
wars.*

The first request I made, after I had obtained my
liberty, was, that I might have licence to see Mildendo,
the metropolis; which the Emperor easily granted me,
but with a special charge to do no hurt either to the
inhabitants or their houses. The people had notice by
proclamation of my design to visit the town. The wall
which encompassed it, is two foot and an half high, and
at least eleven inches broad, so that a coach and horses
may be driven very safely round it; and it is flanked
with strong towers at ten foot distance. I stepped over
the great Western Gate, and passed very gently, and
sideling through the two principal streets, only in my
short waistcoat, for fear of damaging the roofs and eaves
of the houses with the skirts of my coat. I walked with
the utmost circumspection, to avoid treading on any
stragglers, that might remain in the streets, although the
orders were very strict, that all people should keep in
their houses, at their own peril. The garret windows
and tops of houses were so crowded with spectators,
that I thought in all my travels I had not seen a more
populous place. The city is an exact square, each side
of the wall being five hundred foot long. The two great
streets, which run cross and divide it into four quarters,
are five foot wide. The lanes and alleys, which I could
not enter, but only viewed them as I passed, are from
twelve to eighteen inches. The town is capable of hold-

ing five hundred thousand souls. The houses are from
three to five stories. The shops and markets well provided.

The Emperor's palace is in the centre of the city,
where the two great streets meet. It is inclosed by a
wall of two foot high, and twenty foot distant from the
buildings. I had his Majesty's permission to step over
this wall; and the space being so wide between that and
the palace, I could easily view it on every side. The outward court is a square of forty foot, and includes two
other courts: in the inmost are the royal apartments,
which I was very desirous to see, but found it extremely
difficult; for the great gates, from one square into another, were but eighteen inches high, and seven inches
wide. Now the buildings of the outer court were at least
five foot high, and it was impossible for me to stride
over them without infinite damage to the pile, though
the walls were strongly built of hewn stone, and four
inches thick. At the same time the Emperor had a great
desire that I should see the magnificence of his palace;
but this I was not able to do till three days after, which
I spent in cutting down with my knife some of the
largest trees in the royal park, about an hundred yards
distant from the city. Of these trees I made two stools,
each about three foot high, and strong enough to bear
my weight. The people having received notice a second
time, I went again through the city to the palace, with
my two stools in my hands. When I came to the side of
the outer court, I stood upon one stool, and took the
other in my hand: this I lifted over the roof, and gently
set it down on the space between the first and second
court, which was eight foot wide. I then stept over the
buildings very conveniently from one stool to the other,
and drew up the first after me with a hooked stick. By
this contrivance I got into the inmost court; and lying

down upon my side, I applied my face to the windows of the middle stories, which were left open on purpose, and discovered the most splendid apartments that can be imagined. There I saw the Empress and the young Princes, in their several lodgings, with their chief attendants about them. Her Imperial Majesty was pleased to smile very graciously upon me, and gave me out of the window her hand to kiss.

But I shall not anticipate the reader with farther descriptions of this kind, because I reserve them for a greater work, which is now almost ready for the press, containing a general description of this empire, from its first erection, through a long series of princes, with a particular account of their wars and politics, laws, learning, and religion: their plants and animals, their peculiar manners and customs, with other matters very curious and useful; my chief design at present being only to relate such events and transactions as happened to the public, or to myself, during a residence of about nine months in that empire.

One morning, about a fortnight after I had obtained my liberty, Reldresal, principal Secretary (as they style him) of private Affairs, came to my house attended only by one servant. He ordered his coach to wait at a distance, and desired I would give him an hour's audience; which I readily consented to, on account of his quality and personal merits, as well as the many good offices he had done me during my solicitations at court. I offered to lie down, that he might the more conveniently reach my ear; but he chose rather to let me hold him in my hand during our conversation. He began with compliments on my liberty: said he might pretend to some merit in it: but, however, added, that if it had not been for the present situation of things at court, perhaps I might not have obtained it so soon. For, said he, as flourishing a condition as we may appear to be in to foreigners, we labour under two mighty evils; a violent faction at home, and the danger of an invasion by a most potent enemy from abroad. As to the first, you are to understand, that for about seventy moons past there have been two struggling parties in this empire, under the names of *Tramecksan* and *Slamecksan*, from the high and low heels on their shoes, by which they distinguish themselves. It is alleged indeed, that the high heels are most agreeable to our ancient constitution: but however this be, his Majesty hath determined to make use of only low heels in the administration of the government, and all offices in the gift of the Crown, as you cannot but observe; and particularly, that his Majesty's Imperial heels are lower at least by a *drurr* than any of his court; (*drurr* is a measure about the fourteenth part of an inch). The animosities between these two parties run so high, that they will neither eat nor drink, nor talk with each other. We compute the *Tramecksan*, or High-Heels, to exceed us in number; but the power is wholly on our side. We apprehend his Imperial Highness, the Heir to the Crown, to have some tendency towards the High-Heels; at least we can plainly discover one of his heels higher than the other, which gives him a hobble in his gait. Now, in the midst of these intestine disquiets, we are threatened with an invasion from the Island of Blefuscu, which is the other great empire of the universe, almost as large and powerful as this of his Majesty. For as to what we have heard you affirm, that there are other kingdoms and states in the world inhabited by human creatures as large as yourself, our philosophers are in much doubt, and would rather conjecture that you dropped from the moon, or one of the stars; because it is certain, that an hundred mortals of your bulk would, in a short time, destroy all the fruits and cattle of his Majesty's dominions. Besides, our histories of six thousand moons make no mention of any other regions, than the two great empires of Lilliput and Blefuscu. Which two mighty powers have, as I was going to tell you, been engaged in a most obstinate war for six and thirty moons past. It began upon the following occasion. It is allowed on all hands, that the primitive way of breaking eggs before we eat them, was upon the larger end: but his present Majesty's grandfather, while he was a boy, going to eat an egg, and breaking it according to the ancient practice, happened to cut one of his fingers. Whereupon the Emperor his father published an edict, commanding all his subjects, upon great penalties, to break the smaller end of their eggs. The people so highly resented this law, that our histories tell us there have been six rebellions raised on that account; wherein one Emperor lost his life, and another his crown. These civil commotions were constantly fomented by the monarchs of Blefuscu; and when they were quelled, the exiles always fled for refuge to that empire. It is computed, that eleven thousand persons have, at several times, suffered death, rather than submit to break their eggs at the smaller end. Many hundred large volumes have been published upon this controversy: but the books of the Big-Endians have been long forbidden, and the whole party rendered incapable by law of holding employments. During the course of these troubles, the Emperors of Blefuscu did frequently expostulate by their ambassadors, accusing us of making a schism in religion, by offending against a fundamental doctrine of our great prophet Lustrog, in the fifty-fourth chapter of the Blundecral (which is their Alcoran). This, however, is thought to be a mere strain upon the text: for the words are these; *That all true believers break their eggs at the convenient end*: and which is the

convenient end, seems, in my humble opinion, to be left
to every man's conscience, or at least in the power of
the chief magistrate to determine. Now the Big-Endian exiles have found so much credit in the Emperor
of Blefuscu's court, and so much private assistance and
encouragement from their party here at home, that a
bloody war has been carried on between the two empires for six and thirty moons with various success; during which time we have lost forty capital ships, and a
much greater number of smaller vessels, together with
thirty thousand of our best seamen and soldiers; and the
damage received by the enemy is reckoned to be somewhat greater than ours. However, they have now
equipped a numerous fleet, and are just preparing to
make a descent upon us; and his Imperial Majesty,
placing great confidence in your valour and strength,
has commanded me to lay this account of his affairs before you.

I desired the Secretary to present my humble duty
to the Emperor, and to let him know, that I thought it
would not become me, who was a foreigner, to interfere
with parties; but I was ready, with the hazard of my life,
to defend his person and state against all invaders.

CHAP. V

*The Author, by an extraordinary stratagem, prevents an in-
vasion. A high title of honour is conferred upon him. Ambassadors arrive from the Emperor of Blefuscu, and sue for
peace. The Empress's apartment on fire by an accident;
the Author instrumental in saving the rest of the palace.*

The Empire of Blefuscu is an island situated to the
north north-east side of Lilliput, from whence it is
parted only by a channel of eight hundred yards wide.

I had not yet seen it, and upon this notice of an intended invasion, I avoided appearing on that side of the coast, for fear of being discovered by some of the enemy's ships, who had received no intelligence of me, all intercourse between the two empires having been strictly forbidden during the war, upon pain of death, and an embargo laid by our Emperor upon all vessels whatsoever. I communicated to his Majesty a project I had formed of seizing the enemy's whole fleet: which, as our scouts assured us, lay at anchor in the harbour ready to sail with the first fair wind. I consulted the most experienced seamen, upon the depth of the channel, which they had often plumbed, who told me, that in the middle at highwater it was seventy *glumgluffs* deep, which is about six foot of European measure; and the rest of it fifty *glumgluffs* at most. I walked towards the north-east coast over against Blefuscu; and lying down behind a hillock, took out my small pocket perspective-glass, and viewed the enemy's fleet at anchor, consisting of about fifty men of war, and a great number of transports: I then came back to my house, and gave order (for which I had a warrant) for a great quantity of the strongest cable and bars of iron. The cable was about as thick as packthread, and the bars of the length and size of a knitting-needle. I trebled the cable to make it stronger, and for the same reason I twisted three of the iron bars together, binding the extremities into a hook. Having thus fixed fifty hooks to as many cables, I went back to the north-east coast, and putting off my coat, shoes, and stockings, walked into the sea in my leathern jerkin, about half an hour before high water. I waded with what haste I could, and swam in the middle about thirty yards till I felt ground; I arrived at the fleet in less than half an hour. The enemy was so frighted when they saw me, that they leaped out of their ships, and swam to shore, where there could not be fewer than thirty thousand souls. I then took my tackling, and fastening a hook to the hole at the prow of each, I tied all the cords together at the end. While I was thus employed, the enemy discharged several thousand arrows, many of which stuck in my hands and face; and besides the excessive smart, gave me much disturbance in my work. My greatest apprehension was for my eyes, which I should have infallibly lost, if I had not suddenly thought of an expedient. I kept among other little necessaries a pair of spectacles in a private pocket, which, as I observed before, had scaped the Emperor's searchers. These I took out and fastened as strongly as I could upon my nose, and thus armed went on boldly with my work in spite of the enemy's arrows, many of which struck against the glasses of my spectacles, but without any other effect, further than a little to discompose them. I had now fastened all the hooks, and taking the knot in my hand, began to pull; but not a ship would stir, for they were all too fast held by their anchors, so that the boldest part of my enterprise remained. I therefore let go the cord, and leaving the hooks fixed to the ships, I resolutely cut with my knife the cables that fastened the anchors, receiving about two hundred shots in my face and hands; then I took up the knotted end of the cables, to which my hooks were tied, and with great ease drew fifty of the enemy's largest men of war after me.

The Blefuscudians, who had not the least imagination of what I intended, were at first confounded with astonishment. They had seen me cut the cables, and thought my design was only to let the ships run a-drift, or fall foul on each other: but when they perceived the whole fleet moving in order, and saw me pulling at the end, they set up such a scream of grief and despair, that it is almost impossible to describe or conceive. When I had got out of danger, I stopped awhile to pick out the arrows that stuck in my hands and face; and rubbed on some of the same ointment that was given me at my first arrival, as I have formerly mentioned. I then took off my spectacles, and waiting about an hour, till the tide was a little fallen, I waded through the middle with my cargo, and arrived safe at the royal port of Lilliput.

The Emperor and his whole court stood on the shore, expecting the issue of this great adventure. They saw the ships move forward in a large half-moon, but could not discern me, who was up to my breast in water. When I advanced to the middle of the channel, they were yet in more pain, because I was under water to my neck. The Emperor concluded me to be drowned, and that the enemy's fleet was approaching in a hostile manner: but he was soon eased of his fears, for the channel growing shallower every step I made, I came in a short time within hearing, and holding up the end of the cable by which the fleet was fastened, I cried in a loud voice, *Long live the most puissant Emperor of Lilliput!* This great prince received me at my landing with all possible encomiums, and created me a *Nardac* upon the spot, which is the highest title of honour among them.

His Majesty desired I would take some other opportunity of bringing all the rest of his enemy's ships into his ports. And so unmeasurable is the ambition of princes, that he seemed to think of nothing less than reducing the whole empire of Blefuscu into a province, and governing it by a viceroy; of destroying the Big-Endian exiles, and compelling that people to break the smaller end of their eggs, by which he would remain the sole monarch of the whole world. But I endeavoured to divert him from this design, by many arguments drawn from the topics of policy as well as justice; and

I plainly protested, that I would never be an instrument of bringing a free and brave people into slavery. And when the matter was debated in council, the wisest part of the ministry were of my opinion.

This open bold declaration of mine was so opposite to the schemes and politics of his Imperial Majesty, that he could never forgive it; he mentioned it in a very artful manner at council, where I was told that some of the wisest appeared, at least by their silence, to be of my opinion; but others, who were my secret enemies, could not forbear some expressions, which by a side-wind reflected on me. And from this time began an intrigue between his Majesty and a junto of ministers maliciously bent against me, which broke out in less than two months, and had like to have ended in my utter destruction. Of so little weight are the greatest services to princes, when put into the balance with a refusal to gratify their passions.

About three weeks after this exploit, there arrived a solemn embassy from Blefuscu, with humble offers of a peace; which was soon concluded upon conditions very advantageous to our Emperor, wherewith I shall not trouble the reader. There were six ambassadors, with a train of about five hundred persons, and their entry was very magnificent, suitable to the grandeur of their master, and the importance of their business. When their treaty was finished, wherein I did them several good offices by the credit I now had, or at least appeared to have at court, their Excellencies, who were privately told how much I had been their friend, made me a visit in form. They began with many compliments upon my valour and generosity, invited me to that kingdom in the Emperor their master's name, and desired me to show them some proofs of my prodigious strength, of which they had heard so many wonders; wherein I readily obliged them, but shall not trouble the reader with the particulars.

When I had for some time entertained their Excellencies, to their infinite satisfaction and surprise, I desired they would do me the honour to present my most humble respects to the Emperor their master, the renown of whose virtues had so justly filled the whole world with admiration, and whose royal person I resolved to attend before I returned to my own country: accordingly, the next time I had the honour to see our Emperor, I desired his general licence to wait on the Blefuscudian monarch, which he was pleased to grant me, as I could perceive, in a very cold manner; but could not guess the reason, till I had a whisper from a certain person, that Flimnap and Bolgolam had represented my intercourse with those ambassadors as a mark of disaffection, from which I am sure my heart was wholly free. And this was the first time I began to conceive some imperfect idea of courts and ministers.

It is to be observed, that these ambassadors spoke to me by an interpreter, the languages of both empires differing as much from each other as any two in Europe, and each nation priding itself upon the antiquity, beauty, and energy of their own tongues, with an avowed contempt for that of their neighbour; yet our Emperor, standing upon the advantage he had got by the seizure of their fleet, obliged them to deliver their credentials, and make their speech in the Lilliputian tongue. And it must be confessed, that from the great intercourse of trade and commerce between both realms, from the continual reception of exiles, which is mutual among them, and from the custom in each empire to send their young nobility and richer gentry to the other, in order to polish themselves by seeing the world, and understanding men and manners; there are few persons of distinction, or merchants, or seamen, who dwell in the maritime parts, but what can hold conversation in both tongues; as I found some weeks after, when I went to pay my respects to the Emperor of Blefuscu, which in the midst of great misfortunes, through the malice of my enemies, proved a very happy adventure to me, as I shall relate in its proper place.

The reader may remember, that when I signed those articles upon which I recovered my liberty, there were some which I disliked upon account of their being too servile, neither could anything but an extreme necessity have forced me to submit. But being now a *Nardac* of the highest rank in that empire, such offices were looked upon as below my dignity, and the Emperor (to do him justice) never once mentioned them to me. However, it was not long before I had an opportunity of doing his Majesty, at least, as I then thought, a most signal service. I was alarmed at midnight with the cries of many hundred people at my door; by which being suddenly awaked, I was in some kind of terror. I heard the word *burglum* repeated incessantly: several of the Emperor's court, making their way through the crowd, entreated me to come immediately to the palace, where her Imperial Majesty's apartment was on fire, by the carelessness of a maid of honour, who fell asleep while she was reading a romance. I got up in an instant; and orders being given to clear the way before me, and it being likewise a moonshine night, I made a shift to get to the Palace without trampling on any of the people. I found they had already applied ladders to the walls of the apartment, and were well provided with buckets, but the water was at some distance. These buckets were about the size of a large thimble, and the poor people supplied me with them as fast as they could; but the flame was so violent that they did little good. I might easily have stifled it with my coat, which I unfortunately left behind me for haste, and came away only in my leathern jerkin. The case seemed wholly desperate and deplorable; and this magnificent palace would have infallibly been burnt down to the ground, if, by a presence of mind, unusual to me, I had not suddenly thought of an expedient. I had the evening before drunk plentifully of a most delicious wine, called *glimigrim* (the Blefuscudians call it *flunec*, but ours is esteemed the better sort), which is very diuretic. By the luckiest chance in the world, I had not discharged myself of any part of it. The heat I had contracted by coming very near the flames, and by labouring to quench them, made the wine begin to operate by urine; which I voided in such a quantity, and applied so well to the proper places, that in three minutes the fire was wholly extinguished, and the rest of that noble pile, which had cost so many ages in erecting, preserved from destruction.

It was now day-light, and I returned to my house without waiting to congratulate with the Emperor: because, although I had done a very eminent piece of service, yet I could not tell how his Majesty might resent the manner by which I had performed it: for, by the fundamental laws of the realm, it is capital in any person, of what quality soever, to make water within the precincts of the palace. But I was a little comforted by a message from his Majesty, that he would give orders to the Grand Justiciary for passing my pardon in form; which, however, I could not obtain. And I was privately assured, that the Empress, conceiving the greatest abhorrence of what I had done, removed to the most distant side of the court, firmly resolved that those buildings should never be repaired for her use: and, in the presence of her chief confidents could not forbear vowing revenge.

CHAP. VI

Of the inhabitants of Lilliput; *their learning, laws, and customs, the manner of educating their children. The Author's way of living in that country. His vindication of a great lady.*

Although I intend to leave the description of this empire to a particular treatise, yet in the mean time I am content to gratify the curious reader with some general ideas. As the common size of the natives is somewhat under six inches high, so there is an exact proportion in all other animals, as well as plants and trees: for instance, the tallest horses and oxen are between four and five inches in height, the sheep an inch and a half, more or less: their geese about the bigness of a sparrow, and so the several gradations downwards till you come to the smallest, which, to my sight, were almost invisible; but nature hath adapted the eyes of the Lilliputians to all objects proper for their view: they see with great exactness, but at no great distance. And to show the sharpness of their sight towards objects that are near, I have been much pleased with observing a cook pulling a lark, which was not so large as a common fly; and a young girl threading an invisible needle with invisible silk. Their tallest trees are about seven foot high: I mean some of those in the great royal park, the tops whereof I could but just reach with my fist clinched. The other vegetables are in the same proportion; but this I leave to the reader's imagination.

I shall say but little at present of their learning, which for many ages hath flourished in all its branches among them: but their manner of writing is very peculiar, being neither from the left to the right, like the Europeans;

nor from the right to the left, like the Arabians; nor from up to down, like the Chinese; nor from down to up, like the Cascagians; but aslant from one corner of the paper to the other, like ladies in England.

They bury their dead with their heads directly downwards, because they hold an opinion, that in eleven thousand moons they are all to rise again, in which period the earth (which they conceive to be flat) will turn upside down, and by this means they shall, at their resurrection, be found ready standing on their feet. The learned among them confess the absurdity of this doctrine, but the practice still continues, in compliance to the vulgar.

There are some laws and customs in this empire very peculiar; and if they were not so directly contrary to those of my own dear country, I should be tempted to say a little in their justification. It is only to be wished that they were as well executed. The first I shall mention, relates to informers. All crimes against the state are punished here with the utmost severity; but if the person accused maketh his innocence plainly to appear upon his trial, the accuser is immediately put to an ignominious death; and out of his goods or lands, the innocent person is quadruply recompensed for the loss of his time, for the danger he underwent, for the hardship of his imprisonment, and for all the charges he hath been at in making his defence. Or, if that fund be deficient, it is largely supplied by the Crown. The Emperor does also confer on him some public mark of his favour, and proclamation is made of his innocence through the whole city.

They look upon fraud as a greater crime than theft, and therefore seldom fail to punish it with death; for they allege, that care and vigilance, with a very com-

mon understanding, may preserve a man's goods from
thieves, but honesty has no fence against superior cunning; and since it is necessary that there should be a
perpetual intercourse of buying and selling, and dealing
upon credit, where fraud is permitted and connived at,
or hath no law to punish it, the honest dealer is always
undone, and the knave gets the advantage. I remember
when I was once interceding with the Emperor for a
criminal who had wronged his master of a great sum
of money, which he had received by order, and ran
away with; and happening to tell his Majesty, by way
of extension, that it was only a breach of trust; the Emperor thought it monstrous in me to offer, as a defence,
the greatest aggravation of the crime: and truly I had
little to say in return, farther than the common answer,
that different nations had different customs; for, I confess, I was heartily ashamed.

Although we usually call reward and punishment the
two hinges upon which all government turns, yet I could
never observe this maxim to be put in practice by any
nation except that of Lilliput. Whoever can there bring
sufficient proof that he hath strictly observed the laws
of his country for seventy-three moons, hath a claim to
certain privileges, according to his quality and condition of life, with a proportionable sum of money out of a
fund appropriated for that use: he likewise acquires the
title of *Snilpall,* or Legal, which is added to his name,
but does not descend to his posterity. And these people
thought it a prodigious defect of policy among us, when
I told them that our laws were enforced only by penalties, without any mention of reward. It is upon this account that the image of Justice, in their courts of judicature, is formed with six eyes, two before, as many
behind, and on each side one, to signify circumspection;

with a bag of gold open in her right hand, and a sword
sheathed in her left, to show she is more disposed to reward than to punish.

In choosing persons for all employments, they have
more regard to good morals than to great abilities; for,
since government is necessary to mankind, they believe
that the common size of human understandings is fitted
to some station or other, and that Providence never intended to make the management of public affairs a
mystery, to be comprehended only by a few persons of
sublime genius, of which there seldom are three born in
an age: but they suppose truth, justice, temperance, and
the like, to be in every man's power; the practice of
which virtues, assisted by experience and a good intention, would qualify any man for the service of his country, except where a course of study is required. But they
thought the want of moral virtues was so far from being supplied by superior endowments of the mind, that
employments could never be put into such dangerous
hands as those of persons so qualified; and at least, that
the mistakes committed by ignorance in a virtuous disposition, would never be of such fatal consequence to
the public weal, as the practices of a man whose inclinations led him to be corrupt, and had great abilities to
manage, and multiply, and defend his corruptions.

In like manner, the disbelief of a Divine Providence
renders a man uncapable of holding any public station;
for, since kings avow themselves to be the deputies of
Providence, the Lilliputians think nothing can be more
absurd than for a prince to employ such men as disown
the authority under which he acts.

In relating these and the following laws, I would only
be understood to mean the original institutions, and not
the most scandalous corruptions into which these people
are fallen by the degenerate nature of man. For as to

that infamous practice of acquiring great employments by dancing on the ropes, or badges of favour and distinction by leaping over sticks and creeping under them, the reader is to observe, that they were first introduced by the grandfather of the Emperor now reigning, and grew to the present height, by the gradual increase of party and faction.

Ingratitude is among them a capital crime, as we read it to have been in some other countries: for they reason thus, that whoever makes ill returns to his benefactor, must needs be a common enemy to the rest of mankind, from whom he hath received no obligation, and therefore such a man is not fit to live.

Their notions relating to the duties of parents and children differ extremely from ours. For, since the conjunction of male and female is founded upon the great law of nature, in order to propagate and continue the species, the Lilliputians will needs have it, that men and women are joined together like other animals, by the motives of concupiscence; and that their tenderness towards their young proceeds from the like natural principle: for which reason they will never allow, that a child is under any obligation to his father for begetting him, or to his mother for bringing him into the world, which, considering the miseries of human life, was neither a benefit in itself, nor intended so by his parents, whose thoughts in their love-encounters were otherwise employed. Upon these, and the like reasonings, their opinion is, that parents are the last of all others to be trusted with the education of their own children; and therefore they have in every town public nurseries, where all parents, except cottagers and labourers, are obliged to send their infants of both sexes to be reared and educated when they come to the age of twenty moons, at which time they are supposed to have some rudiments of docility. These schools are of several kinds, suited to different qualities, and to both sexes. They have certain professors well skilled in preparing children for such a condition of life as befits the rank of their parents, and their own capacities as well as inclinations. I shall first say something of the male nurseries, and then of the female.

The nurseries for males of noble or eminent birth, are provided with grave and learned professors, and their several deputies. The clothes and food of the children are plain and simple. They are bred up in the principles of honour, justice, courage, modesty, clemency, religion, and love of their country; they are always employed in some business, except in the times of eating and sleeping, which are very short, and two hours for diversions, consisting of bodily exercises. They are dressed by men till four years of age, and then are obliged to dress themselves, although their quality be ever so great; and the women attendants, who are aged proportionably to ours at fifty, perform only the most menial offices. They are never suffered to converse with servants, but go together in small or greater numbers to take their diversions, and always in the presence of a professor, or one of his deputies; whereby they avoid those early bad impressions of folly and vice to which our children are subject. Their parents are suffered to see them only twice a year; the visit is to last but an hour. They are allowed to kiss the child at meeting and parting; but a professor, who always stands by on those occasions, will not suffer them to whisper, or use any fondling expressions, or bring any presents of toys, sweetmeats, and the like.

The pension from each family for the education and entertainment of a child, upon failure of due payment, is levied by the Emperor's officers.

The nurseries for children of ordinary gentlemen,

merchants, traders, and handicrafts, are managed proportionably after the same manner; only those designed for trades, are put out apprentices at eleven years old, whereas those of persons of quality continue in their exercises till fifteen, which answers to one and twenty with us: but the confinement is gradually lessened for the last three years.

In the female nurseries, the young girls of quality are educated much like the males, only they are dressed by orderly servants of their own sex; but always in the presence of a professor or deputy, till they come to dress themselves, which is at five years old. And if it be found that these nurses ever presume to entertain the girls with frightful or foolish stories, or the common follies practised by chambermaids among us, they are publicly whipped thrice about the city, imprisoned for a year, and banished for life to the most desolate part of the country. Thus the young ladies there are as much ashamed of being cowards and fools, as the men, and despise all personal ornaments beyond decency and cleanliness: neither did I perceive any difference in their education, made by their difference of sex, only that the exercises of the females were not altogether so robust; and that some rules were given them relating to domestic life, and a smaller compass of learning was enjoined them: for their maxim is, that among people of quality, a wife should be always a reasonable and agreeable companion, because she cannot always be young. When the girls are twelve years old, which among them is the marriageable age, their parents or guardians take them home, with great expressions of gratitude to the professors, and seldom without tears of the young lady and her companions.

In the nurseries of females of the meaner sort, the children are instructed in all kinds of works proper for their sex, and their several degrees: those intended for apprentices, are dismissed at seven years old, the rest are kept to eleven.

The meaner families who have children at these nurseries, are obliged, besides their annual pension, which is as low as possible, to return to the steward of the nursery a small monthly share of their gettings, to be a portion for the child; and therefore all parents are limited in their expenses by the law. For the Lilliputians think nothing can be more unjust, than for people, in subservience to their own appetites, to bring children into the world, and leave the burthen of supporting them on the public. As to persons of quality, they give security to appropriate a certain sum for each child, suitable to their condition; and these funds are always managed with good husbandry, and the most exact justice.

The cottagers and labourers keep their children at home, their business being only to till and cultivate the earth, and therefore their education is of little consequence to the public; but the old and diseased among them are supported by hospitals: for begging is a trade unknown in this empire.

And here it may perhaps divert the curious reader, to give some account of my domestic, and my manner of living in this country, during a residence of nine months and thirteen days. Having a head mechanically turned, and being likewise forced by necessity, I had made for myself a table and chair convenient enough, out of the largest trees in the royal park. Two hundred sempstresses were employed to make me shirts, and linen for my bed and table, all of the strongest and coarsest kind they could get; which, however, they were forced to quilt together in several folds, for the thickest was some degrees finer than lawn. Their linen is usually three inches wide, and three foot make a piece. The sempstresses took my measure as I lay on the ground, one standing at my neck, and another at my mid-leg, with a strong cord extended, that each held by the end, while the third measured the length of the cord with a rule of an inch long. Then they measured my right thumb, and desired no more; for by a mathematical computation, that twice round the thumb is once round the wrist, and so on to the neck and the waist; and by the help of my old shirt, which I displayed on the ground before them for a pattern, they fitted me exactly. Three hundred tailors were employed in the same manner to make me clothes; but they had another contrivance for taking my measure. I kneeled down, and they raised a ladder from the ground to my neck; upon this ladder one of them mounted, and let fall a plumb-line from my collar to the floor, which just answered the length of my coat: but my waist and arms I measured myself. When my clothes were finished, which was done in my house (for the largest of theirs would not have been able to hold them), they looked like the patch-work made by the ladies in England, only that mine were all of a colour.

I had three hundred cooks to dress my victuals, in little convenient huts built about my house, where they and their families lived, and prepared me two dishes a-piece. I took up twenty waiters in my hand, and placed them on the table: an hundred more attended below on the ground, some with dishes of meat, and some with barrels of wine, and other liquors, slung on their shoulders; all which the waiters above drew up as I wanted, in a very ingenious manner, by certain cords, as we draw the bucket up a well in Europe. A dish of their meat was a good mouthful, and a barrel of their liquor a reasonable draught. Their mutton yields to ours, but their beef is excellent. I have had a sirloin so large, that I have been forced to make three bits of it; but this is rare. My servants were astonished to see me eat it bones and all, as in our country we do the leg of a lark. Their geese and turkeys I usually eat at a mouthful, and I must confess they far exceed ours. Of their smaller fowl I could take up twenty or thirty at the end of my knife.

One day his Imperial Majesty, being informed of my way of living, desired that himself and his Royal Consort, with the young Princes of the blood of both sexes, might have the happiness (as he was pleased to call it) of dining with me. They came accordingly, and I placed them in chairs of state on my table, just over against me, with their guards about them. Flimnap, the Lord High Treasurer, attended there likewise with his white staff; and I observed he often looked on me with a sour countenance, which I would not seem to regard, but eat more than usual, in honour to my dear country, as well as to fill the court with admiration. I have some private reasons to believe, that this visit from his Majesty gave Flimnap an opportunity of doing me ill offices to his master. That minister had always been my secret enemy, though he outwardly caressed me more than was usual to the moroseness of his nature. He represented to the Emperor the low condition of his treasury; that he was forced to take up money at great discount; that exchequer bills would not circulate under nine *per cent.* below par; that in short I had cost his Majesty above a million and a half of *sprugs* (their greatest gold coin, about the bigness of a spangle); and upon the whole, that it would be advisable in the Emperor to take the first occasion of dismissing me.

I am here obliged to vindicate the reputation of an excellent lady, who was an innocent sufferer upon my account. The Treasurer took a fancy to be jealous of his wife, from the malice of some evil tongues, who in-

formed him that her Grace had taken a violent affection
for my person; and the court-scandal ran for some time,
that she once came privately to my lodging. This I
solemnly declare to be a most infamous falsehood, without any grounds, farther than that her Grace was
pleased to treat me with all innocent marks of freedom
and friendship. I own she came often to my house, but
always publicly, nor ever without three more in the
coach, who were usually her sister and young daughter,
and some particular acquaintance; but this was common
to many other ladies of the court. And I still appeal to
my servants round, whether they at any time saw a
coach at my door without knowing what persons were in
it. On those occasions, when a servant had given me
notice, my custom was to go immediately to the door;
and, after paying my respects, to take up the coach and
two horses very carefully in my hands (for, if there were
six horses, the postillion always unharnessed four) and
place them on a table, where I had fixed a moveable
rim quite round, of five inches high, to prevent accidents. And I have often had four coaches and horses at
once on my table full of company, while I sat in my
chair leaning my face towards them; and when I was
engaged with one set, the coachmen would gently drive
the others round my table. I have passed many an afternoon very agreeably in these conversations. But I defy
the Treasurer, or his two informers (I will name them,
and let them make their best of it) Clustril and Drunlo,
to prove that any person ever came to me *incognito*, except the secretary Reldresal, who was sent by express
command of his Imperial Majesty, as I have before related. I should not have dwelt so long upon this particular, if it had not been a point wherein the reputation
of a great lady is so nearly concerned, to say nothing of
my own; though I then had the honour to be a *Nardac*,

which the Treasurer himself is not; for all the world knows he is only a *Glumglum,* a title inferior by one degree, as that of a Marquis is to a Duke in England, although I allow he preceded me in right of his post. These false informations, which I afterwards came to the knowledge of, by an accident not proper to mention, made Flimnap, the Treasurer, show his lady for some time an ill countenance, and me a worse; and although he were at last undeceived and reconciled to her, yet I lost all credit with him, and found my interest decline very fast with the Emperor himself, who was indeed too much governed by that favourite.

CHAP. VII

The Author, being informed of a design to accuse him of high-treason, makes his escape to Blefuscu. *His reception there.*

Before I proceed to give an account of my leaving this kingdom, it may be proper to inform the reader of a private intrigue which had been for two months forming against me.

I had been hitherto all my life a stranger to courts, for which I was unqualified by the meanness of my condition. I had indeed heard and read enough of the dispositions of great princes and ministers; but never expected to have found such terrible effects of them in so remote a country, governed, as I thought, by very different maxims from those in Europe.

When I was just preparing to pay my attendance on the Emperor of Blefuscu, a considerable person at court (to whom I had been very serviceable at a time when he lay under the highest displeasure of his Imperial Maj-

esty) came to my house very privately at night in a
close chair, and without sending his name, desired admittance. The chairmen were dismissed; I put the chair,
with his Lordship in it, into my coat-pocket: and giving
orders to a trusty servant to say I was indisposed and
gone to sleep, I fastened the door of my house, placed
the chair on the table, according to my usual custom,
and sat down by it. After the common salutations were
over, observing his Lordship's countenance full of concern, and enquiring into the reason, he desired I would
hear him with patience in a matter that highly concerned my honour and my life. His speech was to the
following effect, for I took notes of it as soon as he left
me.

You are to know, said he, that several Committees of
Council have been lately called in the most private manner on your account; and it but two days since his Majesty came to a full resolution.

You are very sensible that Syresh Bolgolam (*Galbet*,
or High-Admiral) hath been your mortal enemy almost
ever since your arrival. His original reasons I know not;
but his hatred is much increased since your great success against Blefuscu, by which his glory, as Admiral, is
obscured. This Lord, in conjunction with Flimnap the
High-Treasurer, whose enmity against you is notorious
on account of his lady, Limtoc the General, Lalcon the
Chamberlain, and Balmuff the Grand Justiciary, have
prepared articles of impeachment against you, for treason, and other capital crimes.

This preface made me so impatient, being conscious
of my own merits and innocence, that I was going to interrupt; when he entreated me to be silent, and thus
proceeded.

Out of gratitude for the favours you have done me, I procured information of the whole proceedings, and a copy of the articles, wherein I venture my head for your service.

ARTICLES OF IMPEACHMENT AGAINST QUINBUS FLESTRIN (THE MAN-MOUNTAIN.)

ARTICLE I

Whereas, by a statute made in the reign of his Imperial Majesty Calin Deffar Plune, it is enacted, that whoever shall make water within the precincts of the royal palace, shall be liable to the pains and penalties of high treason; notwithstanding, the said Quinbus Flestrin, in open breach of the said law, under colour of extinguishing the fire kindled in the apartment of his Majesty's most dear Imperial Consort, did maliciously, traitorously, and devilishly, by discharge of his urine, put out the said fire kindled in the said apartment, lying and being within the precincts of the said royal palace, against the statute in that case provided, *etc.* against the duty, *etc.*

ARTICLE II

That the said Quinbus Flestrin having brought the imperial fleet of Blefuscu into the royal port, and being afterwards commanded by his Imperial Majesty to seize all the other ships of the said empire of Blefuscu, and reduce that empire to a province, to be governed by a viceroy from hence, and to destroy and put to death not only all the Big-Endian exiles, but likewise all the people of that empire, who would not immediately forsake the Big-Endian heresy: He, the said Flestrin, like a false traitor against his most Auspicious, Serene, Imperial Majesty, did petition to be excused from the said service, upon pretence of unwillingness to force the consciences, or destroy the liberties and lives of an innocent people.

Article III

That, whereas certain ambassadors arrived from the court of Blefuscu, to sue for peace in his Majesty's court: He, the said Flestrin, did, like a false traitor, aid, abet, comfort, and divert the said ambassadors, although he knew them to be servants to a prince who was lately an open enemy to his Imperial Majesty, and in open war against his said Majesty.

Article IV

That the said Quinbus Flestrin, contrary to the duty of a faithful subject, is now preparing to make a voyage to the court and empire of Blefuscu, for which he hath received only verbal licence from his Imperial Majesty; and under colour of the said licence, doth falsely and traitorously intend to take the said voyage, and thereby to aid, comfort, and abet the Emperor of Blefuscu, so late an enemy, and in open war with his Imperial Majesty aforesaid.

There are some other articles, but these are the most important, of which I have read you an abstract.

In the several debates upon this impeachment, it must be confessed that his Majesty gave many marks of his great lenity, often urging the services you had done him, and endeavouring to extenuate your crimes. The Treasurer and Admiral insisted that you should be put to the most painful and ignominious death, by setting fire on your house at night, and the General was to attend with twenty thousand men armed with poisoned arrows to shoot you on the face and hands. Some of your servants were to have private orders to strew a poisonous juice on your shirts, which would soon make you tear your own flesh, and die in the utmost torture. The General came into the same opinion; so that for a long time there was a majority against you. But his Majesty resolving, if possible, to spare your life, at last brought off the Chamberlain.

Upon this incident, Reldresal, principal Secretary for private Affairs, who always approved himself your true friend, was commanded by the Emperor to deliver his opinion, which he accordingly did; and therein justified the good thoughts you have of him. He allowed your crimes to be great, but that still there was room for mercy, the most commendable virtue in a prince, and for which his Majesty was so justly celebrated. He said, the friendship between you and him was so well known to the world, that perhaps the most honourable board might think him partial: however, in obedience to the command he had received, he would freely offer his sentiments. That if his Majesty, in consideration of your services, and pursuant to his own merciful disposition, would please to spare your life, and only give orders to put out both your eyes, he humbly conceived, that by this expedient, justice might in some measure be satisfied, and all the world would applaud the lenity of the Emperor, as well as the fair and generous proceedings of those who have the honour to be his counsellors. That the loss of your eyes would be no impediment to your bodily strength, by which you might still be useful to his Majesty. That blindness is an addition to courage, by concealing dangers from us; that the fear you had for your eyes was the greatest difficulty in bringing over the enemy's fleet, and it would be sufficient for you to see by the eyes of the ministers, since the greatest princes do no more.

This proposal was received with the utmost disapprobation by the whole board. Bolgolam, the Admiral, could not preserve his temper; but rising up in fury, said, he wondered how the Secretary durst presume to give his opinion for preserving the life of a traitor: that the services you had performed, were, by all true reasons of state, the great aggravation of your crimes; that you, who were able to extinguish the fire, by discharge of urine in her Majesty's apartment (which he mentioned with horror), might, at another time, raise an inundation by the same means, to drown the whole palace; and the same strength which enabled you to bring over the enemy's fleet, might serve, upon the first discontent, to carry it back: that he had good reasons to think you were a Big-Endian in your heart; and as treason begins in the heart, before it appears in overt acts, so he accused you as a traitor on that account, and therefore insisted you should be put to death.

The Treasurer was of the same opinion; he showed to what straits his Majesty's revenue was reduced by the charge of maintaining you, which would soon grow insupportable: that the Secretary's expedient of putting out your eyes was so far from being a remedy against this evil, that it would probably increase it, as it is manifest from the common practice of blinding some kind of fowl, after which they fed the faster, and grew sooner fat: that his sacred Majesty and the Council, who are your judges, were in their own consciences fully convinced of your guilt, which was a sufficient argument to condemn you to death, without the formal proofs required by the strict letter of the law.

But his Imperial Majesty, fully determined against capital punishment, was graciously pleased to say, that since the Council thought the loss of your eyes too easy a censure, some other may be inflicted hereafter. And your friend the Secretary humbly desiring to be heard again, in answer to what the Treasurer had objected concerning the great charge his Majesty was at in maintaining you, said, that his Excellency, who had the sole disposal of the Emperor's revenue, might easily provide against the evil, by gradually lessening your establishment; by which, for want of sufficient food, you would grow weak and faint, and lose your appetite, and consequently decay and consume in a few months; neither would the stench of your carcass be then so dangerous, when it should become more than half diminished; and immediately upon your death, five or six thousand of his Majesty's subjects might, in two or three days, cut your flesh from your bones, take it away by cart-loads, and bury it in distant parts to prevent infection, leaving the skeleton as a monument of admiration to posterity.

Thus by the great friendship of the Secretary, the whole affair was compromised. It was strictly enjoined, that the project of starving you by degrees should be kept a secret, but the sentence of putting out your eyes was entered on the books; none dissenting except Bolgolam the Admiral, who, being a creature of the Empress, was perpetually instigated by her Majesty to insist upon your death, she having borne perpetual malice against you, on account of that infamous and illegal method you took to extinguish the fire in her apartment.

In three days your friend the Secretary will be directed to come to your house, and read before you the articles of impeachment; and then to signify the great lenity and favour of his Majesty and Council, whereby you are only condemned to the loss of your eyes, which his Majesty doth not question you will gratefully and humbly submit to; and twenty of his Majesty's surgeons will attend, in order to see the operation well performed, by discharging very sharp-pointed arrows into the balls of your eyes, as you lie on the ground.

I leave to your prudence what measures you will take; and to avoid suspicion, I must immediately return in as private a manner as I came.

His Lordship did so, and I remained alone, under many doubts and perplexities of mind.

It was a custom introduced by this prince and his ministry (very different, as I have been assured, from the practices of former times), that after the court had decreed any cruel execution, either to gratify the monarch's resentment, or the malice of a favourite, the Emperor always made a speech to his whole Council, expressing his great lenity and tenderness, as qualities known and confessed by all the world. This speech was immediately published through the kingdom; nor did any thing terrify the people so much as those encomiums on his Majesty's mercy; because it was observed, that the more these praises were enlarged and insisted on, the more inhuman was the punishment, and the sufferer more innocent. And as to myself, I must confess, having never been designed for a courtier either by my birth or education, I was so ill a judge of things, that I could not discover the lenity and favour of this sentence, but conceived it (perhaps erroneously) rather to be rigorous than gentle. I sometimes thought of standing my trial, for although I could not deny the facts alleged in the several articles, yet I hoped they would admit of some extenuations. But having in my life perused many state trials, which I ever observed to terminate as the judges thought fit to direct, I durst not rely on so dangerous a decision, in so critical a juncture, and against such powerful enemies. Once I was strongly bent upon resistance, for while I had liberty, the whole strength of that empire could hardly subdue me, and I might easily with stones pelt the metropolis to pieces; but I soon rejected that project with horror, by remembering the oath I had made to the Emperor, the favours I received from him, and the high title of *Nardac* he conferred upon me. Neither had I so soon learned the gratitude of courtiers, to persuade myself that his Majesty's present severities acquitted me of all past obligations.

At last I fixed upon a resolution, for which it is probable I may incur some censure, and not unjustly; for I confess I owe the preserving my eyes, and consequently my liberty, to my own great rashness and want of experience: because if I had then known the nature of princes and ministers, which I have since observed in many other courts, and their methods of treating criminals less obnoxious than myself, I should with great alacrity and readiness have submitted to so easy a punishment. But hurried on by the precipitancy of youth, and having his Imperial Majesty's licence to pay my attendance upon the Emperor of Blefuscu, I took this opportunity, before the three days were elapsed, to send a letter to my friend the Secretary, signifying my resolution of setting out that morning for Blefuscu pursuant to the leave I had got; and without waiting for an answer, I went to that side of the island where our fleet lay. I seized a large man of war, tied a cable to the prow, and, lifting up the anchors, I stripped myself, put my clothes (together with my coverlet, which I brought under my arm) into the vessel, and drawing it after me between wading and swimming, arrived at the royal port of Blefuscu, where the people had long expected me: they lent me two guides to direct me to the capital city, which is of the same name. I held them in my hands till I came within two hundred yards of the gate, and desired them to signify my arrival to one of the secretaries, and let him know, I there waited his Majesty's command. I had an answer in about an hour, that his Majesty, attended by the Royal Family, and great officers of the court, was coming out to receive me. I advanced a hundred yards. The Emperor and his train alighted from their horses, the Empress and ladies from their coaches, and I did not perceive they were in any fright or concern. I lay on the ground to kiss his Majesty's and the Empress's hands. I told his Majesty, that I was come according to my promise, and with the licence of the Emperor my master, to have the honour of seeing so mighty a monarch, and to offer him any service in my power, consistent with my duty to my own prince; not mentioning a word of my disgrace, because I had hitherto no regular information of it, and might suppose myself wholly ignorant of any such design; neither could I reasonably conceive that the Emperor would discover the secret while I was out of his power: wherein, however, it soon appeared I was deceived.

I shall not trouble the reader with the particular account of my reception at this court, which was suitable to the generosity of so great a prince; nor of the difficulties I was in for want of a house and bed, being forced to lie on the ground, wrapped up in my coverlet.

CHAP. VIII

The Author, by a lucky accident, finds means to leave Ble-fuscu; and, after some difficulties, returns safe to his native country.

Three days after my arrival, walking out of curiosity to the north-east coast of the island, I observed, about half a league off, in the sea, somewhat that looked like a boat overturned. I pulled off my shoes and stockings, and wading two or three hundred yards, I found the object to approach nearer by force of the tide; and then plainly saw it to be a real boat, which I supposed might, by some tempest, have been driven from a ship; whereupon

I returned immediately towards the city, and desired his
Imperial Majesty to lend me twenty of the tallest vessels
he had left after the loss of his fleet, and three thousand
seamen under the command of his Vice-Admiral. This
fleet sailed round, while I went back the shortest way to
the coast where I first discovered the boat; I found the
tide had driven it still nearer. The seamen were all provided with cordage, which I had beforehand twisted
to a sufficient strength. When the ships came up, I
stripped myself, and waded till I came within an hundred yards of the boat, after which I was forced to swim
till I got up to it. The seamen threw me the end of the
cord, which I fastened to a hole in the fore-part of the
boat, and the other end to a man of war; but I found all
my labour to little purpose; for being out of my depth,
I was not able to work. In this necessity, I was forced to
swim behind, and push the boat forwards as often as I
could, with one of my hands; and the tide favouring me,
I advanced so far, that I could just hold up my chin and
feel the ground. I rested two or three minutes, and then
gave the boat another shove, and so on till the sea was
no higher than my arm-pits; and now the most laborious
part being over, I took out my other cables, which were
stowed in one of the ships, and fastening them first to
the boat, and then to nine of the vessels which attended
me; the wind being favourable, the seamen towed, and
I shoved till we arrived within forty yards of the shore;
and waiting till the tide was out, I got dry to the
boat, and by the assistance of two thousand men, with
ropes and engines, I made a shift to turn it on its bottom, and found it was but little damaged.

I shall not trouble the reader with the difficulties I
was under by the help of certain paddles, which cost
me ten days making, to get my boat to the royal port of
Blefuscu, where a mighty concourse of people appeared

upon my arrival, full of wonder at the sight of so prodigious a vessel. I told the Emperor that my good fortune
had thrown this boat in my way, to carry me to some
place from whence I might return into my native country, and begged his Majesty's orders for getting materials to fit it up, together with his licence to depart;
which, after some kind of expostulations, he was pleased
to grant.

I did very much wonder, in all this time, not to have
heard of any express relating to me from our Emperor
to the court of Blefuscu. But I was afterwards given
privately to understand, that his Imperial Majesty, never
imagining I had the least notice of his designs, believed
I was only gone to Blefuscu in performance of my promise, according to the licence he had given me, which
was well known at our court, and would return in a
few days when that ceremony was ended. But he was at
last in pain at my long absence; and after consulting
with the Treasurer, and the rest of that cabal, a person
of quality was dispatched with the copy of the articles
against me. This envoy had instructions to represent to
the monarch of Blefuscu, the great lenity of his master,
who was content to punish me no farther than with the
loss of my eyes; that I had fled from justice, and if I
did not return in two hours, I should be deprived of my
title of *Nardac*, and declared a traitor. The envoy further
added, that in order to maintain the peace and amity
between both empires, his master expected, that his
brother of Blefuscu would give orders to have sent me
back to Lilliput, bound hand and foot, to be punished
as a traitor.

The Emperor of Blefuscu having taken three days to
consult, returned an answer consisting of many civilities
and excuses. He said, that as for sending me bound, his
brother knew it was impossible; that although I had de-

prived him of his fleet, yet he owed great obligations to
me for many good offices I had done him in making the
peace. That however both their Majesties would soon be
made easy; for I had found a prodigious vessel on the
shore, able to carry me on the sea, which he had given
order to fit up with my own assistance and direction;
and he hoped in a few weeks both empires would be
freed from so insupportable an incumbrance.

With this answer the envoy returned to Lilliput, and
the monarch of Blefuscu related to me all that had
passed; offering me at the same time (but under the
strictest confidence) his gracious protection, if I would
continue in his service; wherein although I believed him
sincere, yet I resolved never more to put any confidence
in princes or ministers, where I could possibly avoid it;
and therefore, with all due acknowledgments for his
favourable intentions, I humbly begged to be excused.
I told him, that since fortune, whether good or evil, had
thrown a vessel in my way, I was resolved to venture
myself in the ocean, rather than be an occasion of difference between two such mighty monarchs. Neither
did I find the Emperor at all displeased; and I discovered by a certain accident, that he was very glad of my
resolution, and so were most of his ministers.

These considerations moved me to hasten my departure somewhat sooner than I intended; to which the
court, impatient to have me gone, very readily contributed. Five hundred workmen were employed to make
two sails to my boat, according to my directions, by
quilting thirteen fold of their strongest linen together.
I was at the pains of making ropes and cables, by twist-
ing ten, twenty or thirty of the thickest and strongest
of theirs. A great stone that I happened to find, after a
long search, by the sea-shore, served me for an anchor.
I had the tallow of three hundred cows for greasing my

boat, and other uses. I was at incredible pains in cutting down some of the largest timber-trees for oars and masts, wherein I was, however, much assisted by his Majesty's ship-carpenters, who helped me in smoothing them, after I had done the rough work.

In about a month, when all was prepared, I sent to receive his Majesty's commands, and to take my leave. The Emperor and Royal Family came out of the palace; I lay down on my face to kiss his hand, which he very graciously gave me: so did the Empress and young Princes of the blood. His Majesty presented me with fifty purses of two hundred *sprugs* a-piece, together with his picture at full length, which I put immediately into one of my gloves, to keep it from being hurt. The ceremonies at my departure were too many to trouble the reader with at this time.

I stored the boat with the carcases of an hundred oxen, and three hundred sheep, with bread and drink proportionable, and as much meat ready dressed as four hundred cooks could provide. I took with me six cows and two bulls alive, with as many ewes and rams, intending to carry them into my own country, and propagate the breed. And to feed them on board, I had a good bundle of hay, and a bag of corn. I would gladly have taken a dozen of the natives, but this was a thing the Emperor would by no means permit; and besides a diligent search into my pockets, his Majesty engaged my honour not to carry away any of his subjects, although with their own consent and desire.

Having thus prepared all things as well as I was able, I set sail on the twenty-fourth day of September 1701, at six in the morning; and when I had gone about four leagues to the northward, the wind being at south-east, at six in the evening I descried a small island about half a league to the north-west. I advanced forward, and cast anchor on the lee-side of the island, which seemed to be uninhabited. I then took some refreshment, and went to my rest. I slept well, and as I conjecture at least six hours, for I found the day broke in two hours after I awaked. It was a clear night. I eat my breakfast before the sun was up; and heaving anchor, the wind being favourable, I steered the same course that I had done the day before, wherein I was directed by my pocket-compass. My intention was to reach, if possible, one of those islands, which I had reason to believe lay to the north-east of Van Diemen's Land. I discovered nothing all that day; but upon the next, about three in the afternoon, when I had by my computation made twenty-four leagues from Blefuscu, I desired a sail steering to the south-east; my course was due east. I hailed her, but could get no answer; yet I found I gained upon her, for the wind slackened. I made all the sail I could, and in half an hour she spied me, then hung out her ancient, and discharged a gun. It is not easy to express the joy I was in upon the unexpected hope of once more seeing my beloved country, and the dear pledges I had left in it. The ship slackened her sails, and I came up with her between five and six in the evening, September 26; but my heart leaped within me to see her English colours. I put my cows and sheep into my coat-pockets, and got on board with all my little cargo of provisions. The vessel was an English merchant-man, returning from Japan by the North and South Seas; the Captain, Mr. John Biddel of Deptford, a very civil man, and an excellent sailor. We were now in the latitude of thirty degrees south; there were about fifty men in the ship; and here I met an old comrade of mine, one Peter Williams, who gave me a good character to the Captain. This gentleman treated me with kindness, and desired I would let him know what place I came from last, and whither I was bound; which I did in a few words, but he thought I was raving, and that the dangers I underwent had disturbed my head; whereupon I took my black cattle and sheep out of my pocket, which, after great astonishment, clearly convinced him of my veracity. I then showed him the gold given me by the Emperor of Blefuscu, together with his Majesty's picture at full length, and some other rarities of that country. I gave him two purses of two hundred *sprugs* each, and promised, when we arrived in England, to make him a present of a cow and a sheep big with young.

I shall not trouble the reader with a particular account of this voyage, which was very prosperous for the most part. We arrived in the Downs on the 13th of April, 1702. I had only one misfortune, that the rats on board carried away one of my sheep; I found her bones in a hole, picked clean from the flesh. The rest of my cattle I got safe on shore, and set them a grazing in a bowling-green at Greenwich, where the fineness of the grass made them feed very heartily, though I had always feared the contrary: neither could I possibly have preserved them in so long a voyage, if the Captain had not allowed me some of his best biscuit, which, rubbed to powder, and mingled with water, was their constant food. The short time I continued in England, I made a considerable profit by showing my cattle to many persons of quality, and others: and before I began my second voyage, I sold them for six hundred pounds. Since my last return, I find the breed is considerably increased, especially the sheep; which I hope will prove much to the advantage of the woollen manufacture, by the fineness of the fleeces.

I stayed but two months with my wife and family; for my insatiable desire of seeing foreign countries would suffer me to continue no longer. I left fifteen hundred pounds with my wife, and fixed her in a good house at Redriff. My remaining stock I carried with me, part in money, and part in goods, in hopes to improve my fortunes. My eldest uncle John had left me an estate in land, near Epping, of about thirty pounds a year; and I had a long lease of the Black Bull in Fetter-Lane, which yielded me as much more; so that I was not in any danger of leaving my family upon the parish. My son Johnny, named so after his uncle, was at the Grammar School, and a towardly child. My daughter Betty (who is now well married, and has children) was then at her needle-work. I took leave of my wife, and boy and girl, with tears on both sides, and went on board the *Adventure*, a merchant-ship of three hundred tons, bound for Surat, Captain John Nicholas, of Liverpool, Commander. But my account of this voyage must be referred to the second part of my Travels.

THE END OF THE FIRST PART.

PART II

A Voyage to Brobdingnag

CHAP. I

A great storm described, the long-boat sent to fetch water, the Author goes with it to discover the country. He is left on shore, is seized by one of the natives, and carried to a farmer's house. His reception there, with several accidents that happened there. A description of the inhabitants.

HAVING been condemned by nature and fortune to an active and restless life, in two months after my return, I again left my native country, and took shipping in the Downs on the 20th day of June, 1702, in the *Adventure*, Captain John Nicholas, a Cornish man, Commander, bound for Surat. We had a very prosperous gale till we arrived at the Cape of Good Hope, where we landed for fresh water, but discovering a leak we unshipped our goods and wintered there; for the Captain falling sick of an ague, we could not leave the Cape till the end of March. We then set sail, and had a good voyage till we passed the Straits of Madagascar; but having got northward of that island, and to about five degrees south latitude, the winds, which in those seas are observed to blow a constant equal gale between the north and west from the beginning of December to the beginning of May, on the 19th of April began to blow with much greater violence, and more westerly than usual, continuing so for twenty days together, during which time we were driven a little to the east of the Molucca Islands, and about three degrees northward of the Line, as our Captain found by an observation he took the 2nd of May, at which time the wind ceased, and it was a perfect calm, whereat I was not a little rejoiced. But he, being a man well experienced in the navigation of those seas, bid us all prepare against a storm, which accordingly happened the day following: for a southern wind, called the southern monsoon, began to set in.

Finding it was likely to overblow, we took in our sprit-sail, and stood by to hand the fore-sail; but making foul weather, we looked the guns were all fast, and handed the mizen. The ship lay very broad off, so we thought it better spooning before the sea, than trying or hulling. We reefed the fore-sail and set him, we hawled aft the fore-sheet; the helm was hard a weather. The ship wore bravely. We belayed the fore-down-hall; but the sail was split, and we hawled down the yard, and got the sail into the ship, and unbound all the things clear of it. It was a very fierce storm; the sea broke strange and dangerous. We hawled off upon the laniard of the whipstaff, and helped the man at helm. We would not get down our top-cast, but let all stand, because she scudded before the sea very well, and we knew that the top-mast being aloft, the ship was the wholesomer, and made better way through the sea, seeing we had sea-room. When the storm was over, we set fore-sail and main-sail, and brought the ship to. Then we set the mizen, main-top-sail, and the fore-top-sail. Our course was east north-east, the wind was at south-west. We got the starboard tacks aboard, we cast off our weather-braces and lifts; we set in the lee-braces, and hawled forward by the weather-bowlings, and hawled them tight, and belayed them, and hawled over the mizen

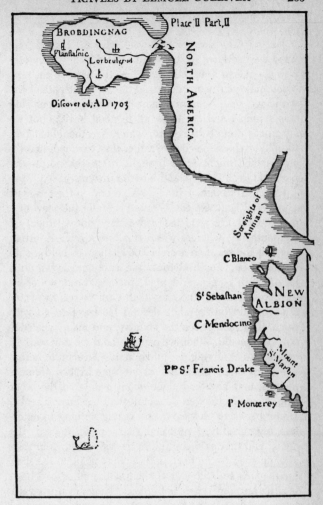

Plate II Part.II

BROBDINGNAG

Flanflasnic

Lorbrulgrud

Discovered, A.D. 1703

NORTH AMERICA

Streights of Annian

C Blanco

St Sebastian

NEW ALBION

C Mendocino

Mount St Martin

Pᵖ Sᵗ Francis Drake

P Monterey

tack to windward, and kept her full and by as near as she would lie.

During this storm, which was followed by a strong wind west south-west, we were carried by my computation about five hundred leagues to the east, so that the oldest sailor on board could not tell in what part of the world we were. Our provisions held out well, our ship was staunch, and our crew all in good health; but we lay in the utmost distress for water. We thought it best to hold on the same course, rather than turn more northerly, which might have brought us to the north-west parts of Great Tartary, and into the frozen sea.

On the 16th day of June, 1703, a boy on the top-mast discovered land. On the 17th we came in full view of a great island or continent (for we knew not whether) on the south side whereof was a small neck of land jutting out into the sea, and a creek too shallow to hold a ship of above one hundred tons. We cast anchor within a league of this creek, and our Captain sent a dozen of his men well armed in the long-boat, with vessels for water if any could be found. I desired his leave to go with them, that I might see the country, and make what discoveries I could. When we came to land we saw no river or spring, nor any sign of inhabitants. Our men therefore wandered on the shore to find out some fresh water near the sea, and I walked alone about a mile on the other side, where I observed the country all barren and rocky. I now began to be weary, and seeing nothing to entertain my curiosity, I returned gently down towards the creek; and the sea being full in my view, I saw our men already got into the boat, and rowing for life to the ship. I was going to hollow after them, although it had been to little purpose, when I observed a huge creature walking after them in the sea, as fast as he could: he waded not much deeper than his knees, and took prodigious strides: but our men had the start of him half a league, and the sea thereabouts being full of sharp-pointed rocks, the monster was not able to overtake the boat. This I was afterwards told, for I durst not stay to see the issue of that adventure; but ran as fast as I could the way I first went, and then climbed up a steep hill, which gave me some prospect of the country. I found it fully cultivated; but that which first surprised me was the length of the grass, which in those grounds that seemed to be kept for hay, was about twenty foot high.

I fell into a high road, for so I took it to be, though it served to the inhabitants only as a foot-path through a field of barley. Here I walked on for some time, but could see little on either side, it being now near harvest, and the corn rising at least forty foot. I was an hour walking to the end of this field, which was fenced in with a hedge of at least one hundred and twenty foot high, and the trees so lofty that I could make no computation of their altitude. There was a stile to pass from this field into the next. It had four steps, and a stone to cross over when you came to the uppermost. It was impossible for me to climb this stile, because every step was six foot high, and the upper stone above twenty. I was endeavouring to find some gap in the hedge, when I discovered one of the inhabitants in the next field, advancing towards the stile, of the same size with him whom I saw in the sea pursuing our boat. He appeared as tall as an ordinary spire-steeple, and took about ten yards at every stride, as near as I could guess. I was struck with the utmost fear and astonishment, and ran to hide myself in the corn, from whence I saw him at the top of the stile, looking back into the next field on the right hand, and heard him call in a voice many degrees louder than a speaking-trumpet: but the noise was so high in the air, that at first I certainly thought it was thunder. Whereupon seven monsters like himself came towards him with reaping-hooks in their hands, each hook about the largeness of six scythes. These people were not so well clad as the first, whose servants or labourers they seemed to be: for, upon some words he spoke, they went to reap the corn in the field where I lay. I kept from them at as great a distance as I could, but was forced to move with extreme difficulty, for the stalks of the corn were sometimes not above a foot distant, so that I could hardly squeeze my body betwixt them. However, I made a shift to go forward till I came to a part of the field where the corn had been laid by the rain and wind. Here it was impossible for me to advance a step; for the stalks were so interwoven that I could not creep through, and the beards of the fallen ears so strong and pointed that they pierced through my clothes into my flesh. At the same time I heard the reapers not above an hundred yards behind me. Being quite dispirited with toil, and wholly overcome by grief and despair, I lay down between two ridges, and heartily wished I might there end my days. I bemoaned my desolate widow, and fatherless children. I lamented my own folly and wilfulness in attempting a second voyage against the advice of all my friends and relations. In this terrible agitation of mind I could not forbear thinking of Lilliput, whose inhabitants looked upon me as the greatest prodigy that ever appeared in the world; where I was able to draw an Imperial Fleet in my hand, and perform those other actions which will be recorded for ever in the chronicles of that empire, while posterity shall hardly believe them, although attested by millions. I reflected what a mortification it must prove to me to appear as inconsiderable in this nation as one single Lilliputian would be among us. But this I conceived was to be the least of my misfortunes: for, as human crea-

tures are observed to be more savage and cruel in proportion to their bulk, what could I expect but to be a
morsel in the mouth of the first among these enormous
barbarians that should happen to seize me? Undoubtedly
philosophers are in the right when they tell us, that
nothing is great or little otherwise than by comparison.
It might have pleased fortune to have let the Lilliputians
find some nation, where the people were as diminutive
with respect to them, as they were to me. And who
knows but that even this prodigious race of mortals
might be equally overmatched in some distant part of
the world, whereof we have yet no discovery?

Scared and confounded as I was, I could not forbear
going on with these reflections, when one of the reapers
approaching within ten yards of the ridge where I lay,
made me apprehend that with the next step I should be
squashed to death under his foot, or cut in two with his
reaping-hook. And therefore when he was again about
to move, I screamed as loud as fear could make me.
Whereupon the huge creature trod short, and looking
round under him for some time, at last espied me as I
lay on the ground. He considered a while with the caution of one who endeavours to lay hold on a small dangerous animal in such a manner that it shall not be able
either to scratch or bite him, as I myself have sometimes
done with a weasel in England. At length he ventured
to take me up behind by the middle between his fore-
finger and thumb, and brought me within three yards of
his eyes, that he might behold my shape more perfectly.
I guessed his meaning, and my good fortune gave me
so much presence of mind, that I resolved not to struggle in the least as he held me in the air about sixty foot
from the ground, although he grievously pinched my
sides, for fear I should slip through his fingers. All I
ventured was to raise my eyes towards the sun, and

place my hands together in a supplicating posture, and to speak some words in an humble melancholy tone, suitable to the condition I then was in. For I apprehended every moment that he would dash me against the ground, as we usually do any little hateful animal which we have a mind to destroy. But my good star would have it, that he appeared pleased with my voice and gestures, and began to look upon me as a curiosity, much wondering to hear me pronounce articulate words, although he could not understand them. In the mean time I was not able to forbear groaning and shedding tears, and turning my head towards my sides; letting him know, as well as I could, how cruelly I was hurt by the pressure of his thumb and finger. He seemed to apprehend my meaning; for, lifting up the lappet of his coat, he put me gently into it, and immediately ran along with me to his master, who was a substantial farmer, and the same person I had first seen in the field.

The farmer having (as I supposed by their talk) received such an account of me as his servant could give him, took a piece of a small straw, about the size of a walking staff, and therewith lifted up the lappets of my coat; which it seems he thought to be some kind of covering that nature had given me. He blew my hairs aside to take a better view of my face. He called his hinds about him, and asked them (as I afterwards learned) whether they had ever seen in the fields any little creature that resembled me. He then placed me softly on the ground upon all four, but I got immediately up, and walked slowly backwards and forwards, to let those people see I had no intent to run away. They all sat down in a circle about me, the better to observe my motions. I pulled off my hat, and made a low bow towards the farmer. I fell on my knees, and lifted up my hands and eyes, and spoke several words as loud as I could: I took a purse of gold out of my pocket, and humbly presented it to him. He received it on the palm of his hand, then applied it close to his eye, to see what it was, and afterwards turned it several times with the point of a pin (which he took out of his sleeve), but could make nothing of it. Whereupon I made a sign that he should place his hand on the ground. I then took the purse, and opening it, poured all the gold into his palm. There were six Spanish pieces of four pistoles each, beside twenty or thirty smaller coins. I saw him wet the tip of his little finger upon his tongue, and take up one of my largest pieces, and then another, but he seemed to be wholly ignorant what they were. He made me a sign to put them again to my purse, and the purse again into my pocket, which after offering to him several times, I thought it best to do.

The farmer by this time was convinced I must be a rational creature. He spoke often to me, but the sound of his voice pierced my ears like that of a water-mill, yet his words were articulate enough. I answered as loud as I could, in several languages, and he often laid his ear within two yards of me, but all in vain, for we were wholly unintelligible to each other. He then sent his servants to their work, and taking his handkerchief out of his pocket, he doubled and spread it on his left hand, which he placed flat on the ground, with the palm up-wards, making me a sign to step into it, as I could easily do, for it was not above a foot in thickness. I thought it my part to obey, and for fear of falling, laid myself at length upon the handkerchief, with the remainder of which he lapped me up to the head for further security, and in this manner carried me home to his house. There he called his wife, and showed me to her; but she screamed and ran back, as women in England do at the sight of a toad or a spider. However, when she had a while seen my behaviour, and how well I observed the signs her husband made, she was soon reconciled, and by degrees grew extremely tender of me.

It was about twelve at noon, and a servant brought in dinner. It was only one substantial dish of meat (fit for the plain condition of an husbandman) in a dish of about four-and-twenty foot diameter. The company were the farmer and his wife, three children, and an old grandmother. When they were sat down, the farmer placed me at some distance from him on the table, which was thirty foot high from the floor. I was in a terrible fright, and kept as far as I could from the edge for fear of falling. The wife minced a bit of meat, then crumbled some bread on a trencher, and placed it before me. I made her a low bow, took out my knife and fork, and fell to eat, which gave them exceeding delight. The mistress sent her maid for a small dram cup, which held about two gallons, and filled it with drink; I took up the vessel with much difficulty in both hands, and in a most respectful manner drank to her ladyship's health, expressing the words as loud as I could in English, which made the company laugh so heartily that I was almost deafened with the noise. This liquor tasted like a small cyder, and was not unpleasant. Then the master made me a sign to come to his trencher side; but as I walked on the table, being in great surprise all the time, as the indulgent reader will easily conceive and excuse, I happened to stumble against a crust, and fell flat on my face, but received no hurt. I got up immediately, and observing the good people to be in much concern, I took my hat (which I held under my arm out of good manners) and waving it over my head, made three huzzas, to show I had got no mischief by my fall. But advancing forwards toward my master (as I shall henceforth call him), his youngest son who sat next to him,

an arch boy of about ten years old, took me up by the
legs, and held me so high in the air, that I trembled
every limb; but his father snatched me from him, and
at the same time gave him such a box on the left ear, as
would have felled an European troop of horse to the
earth, ordering him to be taken from the table. But being afraid the boy might owe me a spite, and well remembering how mischievous all children among us naturally are to sparrows, rabbits, young kittens, and puppy
dogs, I fell on my knees, and pointing to the boy, made
my master to understand, as well as I could, that I desired his son might be pardoned. The father complied,
and the lad took his seat again; whereupon I went to
him and kissed his hand, which my master took, and
made him stroke me gently with it.

In the midst of dinner, my mistress's favourite cat
leapt into her lap. I heard a noise behind me like that of
a dozen stocking-weavers at work; and turning my head,
I found it proceeded from the purring of this animal,
who seemed to be three times larger than an ox, as I
computed by the view of her head, and one of her paws,
while her mistress was feeding and stroking her. The
fierceness of this creature's countenance altogether discomposed me; though I stood at the farther end of the
table, above fifty foot off; and although my mistress held
her fast for fear she might give a spring, and seize me in
her talons. But it happened there was no danger; for the
cat took not the least notice of me when my master
placed me within three yards of her. And as I have been
always told, and found true by experience in my travels,
that flying, or discovering fear before a fierce animal, is
a certain way to make it pursue or attack you, so I resolved in this dangerous juncture to show no manner of
concern. I walked with intrepidity five or six times before the very head of the cat, and came within half a

yard of her; whereupon she drew herself back, as if she
were more afraid of me: I had less apprehension concerning the dogs, whereof three or four came into the
room, as it is usual in farmers' houses; one of which was
a mastiff, equal in bulk to four elephants, and a grey-
hound, somewhat taller than the mastiff, but not so
large.

When dinner was almost done, the nurse came in
with a child of a year old in her arms, who immediately
spied me, and began a squall that you might have heard
from London-Bridge to Chelsea, after the usual oratory
of infants, to get me for a plaything. The mother out of
pure indulgence took me up, and put me towards the
child, who presently seized me by the middle, and got
my head in his mouth, where I roared so loud that the
urchin was frighted, and let me drop; and I should infallibly have broke my neck if the mother had not held
her apron under me. The nurse to quiet her babe made
use of a rattle, which was a kind of hollow vessel filled
with great stones, and fastened by a cable to the child's
waist: but all in vain, so that she was forced to apply
the last remedy by giving it suck. I must confess no object ever disgusted me so much as the sight of her monstrous breast, which I cannot tell what to compare with,
so as to give the curious reader an idea of its bulk, shape
and colour. It stood prominent six foot, and could not
be less than sixteen in circumference. The nipple was
about half the bigness of my head, and the hue both of
that and the dug so varified with spots, pimples, and
freckles, that nothing could appear more nauseous: for
I had a near sight of her, she sitting down the more
conveniently to give suck, and I standing on the table.
This made me reflect upon the fair skins of our English
ladies, who appear so beautiful to us, only because they

are of our own size, and their defects not to be seen
but through a magnifying glass, where we find by experiment that the smoothest and whitest skins look
rough and coarse, and ill coloured.

I remember when I was at Lilliput, the complexion
of those diminutive people appeared to me the fairest in
the world; and talking upon this subject with a person
of learning there, who was an intimate friend of mine,
he said that my face appeared much fairer and smoother
when he looked on me from the ground, than it did
upon a nearer view when I took him up in my hand and
brought him close, which he confessed was at first a
very shocking sight. He said he could discover great
holes in my skin; that the stumps of my beard were ten
times stronger than the bristles of a boar, and my complexion made up of several colours altogether disagreeable: although I must beg leave to say for myself, that
I am as fair as most of my sex and country, and very
little sunburnt by all my travels. On the other side, discoursing of the ladies in that Emperor's court, he used
to tell me, one had freckles, another too wide a mouth,
a third too large a nose, nothing of which I was able to
distinguish. I confess this reflection was obvious enough;
which, however, I could not forbear, lest the reader
might think those vast creatures were actually deformed: for I must do them justice to say they are a
comely race of people; and particularly the features
of my master's countenance, although he were but a
farmer, when I beheld him from the height of sixty foot,
appeared very well proportioned.

When dinner was done, my master went out to his
labourers, and as I could discover by his voice and gesture, gave his wife a strict charge to take care of me.
I was very much tired, and disposed to sleep, which my

mistress perceiving, she put me on her own bed, and covered me with a clean white handkerchief, but larger and coarser than the main-sail of a man of war.

I slept about two hours, and dreamed I was at home with my wife and children, which aggravated my sorrows when I awaked and found myself alone in a vast room, between two and three hundred foot wide, and above two hundred high, lying in a bed twenty yards wide. My mistress was gone about her household affairs, and had locked me in. The bed was eight yards from the floor. Some natural necessities required me to get down; I durst not presume to call, and if I had, it would have been in vain, with such a voice as mine, at so great a distance as from the room where I lay to the kitchen where the family kept. While I was under these circumstances, two rats crept up the curtains, and ran smelling backwards and forwards on the bed. One of them came up almost to my face, whereupon I rose in a fright, and drew out my hanger to defend myself. These horrible animals had the boldness to attack me on both sides, and one of them held his fore-feet at my collar; but I had the good fortune to rip up his belly before he could do me any mischief. He fell down at my feet, and the other seeing the fate of his comrade, made his escape, but not without one good wound on the back, which I gave him as he fled, and made the blood run trickling from him. After this exploit, I walked gently to and fro on the bed, to recover my breath and loss of spirits. These creatures were of the size of a large mastiff, but infinitely more nimble and fierce, so that if I had taken off my belt before I went to sleep, I must have infallibly been torn to pieces and devoured. I measured the tail of the dead rat, and found it to be two yards long, wanting an inch; but it went against my stomach to drag the carcass off the bed, where it lay still bleeding; I observed it had yet some life, but with a strong slash across the neck, I thoroughly dispatched it.

Soon after my mistress came into the room, who seeing me all bloody, ran and took me up in her hand. I pointed to the dead rat, smiling and making other signs to show I was not hurt, whereat she was extremely rejoiced, calling the maid to take up the dead rat with a pair of tongs, and throw it out of the window. Then she set me on a table, where I showed her my hanger all bloody, and wiping it on the lappet of my coat, returned it to the scabbard. I was pressed to do more than one thing, which another could not do for me, and therefore endeavoured to make my mistress understand that I desired to be set down on the floor; which after she had done, my bashfulness would not suffer me to express myself farther than by pointing to the door, and bowing several times. The good woman with much difficulty at last perceived what I would be at, and taking me up again in her hand, walked into the garden, where she set me down. I went on one side about two hundred yards, and beckoning to her not to look or to follow me, I hid myself between two leaves of sorrel, and there discharged the necessities of nature.

I hope the gentle reader will excuse me for dwelling on these and the like particulars, which however insignificant they may appear to grovelling vulgar minds, yet will certainly help a philosopher to enlarge his thoughts and imagination, and apply them to the benefit of public as well as private life, which was my sole design in presenting this and other accounts of my travels to the world; wherein I have been chiefly studious of truth, without affecting any ornaments of learning or of style. But the whole scene of this voyage made so strong an impression on my mind, and is so deeply fixed in my memory, that in committing it to paper I did not omit one material circumstance: however, upon a strict review, I blotted out several passages of less moment which were in my first copy, for fear of being censured as tedious and trifling, whereof travellers are often, perhaps not without justice, accused.

CHAP. II

A description of the farmer's daughter. The Author carried to a market-town, and then to the metropolis. The particulars of his journey.

My mistress had a daughter of nine years old, a child of forward parts for her age, very dexterous at her needle, and skilful in dressing her baby. Her mother and she contrived to fit up the baby's cradle for me against night: the cradle was put into a small drawer of a cabinet, and the drawer placed upon a hanging shelf for fear of the rats. This was my bed all the time I stayed with those people, though made more convenient by degrees, as I began to learn their language, and make my wants known. This young girl was so handy, that after I had once or twice pulled off my clothes before her, she was able to dress and undress me, though I never gave her that trouble when she would let me do either myself. She made me seven shirts, and some other linen, of as fine cloth as could be got, which indeed was coarser than sackcloth; and these she constantly washed for me with her own hands. She was likewise my schoolmistress to teach me the language: when I pointed to any thing, she told me the name of it in her own tongue, so that in a few days I was able to call for whatever I had a mind to. She was very good-natured, and not above forty foot high, being little for her age. She gave me the name of *Grildrig,* which the family took up, and afterwards the whole kingdom. The word imports what the Latins call *nanunculus,* the Italians *homunceletino,* and the English *mannikin.* To her I chiefly owe my preservation in that country: we never parted while I was there; I called her my *Glumdalclitch,* or little nurse: and I should be guilty of great ingratitude, if I omitted this honourable mention of her care and affection towards me, which I heartily wish it lay in my power to requite as she deserves, instead of being the innocent but unhappy instrument of her disgrace, as I have too much reason to fear.

It now began to be known and talked of in the neighbourhood, that my master had found a strange animal in the field, about the bigness of a *splacknuck,* but exactly shaped in every part like a human creature; which it likewise imitated in all its actions; seemed to speak in a little language of its own, had already learned several words of theirs, went erect upon two legs, was tame and gentle, would come when it was called, do whatever it was bid, had the finest limbs in the world, and a complexion fairer than a nobleman's daughter of three years old. Another farmer who lived hard by, and was a particular friend of my master, came on a visit on purpose to enquire into the truth of this story. I was immediately produced, and placed upon a table, where I walked as I was commanded, drew my hanger, put it up again, made my reverence to my master's guest, asked him in his own language how he did, and told him he was welcome, just as my little nurse had instructed me. This man who was old and dim-sighted, put on his spectacles to behold me better, at which I could not forbear laughing very heartily, for his eyes appeared like the full moon shining into a chamber at two windows. Our people, who discovered the cause of my mirth, bore me company in laughing, at which the old fellow was fool enough to be angry and out of countenance. He had the character of a great miser, and to my misfortune he well deserved it, by the cursed advice he gave my master to show me as a sight upon a market-day in the next town, which was half an hour's riding, about two and twenty miles from our house. I guessed there was some mischief contriving, when I observed my master and his friend whispering long together, sometimes pointing at me; and my fears made me fancy that I overheard and understood some of their words. But the next morning Glumdalclitch, my little nurse, told me the whole matter, which she had cunningly picked out from her mother. The poor girl laid me on her bosom, and fell a weeping with shame and grief. She apprehended some mischief would happen to me from rude vulgar folks, who might squeeze me to death, or break one of my limbs by taking me in their hands. She had also observed how modest I was in my nature, how nicely I regarded my honour, and what an indignity I should conceive it to be exposed for money as a public spectacle to the meanest of the people. She said, her papa and mamma had promised that Grildrig should be hers, but now she found they meant to serve her as they did last year, when they pretended to give her a lamb, and yet, as soon as it was fat, sold it to a butcher. For my own part, I may truly affirm that I was less concerned than my nurse. I had a strong hope, which never left me, that I should one day recover my liberty; and as to the ignominy of being carried about for a monster, I considered myself to be a perfect stranger in the country, and that such a misfortune could never be charged upon me as a reproach, if ever I should return to England; since the King of Great Britain himself, in my condition, must have undergone the same distress.

My master, pursuant to the advice of his friend, carried me in a box the next market-day to the neighbouring town, and took along with him his little daughter, my nurse, upon a pillion behind him. The box was close on every side, with a little door for me to go in and out, and a few gimlet-holes to let in air. The girl had been so careful to put the quilt of her baby's bed into it, for me to lie down on. However, I was terribly shaken and discomposed in this journey, though it were but of half an hour. For the horse went about forty foot at every step, and trotted so high, that the agitation was equal to the rising and falling of a ship in a great storm, but much more frequent. Our journey was somewhat further than from London to St. Albans. My master alighted at an inn which he used to frequent; and after consulting a while with the inn-keeper, and making some necessary preparations, he hired the *Grultrud,* or crier, to give notice through the town of a strange creature to be seen at the Sign of the Green Eagle, not so big as a *splacknuck* (an animal in that country very finely shaped, about six foot long), and in every part of the body resembling an human creature, could speak several words, and perform an hundred diverting tricks.

I was placed upon a table in the largest room of the inn, which might be near three hundred foot square. My little nurse stood on a low stool close to the table, to take care of me, and direct what I should do. My master, to avoid a crowd, would suffer only thirty people at a time to see me. I walked about on the table as the girl commanded: she asked me questions as far as she knew my understanding of the language reached, and I answered them as loud as I could. I turned about several times to the company, paid my humble respects, said they were welcome, and used some other speeches I had been taught. I took up a thimble filled with liquor, which Glumdalclitch had given me for a cup, and drank their health. I drew out my hanger, and flourished with it after the manner of fencers in England. My nurse gave me part of a straw, which I exercised as a pike, having learned the art in my youth. I was that day shown to twelve sets of company, and as often forced to go over again with the same fopperies, till I was half dead with weariness and vexation. For those who had seen me made such wonderful reports, that the people were ready to break down the doors to come in. My master for his own interest would not suffer any one to touch me except my nurse; and, to prevent danger, benches were set round the table at such a distance as put me out of every body's reach. However, an unlucky school-boy aimed a hazel nut directly at my head, which very narrowly missed me; otherwise, it came with so much violence, that it would have infallibly knocked out my brains, for it was almost as large as a small pumpion: but I had the satisfaction to see the young rogue well beaten, and turned out of the room.

My master gave public notice, that he would show me again the next market-day, and in the meantime he prepared a more convenient vehicle for me, which he had reason enough to do; for I was so tired with my first journey, and with entertaining company for eight hours together, that I could hardly stand upon my legs, or speak a word. It was at least three days before I recovered my strength; and that I might have no rest at home, all the neighbouring gentlemen from an hundred miles round, hearing of my fame, came to see me at my master's own house. There could not be fewer than thirty persons with their wives and children (for the country is very populous); and my master demanded the rate of a full room whenever he showed me at home, although it were only to a single family; so that for some time I had but little ease every day of the week (except Wednesday, which is their Sabbath) although I were not carried to the town.

My master finding how profitable I was likely to be, resolved to carry me to the most considerable cities of the kingdom. Having therefore provided himself with all things necessary for a long journey, and settled his affairs at home, he took leave of his wife, and upon the 17th of August, 1703, about two months after my arrival, we set out for the metropolis, situated near the middle of that empire, and about three thousand miles distance from our house. My master made his daughter Glumdalclitch ride behind him. She carried me on her lap in a box tied about her waist. The girl had lined it on all sides with the softest cloth she could get, well quilted underneath, furnished it with her baby's bed, provided me with linen and other necessaries, and made everything as convenient as she could. We had no other company but a boy of the house, who rode after us with the luggage.

My master's design was to show me in all the towns by the way, and to step out of the road for fifty or an hundred miles, to any village or person of quality's house where he might expect custom. We made easy journeys of not above seven or eight score miles a day: for Glumdalclitch, on purpose to spare me, complained she was tired with the trotting of the horse. She often took me out of my box, at my own desire, to give me air, and show me the country, but always held me fast by a leading-string. We passed over five or six rivers many degrees broader and deeper than the Nile or the Ganges; and there was hardly a rivulet so small as the Thames at London-Bridge. We were ten weeks in our journey, and I was shown in eighteen large towns besides many villages and private families.

On the 26th day of October, we arrived at the metropolis, called in their language *Lorbrulgrud,* or Pride of the Universe. My master took a lodging in the principal street of the city, not far from the royal palace, and put out bills in the usual form, containing an exact description of my person and parts. He hired a large room between three and four hundred foot wide. He provided a table sixty foot in diameter, upon which I was to act my part, and pallisadoed it round three foot from the edge, and as many high, to prevent my falling over. I was shown ten times a day to the wonder and satisfaction of all people. I could now speak the language tolerably well, and perfectly understood every word that was spoken to me. Besides, I had learnt their alphabet, and could make a shift to explain a sentence here and there; for Glumdalclitch had been my instructor while we were at home, and at leisure hours during our journey. She carried a little book in her pocket, not much larger than a Sanson's Atlas; it was a common treatise for the use of young girls, giving a short account of their religion: out of this she taught me my letters, and interpreted the words.

CHAP. III

The Author sent for to Court. The Queen buys him of his master the farmer, and presents him to the King. He disputes with his Majesty's great scholars. An apartment at Court provided for the Author. He is in high favour with the Queen. He stands up for the honour of his own country. His quarrels with the Queen's dwarf.

The frequent labours I underwent every day made in a few weeks a very considerable change in my health: the more my master got by me, the more insatiable he

grew. I had quite lost my stomach, and was almost reduced to a skeleton. The farmer observed it, and con-
cluding I soon must die, resolved to make as good a
hand of me as he could. While he was thus reasoning
and resolving with himself, a *Slardral*, or Gentleman
Usher, came from court, commanding my master to
carry me immediately thither for the diversion of the
Queen and her ladies. Some of the latter had already
been to see me, and reported strange things of my
beauty, behaviour, and good sense. Her Majesty and
those who attended her were beyond measure delighted
with my demeanour. I fell on my knees, and begged the
honour of kissing her Imperial foot; but this gracious
princess held out her little finger towards me (after I
was set on a table), which I embraced in both my arms,
and put the tip of it, with the utmost respect, to my lip.
She made me some general questions about my country
and my travels, which I answered as distinctly and in
as few words as I could. She asked whether I would be
content to live at court. I bowed down to the board of
the table, and humbly answered, that I was my master's
slave, but if I were at my own disposal, I should be
proud to devote my life to her Majesty's service. She
then asked my master whether he were willing to sell
me at a good price. He, who apprehended I could not
live a month, was ready enough to part with me, and
demanded a thousand pieces of gold, which were ordered him on the spot, each piece being about the bigness of eight hundred moidores; but, allowing for the
proportion of all things between that country and Europe, and the high price of gold among them, was
hardly so great a sum as a thousand guineas would be in
England. I then said to the Queen, since I was now her
Majesty's most humble creature and vassal, I must beg
the favour, that Glumdalclitch, who had always tended

me with so much care and kindness, and understood to do it so well, might be admitted into her service, and continue to be my nurse and instructor. Her Majesty agreed to my petition, and easily got the farmer's consent, who was glad enough to have his daughter preferred at court: and the poor girl herself was not able to hide her joy. My late master withdrew, bidding me farewell, and saying he had left me in a good service; to which I replied not a word, only making him a slight bow.

The Queen observed my coldness, and when the farmer was gone out of the apartment, asked me the reason. I made bold to tell her Majesty that I owed no other obligation to my late master, than his not dashing out the brains of a poor harmless creature found by chance in his field; which obligation was amply recompensed by the gain he had made in showing me through half the kingdom, and the price he had now sold me for. That the life I had since led, was laborious enough to kill an animal of ten times my strength. That my health was much impaired by the continual drudgery of entertaining the rabble every hour of the day, and that if my master had not thought my life in danger, her Majesty perhaps would not have got so cheap a bargain. But as I was out of all fear of being ill treated under the protection of so great and good an Empress, the Ornament of Nature, the Darling of the World, the Delight of her Subjects, the Phœnix of the Creation; so I hoped my late master's apprehensions would appear to be groundless, for I already found my spirits to revive by the influence of her most august presence.

This was the sum of my speech, delivered with great improprieties and hesitation; the latter part was altogether framed in the style peculiar to that people, whereof I learned some phrases from Glumdalclitch, while she was carrying me to court.

The Queen giving great allowance for my defectiveness in speaking, was however surprised at so much wit and good sense in so diminutive an animal. She took me in her own hand, and carried me to the King, who was then retired to his cabinet. His Majesty, a prince of much gravity, and austere countenance, not well observing my shape at first view, asked the Queen after a cold manner, how long it was since she grew fond of a *splacknuck;* for such it seems he took me to be, as I lay upon my breast in her Majesty's right hand. But this princess, who hath an infinite deal of wit and humour, set me gently on my feet upon the scrutore, and commanded me to give his Majesty an account of myself, which I did in a very few words; and Glumdalclitch, who attended at the cabinet door, and could not endure I should be out of her sight, being admitted, confirmed all that had passed from my arrival at her father's house.

The King, although he be as learned a person as any in his dominions, and had been educated in the study of philosophy, and particularly mathematics; yet when he observed my shape exactly, and saw me walk erect, before I began to speak, conceived I might be a piece of clock-work (which is in that country arrived to a very great perfection), contrived by some ingenious artist. But when he heard my voice, and found what I delivered to be regular and rational, he could not conceal his astonishment. He was by no means satisfied with the relation I gave him of the manner I came into his kingdom, but thought it a story concerted between Glumdalclitch and her father, who had taught me a set of words to make me sell at a higher price. Upon this imagination he put several other questions to me, and still received rational answers, no otherwise defective than by a foreign accent, and an imperfect knowledge in the language, with some rustic phrases which I had learned at the farmer's house, and did not suit the polite style of a court.

His Majesty sent for three great scholars who were then in their weekly waiting, according to the custom in that country. These gentlemen, after they had a while examined my shape with much nicety, were of different opinions concerning me. They all agreed that I could not be produced according to the regular laws of nature, because I was not framed with a capacity of preserving my life, either by swiftness, or climbing of trees, or digging holes in the earth. They observed by my teeth, which they viewed with great exactness, that I was a carnivorous animal; yet most quadrupeds being an over-match for me, and field mice, with some others, too nimble, they could not imagine how I should be able to support myself, unless I fed upon snails and other insects, which they offered, by many learned arguments, to evince that I could not possibly do. One of these virtuosi seemed to think that I might be an embryo, or abortive birth. But this opinion was rejected by the other two, who observed my limbs to be perfect and finished, and that I had lived several years, as it was manifest from my beard, the stumps whereof they plainly discovered through a magnifying-glass. They would not allow me to be a dwarf, because my littleness was beyond all degrees of comparison; for the Queen's favourite dwarf, the smallest ever known in that kingdom, was near thirty foot high. After much debate, they concluded unanimously that I was only *relplum scalcath,* which is interpreted literally, *lusus naturæ;* a determination exactly agreeable to the modern philosophy of Europe, whose professors, disdaining the old evasion of *occult causes*, whereby the followers of Aristotle endeavour in vain to disguise their ignorance, have invented this wonderful solution of all difficulties, to the unspeakable advancement of human knowledge.

After this decisive conclusion, I entreated to be heard a word or two. I applied myself to the King, and assured his Majesty, that I came from a country which abounded with several millions of both sexes, and of my own stature; where the animals, trees, and houses were all in proportion, and where by consequence I might be as able to defend myself, and to find sustenance, as any of his Majesty's subjects could do here; which I took for a full answer to those gentlemen's arguments. To this they only replied with a smile of contempt, saying, that the farmer had instructed me very well in my lesson. The King, who had a much better understanding, dismissing his learned men, sent for the farmer, who by good fortune was not yet gone out of town. Having therefore first examined him privately, and then confronted him with me and the young girl, his Majesty began to think that what we told him might possibly be true. He desired the Queen to order that a particular care should be taken of me, and was of opinion that Glumdalclitch should still continue in her office of tending me, because he observed we had a great affection for each other. A convenient apartment was provided for her at court: she had a sort of governess appointed to take care of her education, a maid to dress her, and two other servants for menial offices; but the care of me was wholly appropriated to herself. The Queen commanded her own cabinet-maker to contrive a box that might serve me for a bed-chamber, after the model that Glumdalclitch and I should agree upon. This man was a most ingenious artist, and according to my directions, in

three weeks finished for me a wooden chamber of sixteen foot square, and twelve high, with sash-windows,
a door, and two closets, like a London bed-chamber.
The board that made the ceiling was to be lifted up and
down by two hinges, to put in a bed ready furnished by
her Majesty's upholsterer, which Glumdalclitch took out
every day to air, made it with her own hands, and letting it down at night, locked up the roof over me. A nice
workman, who was famous for little curiosities, under-
took to make me two chairs, with backs and frames, of
a substance not unlike ivory, and two tables, with a
cabinet to put my things in. The room was quilted on
all sides, as well as the floor and the ceiling, to prevent
any accident from the carelessness of those who carried
me, and to break the force of a jolt when I went in a
coach. I desired a lock for my door, to prevent rats and
mice from coming in: the smith, after several attempts,
made the smallest that ever was seen among them, for
I have known a larger at the gate of a gentleman's house
in England. I made a shift to keep the key in a pocket of
my own, fearing Glumdalclitch might lose it. The Queen
likewise ordered the thinnest silks that could be gotten,
to make me clothes, not much thicker than an English
blanket, very cumbersome till I was accustomed to
them. They were after the fashion of the kingdom,
partly resembling the Persian, and partly the Chinese,
and are a very grave and decent habit.

The Queen became so fond of my company, that she
could not dine without me. I had a table placed upon
the same at which her Majesty eat, just at her left elbow,
and a chair to sit on. Glumdalclitch stood upon a stool
on the floor, near my table, to assist and take care of
me. I had an entire set of silver dishes and plates, and
other necessaries, which, in proportion to those of the
Queen, were not much bigger than what I have seen of

the same kind in a London toy-shop, for the furniture of
a baby-house: these my little nurse kept in her pocket,
in a silver box, and gave me at meals as I wanted them,
always cleaning them herself. No person dined with the
Queen but the two Princesses Royal, the elder sixteen
years old, and the younger at that time thirteen and a
month. Her Majesty used to put a bit of meat upon one
of my dishes, out of which I carved for myself, and her
diversion was to see me eat in miniature. For the Queen
(who had indeed but a weak stomach) took up at one
mouthful, as much as a dozen English farmers could eat
at a meal, which to me was for some time a very nauseous sight. She would craunch the wing of a lark, bones
and all, between her teeth, although it were nine times
as large as that of a full-grown turkey; and put a bit
of bread into her mouth, as big as two twelve-penny
loaves. She drank out of a golden cup, above a hogshead at a draught. Her knives were twice as long as a
scythe set straight upon the handle. The spoons, forks,
and other instruments were all in the same proportion.
I remember when Glumdalclitch carried me out of curiosity to see some of the tables at court, where ten or
a dozen of these enormous knives and forks were lifted
up together, I thought I had never till then beheld so
terrible a sight.

It is the custom that every Wednesday (which, as I
have before observed, was their Sabbath) the King and
Queen, with the royal issue of both sexes, dine together
in the apartment of his Majesty, to whom I was now
become a great favourite; and at these times my little
chair and table were placed at his left hand, before one
of the salt-cellars. This prince took a pleasure in conversing with me, enquiring into the manners, religion,
laws, government, and learning of Europe; wherein I
gave him the best account I was able. His apprehension

was so clear, and his judgment so exact, that he made very wise reflections and observations upon all I said. But, I confess, that after I had been a little too copious in talking of my own beloved country, of our trade, and wars by sea and land, of our schisms in religion, and parties in the state; the prejudices of his education prevailed so far, that he could not forbear taking me up in his right hand, and stroking me gently with the other, after an hearty fit of laughing, asked me, whether I were a Whig or a Tory. Then turning to his first minister, who waited behind him with a white staff, near as tall as the main-mast of the *Royal Sovereign,* he observed how contemptible a thing was human grandeur, which could be mimicked by such diminutive insects as I: and yet, said he, I dare engage, these creatures have their titles and distinctions of honour, they contrive little nests and burrows, that they call houses and cities; they make a figure in dress and equipage; they love, they fight, they dispute, they cheat, they betray. And thus he continued on, while my colour came and went several times, with indignation to hear our noble country, the mistress of arts and arms, the scourge of France, the arbitress of Europe, the seat of virtue, piety, honour, and truth, the pride and envy of the world, so contemptuously treated.

But as I was not in a condition to resent injuries, so, upon mature thoughts, I began to doubt whether I were injured or no. For, after having been accustomed several months to the sight and converse of this people, and observed every object upon which I cast my eyes, to be of proportionable magnitude, the horror I had first conceived from their bulk and aspect was so far worn off, that if I had then beheld a company of English lords and ladies in their finery and birth-day clothes, acting their several parts in the most courtly manner, of strutting, and bowing, and prating; to say the truth, I should have been strongly tempted to laugh as much at them as the King and his grandees did at me. Neither indeed could I forbear smiling at myself, when the Queen used to place me upon her hand towards a looking-glass, by which both our persons appeared before me in full view together; and there could be nothing more ridiculous than the comparison; so that I really began to imagine myself dwindled many degrees below my usual size.

Nothing angered and mortified me so much as the Queen's dwarf, who being of the lowest stature that was ever in that country (for I verily think he was not full thirty foot high) became insolent at seeing a creature so much beneath him, that he would always affect to swagger and look big as he passed by me in the Queen's antechamber, while I was standing on some table talking with the lords or ladies of the court, and he seldom failed of a smart word or two upon my littleness; against which I could only revenge myself by calling him brother, challenging him to wrestle, and such repartees as are usual in the mouths of court pages. One day at dinner this malicious little cub was so nettled with something I had said to him, that raising himself upon the frame of her Majesty's chair, he took me up by the middle, as I was sitting down, not thinking any harm, and let me drop into a large silver bowl of cream, and then ran away as fast as he could. I fell over head and ears, and if I had not been a good swimmer, it might have gone very hard with me; for Glumdalclitch in that instant happened to be at the other end of the room, and the Queen was in such a fright that she wanted presence of mind to assist me. But my little nurse ran to my relief, and took me out, after I had swallowed above a quart of cream. I was put to bed; however, I received no other damage than the loss of a suit of clothes, which was utterly spoiled. The dwarf was soundly whipped, and as a farther punishment, forced to drink up the bowl of cream, into which he had thrown me: neither was he ever restored to favour: for, soon after the Queen bestowed him on a lady of high quality, so that I saw him no more, to my very great satisfaction; for I could not tell to what extremity such a malicious urchin might have carried his resentment.

He had before served me a scurvy trick, which set the Queen a laughing, although at the same time she was heartily vexed, and would have immediately cashiered him, if I had not been so generous as to intercede. Her Majesty had taken a marrow-bone upon her plate, and after knocking out the marrow, placed the bone again in the dish erect as it stood before; the dwarf watching his opportunity, while Glumdalclitch was gone to the sideboard, mounted the stool she stood on to take care of me at meals, took me up in both hands, and squeezing my legs together, wedged them into the marrow bone above my waist, where I stuck for some time, and made a very ridiculous figure. I believe it was near a minute before any one knew what was become of me, for I thought it below me to cry out. But, as princes seldom get their meat hot, my legs were not scalded, only my stockings and breeches in a sad condition. The dwarf, at my entreaty, had no other punishment than a sound whipping.

I was frequently rallied by the Queen upon account of my fearfulness, and she used to ask me whether the people of my country were as great cowards as myself. The occasion was this: the kingdom is much pestered with flies in summer; and these odious insects, each of them as big as a Dunstable lark, hardly gave me any rest while I sat at dinner, with their continual humming and buzzing about my ears. They would sometimes alight

upon my victuals, and leave their loathsome excrement
or spawn behind, which to me was very visible, though
not to the natives of that country, whose large optics
were not so acute as mine in viewing smaller objects.
Sometimes they would fix upon my nose or forehead,
where they stung me to the quick, smelling very offensively, and I could easily trace that viscous matter, which
our naturalists tell us enables those creatures to walk
with their feet upwards upon a ceiling. I had much
ado to defend myself against these detestable animals,
and could not forbear starting when they came on my
face. It was the common practice of the dwarf to catch
a number of these insects in his hand, as schoolboys do
among us, and let them out suddenly under my nose,
on purpose to frighten me, and divert the Queen. My
remedy was to cut them in pieces with my knife as they
flew in the air, wherein my dexterity was much admired.

I remember one morning when Glumdalclitch had set
me in my box upon a window, as she usually did in fair
days to give me air (for I durst not venture to let the
box be hung on a nail out of the window, as we do with
cages in England), after I had lifted up one of my
sashes, and sat down at my table to eat a piece of sweet
cake for my breakfast, above twenty wasps, allured by
the smell, came flying into the room, humming louder
than the drones of as many bagpipes. Some of them
seized my cake, and carried it piecemeal away, others
flew about my head and face, confounding me with the
noise, and putting me in the utmost terror of their stings.
However I had the courage to rise and draw my hanger,
and attack them in the air. I dispatched four of them,
but the rest got away, and I presently shut my window.
These insects were as large as partridges: I took out
their stings, found them an inch and a half long, and as
sharp as needles. I carefully preserved them all, and

having since shown them with some other curiosities in several parts of Europe; upon my return to England I gave three of them to Gresham College, and kept the fourth for myself.

CHAP. IV

The country described. A proposal for correcting modern maps. The King's palace, and some account of the metropolis. The Author's way of travelling. The chief temple described.

I now intend to give the reader a short description of this country, as far as I travelled in it, which was not above two thousand miles round Lorbrulgrud the metropolis. For the Queen, whom I always attended, never went further when she accompanied the King in his progresses, and there stayed till his Majesty returned from viewing his frontiers. The whole extent of this prince's dominions reacheth about six thousand miles in length, and from three to five in breadth. From whence I cannot but conclude that our geographers of Europe are in a great error, by supposing nothing but sea between Japan and California; for it was ever my opinion, that there must be a balance of earth to counterpoise the great continent of Tartary; and therefore they ought to correct their maps and charts, by joining this vast tract of land to the north-west parts of America, wherein I shall be ready to lend them my assistance.

The kingdom is a peninsula, terminated to the northeast by a ridge of mountains thirty miles high, which are altogether impassable by reason of the volcanoes upon the tops. Neither do the most learned know what sort of mortals inhabit beyond those mountains, or whether they be inhabited at all. On the three other sides it is bounded by the ocean. There is not one sea-port in the whole kingdom, and those parts of the coasts into which the rivers issue are so full of pointed rocks, and the sea generally so rough, that there is no venturing with the smallest of their boats, so that these people are wholly excluded from any commerce with the rest of the world. But the large rivers are full of vessels, and abound with excellent fish, for they seldom get any from the sea, because the sea-fish are of the same size with those in Europe, and consequently not worth catching; whereby it is manifest, that nature, in the production of plants and animals of so extraordinary a bulk, is wholly confined to this continent, of which I leave the reasons to be determined by philosophers. However, now and then they take a whale that happens to be dashed against the rocks, which the common people feed on heartily. These whales I have known so large that a man could hardly carry one upon his shoulders; and sometimes for curiosity they are brought in hampers to Lorbrulgrud: I saw one of them in a dish at the King's table, which passed for a rarity, but I did not observe he was fond of it; for I think indeed the bigness disgusted him, although I have seen one somewhat larger in Greenland.

The country is well inhabited, for it contains fifty-one cities, near an hundred walled towns, and a great number of villages. To satisfy my curious reader, it may be sufficient to describe Lorbrulgrud. This city stands upon almost two equal parts on each side the river that passes through. It contains above eighty thousand houses, and about six hundred thousand inhabitants. It is in length three *glonglungs* (which make about fifty-four English miles) and two and a half in breadth, as I measured it myself in the royal map made by the King's order, which was laid on the ground on purpose for me, and extended an hundred feet: I paced the diameter and circumference several times bare-foot, and computing by the scale, measured it pretty exactly.

The King's palace is no regular edifice, but an heap of buildings about seven miles round: the chief rooms are generally two hundred and forty foot high, and broad and long in proportion. A coach was allowed to Glumdalclitch and me, wherein her governess frequently took her out to see the town, or go among the shops; and I was always of the party, carried in my box; although the girl at my own desire would often take me out, and hold me in her hand, that I might more conveniently view the houses and the people, as we passed along the streets. I reckoned our coach to be about a square of Westminster-Hall, but not altogether so high; however, I cannot be very exact. One day the governess ordered our coachman to stop at several shops, where the beggars, watching their opportunity, crowded to the sides of the coach, and gave me the most horrible spectacles that ever an European eye beheld. There was a woman with a cancer in her breast, swelled to a monstrous size, full of holes, in two or three of which I could have easily crept, and covered my whole body. There was a fellow with a wen in his neck, larger than five wool-packs, and another with a couple of wooden legs, each about twenty foot high. But the most hateful sight of all was the lice crawling on their clothes. I could see distinctly the limbs of these vermin with my naked eye, much better than those of an European louse through a microscope, and their snouts with which they rooted like swine. They were the first I had ever beheld, and I should have been curious enough to dissect one of them, if I had proper instruments (which I unluckily left behind me in the ship), although indeed the sight was so nauseous, that it perfectly turned my stomach.

Besides the large box in which I was usually carried,

the Queen ordered a smaller one to be made for me, of
about twelve foot square, and ten high, for the convenience of travelling, because the other was somewhat too
large for Glumdalclitch's lap, and cumbersome in the
coach; it was made by the same artist, whom I directed
in the whole contrivance. This travelling closet was an
exact square with a window in the middle of three of
the squares, and each window was latticed with iron
wire on the outside, to prevent accidents in long journeys. On the fourth side, which had no window, two
strong staples were fixed, through which the person that
carried me, when I had a mind to be on horseback, put
in a leathern belt, and buckled it about his waist. This
was always the office of some grave trusty servant in
whom I could confide, whether I attended the King and
Queen in their progresses, or were disposed to see the
gardens, or pay a visit to some great lady or minister
of state in the court, when Glumdalclitch happened to
be out of order: for I soon began to be known and
esteemed among the greatest officers, I suppose more
upon account of their Majesties' favour, than any merit
of my own. In journeys, when I was weary of the coach,
a servant on horseback would buckle on my box, and
place it on a cushion before him; and there I had a full
prospect of the country on three sides from my three
windows. I had in this closet a field-bed and a hammock
hung from the ceiling, two chairs and a table, neatly
screwed to the floor, to prevent being tossed about by
the agitation of the horse or the coach. And having been
long used to sea-voyages, those motions, although sometimes very violent, did not much discompose me.

Whenever I had a mind to see the town, it was always
in my travelling-closet, which Glumdalclitch held in her
lap in a kind of open sedan, after the fashion of the
country, borne by four men, and attended by two others

in the Queen's livery. The people who had often heard
of me, were very curious to crowd about the sedan, and
the girl was complaisant enough to make the bearers
stop, and to take me in her hand that I might be more
conveniently seen.

I was very desirous to see the chief temple, and particularly the tower belonging to it, which is reckoned
the highest in the kingdom. Accordingly one day my
nurse carried me thither, but I may truly say I came
back disappointed; for the height is not above three
thousand foot, reckoning from the ground to the highest
pinnacle top; which allowing for the difference between
the size of those people, and us in Europe, is no great
matter for admiration, nor at all equal in proportion (if
I rightly remember) to Salisbury steeple. But, not to
detract from a nation to which during my life I shall
acknowledge myself extremely obliged, it must be allowed, that whatever this famous tower wants in height
is amply made up in beauty and strength. For the walls
are near an hundred foot thick, built of hewn stone,
whereof each is about forty foot square, and adorned
on all sides with statues of Gods and Emperors cut in
marble larger than the life, placed in their several niches.
I measured a little finger which had fallen down from
one of these statues, and lay unperceived among some
rubbish, and found it exactly four foot and an inch in
length. Glumdalclitch wrapped it up in a handkerchief,
and carried it home in her pocket to keep among other
trinkets, of which the girl was very fond, as children at
her age usually are.

The King's kitchen is indeed a noble building, vaulted
at top, and about six hundred foot high. The great oven
is not so wide by ten paces as the cupola at St. Paul's:
for I measured the latter on purpose after my return.
But if I should describe the kitchen-grate, the prodigious

pots and kettles, the joints of meat turning on the spits, with many other particulars, perhaps I should be hardly believed; at least a severe critic would be apt to think I enlarged a little, as travellers are often suspected to do. To avoid which censure, I fear I have run too much into the other extreme; and that if this treatise should happen to be translated into the language of Brobdingnag (which is the general name of that kingdom) and transmitted thither, the King and his people would have reason to complain that I had done them an injury by a false and diminutive representation.

His Majesty seldom keeps above six hundred horses in his stables: they are generally from fifty-four to sixty foot high. But when he goes abroad on solemn days, he is attended for state by a militia guard of five hundred horse, which indeed I thought was the most splendid sight that could be ever beheld, till I saw part of his army in battalia, whereof I shall find another occasion to speak.

CHAP. V

Several adventures that happened to the Author. The execution of a criminal. The Author shows his skill in navigation.

I should have lived happy enough in that country, if my littleness had not exposed me to several ridiculous and troublesome accidents: some of which I shall venture to relate. Glumdalclitch often carried me into the gardens of the court in my smaller box, and would sometimes take me out of it and hold me in her hand, or set me down to walk. I remember, before the dwarf left the Queen, he followed us one day into those gardens, and my nurse having set me down, he and I being close together, near some dwarf apple-trees, I must needs show my wit by a silly allusion between him and the trees, which happens to hold in their language as it doth in ours. Whereupon, the malicious rogue watching his opportunity, when I was walking under one of them, shook it directly over my head, by which a dozen apples, each of them near as large as a Bristol barrel, came tumbling about my ears; one of them hit me on the back as I chanced to stoop, and knocked me down flat on my face, but I received no other hurt, and the dwarf was pardoned at my desire, because I had given the provocation.

Another day Glumdalclitch left me on a smooth grassplot to divert myself while she walked at some distance with her governess. In the meantime there suddenly fell such a violent shower of hail, that I was immediately by the force of it struck to the ground: and when I was down, the hailstones gave me such cruel bangs all over the body, as if I had been pelted with tennis-balls; however I made a shift to creep on all four, and shelter myself by lying flat on my face on the lee-side of a border of lemon thyme, but so bruised from head to foot that I could not go abroad in ten days. Neither is this at all to be wondered at, because nature in that country observing the same proportion through all her operations, a hailstone is near eighteen hundred times as large as one in Europe, which I can assert upon experience, having been so curious to weigh and measure them.

But a more dangerous accident happened to me in the same garden, when my little nurse believing she had put me in a secure place, which I often entreated her to do, that I might enjoy my own thoughts, and having left my box at home to avoid the trouble of carrying it, went to another part of the garden with her governess and some ladies of her acquaintance. While she was absent, and out of hearing, a small white spaniel belonging to one of the chief gardeners, having got by accident into the garden, happened to range near the place where I lay. The dog following the scent, came directly up, and taking me in his mouth, ran straight to his master, wagging his tail, and set me gently on the ground. By good fortune he had been so well taught, that I was carried between his teeth without the least hurt, or even tearing my clothes. But the poor gardener, who knew me well, and had a great kindness for me, was in a terrible fright. He gently took me up in both his hands, and asked me how I did; but I was so amazed and out of breath, that I could not speak a word. In a few minutes I came to myself, and he carried me safe to my little nurse, who by this time had returned to the place where she left me, and was in cruel agonies when I did not appear, nor answer when she called: she severely reprimanded the gardener on account of his dog. But the thing was hushed up, and never known at court; for the girl was afraid of the Queen's anger, and truly as to myself, I thought it would not be for my reputation that such a story should go about.

This accident absolutely determined Glumdalclitch never to trust me abroad for the future out of her sight. I had been long afraid of this resolution, and therefore concealed from her some little unlucky adventures that happened in those times when I was left by myself. Once a kite hovering over the garden made a stoop at me, and if I had not resolutely drawn my hanger, and run under a thick espalier, he would have certainly carried me away in his talons. Another time walking to the top of a fresh mole-hill, I fell to my neck in the hole through which that animal had cast up the earth, and coined some lie, not worth remembering, to excuse myself for spoiling my clothes. I likewise broke my right shin against the shell of a snail, which I happened to stumble over, as I was walking alone, and thinking on poor England.

I cannot tell whether I were more pleased or mortified, to observe in those solitary walks, that the smaller birds did not appear to be at all afraid of me, but would hop about within a yard distance, looking for worms, and other food, with as much indifference and security, as if no creature at all were near them. I remember, a thrush had the confidence to snatch out of my hand, with his bill, a piece of cake that Glumdalclitch had just given me for my breakfast. When I attempted to catch any of these birds, they would boldly turn against me, endeavouring to pick my fingers, which I durst not venture within their reach; and then they would hop back unconcerned, to hunt for worms or snails, as they did before. But one day I took a thick cudgel, and threw it with all my strength so luckily at a linnet, that I knocked him down, and seizing him by the neck with both my hands, ran with him in triumph to my nurse. However, the bird, who had only been stunned, recovering himself, gave me so many boxes with his wings on both sides of my head and body, though I held him at arm's length, and was out of the reach of his claws, that I was twenty times thinking to let him go. But I was soon relieved by one of our servants, who wrung off the bird's neck, and I had him next day for dinner, by the Queen's command. This linnet, as near as I can remember, seemed to be somewhat larger than an English swan.

The Maids of Honour often invited Glumdalclitch to their apartments, and desired she would bring me along with her, on purpose to have the pleasure of seeing and touching me. They would often strip me naked from top to toe, and lay me at full length in their bosoms; wherewith I was much disgusted; because, to say the truth, a very offensive smell came from their skins; which I do not mention or intend to the disadvantage of those excellent ladies, for whom I have all manner of respect; but I conceive that my sense was more acute in proportion to my littleness, and that those illustrious persons were no more disagreeable to their lovers, or to each other, than people of the same quality are with us in England. And, after all, I found their natural smell was much more supportable than when they used perfumes, under which I immediately swooned away. I cannot forget that an intimate friend of mine in Lilliput took the freedom in a warm day, when I had used a good deal of exercise, to complain of a strong smell about me, although I am as little faulty that way as most of my sex: but I suppose his faculty of smelling was as nice with regard to me, as mine was to that of this people. Upon this point, I cannot forbear doing justice to the Queen my mistress, and Glumdalclitch my nurse, whose persons were as sweet as those of any lady in England.

That which gave me most uneasiness among these Maids of Honour (when my nurse carried me to visit them) was to see them use me without any manner of ceremony, like a creature who had no sort of consequence. For they would strip themselves to the skin, and put on their smocks in my presence, while I was placed on their toilet directly before their naked bodies, which, I am sure, to me was very far from being a tempting sight, or from giving me any other emotions than those of horror and disgust. Their skins appeared so coarse and uneven, so variously coloured, when I saw them near, with a mole here and there as broad as a trencher, and hairs hanging from it thicker than packthreads, to say nothing further concerning the rest of their persons. Neither did they at all scruple, while I was by, to discharge what they had drunk, to the quantity of at least two hogsheads, in a vessel that held above three tuns.

The handsomest among these Maids of Honour, a pleasant frolicsome girl of sixteen, would sometimes set me
astride upon one of her nipples, with many other tricks,
wherein the reader will excuse me for not being over
particular. But I was so much displeased, that I entreated Glumdalclitch to contrive some excuse for not
seeing that young lady any more.

One day a young gentleman, who was nephew to my
nurse's governess, came and pressed them both to see an
execution. It was of a man who had murdered one of
that gentleman's intimate acquaintance. Glumdalclitch
was prevailed on to be of the company, very much
against her inclination, for she was naturally tender-
hearted: and as for myself, although I abhorred such
kind of spectacles, yet my curiosity tempted me to see
something that I thought must be extraordinary. The
malefactor was fixed in a chair upon a scaffold erected
for the purpose, and his head cut off at a blow with a
sword of about forty foot long. The veins and arteries
spouted up such a prodigious quantity of blood, and so
high in the air, that the great *jet d'eau* at Versailles was
not equal for the time it lasted; and the head, when it
fell on the scaffold floor, gave such a bounce, as made
me start, although I were at least half an English mile
distant.

The Queen, who often used to hear me talk of my
sea-voyages, and took all occasions to divert me when I
was melancholy, asked me whether I understood how
to handle a sail, or an oar, and whether a little exercise
of rowing might not be convenient for my health. I answered, that I understood both very well: for although
my proper employment had been to be surgeon or doctor to the ship, yet often, upon a pinch, I was forced to
work like a common mariner. But I could not see how
this could be done in their country, where the smallest

wherry was equal to a first-rate man of war among us,
and such a boat as I could manage would never live in
any of their rivers. Her Majesty said, if I would contrive
a boat, her own joiner should make it, and she would
provide a place for me to sail in. The fellow was an ingenious workman, and, by my instructions, in ten days
finished a pleasure-boat, with all its tackling, able conveniently to hold eight Europeans. When it was finished,
the Queen was so delighted, that she ran with it in her
lap to the King, who ordered it to be put in a cistern
full of water, with me in it, by way of trial; where I
could not manage my two sculls, or little oars, for want
of room. But the Queen had before contrived another
project. She ordered the joiner to make a wooden trough
of three hundred foot long, fifty broad, and eight deep;
which being well pitched to prevent leaking, was placed
on the floor along the wall, in an outer room of the
palace. It had a cock near the bottom to let out the
water when it began to grow stale, and two servants
could easily fill it in half an hour. Here I often used to
row for my own diversion, as well as that of the Queen
and her ladies, who thought themselves well entertained
with my skill and agility. Sometimes I would put up
my sail, and then my business was only to steer, while
the ladies gave me a gale with their fans; and when they
were weary, some of the pages would blow my sail
forward with their breath, while I showed my art by
steering starboard or larboard as I pleased. When I had
done, Glumdalclitch always carried my boat into her
closet, and hung it on a nail to dry.

In this exercise I once met an accident which had like
to have cost me my life: for, one of the pages having
put my boat into the trough, the governess, who attended Glumdalclitch, very officiously lifted me up to
place me in the boat, but I happened to slip through her

fingers, and should have infallibly fallen down forty feet upon the floor, if by the luckiest chance in the world, I had not been stopped by a corking-pin that stuck in the good gentlewoman's stomacher; the head of the pin passed between my shirt and the waistband of my breeches, and thus I was held by the middle in the air till Glumdalclitch ran to my relief.

Another time, one of the servants, whose office it was to fill my trough every third day with fresh water, was so careless to let a huge frog (not perceiving it) slip out of his pail. The frog lay concealed till I was put into my boat, but then seeing a resting-place, climbed up, and made it lean so much on one side, that I was forced to balance it with all my weight on the other, to prevent overturning. When the frog was got in, it hopped at once half the length of the boat, and then over my head, backwards and forwards, daubing my face and clothes with its odious slime. The largeness of its features made it appear the most deformed animal that can be conceived. However, I desired Glumdalclitch to let me deal with it alone. I banged it a good while with one of my sculls, and at last forced it to leap out of the boat.

But the greatest danger I ever underwent in that kingdom, was from a monkey, who belonged to one of the clerks of the kitchen. Glumdalclitch had locked me up in her closet, while she went somewhere upon business, or a visit. The weather being very warm, the closet-window was left open, as well as the windows and the door of my bigger box, in which I usually lived, because of its largeness and conveniency. As I sat quietly meditating at my table, I heard something bounce in at the closet-window, and skip about from one side to the other; whereat, although I were much alarmed, yet I ventured to look out, but not stirring from my seat; and then I saw this frolicsome animal, frisking and leaping

up and down, till at last he came to my box, which he
seemed to view with great pleasure and curiosity, peeping in at the door and every window. I retreated to the
farther corner of my room, or box, but the monkey looking in at every side, put me into such a fright, that I
wanted presence of mind to conceal myself under the
bed, as I might easily have done. After some time spent
in peeping, grinning, and chattering, he at last espied
me, and reaching one of his paws in at the door, as a cat
does when she plays with a mouse, although I often
shifted place to avoid him, he at length seized the lappet
of my coat (which being made of that country silk, was
very thick and strong) and dragged me out. He took me
up in his right fore-foot, and held me as a nurse does a
child she is going to suckle, just as I have seen the same
sort of creature do with a kitten in Europe: and when
I offered to struggle, he squeezed me so hard, that I
thought it more prudent to submit. I have good reason
to believe that he took me for a young one of his own
species, by his often stroking my face very gently with
his other paw. In these diversions he was interrupted
by a noise at the closet door, as if somebody were opening it; whereupon he suddenly leaped up to the window, at which he had come in, and thence upon the
leads and gutters, walking upon three legs, and holding
me in the fourth, till he clambered up to a roof that was
next to ours. I heard Glumdalclitch give a shriek at the
moment he was carrying me out. The poor girl was almost distracted: that quarter of the palace was all in an
uproar; the servants ran for ladders; the monkey was
seen by hundreds in the court, sitting upon the ridge of
a building, holding me like a baby in one of his fore-
paws, and feeding me with the other, by cramming into
my mouth some victuals he had squeezed out of the bag
on one side of his chaps, and patting me when I would

not eat; whereat many of the rabble below could not forbear laughing; neither do I think they justly ought to be blamed, for without question the sight was ridiculous enough to every body but myself. Some of the people threw up stones, hoping to drive the monkey down; but this was strictly forbidden, or else very probably my brains had been dashed out.

The ladders were now applied, and mounted by several men, which the monkey observing, and finding himself almost encompassed; not being able to make speed enough with his three legs, let me drop on a ridge tile, and made his escape. Here I sat for some time, three hundred yards from the ground, expecting every moment to be blown down by the wind, or to fall by my own giddiness, and come tumbling over and over from the ridge to the eaves; but an honest lad, one of my nurse's footmen, climbed up, and putting me into his breeches pocket, brought me down safe.

I was almost choked with the filthy stuff the monkey had crammed down my throat: but my dear little nurse picked it out of my mouth with a small needle, and then I fell a vomiting, which gave me great relief. Yet I was so weak and bruised in the sides with the squeezes given ,me by this odious animal, that I was forced to keep my bed a fortnight. The King, Queen, and all the court, sent every day to enquire after my health, and her Majesty made me several visits during my sickness. The monkey was killed, and an order made that no such animal should be kept about the palace.

When I attended the King after my recovery, to return him thanks for his favours, he was pleased to rally me a good deal upon this adventure. He asked me what my thoughts and speculations were while I lay in the monkey's paw; how I liked the victuals he gave me; his manner of feeding; and whether the fresh air on the roof had sharpened my stomach. He desired to know what I would have done upon such an occasion in my own country. I told his Majesty, that in Europe we had no monkeys, except such as were brought for curiosities from other places, and so small, that I could deal with a dozen of them together, if they presumed to attack me. And as for that monstrous animal with whom I was so lately engaged (it was indeed as large as an elephant), if my fears had suffered me to think so far as to make use of my hanger (looking fiercely and clapping my hand upon the hilt as I spoke), when he poked his paw into my chamber, perhaps I should have given him such a wound, as would have made him glad to withdraw it with more haste than he put it in. This I delivered in a firm tone, like a person who was jealous lest his courage should be called in question. However, my speech produced nothing else besides a loud laughter, which all the respect due to his Majesty from those about him could not make them contain. This made me reflect how vain an attempt it is for a man to endeavour doing himself honour among those who are out of all degree of equality or comparison with him. And yet I have seen the moral of my own behaviour very frequent in England since my return, where a little contemptible varlet, without the least title to birth, person, wit, or common sense, shall presume to look with importance, and put himself upon a foot with the greatest persons of the kingdom.

I was every day furnishing the court with some ridiculous story: and Glumdalclitch, although she loved me to excess, yet was arch enough to inform the Queen, whenever I committed any folly that she thought would be diverting to her Majesty. The girl, who had been out of order, was carried by her governess to take the air about an hour's distance, or thirty miles from town. They

alighted out of the coach near a small foot-path in a
field, and Glumdalclitch setting down my travelling-box,
I went out of it to walk. There was a cow-dung in the
path, and I must needs try my activity by attempting to
leap over it. I took a run, but unfortunately jumped
short, and found myself just in the middle up to my
knees. I waded through with some difficulty, and one
of the footmen wiped me as clean as he could with his
handkerchief; for I was filthily bemired, and my nurse
confined me to my box till we returned home; where the
Queen was soon informed of what had passed, and the
footmen spread it about the court: so that all the mirth,
for some days, was at my expense.

CHAP. VI

*Several contrivances of the Author to please the King and
Queen. He shows his skill in music. The King enquires
into the state of Europe, which the Author relates to him.
The King's observations thereon.*

I used to attend the King's levee once or twice a week,
and had often seen him under the barber's hand, which
indeed was at first very terrible to behold: for the razor
was almost twice as long as an ordinary scythe. His
Majesty, according to the custom of the country, was
only shaved twice a week. I once prevailed on the barber to give me some of the suds or lather, out of which
I picked forty or fifty of the strongest stumps of hair.
I then took a piece of fine wood, and cut it like the
back of a comb, making several holes in it at equal distance with as small a needle as I could get from Glumdalclitch. I fixed in the stumps so artificially, scraping
and sloping them with my knife toward the points, that
I made a very tolerable comb; which was a seasonable

supply, my own being so much broken in the teeth, that it was almost useless: neither did I know any artist in that country so nice and exact, as would undertake to make me another.

And this puts me in mind of an amusement wherein I spent many of my leisure hours. I desired the Queen's woman to save for me the combings of her Majesty's hair, whereof in time I got a good quantity, and consulting with my friend the cabinet-maker, who had received general orders to do little jobs for me, I directed him to make two chair-frames, no larger than those I had in my box, and then to bore little holes with a fine awl round those parts where I designed the backs and seats; through these holes I wove the strongest hairs I could pick out, just after the manner of cane-chairs in England. When they were finished, I made a present of them to her Majesty, who kept them in her cabinet, and used to show them for curiosities, as indeed they were the wonder of every one that beheld them. The Queen would have had me sit upon one of these chairs, but I absolutely refused to obey her, protesting I would rather die a thousand deaths than place a dishonourable part of my body on those precious hairs that once adorned her Majesty's head. Of these hairs (as I had always a mechanical genius) I likewise made a neat little purse about five foot long, with her Majesty's name deciphered in gold letters, which I gave to Glumdalclitch, by the Queen's consent. To say the truth, it was more for show than use, being not of strength to bear the weight of the larger coins, and therefore she kept nothing in it but some little toys that girls are fond of.

The King, who delighted in music, had frequent concerts at court, to which I was sometimes carried, and set in my box on a table to hear them: but the noise was so great, that I could hardly distinguish the tunes. I am confident that all the drums and trumpets of a royal army, beating and sounding together just at your ears, could not equal it. My practice was to have my box removed from the places where the performers sat, as far as I could, then to shut the doors and windows of it, and draw the window curtains; after which I found their music not disagreeable.

I had learned in my youth to play a little upon the spinet. Glumdalclitch kept one in her chamber, and a master attended twice a week to teach her: I call it a spinet, because it somewhat resembled that instrument, and was played upon in the same manner. A fancy came into my head that I would entertain the King and Queen with an English tune upon this instrument. But this appeared extremely difficult: for the spinet was near sixty foot long, each key being almost a foot wide, so that, with my arms extended, I could not reach to above five keys, and to press them down required a good smart stroke with my fist, which would be too great a labour, and to no purpose. The method I contrived was this. I prepared two round sticks about the bigness of common cudgels; they were thicker at one end than the other, and I covered the thicker ends with a piece of a mouse's skin, that by rapping on them I might neither damage the tops of the keys, nor interrupt the sound. Before the spinet a bench was placed, about four foot below the keys, and I was put upon the bench. I ran sideling upon it that way and this, as fast as I could, banging the proper keys with my two sticks, and made a shift to play a jig, to the great satisfaction of both their Majesties: but it was the most violent exercise I ever underwent, and yet I could not strike above sixteen keys, nor, consequently, play the bass and treble together, as other artists do; which was a great disadvantage to my performance.

The King, who, as I before observed, was a prince of excellent understanding, would frequently order that I should be brought in my box, and set upon the table in his closet. He would then command me to bring one of my chairs out of the box, and sit down within three yards distance upon the top of the cabinet, which brought me almost to a level with his face. In this manner I had several conversations with him. I one day took the freedom to tell his Majesty, that the contempt he discovered towards Europe, and the rest of the world, did not seem answerable to those excellent qualities of the mind he was master of. That reason did not extend itself with the bulk of the body: on the contrary, we observed in our country, that the tallest persons were usually least provided with it. That among other animals, bees and ants had the reputation of more industry, art and sagacity, than many of the larger kinds. And that, as inconsiderable as he took me to be, I hoped I might live to do his Majesty some signal service. The King heard me with attention, and began to conceive a much better opinion of me than he had ever before. He desired I would give him as exact an account of the government of England as I possibly could; because, as fond as princes commonly are of their own customs (for so he conjectured of other monarchs, by my former discourses), he should be glad to hear of any thing that might deserve imitation.

Imagine with thyself, courteous reader, how often I then wished for the tongue of Demosthenes or Cicero, that might have enabled me to celebrate the praise of my own dear native country in a style equal to its merits and felicity.

I began my discourse by informing his Majesty, that our dominions consisted of two islands, which composed three mighty kingdoms under one sovereign, beside our plantations in America. I dwelt long upon the fertility of our soil, and the temperature of our climate. I then spoke at large upon the constitution of an English Parliament, partly made up of an illustrious body called the House of Peers, persons of the noblest blood, and of the most ancient and ample patrimonies. I described that extraordinary care always taken of their education in arts and arms, to qualify them for being counsellors born to the king and kingdom; to have a share in the legislature; to be members of the highest Court of Judicature, from whence there could be no appeal; and to be champions always ready for the defence of their prince and country, by their valour, conduct, and fidelity. That these were the ornament and bulwark of the kingdom, worthy followers of their most renowned ancestors, whose honour had been the reward of their virtue, from which their posterity were never once known to degenerate. To these were joined several holy persons, as part of that assembly, under the title of Bishops, whose peculiar business it is to take care of religion, and of those who instruct the people therein. These were searched and sought out through the whole nation, by the prince and his wisest counsellors, among such of the priesthood as were most deservedly distinguished by the sanctity of their lives, and the depth of their erudition; who were indeed the spiritual fathers of the clergy and the people.

That the other part of the Parliament consisted of an assembly called the House of Commons, who were all principal gentlemen, freely picked and culled out by the people themselves, for their great abilities and love of their country, to represent the wisdom of the whole nation. And these two bodies make up the most august assembly in Europe, to whom, in conjunction with the prince, the whole legislature is committed.

I then descended to the Courts of Justice, over which the Judges, those venerable sages and interpreters of the law, presided, for determining the disputed rights and properties of men, as well as for the punishment of vice, and protection of innocence. I mentioned the prudent management of our treasury; the valour and achievements of our forces by sea and land. I computed the number of our people, by reckoning how many millions there might be of each religious sect, or political party among us. I did not omit even our sports and pastimes, or any other particular which I thought might redound to the honour of my country. And I finished all with a brief historical account of affairs and events in England for about an hundred years past.

This conversation was not ended under five audiences, each of several hours, and the King heard the whole with great attention, frequently taking notes of what I spoke, as well as memorandums of what questions he intended to ask me.

When I had put an end to these long discourses, his Majesty in a sixth audience consulting his notes, proposed many doubts, queries, and objections, upon every article. He asked what methods were used to cultivate the minds and bodies of our young nobility, and in what kind of business they commonly spent the first and teachable part of their lives. What course was taken to supply that assembly when any noble family became extinct. What qualifications were necessary in those who are to be created new lords: whether the humour of the prince, a sum of money to a court lady, or a prime minister, or a design of strengthening a party opposite to the public interest, ever happened to be motives in those advancements. What share of knowledge these lords had in the laws of their country, and how they came by it, so as to enable them to decide the properties of their fellow-subjects in the last resort. Whether they were always so free from avarice, partialities, or want, that a bribe, or some other sinister view, could have no place among them. Whether those holy lords I spoke of were always promoted to that rank upon account of their knowledge in religious matters, and the sanctity of their lives, had never been compliers with the times, while they were common priests, or slavish prostitute chaplains to some nobleman, whose opinions they continued servilely to follow after they were admitted into that assembly.

He then desired to know what arts were practised in electing those whom I called commoners: whether a stranger with a strong purse might not influence the vulgar voters to choose him before their own landlord, or the most considerable gentleman in the neighbourhood. How it came to pass, that people were so violently bent upon getting into this assembly, which I allowed to be a great trouble and expense, often to the ruin of their families, without any salary or pension: because this appeared such an exalted strain of virtue and public spirit, that his Majesty seemed to doubt it might possibly not be always sincere: and he desired to know whether such zealous gentlemen could have any views of refunding themselves for the charges and trouble they were at, by sacrificing the public good to the designs of a weak and vicious prince in conjunction with a corrupted ministry. He multiplied his questions, and sifted me thoroughly upon every part of this head, proposing numberless enquiries and objections, which I think it not prudent or convenient to repeat.

Upon what I said in relation to our Courts of Justice, his Majesty desired to be satisfied in several points: and this I was the better able to do, having been formerly almost ruined by a long suit in chancery, which was decreed for me with costs. He asked, what time was usually spent in determining between right and wrong, and what degree of expense. Whether advocates and orators had liberty to plead in causes manifestly known to be unjust, vexatious, or oppressive. Whether party in religion or politics were observed to be of any weight in the scale of justice. Whether those pleading orators were persons educated in the general knowledge of equity, or only in provincial, national, and other local customs. Whether they or their judges had any part in penning those laws which they assumed the liberty of interpreting and glossing upon at their pleasure. Whether they had ever at different times pleaded for and against the same cause, and cited precedents to prove contrary opinions. Whether they were a rich or a poor corporation. Whether they received any pecuniary reward for pleading or delivering their opinions. And particularly, whether they were ever admitted as members in the lower senate.

He fell next upon the management of our treasury; and said, he thought my memory had failed me, because I computed our taxes at about five or six millions a year, and when I came to mention the issues, he found they sometimes amounted to more than double; for the notes he had taken were very particular in this point, because he hoped, as he told me, that the knowledge of our conduct might be useful to him, and he could not be deceived in his calculations. But, if what I told him were true, he was still at a loss how a kingdom could run out of its estate like a private person. He asked me, who were our creditors; and where we should find money to pay them. He wondered to hear me talk of such chargeable and expensive wars; that certainly we must be a quarrelsome people, or live among very bad neighbours, and that our generals must needs be richer than our kings. He asked what business we had out of our own islands, unless upon the score of trade or treaty, or to defend the coasts with our fleet. Above all, he was amazed to hear me talk of a mercenary standing army in the midst of peace, and among a free people. He said, if we were governed by our own consent in the persons of our representatives, he could not imagine of whom we were afraid, or against whom we were to fight; and would hear my opinion, whether a private man's house might not better be defended by himself, his children, and family, than by half a dozen rascals picked up at a venture in the streets, for small wages, who might get an hundred times more by cutting their throats.

He laughed at my odd kind of arithmetic (as he was pleased to call it) in reckoning the numbers of our people by a computation drawn from the several sects among us in religion and politics. He said, he knew no reason, why those who entertain opinions prejudicial to the public, should be obliged to change, or should not be obliged to conceal them. And as it was tyranny in any government to require the first, so it was weakness not to enforce the second: for a man may be allowed to keep poisons in his closet, but not to vend them about for cordials.

He observed, that among the diversions of our nobility and gentry, I had mentioned gaming. He desired to know at what age this entertainment was usually taken up, and when it was laid down; how much of their time it employed; whether it ever went so high as to affect their fortunes; whether mean vicious people, by their dexterity in that art, might not arrive at great riches, and sometimes keep our very nobles in dependence, as well as habituate them to vile companions, wholly take them from the improvement of their minds, and force them, by the losses they have received, to learn and practise that infamous dexterity upon others.

He was perfectly astonished with the historical account I gave him of our affairs during the last century, protesting it was only an heap of conspiracies, rebellions, murders, massacres, revolutions, banishments, the very worst effects that avarice, faction, hypocrisy, perfidiousness, cruelty, rage, madness, hatred, envy, lust, malice, or ambition, could produce.

His Majesty, in another audience, was at the pains to recapitulate the sum of all I had spoken; compared the questions he made with the answers I had given; then taking me into his hands, and stroking me gently, delivered himself in these words, which I shall never forget, nor the manner he spoke them in: My little friend Grildrig, you have made a most admirable panegyric upon your country; you have clearly proved that ignorance, idleness, and vice, are the proper ingredients for qualifying a legislator: that laws are best explained, interpreted, and applied by those whose interest and abilities lie in perverting, confounding, and eluding them. I observe among you some lines of an institution, which in its original might have been tolerable, but these half erased, and the rest wholly blurred and blotted by corruptions. It doth not appear from all you have said, how any one virtue is required towards the procurement of any one station among you; much less that men are ennobled on account of their virtue, that priests are advanced for their piety or learning, soldiers for their conduct or valour, judges for their integrity, senators for the love of their country, or counsellors for their wisdom. As for yourself (continued the King), who have spent the greatest part of your life in travelling, I am well disposed to hope you may hitherto have escaped many vices of your country. But by what I have gathered from your own relation, and the answers I have with much pains wringed and extorted from you, I cannot but conclude the bulk of your natives to be the most pernicious race of little odious vermin that nature ever suffered to crawl upon the surface of the earth.

CHAP. VII

The Author's love of his country. He makes a proposal of much advantage to the King, which is rejected. The King's great ignorance in politics. The learning of that country very imperfect and confined. Their laws, and military affairs, and parties in the State.

Nothing but an extreme love of truth could have hindered me from concealing this part of my story. It was in vain to discover my resentments, which were always turned into ridicule; and I was forced to rest with patience while my noble and most beloved country was so injuriously treated. I am heartily sorry as any of my readers can possibly be, that such an occasion was given: but this prince happened to be so curious and inquisitive upon every particular, that it could not consist either with gratitude or good manners to refuse giving him what satisfaction I was able. Yet thus much I may be allowed to say in my own vindication, that I artfully eluded many of his questions, and gave to every point a more favourable turn by many degrees than the strictness of truth would allow. For I have always borne that laudable partiality to my own country, which Dionysius Halicarnassensis with so much justice recommends to an historian: I would hide the frailties and deformities of my political mother, and place her virtues and beauties in the most advantageous light. This was my sincere endeavour in those many discourses I had with that mighty monarch, although it unfortunately failed of success.

But great allowances should be given to a King who lives wholly secluded from the rest of the world, and must therefore be altogether unacquainted with the manners and customs that most prevail in other nations: the want of which knowledge will ever produce many prejudices, and a certain narrowness of thinking, from which we and the politer countries of Europe are wholly exempted. And it would be hard indeed, if so remote a prince's notions of virtue and vice were to be offered as a standard for all mankind.

To confirm what I have now said, and further, to show the miserable effects of a confined education, I shall here insert a passage which will hardly obtain belief. In hopes to ingratiate myself farther into his Majesty's favour, I told him of an invention discovered between three and four hundred years ago, to make a certain powder, into an heap of which the smallest spark of fire falling, would kindle the whole in a moment, although it were as big as a mountain, and make it all fly up in the air together, with a noise and agitation greater than thunder. That a proper quantity of this powder rammed into an hollow tube of brass or iron, according to its bigness, would drive a ball of iron or lead with such violence and speed, as nothing was able to sustain its force. That the largest balls thus discharged, would not only destroy whole ranks of an army at once, but batter the strongest walls to the ground, sink down ships, with a thousand men in each, to the bottom of the sea; and, when linked together by a chain, would cut through masts and rigging, divide hundreds of bodies in the middle, and lay all waste before them. That we often put this powder into large hollow balls of iron, and discharged them by an engine into some city we were besieging, which would rip up the pavements, tear the houses to pieces, burst and throw splinters on every side, dashing out the brains of all who came near. That I knew the ingredients very well, which were cheap, and common; I understood the manner of compounding them, and could direct his workmen how to make those tubes, of a size proportionable to all other things in his Majesty's kingdom, and the largest need not be above an hundred foot long; twenty or thirty of which tubes, charged with the proper quantity of powder and balls, would batter down the walls of the strongest town in his dominions in a few hours, or destroy the whole metropolis, if ever it should pretend to dispute his absolute commands. This I humbly offered to his Majesty, as a small tribute of acknowledgment in return of so many marks that I had received of his royal favour and protection.

The King was struck with horror at the description I had given of those terrible engines, and the proposal I had made. He was amazed how so impotent and grovelling an insect as I (these were his expressions) could maintain such inhuman ideas, and in so familiar a manner as to appear wholly unmoved at all the scenes of blood and desolation, which I had painted as the common effects of those destructive machines, whereof he said, some evil genius, enemy to mankind, must have been the first contriver. As for himself, he protested, that although few things delighted him so much as new discoveries in art or in nature, yet he would rather lose half his kingdom than be privy to such a secret, which he commanded me, as I valued my life, never to mention any more.

A strange effect of narrow principles and short views! that a prince possessed of every quality which procures veneration, love, and esteem; of strong parts, great wisdom, and profound learning, endued with admirable talents for government, and almost adored by his subjects, should from a nice unnecessary scruple, whereof in Europe we can have no conception, let slip an opportunity put into his hands, that would have made him absolute master of the lives, the liberties, and the fortunes of his people. Neither do I say this with the least intention to detract from the many virtues of that excellent King, whose character I am sensible will on this account be very much lessened in the opinion of an English reader: but I take this defect among them to have risen from their ignorance, they not having hitherto reduced politics into a science, as the more acute wits of Europe have done. For, I remember very well, in a discourse one day with the King, when I happened to say there were several thousand books among us written upon the art of government, it gave him (directly contrary to my intention) a very mean opinion of our understandings. He professed both to abominate and despise all mystery, refinement, and intrigue, either in a prince or a minister. He could not tell what I meant by secrets of state, where an enemy or some rival nation were not in the case. He confined the knowledge of governing within very narrow bounds; to common sense and reason, to justice and lenity, to the speedy determination of civil and criminal causes; with some other obvious topics, which are not worth considering. And he gave it for his opinion, that whoever could make two ears of corn, or two blades of grass to grow upon a spot of ground where only one grew before, would deserve better of mankind, and do more essential service to his country, than the whole race of politicians put together.

The learning of this people is very defective, consisting only in morality, history, poetry, and mathematics, wherein they must be allowed to excel. But the last of these is wholly applied to what may be useful in life, to the improvement of agriculture, and all mechanical arts; so that among us it would be little esteemed. And as to ideas, entities, abstractions, and transcendentals, I could never drive the least conception into their heads.

No law of that country must exceed in words the number of letters in their alphabet, which consists only in two and twenty. But, indeed, few of them extend even to that length. They are expressed in the most plain and simple terms, wherein those people are not mercurial enough to discover above one interpretation: and to write a comment upon any law is a capital crime. As to the decision of civil causes, or proceedings against criminals, their precedents are so few, that they have little reason to boast of any extraordinary skill in either.

They have had the art of printing, as well as the Chinese, time out of mind: but their libraries are not very large; for that of the King's, which is reckoned the biggest, doth not amount to above a thousand volumes, placed in a gallery of twelve hundred foot long, from whence I had liberty to borrow what books I pleased. The Queen's joiner had contrived in one of Glumdal-clitch's rooms a kind of wooden machine five and twenty foot high, formed like a standing ladder; the steps were each fifty foot long. It was indeed a moveable pair of stairs, the lowest end placed at ten foot distance from the wall of the chamber. The book I had a mind to read was put up leaning against the wall. I first mounted to the upper step of the ladder, and turning my face towards the book, began at the top of the page, and so walking to the right and left about eight or ten paces, according to the length of the lines, till I had gotten a little below the level of my eyes, and then descending gradually till I came to the bottom: after which I mounted again, and began the other page in the same manner, and so turned over the leaf, which I could easily do with both my hands, for it was as thick and stiff as a pasteboard, and in the largest folios not above eighteen or twenty foot long.

Their style is clear, masculine, and smooth, but not florid, for they avoid nothing more than multiplying unnecessary words, or using various expressions. I have perused many of their books, especially those in history and morality. Among the rest, I was much diverted with a little old treatise, which always lay in Glumdalclitch's bed-chamber, and belonged to her governess, a grave elderly gentlewoman, who dealt in writings of morality and devotion. The book treats of the weakness of human kind, and is in little esteem, except among the women and the vulgar. However, I was curious to see what an author of that country could say upon such a subject. This writer went through all the usual topics of European moralists, showing how diminutive, contemptible, and helpless an animal was man in his own nature; how unable to defend himself from the inclemencies of the air, or the fury of wild beasts: how much he was excelled by one creature in strength, by another in speed, by a third in foresight, by a fourth in industry. He added, that nature was degenerated in these latter declining ages of the world, and could now produce only small abortive births in comparison of those in ancient times. He said, it was very reasonable to think, not only that the species of men were originally much larger, but also, that there must have been giants in former ages, which, as it is asserted by history and tradition, so it hath been confirmed by huge bones and skulls casually dug up in several parts of the kingdom, far exceeding the common dwindled race of man in our days. He argued, that the very laws of nature absolutely required we should have

been made in the beginning, of a size more large and
robust, not so liable to destruction from every little accident of a tile falling from a house, or a stone cast from
the hand of a boy, or of being drowned in a little brook.
From this way of reasoning the author drew several
moral applications useful in the conduct of life, but
needless here to repeat. For my own part, I could not
avoid reflecting how universally this talent was spread,
of drawing lectures in morality, or indeed rather matter
of discontent and repining, from the quarrels we raise
with nature. And I believe, upon a strict enquiry, those
quarrels might be shown as ill grounded among us, as
they are among that people.

As to their military affairs, they boast that the King's
army consists of an hundred and seventy-six thousand
foot, and thirty-two thousand horse: if that may be
called an army which is made up of tradesmen in the
several cities, and farmers in the country, whose com-
manders are only the nobility and gentry, without pay
or reward. They are indeed perfect enough in their
exercises, and under very good discipline, wherein I saw
no great merit; for how should it be otherwise, where
every farmer is under the command of his own landlord,
and every citizen under that of the principal men in his
own city, chosen after the manner of Venice by ballot?

I have often seen the militia of Lorbrulgrud drawn
out to exercise in a great field near the city of twenty
miles square. They were in all not above twenty-five
thousand foot, and six thousand horse; but it was impossible for me to compute their number, considering
the space of ground they took up. A cavalier mounted
on a large steed, might be about an hundred foot high.
I have seen this whole body of horse, upon a word of
command, draw their swords at once, and brandish
them in the air. Imagination can figure nothing so

grand, so surprising, and so astonishing! It looked as if ten thousand flashes of lightning were darting at the same time from every quarter of the sky.

I was curious to know how this prince, to whose dominions there is no access from any other country, came to think of armies, or to teach his people the practice of military discipline. But I was soon informed, both by conversation, and reading their histories. For, in the course of many ages they have been troubled with the same disease to which the whole race of mankind is subject; the nobility often contending for power, the people for liberty, and the King for absolute dominion. All which, however happily tempered by the laws of that kingdom, have been sometimes violated by each of the three parties, and have once or more occasioned civil wars, the last whereof was happily put an end to by this prince's grandfather by a general composition; and the militia, then settled with common consent, hath been ever since kept in the strictest duty.

CHAP. VIII

The King and Queen make a progress to the frontiers. The Author attends them. The manner in which he leaves the country very particularly related. He returns to England.

I had always a strong impulse that I should some time recover my liberty, though it was impossible to conjecture by what means, or to form any project with the least hope of succeeding. The ship in which I sailed was the first ever known to be driven within sight of that coast, and the King had given strict orders, that if at any time another appeared, it should be taken ashore, and with all its crew and passengers brought in a tum-

bril to Lorbrulgrud. He was strongly bent to get me
a women of my own size, by whom I might propagate
the breed: but I think I should rather have died than
undergone the disgrace of leaving a posterity to be kept
in cages like tame canary birds, and perhaps, in time,
sold about the kingdom to persons of quality for curiosities. I was, indeed, treated with much kindness: I
was the favourite of a great King and Queen, and the
delight of the whole court, but it was upon such a foot
as ill became the dignity of human kind. I could never
forget those domestic pledges I had left behind me. I
wanted to be among people with whom I could converse
upon even terms, and walk about the streets and fields
without fear of being trod to death like a frog or a young
puppy. But my deliverance came sooner than I expected, and in a manner not very common: the whole
story and circumstances of which I shall faithfully relate.

I had now been two years in this country; and about
the beginning of the third, Glumdalclitch and I attended
the King and Queen in a progress to the south coast of
the kingdom. I was carried, as usual, in my travelling-
box, which, as I have already described, was a very convenient closet of twelve foot wide. And I had ordered a
hammock to be fixed by silken ropes from the four corners at the top, to break the jolts, when a servant carried
me before him on horseback, as I sometimes desired,
and would often sleep in my hammock while we were
upon the road. On the roof of my closet, just over the
middle of the hammock, I ordered the joiner to cut out
a hole of a foot square, to give me air in hot weather, as
I slept; which hole I shut at pleasure with a board that
drew backwards and forwards through a groove.

When we came to our journey's end, the King thought
proper to pass a few days at a palace he hath near Flan-

flasnic, a city within eighteen English miles of the sea-side. Glumdalclitch and I were much fatigued; I had gotten a small cold, but the poor girl was so ill as to be confined to her chamber. I longed to see the ocean, which must be the only scene of my escape, if ever it should happen. I pretended to be worse than I really was, and desired leave to take the fresh air of the sea, with a page whom I was very fond of, and who had sometimes been trusted with me. I shall never forget with what unwillingness Glumdalclitch consented, nor the strict charge she gave the page to be careful of me, bursting at the same time into a flood of tears, as if she had some foreboding of what was to happen. The boy took me out in my box about half an hour's walk from the palace, towards the rocks on the sea-shore. I ordered him to set me down, and lifting up one of my sashes, cast many a wistful melancholy look towards the sea. I found myself not very well, and told the page that I had a mind to take a nap in my hammock, which I hoped would do me good. I got in, and the boy shut the window close down to keep out the cold. I soon fell asleep, and all I can conjecture is, that while I slept, the page, thinking no danger could happen, went among the rocks to look for birds' eggs, having before observed him from my window searching about, and picking up one or two in the clefts. Be that as it will, I found myself suddenly awaked with a violent pull upon the ring which was fastened at the top of my box for the con-veniency of carriage. I felt my box raised very high in the air, and then borne forward with prodigious speed. The first jolt had like to have shaken me out of my ham-mock, but afterwards the motion was easy enough. I called out several times, as loud as I could raise my voice, but all to no purpose. I looked towards my win-dows, and could see nothing but the clouds and sky.

I heard a noise just over my head like the clapping of wings, and then began to perceive the woful condition I was in; that some eagle had got the ring of my box in his beak, with an intent to let it fall on a rock like a tortoise in a shell, and then pick out my body, and devour it. For the sagacity and smell of this bird enable him to discover his quarry at a great distance, though better concealed than I could be within a two-inch board.

In a little time I observed the noise and flutter of wings to increase very fast, and my box was tossed up and down, like a sign-post in a windy day. I heard several bangs or buffets, as I thought, given to the eagle (for such I am certain it must have been that held the ring of my box in his beak), and then all on a sudden felt myself falling perpendicularly down for above a minute, but with such incredible swiftness that I almost lost my breath. My fall was stopped by a terrible squash, that sounded louder to my ears than the cataract of Niagara; after which I was quite in the dark for another minute, and then my box began to rise so high that I could see light from the tops of my windows. I now perceived that I was fallen into the sea. My box, by the weight of my body, the goods that were in, and the broad plates of iron fixed for strength at the four corners of the top and bottom, floated about five foot deep in water. I did then, and do now suppose that the eagle which flew away with my box was pursued by two or three others, and forced to let me drop while he was defending himself against the rest, who hoped to share in the prey. The plates of iron fastened at the bottom of the box (for those were the strongest) preserved the balance while it fell, and hindered it from being broken on the surface of the water. Every joint of it was well grooved, and the door did not move on hinges, but up and down like a sash, which kept my closet so tight that very little water came in. I got with much difficulty out of my hammock, having first ventured to draw back the slip-board on the roof already mentioned, contrived on purpose to let in air, for want of which I found myself almost stifled.

How often did I then wish myself with my dear Glumdalclitch, from whom one single hour had so far divided me! And I may say with truth, that in the midst of my own misfortunes I could not forbear lamenting my poor nurse, the grief she would suffer for my loss, the displeasure of the Queen, and the ruin of her fortune. Perhaps many travellers have not been under greater difficulties and distress than I was at this juncture, expecting every moment to see my box dashed in pieces, or at least overset by the first violent blast, or a rising wave. A breach in one single pane of glass would have been immediate death: nor could any thing have preserved the windows, but the strong lattice wires placed on the outside against accidents in travelling. I saw the water ooze in at several crannies, although the leaks were not considerable, and I endeavoured to stop them as well as I could. I was not able to lift up the roof of my closet, which otherwise I certainly should have done, and sat on the top of it, where I might at least preserve myself some hours longer than by being shut up, as I may call it, in the hold. Or, if I escaped these dangers for a day or two, what could I expect but a miserable death of cold and hunger! I was four hours under these circumstances, expecting and indeed wishing every moment to be my last.

I have already told the reader, that there were two strong staples fixed upon that side of my box which had no window, and into which the servant who used to carry me on horseback would put a leathern belt, and buckle it about his waist. Being in this disconsolate state, I heard or at least thought I heard some kind of grating noise on that side of my box where the staples were fixed, and soon after I began to fancy that the box was pulled or towed along in the sea; for I now and then felt a sort of tugging, which made the waves rise near the tops of my windows, leaving me almost in the dark. This gave me some faint hopes of relief, although I was not able to imagine how it could be brought about. I ventured to unscrew one of my chairs, which were always fastened to the floor; and having made a hard shift to screw it down again directly under the slipping-board that I had lately opened, I mounted on the chair, and putting my mouth as near as I could to the hole, I called for help in a loud voice, and in all the languages I understood. I then fastened my handkerchief to a stick I usually carried, and thrusting it up the hole, waved it several times in the air, that if any boat or ship were near, the seamen might conjecture some unhappy mortal to be shut up in the box.

I found no effect from all I could do, but plainly perceived my closet to be moved along; and in the space of an hour, or better, that side of the box where the staples were, and had no window, struck against something that was hard. I apprehended it to be a rock, and found myself tossed more than ever. I plainly heard a noise upon the cover of my closet, like that of a cable, and the grating of it as it passed through the ring. I then found myself hoisted up by degrees at least three foot higher than I was before. Whereupon I again thrust up my stick and handkerchief, calling for help till I was almost hoarse. In return to which, I heard a great shout repeated three times, giving me such transports of joy, as are not to be conceived but by those who feel them. I now heard a trampling over my head, and somebody calling through the hole with a loud voice in the English tongue, If there be any body below, let them speak. I answered, I was an Englishman, drawn by ill fortune into the greatest calamity that ever any creature underwent, and begged, by all that was moving, to be delivered out of the dungeon I was in. The voice replied, I was safe, for my box was fastened to their ship; and the carpenter should immediately come and saw an hole in the cover, large enough to pull me out. I answered, that was needless, and would take up too much time, for there was no more to be done, but let one of the crew put his finger into the ring, and take the box out of the sea into the ship, and so into the captain's cabin. Some of them upon hearing me talk so wildly thought I was mad; others laughed; for indeed it never came into my head that I was now got among people of my own stature and strength. The carpenter came, and in a few minutes sawed a passage about four foot square, then let down a small ladder, upon which I mounted, and from thence was taken into the ship in a very weak condition.

The sailors were all in amazement, and asked me a thousand questions, which I had no inclination to answer. I was equally confounded at the sight of so many pigmies, for such I took them to be, after having so long accustomed my eyes to the monstrous objects I had left. But the Captain, Mr. Thomas Wilcocks, an honest worthy Shropshire man, observing I was ready to faint, took me into his cabin, gave me a cordial to comfort me, and made me turn in upon his own bed, advising me to take a little rest of which I had great need. Before I went to sleep, I gave him to understand that I had some valuable furniture in my box, too good to be lost; a fine hammock, an handsome field-bed, two chairs, a table, and a cabinet: that my closet was hung on all sides, or rather quilted, with silk and cotton: that if he would let one of the crew bring my closet into his cabin, I would open it there before him, and show him my goods. The Captain hearing me utter these absurdities, concluded I was raving: however (I suppose to pacify me), he promised to give order as I desired, and going upon deck sent some of his men down into my closet, from whence (as I afterwards found) they drew up all my goods, and stripped off the quilting; but the chairs, cabinet, and bedstead, being screwed to the floor, were much damaged by the ignorance of the seamen, who tore them up by force. Then they knocked off some of the boards for the use of the ship, and when they had got all they had a mind for, let the hull drop into the sea, which by reason of many breaches made in the bottom and sides, sunk to rights. And indeed I was glad not to have been a spectator of the havoc they made; because I am confident it would have sensibly touched me, by bringing former passages into my mind, which I had rather forget.

I slept some hours, but perpetually disturbed with dreams of the place I had left, and the dangers I had escaped. However, upon waking I found myself much recovered. It was now about eight o'clock at night, and the Captain ordered supper immediately, thinking I had already fasted too long. He entertained me with great kindness, observing me not to look wildly, or talk inconsistently: and when we were left alone, desired I would give him a relation of my travels, and by what accident I came to be set adrift in that monstrous wooden chest. He said, that about twelve o'clock at noon, as he was looking through his glass, he spied it at a distance, and thought it was a sail, which he had a mind to make, being not much out of his course, in hopes of buying some biscuit, his own beginning to fall short. That upon

coming nearer, and finding his error, he sent out his
long-boat to discover what I was; that his men came
back in a fright, swearing they had seen a swimming
house. That he laughed at their folly, and went himself
in the boat, ordering his men to take a strong cable
along with them. That the weather being calm, he
rowed round me several times, observed my windows,
and the wire lattices that defended them. That he discovered two staples upon one side, which was all of
boards, without any passage for light. He then commanded his men to row up to that side, and fastening a
cable to one of the staples, ordered them to tow my
chest (as he called it) towards the ship. When it was
there, he gave directions to fasten another cable to the
ring fixed in the cover, and to raise up my chest with
pulleys, which all the sailors were not able to do above
two or three foot. He said, they saw my stick and handkerchief thrust out of the hole, and concluded that some
unhappy man must be shut up in the cavity. I asked
whether he or the crew had seen any prodigious birds
in the air about the time he first discovered me. To
which he answered, that discoursing this matter with the
sailors while I was asleep, one of them said he had observed three eagles flying towards the north, but re-
marked nothing of their being larger than the usual size,
which I suppose must be imputed to the great height
they were at; and he could not guess the reason of my
question. I then asked the Captain how far he reckoned
we might be from land; he said, by the best computation
he could make, we were at least an hundred leagues. I
assured him, that he must be mistaken by almost half,
for I had not left the country from whence I came above
two hours before I dropt into the sea. Whereupon he
began again to think that my brain was disturbed, of
which he gave me a hint, and advised me to go to bed

in a cabin he had provided. I assured him I was well refreshed with his good entertainment and company, and as much in my senses as ever I was in my life. He then grew serious, and desired to ask me freely whether I were not troubled in mind by the consciousness of some enormous crime, for which I was punished at the command of some prince, by exposing me in that chest, as great criminals in other countries have been forced to sea in a leaky vessel without provisions: for, although he should be sorry to have taken so ill a man into his ship, yet he would engage his word to set me safe on shore in the first port where we arrived. He added, that his suspicions were much increased by some very absurd speeches I had delivered at first to the sailors, and afterwards to himself, in relation to my closet or chest, as well as by my odd looks and behaviour while I was at supper.

I begged his patience to hear me tell my story, which I faithfully did from the last time I left England to the moment he first discovered me. And, as truth always forceth its way into rational minds, so this honest worthy gentleman, who had some tincture of learning, and very good sense, was immediately convinced of my candour and veracity. But further to confirm all I had said, I entreated him to give order that my cabinet should be brought, of which I had the key in my pocket (for he had already informed me how the seamen disposed of my closet). I opened it in his presence, and showed him the small collection of rarities I made in the country from whence I had been so strangely delivered. There was the comb I had contrived out of the stumps of the King's beard, and another of the same materials, but fixed into a paring of her Majesty's thumb-nail, which served for the back. There was a collection of needles and pins from a foot to half a yard long; four wasp-stings, like joiners' tacks; some combings of the Queen's hair; a gold ring which one day she made me a present of in a most obliging manner, taking it from her little finger, and throwing it over my head like a collar. I desired the Captain would please to accept this ring in return of his civilities; which he absolutely refused. I showed him a corn that I had cut off with my own hand, from a maid of honour's toe; it was about the bigness of a Kentish pippin, and grown so hard that when I returned to England, I got it hollowed into a cup, and set in silver. Lastly, I desired him to see the breeches I had then on, which were made of a mouse's skin.

I could force nothing on him but a footman's tooth, which I observed him to examine with great curiosity, and found he had a fancy for it. He received it with abundance of thanks, more than such a trifle could deserve. It was drawn by an unskilful surgeon, in a mistake, from one of Glumdalclitch's men, who was afflicted with the tooth-ache, but it was as sound as any in his head. I got it cleaned, and put it into my cabinet. It was about a foot long, and four inches in diameter.

The Captain was very well satisfied with this plain relation I had given him, and said, he hoped when we returned to England, I would oblige the world by putting it in paper, and making it public. My answer was, that I thought we were already overstocked with books of travels: that nothing could now pass which was not extraordinary; wherein I doubted some authors less consulted truth than their own vanity, or interest, or the diversion of ignorant readers. That my story could contain little besides common events, without those ornamental descriptions of strange plants, trees, birds, and other animals, or of the barbarous customs and idolatry of savage people, with which most writers abound. However, I thanked him for his good opinion, and promised to take the matter into my thoughts.

He said he wondered at one thing very much, which was, to hear me speak so loud, asking me whether the King or Queen of that country were thick of hearing. I told him, it was what I had been used to for above two years past; and that I admired as much at the voices of him and his men, who seemed to me only to whisper, and yet I could hear them well enough. But when I spoke in that country, it was like a man talking in the street to another looking out from the top of a steeple, unless when I was placed on a table, or held in any person's hand. I told him, I had likewise observed another thing, that when I first got into the ship, and the sailors stood all about me, I thought they were the most little contemptible creatures I had ever beheld. For, indeed, while I was in that prince's country, I could never endure to look in a glass after my eyes had been accustomed to such prodigious objects, because the comparison gave me so despicable a conceit of myself. The Captain said, that while we were at supper, he observed me to look at every thing with a sort of wonder, and that I often seemed hardly able to contain my laughter, which he knew not well how to take, but imputed it to some disorder in my brain. I answered, it was very true; and I wondered how I could forbear, when I saw his dishes of the size of a silver three-pence, a leg of pork hardly a mouthful, a cup not so big as a nut-shell; and so I went on, describing the rest of his household-stuff and provisions after the same manner. For, although the Queen had ordered a little equipage of all things necessary for me while I was in her service, yet my ideas were wholly taken up with what I saw on every side of me, and I winked at my own littleness as people do

at their own faults. The Captain understood my raillery very well, and merrily replied with the old English
proverb, that he doubted my eyes were bigger than
my belly, for he did not observe my stomach so good,
although I had fasted all day; and continuing in his
mirth, protested he would have gladly given an hundred
pounds to have seen my closet in the eagle's bill, and
afterwards in its fall from so great an height into the
sea; which would certainly have been a most astonishing object, worthy to have the description of it transmitted to future ages: and the comparison of Phæton
was so obvious, that he could not forbear applying it,
although I did not much admire the conceit.

The Captain having been at Tonquin, was in his return to England driven north-eastward to the latitude
of 44 degrees, and of longitude 143. But meeting a
trade-wind two days after I came on board him, we
sailed southward a long time, and coasting New Holland kept our course west-south-west, and then south-
south-west till we doubled the Cape of Good Hope.
Our voyage was very prosperous, but I shall not trouble
the reader with a journal of it. The Captain called in at
one or two ports, and sent in his long-boat for provisions
and fresh water, but I never went out of the ship till we
came into the Downs, which was on the third day of
June, 1706, about nine months after my escape. I offered to leave my goods in security for payment of my
freight: but the Captain protested he would not receive
one farthing. We took kind leave of each other, and I
made him promise he would come to see me at my
house in Redriff. I hired a horse and guide for five
shillings, which I borrowed of the Captain.

As I was on the road, observing the littleness of the
houses, the trees, the cattle, and the people, I began to
think myself in Lilliput. I was afraid of trampling on

every traveller I met, and often called aloud to have them stand out of the way, so that I had like to have gotten one or two broken heads for my impertinence.

When I came to my own house, for which I was forced to enquire, one of the servants opening the door, I bent down to go in (like a goose under a gate) for fear of striking my head. My wife ran out to embrace me, but I stooped lower than her knees, thinking she could otherwise never be able to reach my mouth. My daughter kneeled to ask my blessing, but I could not see her till she arose, having been so long used to stand with my head and eyes erect to above sixty foot; and then I went to take her up with one hand, by the waist. I looked down upon the servants and one or two friends who were in the house, as if they had been pigmies, and I a giant. I told my wife, she had been too thrifty, for I found she had starved herself and her daughter to nothing. In short, I behaved myself so unaccountably, that they were all of the Captain's opinion when he first saw me, and concluded I had lost my wits. This I mention as an instance of the great power of habit and prejudice.

In a little time I and my family and friends came to a right understanding: but my wife protested I should never go to sea any more; although my evil destiny so ordered that she had not power to hinder me, as the reader may know hereafter. In the mean time I here conclude the second part of my unfortunate voyages.

THE END OF THE SECOND PART.

PART III

A Voyage to Laputa, Balnibarbi, Luggnagg, Glubbdubdrib, and Japan

CHAP. I

The Author sets out on his third voyage, is taken by pirates. The malice of a Dutchman. His arrival at an island. He is received into Laputa.

I HAD not been at home above ten days, when Captain William Robinson, a Cornish man, Commander of the *Hopewell*, a stout ship of three hundred tons, came to my house. I had formerly been surgeon of another ship where he was master, and a fourth part owner, in a voyage to the Levant; he had always treated me more like a brother than an inferior officer, and hearing of my arrival made me a visit, as I apprehended only out of friendship, for nothing passed more than what is usual after long absences. But repeating his visits often, expressing his joy to find me in good health, asking whether I were now settled for life, adding that he intended a voyage to the East Indies in two months; at last he plainly invited me, though with some apologies, to be surgeon of the ship; that I should have another surgeon under me besides our two mates; that my salary should be double to the usual pay; and that hav-

ing experienced my knowledge in sea-affairs to be at
least equal to his, he would enter into any engagement
to follow my advice, as much as if I had share in the
command.

He said so many other obliging things, and I knew
him to be so honest a man, that I could not reject his
proposal; the thirst I had of seeing the world, notwithstanding my past misfortunes, continuing as violent as
ever. The only difficulty that remained, was to persuade
my wife, whose consent however I at last obtained by
the prospect of advantage she proposed to her children.

We set out the 5th day of August, 1706, and arrived
at Fort St. George the 11th of April, 1707. We stayed
there three weeks to refresh our crew, many of whom
were sick. From thence we went to Tonquin, where the
Captain resolved to continue some time, because many
of the goods he intended to buy were not ready, nor
could he expect to be dispatched in several months.
Therefore, in hopes to defray some of the charges he
must be at, he bought a sloop, loaded it with several
sorts of goods, wherewith the Tonquinese usually trade
to the neighbouring islands, and putting fourteen men
on board, whereof three were of the country, he appointed me master of the sloop, and gave me power to
traffic for two months, while he transacted his affairs at
Tonquin.

We had not sailed above three days, when a great
storm arising, we were driven five days to the north-
north-east, and then to the east: after which we had fair
weather, but still with a pretty strong gale from the
west. Upon the tenth day we were chased by two pirates, who soon overtook us; for my sloop was so deep
loaden, that she sailed very slow; neither were we in a
condition to defend ourselves.

We were boarded about the same time by both the

Plate III. Part. III

Parts Unknown

LAND OF
St James Bay
Robin?
IESSO
Salmon
i. Canal
Sea of Corea

Palmers
Straits of
Companys
Land
Stats I

Laputa
BALNIBARBI
Lagad.

Dicovered A.D. 1701

LUGNAGG
St Straldrugs
Clamgrig
Maldoada
Glubbdubdrib

I. Desert
I. Yea

pirates, who entered furiously at the head of their men, but finding us all prostrate upon our faces (for so I gave order), they pinioned us with strong ropes, and setting a guard upon us, went to search the sloop.

I observed among them a Dutchman, who seemed to be of some authority, though he was not Commander of either ship. He knew us by our countenances to be Englishmen, and jabbering to us in his own language, swore we should be tied back to back, and thrown into the sea. I spoke Dutch tolerably well; I told him who we were, and begged him in consideration of our being Christians and Protestants, of neighbouring countries, in strict alliance, that he would move the Captains to take some pity on us. This inflamed his rage; he repeated his threatenings, and turning to his companions, spoke with great vehemence, in the Japanese language, as I suppose, often using the word *Christianos*.

The largest of the two pirate ships was commanded by a Japanese Captain, who spoke a little Dutch, but very imperfectly. He came up to me, and after several questions, which I answered in great humility, he said we should not die. I made the Captain a very low bow, and then turning to the Dutchman, said, I was sorry to find more mercy in a heathen, than in a brother Christian. But I had soon reason to repent those foolish words: for that malicious reprobate, having been endeavoured in vain to persuade both the Captains that I might be thrown into the sea (which they would not yield to after the promise made me, that I should not die), however prevailed so far as to have a punishment inflicted on me, worse in all human appearance than death itself. My men were sent by an equal division into both the pirate ships, and my sloop new manned. As to myself, it was determined that I should be set a-drift in a small canoe, with paddles and a sail, and four days provisions, which last the Japanese Captain was so kind to double out of his own stores, and would permit no man to search me. I got down into the canoe, while the Dutchman standing upon the deck, loaded me with all the curses and injurious terms his language could afford.

About an hour before we saw the pirates, I had taken an observation, and found we were in the latitude of 46 N. and of longitude 183. When I was at some distance from the pirates, I discovered by my pocket-glass several islands to the south-east. I set up my sail, the wind being fair, with a design to reach the nearest of those islands, which I made a shift to do in about three hours. It was all rocky; however, I got many birds' eggs, and striking fire, I kindled some heath and dry sea-weed, by which I roasted my eggs. I eat no other supper, being resolved to spare my provisions as much as I could. I passed the night under the shelter of a rock, strowing some heath under me, and slept pretty well.

The next day I sailed to another island, and thence to a third and fourth, sometimes using my sail, and sometimes my paddles. But not to trouble the reader with a particular account of my distresses, let it suffice, that on the fifth day I arrived at the last island in my sight, which lay south-south-east to the former.

This island was at a greater distance than I expected, and I did not reach it in less than five hours. I encompassed it almost round, before I could find a convenient place to land in, which was a small creek, about three times the wideness of my canoe. I found the island to be all rocky, only a little intermingled with tufts of grass, and sweet-smelling herbs. I took out my small provisions, and after having refreshed myself, I secured the remainder in a cave, whereof there were great numbers. I gathered plenty of eggs upon the rocks, and got a quantity of dry sea-weed, and parched grass, which I

designed to kindle the next day, and roast my eggs as
well as I could (for I had about me my flint, steel,
match, and burning-glass). I lay all night in the cave
where I had lodged my provisions. My bed was the
same dry grass and sea-weed which I intended for fuel.
I slept very little, for the disquiets of my mind prevailed
over my weariness, and kept me awake. I considered
how impossible it was to preserve my life in so desolate
a place, and how miserable my end must be. Yet I
found myself so listless and desponding, that I had not
the heart to rise; and before I could get spirits enough
to creep out of my cave, the day was far advanced. I
walked a while among the rocks; the sky was perfectly
clear, and the sun so hot, that I was forced to turn my
face from it: when all on a sudden it became obscured,
as I thought, in a manner very different from what happens by the interposition of a cloud. I turned back, and
perceived a vast opaque body between me and the sun,
moving forwards towards the island: it seemed to be
about two miles high, and hid the sun six or seven
minutes, but I did not observe the air to be much colder,
or the sky more darkened, than if I had stood under the
shade of a mountain. As it approached nearer over the
place where I was, it appeared to be a firm substance,
the bottom flat, smooth, and shining very bright from
the reflection of the sea below. I stood upon a height
about two hundred yards from the shore, and saw this
vast body descending almost to a parallel with me, at
less than an English mile distance. I took out my pocket-
perspective, and could plainly discover numbers of people moving up and down the sides of it, which appeared
to be sloping, but what those people were doing, I was
not able to distinguish.

The natural love of life gave me some inward motions
of joy, and I was ready to entertain a hope that this ad-

venture might some way or other help to deliver me
from the desolate place and condition I was in. But at
the same time the reader can hardly conceive my astonishment, to behold an island in the air, inhabited by
men, who were able (as it should seem) to raise or sink,
or put it into a progressive motion, as they pleased. But
not being at that time in a disposition to philosophise
upon this phenomenon, I rather chose to observe what
course the island would take, because it seemed for a
while to stand still. Yet soon after, it advanced nearer,
and I could see the sides of it encompassed with several
gradations of galleries and stairs, at certain intervals, to
descend from one to the other. In the lowest gallery, I
beheld some people fishing with long angling rods, and
others looking on. I waved my cap (for my hat was long
since worn out) and my handkerchief towards the island; and upon its nearer approach, I called and shouted
with the utmost strength of my voice; and then looking
circumspectly, I beheld a crowd gather to that side
which was most in my view. I found by their pointing
towards me and to each other, that they plainly discovered me, although they made no return to my shout-
ing. But I could see four or five men running in great
haste up the stairs to the top of the island, who then
disappeared. I happened rightly to conjecture, that these
were sent for orders to some person in authority upon
this occasion.

The number of people increased, and in less than half
an hour, the island was moved and raised in such a manner, that the lowest gallery appeared in a parallel of less
than an hundred yards distance from the height where I
stood. I then put myself into the most supplicating pos-
tures, and spoke in the humblest accent, but received
no answer. Those who stood nearest over against me,
seemed to be persons of distinction, as I supposed by

their habit. They conferred earnestly with each other, looking often upon me. At length one of them called out in a clear, polite, smooth dialect, not unlike in sound to the Italian; and therefore I returned an answer in that language, hoping at least that the cadence might be more agreeable to his ears. Although neither of us understood the other, yet my meaning was easily known, for the people saw the distress I was in.

They made signs for me to come down from the rock, and go towards the shore, which I accordingly did; and the flying island being raised to a convenient height, the verge directly over me, a chain was let down from the lowest gallery, with a seat fastened to the bottom, to which I fixed myself, and was drawn up by pulleys.

CHAP. II

The humours and dispositions of the Laputians *described. An account of their learning. Of the King and his Court. The Author's reception there. The inhabitants subject to fear and disquietudes. An account of the women.*

At my alighting I was surrounded by a crowd of people, but those who stood nearest seemed to be of better quality. They beheld me with all the marks and circumstances of wonder; neither, indeed, was I much in their debt, having never till then seen a race of mortals so singular in their shapes, habits, and countenances. Their heads were all reclined either to the right or the left; one of their eyes turned inward, and the other directly up to the zenith. Their outward garments were adorned with the figures of suns, moons, and stars, interwoven with those of fiddles, flutes, harps, trumpets, guitars, harpsichords, and many other instruments of music, unknown to us in Europe. I observed here and there many in the habit of servants, with a blown bladder fastened like a flail to the end of a short stick, which they carried in their hands. In each bladder was a small quantity of dried pease, or little pebbles (as I was afterwards informed). With these bladders they now and then flapped the mouths and ears of those who stood near them, of which practice I could not then conceive the meaning; it seems, the minds of these people are so taken up with intense speculations, that they neither can speak, nor attend to the discourses of others, without being roused by some external taction upon the organs of speech and hearing; for which reason, those persons who are able to afford it always keep a flapper (the original is *climenole*) in their family, as one of their domestics, nor ever walk abroad or make visits without him. And the business of this officer is, when two or more persons are in company, gently to strike with his bladder the mouth of him who is to speak, and the right ear of him or them to whom the speaker addresseth himself. This flapper is likewise employed diligently to attend his master in his walks, and upon occasion to give him a soft flap on his eyes, because he is always so wrapped up in cogitation, that he is in manifest danger of falling down every precipice, and bouncing his head against every post, and in the streets, of justling others, or being justled himself into the kennel.

It was necessary to give the reader this information, without which he would be at the same loss with me, to understand the proceedings of these people, as they conducted me up the stairs, to the top of the island, and from thence to the royal palace. While we were ascending, they forgot several times what they were about, and left me to myself, till their memories were again roused by their flappers; for they appeared altogether unmoved by the sight of my foreign habit and countenance, and by the shouts of the vulgar, whose thoughts and minds were more disengaged.

At last we entered the palace, and proceeded into the chamber of presence, where I saw the King seated on his throne, attended on each side by persons of prime quality. Before the throne, was a large table filled with globes and spheres, and mathematical instruments of all kinds. His Majesty took not the least notice of us, although our entrance was not without sufficient noise, by the concourse of all persons belonging to the court. But he was then deep in a problem, and we attended at least an hour, before he could solve it. There stood by him on each side, a young page, with flaps in their hands, and when they saw he was at leisure, one of them gently struck his mouth, and the other his right ear; at which he started like one awaked on the sudden, and looking towards me, and the company I was in, recollected the occasion of our coming, whereof he had been informed before. He spoke some words, whereupon immediately a young man with a flap came up to my side, and flapped me gently on the right ear; but I made signs, as well as I could, that I had no occasion for such an instrument; which, as I afterwards found, gave his Majesty and the whole court a very mean opinion of my understanding. The King, as far as I could conjecture, asked me several questions, and I addressed myself to him in all the languages I had. When it was found, that I could neither understand nor be understood, I was conducted by his order to an apartment in his palace (this prince being distinguished above all his predecessors for his hospitality to strangers), where two servants were appointed to attend me. My dinner was brought, and four persons of quality, whom I remembered to have seen very near the King's person, did me the honour to dine with me. We had two courses, of three dishes each. In the first course, there was a shoulder of mutton, cut into an equilateral triangle, a piece of beef into a rhomboides, and a pudding into a cycloid. The second course was two ducks, trussed up into the form of fiddles; sausages and puddings resembling flutes and haut-boys, and a breast of veal in the shape of a harp. The servants cut our bread into cones, cylinders, parallelograms, and several other mathematical figures.

While we were at dinner, I made bold to ask the names of several things in their language; and those noble persons, by the assistance of their flappers, delighted to give me answers, hoping to raise my admiration of their great abilities, if I could be brought to converse with them. I was soon able to call for bread and drink, or whatever else I wanted.

After dinner my company withdrew, and a person was sent to me by the King's order, attended by a flapper. He brought with him pen, ink, and paper, and three or four books, giving me to understand by signs, that he was sent to teach me the language. We sat together four hours, in which time I wrote down a great number of words in columns, with the translations over against them. I likewise made a shift to learn several short sentences. For my tutor would order one of my servants to fetch something, to turn about, to make a bow, to sit, or stand, or walk, and the like. Then I took down the sentence in writing. He showed me also in one of his books, the figures of the sun, moon, and stars, the zodiac, the tropics, and polar circles, together with the denominations of many planes and solids. He gave me the names and descriptions of all the musical instruments, and the general terms of art in playing on each of them. After he had left me, I placed all my words with their interpretations in alphabetical order. And thus in a few days, by the help of a very faithful memory, I got some insight into their language.

The word, which I interpret the *Flying* or *Floating Island,* is in the original *Laputa,* whereof I could never learn the true etymology. *Lap* in the old obsolete language signifieth *high,* and *untuh,* a *governor,* from which they say, by corruption, was derived *Laputa,* from *Lapuntuh.* But I do not approve of this derivation, which seems to be a little strained. I ventured to offer to the learned among them a conjecture of my own, that *Laputa* was *quasi lap outed; lap* signifying properly the dancing of the sunbeams in the sea, and *outed,* a wing, which however I shall not obtrude, but submit to the judicious reader.

Those to whom the King had entrusted me, observing how ill I was clad, ordered a tailor to come next morning, and take my measure for a suit of clothes. This operator did his office after a different manner from those of his trade in Europe. He first took my altitude by a quadrant, and then with a rule and compasses, described the dimensions and outlines of my whole body, all which he entered upon paper, and in six days brought my clothes very ill made, and quite out of shape, by happening to mistake a figure in the calculation. But my comfort was, that I observed such accidents very frequent, and little regarded.

During my confinement for want of clothes, and by an indisposition that held me some days longer, I much enlarged my dictionary; and when I went next to court, was able to understand many things the King spoke, and to return him some kind of answers. His Majesty had given orders that the island should move north-east and by east, to the vertical point over Lagado, the metropolis of the whole kingdom below upon the firm earth. It was about ninety leagues distant, and our voyage lasted four days and an half. I was not in the least sensible of the progressive motion made in the air by the island. On the second morning about eleven o'clock, the King himself in person, attended by his nobility, courtiers, and officers, having prepared all their musical instruments, played on them for three hours without intermission, so that I was quite stunned with the noise; neither could I possibly guess the meaning, till my tutor informed me. He said that the people of their island had their ears adapted to hear the music of the spheres, which always played at certain periods, and the court was now prepared to bear their part in whatever instrument they most excelled.

In our journey towards Lagado, the capital city, his Majesty ordered that the island should stop over certain towns and villages, from whence he might receive the petitions of his subjects. And to this purpose several packthreads were let down with small weights at the bottom. On these packthreads the people strung their petitions, which mounted up directly like scraps of paper fastened by school-boys at the end of the string that holds their kite. Sometimes we received wine and victuals from below, which were drawn up by pulleys.

The knowledge I had in mathematics gave me great assistance in acquiring their phraseology, which depended much upon that science and music; and in the latter I was not unskilled. Their ideas are perpetually conversant in lines and figures. If they would, for example, praise the beauty of a woman, or any other animal, they describe it by rhombs, circles, parallelograms, ellipses, and other geometrical terms, or by words of art drawn from music, needless here to repeat. I observed in the King's kitchen all sorts of mathematical and musical instruments, after the figures of which they cut up the joints that were served to his Majesty's table.

Their houses are very ill built, the walls bevil, without one right angle in any apartment, and this defect ariseth from the contempt they bear to practical geometry, which they despise as vulgar and mechanic, those instructions they give being too refined for the intellectuals of their work-men, which occasions perpetual mistakes. And although they are dexterous enough upon a piece of paper in the management of the rule, the pencil, and the divider, yet in the common actions and behaviour of life, I have not seen a more clumsy, awkward, and unhandy people, nor so slow and perplexed in their conceptions upon all other subjects, except those of mathematics and music. They are very bad reasoners, and vehemently given to opposition, unless when they happen to be of the right opinion, which is seldom their case. Imagination, fancy, and invention, they are wholly strangers to, nor have any words in their language by which those ideas can be expressed; the whole compass of their thoughts and mind being shut up within the two forementioned sciences.

Most of them, and especially those who deal in the astronomical part, have great faith in judicial astrology, although they are ashamed to own it publicly. But what I chiefly admired, and thought altogether unaccountable, was the strong disposition I observed in them towards news and politics, perpetually enquiring into public affairs, giving their judgments in matters of state, and passionately disputing every inch of a party opinion. I have indeed observed the same disposition among most of the mathematicians I have known in Europe, although I could never discover the least analogy between the two sciences; unless those people suppose, that because the smallest circle hath as many degrees as the largest, therefore the regulation and management of the world require no more abilities than the handling and turning of a globe. But I rather take this quality to spring from a very common infirmity of human nature, inclining us to be more curious and conceited in matters where we have least concern, and for which we are least adapted either by study or nature.

These people are under continual disquietudes, never enjoying a minute's peace of mind; and their disturbances proceed from causes which very little affect the rest of mortals. Their apprehensions arise from several changes they dread in the celestial bodies. For instance; that the earth, by the continual approaches of the sun towards it, must in course of time be absorbed, or swallowed up. That the face of the sun will by degrees be encrusted with its own effluvia, and give no more light to the world. That the earth very narrowly escaped a brush from the tail of the last comet, which would have infallibly reduced it to ashes; and that the next, which they have calculated for one and thirty years hence, will probably destroy us. For, if in its perihelion it should approach within a certain degree of the sun (as by their calculations they have reason to dread), it will receive a degree of heat ten thousand times more intense than that of red-hot glowing iron; and in its absence from the sun, carry a blazing tail ten hundred thousand and fourteen miles long; through which if the earth should pass at the distance of one hundred thousand miles from the nucleus or main body of the comet, it must in its passage be set on fire, and reduced to ashes. That the sun daily spending its rays without any nutriment to supply them, will at last be wholly consumed and annihilated; which must be attended with the destruction of this earth, and of all the planets that receive their light from it.

They are so perpetually alarmed with the apprehensions of these and the like impending dangers, that they can neither sleep quietly in their beds, nor have any relish for the common pleasures or amusements of life. When they meet an acquaintance in the morning, the first question is about the sun's health, how he looked at his setting and rising, and what hopes they have to avoid the stroke of the approaching comet. This conversation they are apt to run into with the same temper that boys discover, in delighting to hear terrible stories of spirits and hobgoblins, which they greedily listen to, and dare not go to bed for fear.

The women of the island have abundance of vivacity: they contemn their husbands, and are exceedingly fond of strangers, whereof there is always a considerable number from the continent below, attending at court, either upon affairs of the several towns and corporations or their own particular occasions, but are much despised, because they want the same endowments. Among these the ladies choose their gallants: but the vexation is, that they act with too much ease and security, for the husband is always so rapt in speculation, that the mistress and lover may proceed to the greatest familiarities before his face, if he be but provided with paper and implements, and without his flapper at his side.

The wives and daughters lament their confinement to the island, although I think it the most delicious spot of ground in the world; and although they live in the greatest plenty and magnificence, and are allowed to do whatever they please, they long to see the world, and take the diversions of the metropolis, which they are not allowed to do without a particular licence from the King; and this is not easy to be obtained, because the people of quality have found, by frequent experience, how hard it is to persuade their women to return from below. I was told that a great court lady, who had several children, is married to the prime minister, the richest subject in the kingdom, a very graceful person, extremely fond of her, and lives in the finest palace of the island, went down to Lagado, on the pretence of health, there hid herself for several months, till the King sent a warrant to search for her, and she was found in an obscure eating-house all in rags, having pawned her clothes to maintain an old deformed footman, who beat her every day, and in whose company she was taken much against her will. And although her husband received her with all possible kindness, and without the least reproach, she soon after contrived to steal down again with all her jewels, to the same gallant, and hath not been heard of since.

This may perhaps pass with the reader rather for an European or English story, than for one of a country so remote. But he may please to consider, that the caprices of womankind are not limited by any climate or nation, and that they are much more uniform than can be easily imagined.

In about a month's time I had made a tolerable proficiency in their language, and was able to answer most of the King's questions, when I had the honour to attend him. His Majesty discovered not the least curiosity to enquire into the laws, government, history, religion, or manners of the countries where I had been, but confined his questions to the state of mathematics, and received the account I gave him with great contempt and indifference, though often roused by his flapper on each side.

CHAP. III

A phenomenon solved by modern philosophy and astronomy. The Laputians' great improvements in the latter. The King's method of suppressing insurrections.

I desired leave of this prince to see the curiosities of the island, which he was graciously pleased to grant, and ordered my tutor to attend me. I chiefly wanted to know to what cause in art, or in nature, it owed its several motions, whereof I will now give a philosophical account to the reader.

The Flying or Floating Island is exactly circular, its diameter 7837 yards, or about four miles and an half, and consequently contains ten thousand acres. It is three hundred yards thick. The bottom or under surface, which appears to those who view it below, is one even regular plate of adamant, shooting up to the height of about two hundred yards. Above it lie the several minerals in their usual order, and over all is a coat of rich mould, ten or twelve foot deep. The declivity of the upper surface, from the circumference to the centre, is the natural cause why all the dews and rains which fall upon the island, are conveyed in small rivulets toward the middle, where they are emptied into four large basins, each of about half a mile in circuit, and two hundred yards distant from the centre. From these basins the water is continually exhaled by the sun in the daytime, which effectually prevents their overflowing. Besides, as it is in the power of the monarch to raise the island above the region of clouds and vapours, he can prevent the falling of dews and rains whenever he pleases. For the highest clouds cannot rise above two miles, as naturalists agree, at least they were never known to do so in that country.

At the centre of the island there is a chasm about fifty yards in diameter, from whence the astronomers descend into a large dome, which is therefore called *Flandona Gagnole*, or the Astronomer's Cave, situated at the depth of an hundred yards beneath the upper surface of the adamant. In this cave are twenty lamps continually burning, which from the reflection of the adamant cast a strong light into every part. The place is stored with great variety of sextants, quadrants, telescopes, astrolabes, and other astronomical instruments. But the greatest curiosity, upon which the fate of the island depends, is a loadstone of a prodigious size, in shape resembling a weaver's shuttle. It is in length six yards, and in the thickest part at least three yards over. This magnet is sustained by a very strong axle of adamant passing through its middle, upon which it plays, and is poised so exactly that the weakest hand can turn it. It is hooped round with an hollow cylinder of adamant, four foot deep, as many thick, and twelve yards in diameter, placed horizontally, and supported by eight adamantine feet, each six yards high. In the middle of the concave side there is a groove twelve inches deep, in which the extremities of the axle are lodged, and turned round as there is occasion.

The stone cannot be moved from its place by any force, because the hoop and its feet are one continued piece with that body of adamant which constitutes the bottom of the island.

By means of this loadstone, the island is made to rise and fall, and move from one place to another. For, with respect to that part of the earth over which the monarch presides, the stone is endued at one of its sides with an attractive power, and at the other with a repulsive. Upon placing the magnet erect with its attracting end towards the earth, the island descends; but when the repelling extremity points downwards, the island mounts directly upwards. When the position of the stone is oblique, the motion of the island is so too. For in this magnet the forces always act in lines parallel to its direction.

By this oblique motion, the island is conveyed to different parts of the monarch's dominions. To explain the manner of its progress, let *A B* represent a line drawn across the dominions of Balnibarbi, let the line *c d* represent the loadstone, of which let *d* be the repelling end, and *c* the attracting end, the island being over *C*; let the stone be placed in the position *c d*, with its repelling end downwards; then the island will be driven upwards obliquely towards *D*. When it is arrived at *D*, let the stone be turned upon its axle, till its attracting end points towards *E*, and then the island will be carried obliquely towards *E*; where if the stone be again turned upon its axle till it stands in the position *E F*, with its repelling point downwards, the island will rise obliquely towards *F*, where by directing the attracting end towards *G*, the island may be carried to *G*, and from *G* to *H*, by turning the stone, so as to make its repelling extremity to point directly downwards. And thus by changing the situation of the stone as often as there is occasion, the island is made to rise and fall by turns in an oblique direction, and by those alternate risings and fallings (the obliquity being not considerable) is conveyed from one part of the dominions to the other.

But it must be observed, that this island cannot move beyond the extent of the dominions below, nor can it rise above the height of four miles. For which the astronomers (who have written large systems concerning

Plate III. Part III.

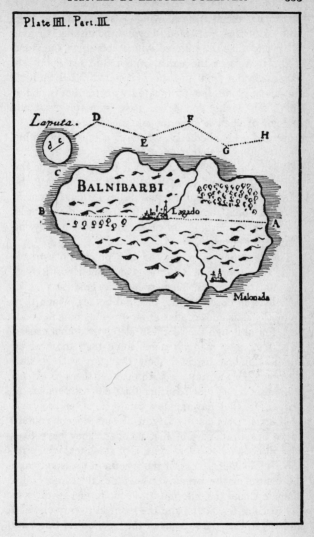

the stone) assign the following reason: that the mag-
netic virtue does not extend beyond the distance of four
miles, and that the mineral which acts upon the stone
in the bowels of the earth, and in the sea about six
leagues distant from the shore, is not diffused through
the whole globe, but terminated with the limits of the
King's dominions; and it was easy from the great advantage of such a superior situation, for a prince to
bring under his obedience whatever country lay within
the attraction of that magnet.

When the stone is put parallel to the plane of the
horizon, the island standeth still; for in that case the
extremities of it being at equal distance from the earth,
act with equal force, the one in drawing downwards,
the other in pushing upwards, and consequently no
motion can ensue.

This loadstone is under the care of certain astronomers, who from time to time give it such positions as
the monarch directs. They spend the greatest part of
their lives in observing the celestial bodies, which they
do by the assistance of glasses far excelling ours in goodness. For although their largest telescopes do not exceed
three feet, they magnify much more than those of an
hundred among us, and show the stars with greater
clearness. This advantage hath enabled them to extend
their discoveries much further than our astronomers in
Europe; for they have made a catalogue of ten thousand
fixed stars, whereas the largest of ours do not contain
above one third part of that number. They have likewise discovered two lesser stars, or satellites, which re-
volve about Mars, whereof the innermost is distant from
the centre of the primary planet exactly three of his
diameters, and the outermost five; the former revolves in
the space of ten hours, and the latter in twenty-one and
an half; so that the squares of their periodical times are

very near in the same proportion with the cubes of their distance from the centre of Mars, which evidently shows them to be governed by the same law of gravitation, that influences the other heavenly bodies.

They have observed ninety-three different comets, and settled their periods with great exactness. If this be true (and they affirm it with great confidence), it is much to be wished that their observations were made public, whereby the theory of comets, which at present is very lame and defective, might be brought to the same perfection with other parts of astronomy.

The King would be the most absolute prince in the universe, if he could but prevail on a ministry to join with him; but these having their estates below on the continent, and considering that the office of a favourite hath a very uncertain tenure, would never consent to the enslaving their country.

If any town should engage in rebellion or mutiny, fall into violent factions, or refuse to pay the usual tribute, the King hath two methods of reducing them to obedience. The first and the mildest course is by keeping the island hovering over such a town, and the lands about it, whereby he can deprive them of the benefit of the sun and the rain, and consequently afflict the inhabitants with dearth and diseases. And if the crime deserve it, they are at the same time pelted from above with great stones, against which they have no defence but by creeping into cellars or caves, while the roofs of their houses are beaten to pieces. But if they still continue obstinate, or offer to raise insurrections, he proceeds to the last remedy, by letting the island drop directly upon their heads, which makes a universal destruction both of houses and men. However, this is an extremity to which the prince is seldom driven, neither, indeed, is he willing to put it in execution, nor dare his ministers advise him to an action, which as it would render them odious to the people, so it would be a great damage to their own estates, which lie all below, for the island is the King's demesne.

But there is still indeed a more weighty reason, why the kings of this country have been always averse from executing so terrible an action, unless upon the utmost necessity. For if the town intended to be destroyed should have in it any tall rocks, as it generally falls out in the larger cities, a situation probably chosen at first with a view to prevent such a catastrophe; or if it abound in high spires, or pillars of stone, a sudden fall might endanger the bottom or under surface of the island, which, although it consists, as I have said, of one entire adamant two hundred yards thick, might happen to crack by too great a choque, or burst by approaching too near the fires from the houses below, as the backs both of iron and stone will often do in our chimneys. Of all this the people are well apprised, and understand how far to carry their obstinacy, where their liberty or property is concerned. And the King, when he is highest provoked, and most determined to press a city to rubbish, orders the island to descend with great gentleness, out of a pretence of tenderness to his people, but indeed for fear of breaking the adamantine bottom; in which case, it is the opinion of all their philosophers, that the loadstone could no longer hold it up, and the whole mass would fall to the ground.

About three years before my arrival among them, while the King was in his progress over his dominions, there happened an extraordinary accident which had like to have put a period to the fate of that monarchy, at least as it is now instituted. Lindalino, the second city in the kingdom, was the first his Majesty visited in his progress. Three days after his departure the inhabitants, who had often complained of great oppressions, shut the town gates, seized on the governor, and with incredible speed and labour erected four large towers, one at every corner of the city (which is an exact square), equal in height to a strong pointed rock that stands directly in the centre of the city. Upon the top of each tower, as well as upon the rock, they fixed a great loadstone, and in case their design should fail, they had provided a vast quantity of the most combustible fuel, hoping to burst therewith the adamantine bottom of the island, if the loadstone project should miscarry.

It was eight months before the King had perfect notice that the Lindalinians were in rebellion. He then commanded that the island should be wafted over the city. The people were unanimous, and had laid in store of provisions, and a great river runs through the middle of the town. The King hovered over them several days to deprive them of the sun and the rain. He ordered many packthreads to be let down, yet not a person offered to send up a petition, but instead thereof, very bold demands, the redress of all their grievances, great immunities, the choice of their own governor, and other the like exorbitances. Upon which his Majesty commanded all the inhabitants of the island to cast great stones from the lower gallery into the town; but the citizens had provided against this mischief by conveying their persons and effects into the four towers, and other strong buildings, and vaults underground.

The King being now determined to reduce this proud people, ordered that the island should descend gently within forty yards of the top of the towers and rock. This was accordingly done; but the officers employed in that work found the descent much speedier than usual, and by turning the loadstone could not without great difficulty keep it in a firm position, but found the island inclining to fall. They sent the King immediate intelligence of this astonishing event, and begged his Majesty's permission to raise the island higher; the King consented, a general council was called, and the officers of the loadstone ordered to attend. One of the oldest and expertest among them obtained leave to try an experiment. He took a strong line of an hundred yards, and the island being raised over the town above the attracting power they had felt, he fastened a piece of adamant to the end of his line, which had in it a mixture of iron mineral, of the same nature with that whereof the bottom or lower surface of the island is composed, and from the lower gallery let it down slowly towards the top of the towers. The adamant was not descended four yards, before the officer felt it drawn so strongly downwards, that he could hardly pull it back. He then threw down several small pieces of adamant, and observed that they were all violently attracted by the top of the tower. The same experiment was made on the other three towers, and on the rock with the same effect.

This incident broke entirely the King's measures, and (to dwell no longer on other circumstances) he was forced to give the town their own conditions.

I was assured by a great minister, that if the island had descended so near the town as not to be able to raise itself, the citizens were determined to fix it for ever, to kill the King and all his servants, and entirely change the government.

By a fundamental law of this realm, neither the king, nor either of his two eldest sons, are permitted to leave the island; nor the queen, till she is past child-bearing.

CHAP. IV

The Author leaves Laputa; *is conveyed to* Balnibarbi, *arrives at the metropolis. A description of the metropolis, and the country adjoining. The Author hospitably received by a great Lord. His conversation with that Lord.*

Although I cannot say that I was ill treated in this island, yet I must confess I thought myself too much neglected, not without some degree of contempt. For neither prince nor people appeared to be curious in any part of knowledge, except mathematics and music, wherein I was far their inferior, and upon that account very little regarded.

On the other side, after having seen all the curiosities of the island, I was very desirous to leave it, being heartily weary of those people. They were indeed excellent in two sciences for which I have great esteem, and wherein I am not unversed; but at the same time so abstracted and involved in speculation, that I never met with such disagreeable companions. I conversed only with women, tradesmen, flappers, and court-pages, during two months of my abode there, by which, at last, I rendered myself extremely contemptible; yet these were the only people from whom I could ever receive a reasonable answer.

I had obtained, by hard study, a good degree of knowledge in their language; I was weary of being confined to an island where I received so little countenance, and resolved to leave it with the first opportunity.

There was a great lord at court, nearly related to the King, and for that reason alone used with respect. He was universally reckoned the most ignorant and stupid person among them. He had performed many eminent services for the crown, had great natural and acquired parts, adorned with integrity and honour, but so ill an ear for music, that his detractors reported he had been often known to beat time in the wrong place; neither could his tutors, without extreme difficulty, teach him to demonstrate the most easy proposition in the mathematics. He was pleased to show me many marks of favour, often did me the honour of a visit, desired to be informed in the affairs of Europe, the laws and customs, the manners and learning of the several countries where I had travelled. He listened to me with great attention, and made very wise observations on all I spoke. He had two flappers attending him for state, but never made use of them except at court, and in visits of ceremony, and would always command them to withdraw when we were alone together.

I entreated this illustrious person to intercede in my behalf with his Majesty for leave to depart, which he accordingly did, as he was pleased to tell me, with regret: for indeed he had made me several offers very advantageous, which however I refused with expressions of the highest acknowledgment.

On the 16th day of February I took leave of his Majesty and the court. The King made me a present to the value of about two hundred pounds English, and my protector his kinsman as much more, together with a letter of recommendation to a friend of his in Lagado, the metropolis. The island being then hovering over a mountain about two miles from it, I was let down from the lowest gallery, in the same manner as I had been taken up.

The continent, as far as it is subject to the monarch of the Flying Island, passes under the general name of *Balnibarbi*, and the metropolis, as I said before, is called *Lagado*. I felt some little satisfaction in finding myself on firm ground. I walked to the city without any concern, being clad like one of the natives, and sufficiently instructed to converse with them. I soon found out the person's house to whom I was recommended, presented my letter from his friend the grandee in the island, and was received with much kindness. This great lord, whose name was Munodi, ordered me an apartment in his own house, where I continued during my stay, and was entertained in a most hospitable manner.

The next morning after my arrival, he took me in his chariot to see the town, which is about half the bigness of London, but the houses very strangely built, and most of them out of repair. The people in the streets walked fast, looked wild, their eyes fixed, and were generally in rags. We passed through one of the town gates, and went about three miles into the country, where I saw many labourers working with several sorts of tools in the ground, but was not able to conjecture what they were about; neither did I observe any expectation either of corn or grass, although the soil appeared to be excellent. I could not forbear admiring at these odd appearances both in town and country, and I made bold to desire my conductor, that he would be pleased to explain to me what could be meant by so many busy heads, hands, and faces, both in the streets and the fields, because I did not discover any good effects they produced; but on the contrary, I never knew a soil so unhappily cultivated, houses so ill contrived and so ruinous, or a people whose countenances and habit expressed so much misery and want.

This Lord Munodi was a person of the first rank, and had been some years Governor of Lagado; but by a cabal of ministers was discharged for insufficiency. However, the King treated him with tenderness, as a well-meaning man, but of a low contemptible understanding.

When I gave that free censure of the country and its inhabitants, he made no further answer than by telling me, that I had not been long enough among them to form a judgment; and that the different nations of the world had different customs, with other common topics to the same purpose. But when we returned to his palace, he asked me how I liked the building, what absurdities I observed, and what quarrel I had with the dress or looks of his domestics. This he might safely do, because every thing about him was magnificent, regular, and polite. I answered that his Excellency's prudence, quality, and fortune, had exempted him from those defects, which folly and beggary had produced in others. He said if I would go with him to his country-house, about twenty miles distant, where his estate lay, there would be more leisure for this kind of conversation. I told his Excellency that I was entirely at his disposal; and accordingly we set out next morning.

During our journey, he made me observe the several methods used by farmers in managing their lands, which to me were wholly unaccountable; for, except in some very few places, I could not discover one ear of corn or blade of grass. But, in three hours travelling, the scene was wholly altered; we came into a most beautiful country; farmers' houses at small distances, neatly built; the fields enclosed, containing vineyards, corn-grounds, and meadows. Neither do I remember to have seen a more delightful prospect. His Excellency observed my countenance to clear up; he told me, with a sigh, that there his estate began, and would continue the same, till we should come to his house. That his countrymen ridiculed and despised him for managing his affairs no better, and for setting so ill an example to the kingdom, which however was followed by very few, such as were old, and wilful, and weak like himself.

We came at length to the house, which was indeed a
noble structure, built according to the best rules of ancient architecture. The fountains, gardens, walks, avenues, and groves, were all disposed with exact judgment
and taste. I gave due praises to every thing I saw,
whereof his Excellency took not the least notice till after
supper, when, there being no third companion, he told
me with a very melancholy air, that he doubted he must
throw down his houses in town and country, to rebuild
them after the present mode, destroy all his plantations,
and cast others into such a form as modern usage required, and give the same directions to all his tenants,
unless he would submit to incur the censure, of pride,
singularity, affectation, ignorance, caprice, and perhaps
increase his Majesty's displeasure.

That the admiration I appeared to be under, would
cease or diminish when he had informed me of some
particulars, which probably I never heard of at court,
the people there being too much taken up in their own
speculations, to have regard to what passed here below.

The sum of his discourse was to this effect. That
about forty years ago, certain persons went up to Laputa, either upon business or diversion, and, after five
months continuance, came back with a very little
smattering in mathematics, but full of volatile spirits acquired in that airy region. That these persons upon their
return began to dislike the management of every thing
below, and fell into schemes of putting all arts, sciences,
languages, and mechanics upon a new foot. To this end
they procured a royal patent for erecting an Academy of
Projectors in Lagado; and the humour prevailed so
strongly among the people, that there is not a town of
any consequence in the kingdom without such an academy. In these colleges, the professors contrive new rules
and methods of agriculture and building, and new in-

struments and tools for all trades and manufactures,
whereby, as they undertake, one man shall do the work
of ten; a palace may be built in a week, of materials so
durable as to last for ever without repairing. All the
fruits of the earth shall come to maturity at whatever
season we think fit to choose, and increase an hundred
fold more than they do at present, with innumerable
other happy proposals. The only inconvenience is, that
none of these projects are yet brought to perfection, and
in the mean time, the whole country lies miserably
waste, the houses in ruins, and the people without food
or clothes. By all which, instead of being discouraged,
they are fifty times more violently bent upon prosecut-
ing their schemes, driven equally on by hope and despair: that as for himself, being not of an enterprising
spirit, he was content to go on in the old forms, to live
in the houses his ancestors had built, and act as they
did in every part of life without innovation. That some
few other persons of quality and gentry had done the
same, but were looked on with an eye of contempt and
ill will, as enemies to art, ignorant, and ill commonwealth's-men, preferring their own ease and sloth before
the general improvement of their country.

His Lordship added, that he would not by any further
particulars prevent the pleasure I should certainly take
in viewing the grand Academy, whither he was resolved
I should go. He only desired me to observe a ruined
building upon the side of a mountain about three miles
distant, of which he gave me this account. That he had
a very convenient mill within half a mile of his house,
turned by a current from a large river, and sufficient for
his own family, as well as a great number of his tenants.
That about seven years ago, a club of those projectors
came to him with proposals to destroy this mill, and
build another on the side of that mountain, on the long

ridge whereof a long canal must be cut for a repository
of water, to be conveyed up by pipes and engines to
supply the mill: because the wind and air upon a height
agitated the water, and thereby made it fitter for motion:
and because the water descending down a reclivity
would turn the mill with half the current of a river
whose course is more upon a level. He said, that being
then not very well with the court, and pressed by many
of his friends, he complied with the proposal; and after
employing an hundred men for two years, the work miscarried, the projectors went off, laying the blame entirely
upon him, railing at him ever since, and putting others
upon the same experiment, with equal assurance of
success, as well as equal disappointment.

In a few days we came back to town, and his Excellency, considering the bad character he had in the
Academy, would not go with me himself, but recommended me to a friend of his to bear me company
thither. My lord was pleased to represent me as a
great admirer of projects, and a person of much curiosity
and easy belief; which, indeed, was not without truth;
for I had myself been a sort of projector in my younger
days.

CHAP. V

The Author permitted to see the Grand Academy of Lagado.
The Academy largely described. The Arts wherein the pro-
fessors employ themselves.

This Academy is not an entire single building, but a continuation of several houses on both sides of a street,
which growing waste was purchased and applied to that
use.

I was received very kindly by the Warden, and went

for many days to the Academy. Every room hath in it one or more projectors, and I believe I could not be in fewer than five hundred rooms.

The first man I saw was of a meagre aspect, with sooty hands and face, his hair and beard long, ragged and singed in several places. His clothes, shirt, and skin, were all of the same colour. He had been eight years upon a project for extracting sun-beams out of cucumbers, which were to be put into vials hermetically sealed, and let out to warm the air in raw inclement summers. He told me, he did not doubt, in eight years more, he should be able to supply the Governor's gardens with sunshine at a reasonable rate; but he complained that his stock was low, and entreated me to give him something as an encouragement to ingenuity, especially since this had been a very dear season for cucumbers. I made him a small present, for my lord had furnished me with money on purpose, because he knew their practice of begging from all who go to see them.

I went into another chamber, but was ready to hasten back, being almost overcome with a horrible stink. My conductor pressed me forward, conjuring me in a whisper to give no offence, which would be highly resented, and therefore I durst not so much as stop my nose. The projector of this cell was the most ancient student of the Academy; his face and beard were of a pale yellow; his hands and clothes daubed over with filth. When I was presented to him, he gave me a close embrace (a compliment I could well have excused). His employment from his first coming into the Academy, was an operation to reduce human excrement to its original food, by separating the several parts, removing the tincture which it receives from the gall, making the odour exhale, and scumming off the saliva. He had a weekly allowance from the society, of a vessel filled with human ordure, about the bigness of a Bristol barrel.

I saw another at work to calcine ice into gunpowder, who likewise showed me a treatise he had written concerning the malleability of fire, which he intended to publish.

There was a most ingenious architect who had contrived a new method for building houses, by beginning at the roof, and working downwards to the foundation, which he justified to me by the like practice of those two prudent insects, the bee and the spider.

There was a man born blind, who had several apprentices in his own condition: their employment was to mix colours for painters, which their master taught them to distinguish by feeling and smelling. It was indeed my misfortune to find them at that time not very perfect in their lessons, and the professor himself happened to be generally mistaken: this artist is much encouraged and esteemed by the whole fraternity.

In another apartment I was highly pleased with a projector, who had found a device for ploughing the ground with hogs, to save the charges of ploughs, cattle, and labour. The method is this: in an acre of ground you bury, at six inches distance and eight deep, a quantity of acorns, dates, chestnuts, and other mast or vegetables whereof these animals are fondest; then you drive six hundred or more of them into the field, where in a few days they will root up the whole ground in search of their food, and make it fit for sowing, at the same time manuring it with their dung. It is true, upon experiment they found the charge and trouble very great, and they had little or no crop. However, it is not doubted that this invention may be capable of great improvement.

I went into another room, where the walls and ceiling were all hung round with cobwebs, except a narrow passage for the artist to go in and out. At my entrance he called aloud to me not to disturb his webs. He lamented the fatal mistake the world had been so long in of using silk-worms, while we had such plenty of domestic insects, who infinitely excelled the former, because they understood how to weave as well as spin. And he proposed farther, that by employing spiders, the charge of dying silks should be wholly saved, whereof I was fully convinced when he showed me a vast number of flies most beautifully coloured, wherewith he fed his spiders, assuring us, that the webs would take a tincture from them; and as he had them in all hues, he hoped to fit everybody's fancy, as soon as he could find proper food for the flies, of certain gums, oils, and other glutinous matter to give a strength and consistence to the threads.

There was an astronomer who had undertaken to place a sun-dial upon the great weathercock on the town-house, by adjusting the annual and diurnal motions of the earth and sun, so as to answer and coincide with all accidental turnings by the wind.

I was complaining of a small fit of colic, upon which my conductor led me into a room, where a great physician resided, who was famous for curing that disease by contrary operations from the same instrument. He had a large pair of bellows with a long slender muzzle of ivory. This he conveyed eight inches up the anus, and drawing in the wind, he affirmed he could make the guts as lank as a dried bladder. But when the disease was more stubborn and violent, he let in the muzzle while the bellows were full of wind, which he discharged into the body of the patient, then withdrew the instrument to replenish it, clapping his thumb strongly against the orifice of the fundament; and this being repeated three or four times, the adventitious wind would rush out, bringing the noxious along with it (like water put into a pump), and the patient recover. I saw him try both experiments upon a dog, but could not discern any effect from the former. After the latter, the animal was ready to burst, and made so violent a discharge, as was very offensive to me and my companions. The dog died on the spot, and we left the doctor endeavouring to recover him by the same operation.

I visited many other apartments, but shall not trouble my reader with all the curiosities I observed, being studious of brevity.

I had hitherto seen only one side of the Academy, the other being appropriated to the advancers of speculative learning, of whom I shall say something when I have mentioned one illustrious person more, who is called among them *the universal artist*. He told us he had been thirty years employing his thoughts for the improvement of human life. He had two large rooms full of wonderful curiosities, and fifty men at work. Some were condensing air into a dry tangible substance, by extracting the nitre, and letting the aqueous or fluid particles percolate; others softening marble for pillows and pincushions; other petrifying the hoofs of a living horse to preserve them from foundering. The artist himself was at that time busy upon two great designs; the first, to sow land with chaff, wherein he affirmed the true seminal virtue to be contained, as he demonstrated by several experiments which I was not skilful enough to comprehend. The other was, by a certain composition of gums, minerals, and vegetables outwardly applied, to prevent the growth of wool upon two young lambs; and he hoped in a reasonable time to propagate the breed of naked sheep all over the kingdom.

We crossed a walk to the other part of the Academy, where, as I have already said, the projectors in speculative learning resided.

The first professor I saw was in a very large room, with forty pupils about him. After salutation, observing me to look earnestly upon a frame, which took up the greatest part of both the length and breadth of the room, he said perhaps I might wonder to see him employed in a project for improving speculative knowledge by practical and mechanical operations. But the world would soon be sensible of its usefulness, and he flattered himself that a more noble exalted thought never sprang in any other man's head. Every one knew how laborious the usual method is of attaining to arts and sciences; whereas, by his contrivance, the most ignorant person at a reasonable charge, and with a little bodily labour, may write books in philosophy, poetry, politics, law, mathematics, and theology, without the least assistance from genius or study. He then led me to the frame, about the sides whereof all his pupils stood in ranks. It was twenty foot square, placed in the middle of the room. The superficies was composed of several bits of wood, about the bigness of a die, but some larger than others. They were all linked together by slender wires. These bits of wood were covered on every square with paper pasted on them, and on these papers were written all the words of their language, in their several moods, tenses, and declensions, but without any order. The professor then desired me to observe, for he was going to set his engine at work. The pupils at his command took each of them hold of an iron handle, whereof there were forty fixed round the edges of the frame, and giving them a sudden turn, the whole disposition of the words was entirely changed. He then commanded six and thirty of the lads to read the several lines softly as they appeared upon the frame; and where they found three or four words together that might make part of a sentence, they dictated to the four remaining boys who were scribes.

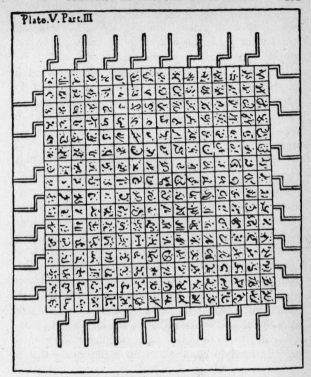

Plate.V.Part.III

This work was repeated three or four times, and at every turn the engine was so contrived, that the words shifted into new places, as the square bits of wood moved upside down.

Six hours a day the young students were employed in this labour, and the professor showed me several volumes in large folio already collected, of broken sentences, which he intended to piece together, and out of those rich materials to give the world a complete body of all arts and sciences; which, however, might be still improved, and much expedited, if the public would raise a fund for making and employing five hundred such frames in Lagado, and oblige the managers to contribute in common their several collections.

He assured me, that this invention had employed all his thoughts from his youth, that he had emptied the whole vocabulary into his frame, and made the strictest computation of the general proportion there is in books between the numbers of particles, nouns, and verbs, and other parts of speech.

I made my humblest acknowledgment to this illustrious person for his great communicativeness, and promised if ever I had the good fortune to return to my native country, that I would do him justice, as the sole inventor of this wonderful machine; the form and contrivance of which I desired leave to delineate upon paper, as in the figure here annexed. I told him, although it were the custom of our learned in Europe to steal inventions from each other, who had thereby at least this advantage, that it became a controversy which was the right owner, yet I would take such caution, that he should have the honour entire without a rival.

We next went to the school of languages, where three professors sat in consultation upon improving that of their own country.

The first project was to shorten discourse by cutting polysyllables into one, and leaving out verbs and participles, because in reality all things imaginable are but nouns.

The other project was a scheme for entirely abolishing all words whatsoever; and this was urged as a great advantage in point of health as well as brevity. For it is plain, that every word we speak is in some degree a diminution of our lungs by corrosion, and consequently contributes to the shortening of our lives. An expedient was therefore offered, that since words are only names for *things*, it would be more convenient for all men to carry about them such things as were necessary to express the particular business they are to discourse on. And this invention would certainly have taken place, to the great ease as well as health of the subject, if the women, in conjunction with the vulgar and illiterate, had not threatened to raise a rebellion, unless they might be allowed the liberty to speak with their tongues, after the manner of their ancestors; such constant irreconcilable enemies to science are the common people. However, many of the most learned and wise adhere to the new scheme of expressing themselves by things, which hath only this inconvenience attending it, that if a man's business be very great, and of various kinds, he must be obliged in proportion to carry a greater bundle of things upon his back, unless he can offord one or two strong servants to attend him. I have often beheld two of those sages almost sinking under the weight of their packs, like pedlars among us; who, when they met in the streets, would lay down their loads, open their sacks, and hold conversation for an hour together; then put up their implements, help each other to resume their burthens, and take their leave.

But for short conversations a man may carry implements in his pockets and under his arms, enough to supply him, and in his house he cannot be at a loss. Therefore the room where company meet who practice this art, is full of all things ready at hand, requisite to furnish matter for this kind of artificial converse.

Another great advantage proposed by this invention, was that it would serve as an universal language to be understood in all civilised nations, whose goods and utensils are generally of the same kind, or nearly resembling, so that their uses might easily be comprehended. And thus ambassadors would be qualified to treat with foreign princes or ministers of state, to whose tongues they were utter strangers.

I was at the mathematical school, where the master taught his pupils after a method scarce imaginable to us in Europe. The proposition and demonstration were fairly written on a thin wafer, with ink composed of a cephalic tincture. This the student was to swallow upon a fasting stomach, and for three days following eat nothing but bread and water. As the wafer digested, the tincture mounted to his brain, bearing the proposition along with it. But the success hath not hitherto been answerable, partly by some error in the *quantum* or composition, and partly by the perverseness of lads, to whom this bolus is so nauseous, that they generally steal aside, and discharge it upwards before it can operate; neither have they been yet persuaded to use so long an abstinence as the prescription requires.

CHAP. VI

A further account of the Academy. The Author proposes some improvements, which are honourably received.

In the school of political projectors I was but ill entertained, the professors appearing in my judgment wholly out of their senses, which is a scene that never fails to make me melancholy. These unhappy people were proposing schemes for persuading monarchs to choose favourites upon the score of their wisdom, capacity, and virtue; of teaching ministers to consult the public good; of rewarding merit, great abilities, eminent services; of instructing princes to know their true interest by placing it on the same foundation with that of

their people; of choosing for employments persons qualified to exercise them; with many other wild impossible
chimæras, that never entered before into the heart of
man to conceive, and confirmed in me the old observation, that there is nothing so extravagant and irra-
tional which some philosophers have not maintained
for truth.

But, however, I shall so far do justice to this part of
the Academy, as to acknowledge that all of them were
not so visionary. There was a most ingenious doctor who
seemed to be perfectly versed in the whole nature and
system of government. This illustrious person had very
usefully employed his studies in finding out effectual
remedies for all diseases and corruptions, to which the
several kinds of public administration are subject by the
vices or infirmities of those who govern, as well as by
the licentiousness of those who are to obey. For instance; whereas all writers and reasoners have agreed,
that there is a strict universal resemblance between the
natural and the political body; can there be any thing
more evident, than that the health of both must be preserved, and the diseases cured by the same prescrip-
tions? It is allowed, that senates and great councils are
often troubled with redundant, ebullient, and other pec-
cant humours, with many diseases of the head, and more
of the heart; with strong convulsions, with grievous con-
tractions of the nerves and sinews in both hands, but
especially the right; with spleen, flatus, vertigos, and
deliriums; with scrofulous tumours full of fœtid puru-
lent matter; with sour frothy ructations, with canine appetites and crudeness of digestion, besides many others
needless to mention. This doctor therefore proposed,
that upon the meeting of a senate, certain physicians
should attend at the three first days of their sitting, and
at the close of each day's debate, feel the pulses of every

senator; after which, having maturely considered, and
consulted upon the nature of the several maladies, and
the methods of cure, they should on the fourth day return to the senate house, attended by their apothecaries
stored with proper medicines; and before the members
sat, administer to each of them lenitives, aperitives, ab-
stersives, corrosives, restringents, palliatives, laxatives,
cephalagics, icterics, apophlegmatics, acoustics, as their
several cases required; and according as these medicines
should operate, repeat, alter, or omit them at the next
meeting.

This project could not be of any great expense to the
public, and would, in my poor opinion, be of much use
for the dispatch of business in those countries where
senates have any share in the legislative power; beget
unanimity, shorten debates, open a few mouths which
are now closed, and close many more which are now
open; curb the petulancy of the young, and correct the
positiveness of the old; rouse the stupid, and damp the
pert.

Again; because it is a general complaint, that the favourites of princes are troubled with short and weak
memories; the same doctor proposed, that whoever attended a first minister, after having told his business
with the utmost brevity and in the plainest words,
should at his departure give the said minister a tweak by
the nose, or a kick in the belly, or tread on his corns,
or lug him thrice by both ears, or run a pin into his
breech, or pinch his arm black and blue, to prevent forgetfulness; and at every levee day repeat the same operation, till the business were done or absolutely refused.

He likewise directed, that every senator in the great
council of a nation, after he had delivered his opinion,
and argued in the defence of it, should be obliged to
give his vote directly contrary; because if that were

done, the result would infallibly terminate in the good of the public.

When parties in a state are violent, he offered a wonderful contrivance to reconcile them. The method is this. You take a hundred leaders of each party, you dispose them into couples of such whose heads are nearest of a size; then let two nice operators saw off the occiput of each couple at the same time, in such a manner that the brain may be equally divided. Let the occiputs thus cut off be interchanged, applying each to the head of his opposite party-man. It seems indeed to be a work that requireth some exactness, but the professor assured us, that if it were dexterously performed, the cure would be infallible. For he argued thus; that the two half brains being left to debate the matter between themselves within the space of one skull, would soon come to a good understanding, and produce that moderation, as well as regularity of thinking, so much to be wished for in the heads of those, who imagine they came into the world only to watch and govern its motion: and as to the difference of brains in quantity or quality, among those who are directors in faction, the doctor assured us from his own knowledge, that it was a perfect trifle.

I heard a very warm debate between two professors, about the most commodious and effectual ways and means of raising money without grieving the subject. The first affirmed the justest method would be to lay a certain tax upon vices and folly, and the sum fixed upon every man, to be rated after the fairest manner by a jury of his neighbours. The second was of an opinion directly contrary, to tax those qualities of body and mind for which men chiefly value themselves, the rate to be more or less according to the degrees of excelling, the decision whereof should be left entirely to their own breast. The highest tax was upon men who are the greatest favourites of the other sex, and the assessments according to the number and natures of the favours they have received; for which they are allowed to be their own vouchers. Wit, valour, and politeness were likewise proposed to be largely taxed, and collected in the same manner, by every person's giving his own word for the quantum of what he possessed. But as to honour, justice, wisdom, and learning, they should not be taxed at all, because they are qualifications of so singular a kind, that no man will either allow them to his neighbour, or value them in himself.

The women were proposed to be taxed according to their beauty and skill in dressing, wherein they had the same privilege with the men, to be determined by their own judgment. But constancy, chastity, good sense, and good nature were not rated, because they would not bear the charge of collecting.

To keep senators in the interest of the crown, it was proposed that the members should raffle for employments, every man first taking an oath, and giving security that he would vote for the court, whether he won or no; after which the losers had in their turn the liberty of raffling upon the next vacancy. Thus hope and expectation would be kept alive, none would complain of broken promises, but impute their disappointments wholly to fortune, whose shoulders are broader and stronger than those of a ministry.

Another professor showed me a large paper of instructions for discovering plots and conspiracies against the government. He advised great statesmen to examine into the diet of all suspected persons; their times of eating; upon which side they lay in bed; with which hand they wiped their posteriors; to take a strict view of their excrements, and, from the colour, the odour, the taste, the consistence, the crudeness of maturity of digestion, form a judgment of their thoughts and designs. Because men are never so serious, thoughtful, and intent, as when they are at stool, which he found by frequent experiment; for in such conjunctures, when he used merely as a trial to consider which was the best way of murdering the king, his ordure would have a tincture of green, but quite different when he thought only of raising an insurrection or burning the metropolis.

The whole discourse was written with great acuteness, containing many observations both curious and useful for politicians, but as I conceived not altogether complete. This I ventured to tell the author, and offered if he pleased to supply him with some additions. He received my proposition with more compliance than is usual among writers, especially those of the projecting species, professing he would be glad to receive farther information.

I told him, that in the kingdom of Tribnia, by the natives called Langden, where I had sojourned some time in my travels, the bulk of the people consist in a manner wholly of discoverers, witnesses, informers, accusers, prosecutors, evidencers, swearers, together with their several subservient and subaltern instruments, all under the colours and conduct of ministers of state and their deputies. The plots in that kingdom are usually the workmanship of those persons who desire to raise their own characters of profound politicians, to restore new vigour to a crazy administration, to stifle or divert general discontents, to fill their pockets with forfeitures, and raise or sink the opinion of public credit, as either shall best answer their private advantage. It is first agreed and settled among them, what suspected persons shall be accused of a plot; then, effectual care is taken to secure all their letters and papers, and put the criminals in chains. These papers are delivered to a set of artists, very dexterous in finding out the mysterious meanings of words, syllables, and letters. For instance, they can discover a close-stool to signify a privy council; a flock of geese, a senate; a lame dog, an invader; a codshead, a ——; the plague, a standing army; a buzzard, a prime minister; the gout, a high priest; a gibbet, a secretary of state; a chamber-pot, a committee of grandees; a sieve, a court lady; a broom, a revolution; a mouse-trap, an employment; a bottomless pit, the treasury; a sink, the court; a cap and bells, a favourite; a broken reed, a court of justice; an empty tun, a general; a running sore, the administration.

When this method fails, they have two others more effectual, which the learned among them call acrostics and anagrams. First they can decipher all initial letters into political meanings. Thus, *N.* shall signify a plot; *B.* a regiment of horse; *L.* a fleet at sea; or secondly by transposing the letters of the alphabet in any suspected paper they can discover the deepest designs of a discontented party. So, for example, if I should say in a letter to a friend, *Our Brother* Tom *has just got the piles,* a skilful decipherer would discover, that the same letters which compose that sentence, may be analysed into the following words; *Resist, a plot is brought home; The tour.* And this is the anagrammatic method.

The professor made me great acknowledgments for communicating these observations, and promised to make honourable mention of me in his treatise.

I saw nothing in this country that could invite me to a longer continuance, and began to think of returning home to England.

CHAP. VII

The Author leaves Lagado, *arrives at* Maldonada. *No ship ready. He takes a short voyage to* Glubbdubdrib. *His reception by the Governor.*

The continent of which this kingdom is a part, extends itself, as I have reason to believe, eastward to that unknown tract of America, westward of California, and north to the Pacific Ocean, which is not above a hundred and fifty miles from Lagado; where there is a good port and much commerce with the great island of Luggnagg, situated to the north-west about 29 degrees north latitude, and 140 longitude. This island of Luggnagg stands south-eastwards of Japan, about an hundred leagues distant. There is a strict alliance between the Japanese Emperor and the King of Luggnagg, which affords frequent opportunities of sailing from one island to the other. I determined therefore to direct my course this way, in order to my return to Europe. I hired two mules with a guide to show me the way, and carry my small baggage. I took leave of my noble protector, who had shown me so much favour, and made me a generous present at my departure.

My journey was without any accident or adventure worth relating. When I arrived at the port of Maldonada (for so it is called), there was no ship in the harbour bound for Luggnagg, nor likely to be in some time. The town is about as large as Portsmouth. I soon fell into some acquaintance, and was very hospitably received. A gentleman of distinction said to me, that since the ships bound for Luggnagg could not be ready in less than a month, it might be no disagreeable amusement for me to take a trip to the little island of Glubbdubdrib, about five leagues off to the south-west. He offered himself and a friend to accompany me, and that I should be provided with a small convenient barque for the voyage.

Glubbdubdrib, as nearly as I can interpret the word signifies the Island of *Sorcerers* or *Magicians*. It is about one third as large as the Isle of Wight, and extremely fruitful: it is governed by the head of a certain tribe, who are all magicians. This tribe marries only among each other, and the eldest in succession is Prince or Governor. He hath a noble palace, and a park of about three thousand acres, surrounded by a wall of hewn stone twenty foot high. In this park are several small enclosures for cattle, corn, and gardening.

The Governor and his family are served and attended by domestics of a kind somewhat unusual. By his skill in necromancy, he hath a power of calling whom he pleaseth from the dead, and commanding their service for twenty-four hours, but no longer; nor can he call the same persons up again in less than three months, except upon very extraordinary occasions.

When we arrived at the island, which was about eleven in the morning, one of the gentlemen who accompanied me, went to the Governor, and desired admittance for a stranger, who came on purpose to have the honour of attending on his Highness. This was immediately granted, and we all three entered the gate of the palace between two rows of guards, armed and dressed after a very antic manner, and something in their countenances that made my flesh creep with a horror I cannot express. We passed through several apartments, between servants of the same sort, ranked on each side as before, till we came to the chamber of presence, where after three profound obeisances, and a few general questions, we were permitted to sit on three stools near the lowest step of his Highness's throne. He understood the language of Balnibarbi, although it were different from that of his island. He desired me to give him some account of my travels; and, to let me see that I should be treated without ceremony, he dismissed all his attendants with a turn of his finger, at which to my great astonishment they vanished in an instant, like visions in a dream, when we awake on a sudden. I could not recover myself in some time, till the Governor assured me that I should receive no hurt; and observing my two companions to be under no concern, who had been often entertained in the same manner, I began to take courage, and related to his Highness a short history of my several adventures, yet not without some hesitation, and frequently looking behind me to the place where I had seen those domestic spectres. I had the honour to dine with the Governor, where a new set of ghosts served up the meat, and waited at table. I now observed myself to be less terrified than I had been in the morning. I stayed till sunset, but humbly desired his Highness to excuse me for not accepting his invitation of lodging in the palace. My two friends and I lay at a private house in the town adjoining, which is the capital of this little island; and the next morning we returned to pay our duty to the Governor, as he was pleased to command us.

After this manner we continued in the island for ten days, most part of every day with the Governor, and at night in our lodging. I soon grew so familiarized to the sight of spirits, that after the third or fourth time they gave me no emotion at all; or, if I had any apprehensions left, my curiosity prevailed over them. For his Highness the Governor ordered me to call up whatever persons I would choose to name, and in whatever numbers among all the dead from the beginning of the world to the present time, and command them to answer any ques-

tions I should think fit to ask; with this condition, that
my questions must be confined within the compass of
the times they lived in. And one thing I might depend
upon, that they would certainly tell me the truth, for
lying was a talent of no use in the lower world.

I made my humble acknowledgments to his Highness for so great a favour. We were in a chamber, from
whence there was a fair prospect into the park. And
because my first inclination was to be entertained with
scenes of pomp and magnificence, I desired to see Alexander the Great, at the head of his army just after the
battle of Arbela; which upon a motion of the Governor's
finger immediately appeared in a large field under the
window, where we stood. Alexander was called up into
the room: it was with great difficulty that I understood
his Greek, and had but little of my own. He assured me
upon his honour that he was not poisoned, but died of a
fever by excessive drinking.

Next I saw Hannibal passing the Alps, who told me
he had not a drop of vinegar in his camp.

I saw Cæsar and Pompey at the head of their troops,
just ready to engage. I saw the former in his last great
triumph. I desired that the senate of Rome might appear before me in one large chamber, and a modern
representative, in counterview in another. The first
seemed to be an assembly of heroes and demi-gods; the
other a knot of pedlars, pickpockets, highway-men, and
bullies.

The Governor at my request gave the sign for Cæsar
and Brutus to advance towards us. I was struck with a
profound veneration at the sight of Brutus, and could
easily discover the most consummate virtue, the greatest
intrepidity and firmness of mind, the truest love of his
country, and general benevolence for mankind in every
lineament of his countenance. I observed with much

pleasure, that these two persons were in good intelligence with each other, and Cæsar freely confessed to me, that the greatest actions of his own life were not equal by many degrees to the glory of taking it away. I had the honour to have much conversation with Brutus; and was told, that his ancestors Junius, Socrates, Epaminondas, Cato the younger, Sir Thomas More, and himself were perpetually together: a sextumvirate to which all the ages of the world cannot add a seventh.

It would be tedious to trouble the reader with relating what vast numbers of illustrious persons were called up, to gratify that insatiable desire I had to see the world in every period of antiquity placed before me. I chiefly fed my eyes with beholding the destroyers of tyrants and usurpers, and the restorers of liberty to oppressed and injured nations. But it is impossible to express the satisfaction I received in my own mind, after such a manner as to make it a suitable entertainment to the reader.

CHAP. VIII

A further account of Glubbdubdrib. *Ancient and modern history corrected.*

Having a desire to see those ancients, who were most renowned for wit and learning, I set apart one day on purpose. I proposed that Homer and Aristotle might appear at the head of all their commentators; but these were so numerous that some hundreds were forced to attend in the court, and outward rooms of the palace. I knew and could distinguish those two heroes at first sight, not only from the crowd, but from each other. Homer was the taller and comelier person of the two, walked very erect for one of his age, and his eyes were the most quick and piercing I ever beheld. Aristotle stooped much, and made use of a staff. His visage was meagre, his hair lank and thin, and his voice hollow. I soon discovered that both of them were perfect strangers to the rest of the company, and had never seen or heard of them before. And I had a whisper from a ghost, who shall be nameless, that these commentators always kept in the most distant quarters from their principals in the lower world, through a consciousness of shame and guilt, because they had so horribly misrepresented the meaning of those authors to posterity. I introduced Didymus and Eustathius to Homer, and prevailed on him to treat them better than perhaps they deserved; for he soon found they wanted a genius to enter into the spirit of a poet. But Aristotle was out of all patience with the account I gave him of Scotus and Ramus, as I presented them to him; and he asked them whether the rest of the tribe were as great dunces as themselves.

I then desired the Governor to call up Descartes and Gassendi, with whom I prevailed to explain their systems to Aristotle. This great philosopher freely acknowledged his own mistakes in natural philosophy, because he proceeded in many things upon conjecture, as all men must do; and he found, that Gassendi, who had made the doctrine of Epicurus as palatable as he could, and the *vortices* of Descartes, were equally exploded. He predicted the same fate to *attraction,* whereof the present learned are such zealous asserters. He said, that new systems of nature were but new fashions, which would vary in every age; and even those who pretend to demonstrate them from mathematical principles, would flourish but a short period of time, and be out of vogue when that was determined.

I spent five days in conversing with many others of the ancient learned. I saw most of the first Roman emperors. I prevailed on the Governor to call up Eliogabalus's cooks to dress us a dinner, but they could not show us much of their skill, for want of materials. A helot of Agesilaus made us a dish of Spartan broth, but I was not able to get down a second spoonful.

The two gentlemen who conducted me to the island, were pressed by their private affairs to return in three days, which I employed in seeing some of the modern dead, who had made the greatest figure for two or three hundred years past in our own and other countries of Europe; and having been always a great admirer of old illustrious families, I desired the Governor would call up a dozen or two of kings with their ancestors in order for eight or nine generations. But my disappointment was grievous and unexpected. For, instead of a long train with royal diadems, I saw in one family two fiddlers, three spruce courtiers, and an Italian prelate. In another, a barber, an abbot, and two cardinals. I have too great a veneration for crowned heads to dwell any longer on so nice a subject. But as to counts, marquesses, dukes, earls, and the like, I was not so scrupulous. And I confess it was not without some pleasure that I found myself able to trace the particular features, by which certain families are distinguished, up to their originals. I could plainly discover from whence one family derives a long chin, why a second hath abounded with knaves for two generations, and fools for two more; why a third happened to be crack-brained, and a fourth to be sharpers. Whence it came what Polydore Virgil says of a certain great house, *Nec vir fortis, nec fœmina casta*. How cruelty, falsehood, and cowardice grew to be characteristics by which certain families are distinguished as much as by their coat of arms. Who first brought the pox into a noble house, which hath lineally descended in scrofulous tumours to their posterity. Neither could I wonder at all this, when I saw such an interruption of lineages by pages, lackeys, valets, coachmen, gamesters, fiddlers, players, captains, and pickpockets.

I was chiefly disgusted with modern history. For having strictly examined all the persons of greatest name in the courts of princes, for an hundred years past, I found how the world had been misled by prostitute writers, to ascribe the greatest exploits in war to cowards, the wisest counsel to fools, sincerity to flatterers, Roman virtue to betrayers of their country, piety to atheists, chastity to sodomites, truth to informers. How many innocent and excellent persons had been condemned to death or banishment, by the practising of great ministers upon the corruption of judges, and the malice of factions. How many villains had been exalted to the highest places of trust, power, dignity, and profit: how great a share in the motions and events of courts, councils, and senates might be challenged by bawds, whores, pimps, parasites, and buffoons. How low an opinion I had of human wisdom and integrity, when I was truly informed of the springs and motives of great enterprises and revolutions in the world, and of the contemptible accidents to which they owed their success.

Here I discovered the roguery and ignorance of those who pretend to write *anecdotes*, or secret history, who send so many kings to their graves with a cup of poison; will repeat the discourse between a prince and chief minister, where no witness was by; unlock the thoughts and cabinets of ambassadors and secretaries of state, and have the perpetual misfortune to be mistaken. Here I discovered the true causes of many great events that have surprised the world, how a whore can govern the back-stairs, the back-stairs a council, and the

council a senate. A general confessed in my presence,
that he got a victory purely by the force of cowardice
and ill conduct; and an admiral, that for want of proper
intelligence, he beat the enemy to whom he intended to
betray the fleet. Three kings protested to me, that in
their whole reigns they never did once prefer any person
of merit, unless by mistake or treachery of some minister in whom they confided: neither would they do it
if they were to live again: and they showed with great
strength of reason, that the royal throne could not be
supported without corruption, because that positive,
confident, restive temper, which virtue infused into man,
was a perpetual clog to public business.

I had the curiosity to enquire in a particular manner,
by what method great numbers had procured to themselves high titles of honour, and prodigious estates; and
I confined my enquiry to a very modern period: however, without grating upon present times, because I
would be sure to give no offence even to foreigners (for
I hope the reader need not be told that I do not in the
least intend my own country in what I say upon this
occasion), a great number of persons concerned were
called up, and upon a very slight examination, discovered such a scene of infamy, that I cannot reflect upon
it without some seriousness. Perjury, oppression, sub-
ornation, fraud, pandarism, and the like infirmities, were
amongst the most excusable arts they had to mention,
and for these I gave, as it was reasonable, great allowance. But when some confessed they owed their greatness and wealth to sodomy or incest; others to the
prostituting of their own wives and daughters; others
to the betraying their country or their prince; some to
poisoning, more to the perverting of justice in order to
destroy the innocent: I hope I may be pardoned if
these discoveries inclined me a little to abate of that

profound veneration which I am naturally apt to pay to persons of high rank, who ought to be treated with the utmost respect due to their sublime dignity, by us their inferiors.

I had often read of some great services done to princes and states, and desired to see the persons by whom those services were performed. Upon enquiry I was told that their names were to be found on no record, except a few of them whom history hath represented as the vilest rogues and traitors. As to the rest, I had never once heard of them. They all appeared with dejected looks, and in the meanest habit, most of them telling me they died in poverty and disgrace, and the rest on a scaffold or a gibbet.

Among others there was one person whose case appeared a little singular. He had a youth about eighteen years old standing by his side. He told me he had for many years been commander of a ship, and in the sea fight at Actium, had the good fortune to break through the enemy's great line of battle, sink three of their capital ships, and take a fourth, which was the sole cause of Antony's flight, and of the victory that ensued; that the youth standing by him, his only son, was killed in the action. He added, that upon the confidence of some merit, the war being at an end, he went to Rome, and solicited at the court of Augustus to be preferred to a greater ship, whose commander had been killed; but without any regard to his pretensions, it was given to a youth who had never seen the sea, the son of Libertina, who waited on one of the emperor's mistresses. Returning back to his own vessel, he was charged with neglect of duty, and the ship given to a favourite page of Publicola, the vice-admiral; whereupon he retired to a poor farm at a great distance from Rome, and there ended his life. I was so curious to know the truth of this story, that I desired Agrippa might be called, who was admiral in that fight. He appeared, and confirmed the whole account, but with much more advantage to the captain, whose modesty had extenuated or concealed a great part of his merit.

I was surprised to find corruption grown so high and so quick in that empire, by the force of luxury so lately introduced, which made me less wonder at many parallel cases in other countries, where vices of all kinds have reigned so much longer, and where the whole praise as well as pillage hath been engrossed by the chief commander, who perhaps had the least title to either.

As every person called up made exactly the same appearance he had done in the world, it gave me melancholy reflections to observe how much the race of human kind was degenerated among us, within these hundred years past. How the pox under all its consequences and denominations had altered every lineament of an English countenance, shortened the size of bodies, unbraced the nerves, relaxed the sinews and muscles, introduced a sallow complexion, and rendered the flesh loose and rancid.

I descended so low as to desire some English yeomen of the old stamp might be summoned to appear, once so famous for the simplicity of their manners, diet and dress, for justice in their dealings, for their true spirit of liberty, for their valour and love of their country. Neither could I be wholly unmoved after comparing the living with the dead, when I considered how all these pure native virtues were prostituted for a piece of money by their grandchildren, who in selling their votes, and managing at elections, have acquired every vice and corruption that can possibly be learned in a court.

CHAP. IX

The Author returns to Maldonada. *Sails to the kingdom of*
Luggnagg. *The Author confined. He is sent for to court.*
The manner of his admittance. The King's great lenity to
his subjects.

The day of our departure being come, I took leave
of his Highness the Governor of Glubbdubdrib, and
returned with by two companions to Maldonada,
where after a fortnight's waiting, a ship was ready
to sail for Luggnagg. The two gentlemen, and some
others, were so generous and kind as to furnish me with
provisions, and see me on board. I was a month in this
voyage. We had one violent storm, and were under a
necessity of steering westward to get into the trade
wind, which holds for about sixty leagues. On the 21st
of April, 1708, we sailed into the river of Clumegnig,
which is a seaport town, at the south-east point of
Luggnagg. We cast anchor within a league of the town,
and made a signal for a pilot. Two of them came on
board in less than half an hour, by whom we were
guided between certain shoals and rocks, which are very
dangerous in the passage to a large basin, where a
fleet may ride in safety within a cable's length of the
town wall.

Some of our sailors, whether out of treachery or
inadvertence, had informed the pilots that I was a
stranger and a great traveller, whereof these gave notice
to a custom-house officer, by whom I was examined very
strictly upon my landing. This officer spoke to me in the
language of Balnibarbi, which by the force of much
commerce is generally understood in that town, especially by seamen, and those employed in the customs. I

gave him a short account of some particulars, and made my story as plausible and consistent as I could; but I thought it necessary to disguise my country, and call myself an Hollander, because my intentions were for Japan, and I knew the Dutch were the only Europeans permitted to enter into that kingdom. I therefore told the officer, that having been shipwrecked on the coast of Balnibarbi, and cast on a rock, I was received up into Laputa, or the Flying Island (of which he had often heard), and was now endeavouring to get to Japan, from whence I might find a convenience of returning to my own country. The officer said, I must be confined till he could receive orders from court, for which he would write immediately, and hoped to receive an answer in a fortnight. I was carried to a convenient lodging, with a sentry placed at the door; however I had the liberty of a large garden, and was treated with humanity enough, being maintained all the time at the King's charge. I was invited by several persons, chiefly out of curiosity, because it was reported that I came from countries very remote of which they had never heard.

I hired a young man who came in the same ship to be an interpreter; he was a native of Luggnagg, but had lived some years at Maldonada, and was a perfect master of both languages. By his assistance I was able to hold a conversation with those who came to visit me; but this consisted only of their questions, and my answers.

The dispatch came from court about the time we expected. It contained a warrant for conducting me and my retinue to Traldragdubh or Trildrogdrib, for it is pronounced both ways as near as I can remember, by a party of ten horse. All my retinue was that poor lad for an interpreter, whom I persuaded into my service, and

at my humble request, we had each of us a mule to ride
on. A messenger was dispatched half a day's journey before us, to give the King notice of my approach, and to
desire that his Majesty would please to appoint a day
and hour, when it would be his gracious pleasure that I
might have the honour to *lick the dust before his foot-
stool.* This is the court style, and I found it to be more
than matter of form. For upon my admittance two days
after my arrival, I was commanded to crawl on my
belly, and lick the floor as I advanced; but on account
of my being a stranger, care was taken to have it made
so clean that the dust was not offensive. However, this
was a peculiar grace, not allowed to any but persons of
the highest rank, when they desire an admittance. Nay,
sometimes the floor is strewed with dust on purpose,
when the person to be admitted happens to have powerful enemies at court. And I have seen a great lord
with his mouth so crammed, that when he had crept to
the proper distance from the throne, he was not able to
speak a word. Neither is there any remedy, because it is
capital for those who receive an audience to spit or wipe
their mouths in his Majesty's presence. There is indeed
another custom, which I cannot altogether approve of.
When the King hath a mind to put any of his nobles to
death in a gentle indulgent manner, he commands to
have the floor strowed with a certain brown powder, of
a deadly composition, which being licked up infallibly
kills him in twenty-four hours. But in justice to this
prince's great clemency, and the care he hath of his subjects' lives (wherein it were much to be wished that the
monarchs of Europe would imitate him), it must be
mentioned for his honour, that strict orders are given to
have the infected parts of the floor well washed after
every such execution; which if his domestics neglect,

they are in danger of incurring his royal displeasure. I myself heard him give directions, that one of his pages should be whipped, whose turn it was to give notice about washing the floor after an execution, but maliciously had omitted it; by which neglect a young lord of great hopes coming to an audience, was unfortunately poisoned, although the King at that time had no design against his life. But this good prince was so gracious, as to forgive the poor page his whipping, upon promise that he would do so no more, without special orders.

To return from this digression; when I had crept within four yards of the throne, I raised myself gently upon my knees, and then striking my forehead seven times on the ground (I pronounced the following words, as they had been taught me the night before, *Ickpling glofthrobb squutserumm blhiop mlashnalt zwin tnodbalkuffh slhiophad gurdlubh asht*. This is the compliment established by the laws of the land for all persons admitted to the King's presence. It may be rendered into English thus: *May your Celestial Majesty outlive the sun, eleven moons and a half*. To this the King returned some answer, which although I could not understand, yet I replied as I had been directed: *Fluft drin yalerick dwuldom prastrad mirpush*, which properly signifies, *My tongue is in the mouth of my friend*, and by this expression was meant that I desired leave to bring my interpreter; whereupon the young man already mentioned was accordingly introduced, by whose intervention I answered as many questions as his Majesty could put in above an hour. I spoke in the Balnibarbian tongue, and my interpreter delivered my meaning in that of Luggnagg.

The King was much delighted with my company, and ordered his *Bliffmarklub*, or High Chamberlain, to

appoint a lodging in the court for me and my interpreter, with a daily allowance for my table, and a large
purse of gold for my common expenses.

I stayed three months in this country out of perfect
obedience to his Majesty, who was pleased highly to
favour me, and made me very honourable offers. But I
thought it more consistent with prudence and justice to
pass the remainder of my days with my wife and family.

CHAP. X

The Luggnaggians *commended. A particular description of
the* Struldbrugs, *with many conversations between the
Author and some eminent persons upon that subject.*

The Luggnaggians are a polite and generous people,
and although they are not without some share of that
pride which is peculiar to all Eastern countries, yet
they show themselves courteous to strangers, especially
such who are countenanced by the court. I had many
acquaintance among persons of the best fashion, and
being always attended by my interpreter, the conversation we had was not disagreeable.

One day in much good company I was asked by a
person of quality, whether I had seen any of their
struldbrugs, or *immortals*. I said I had not, and desired
he would explain to me what he meant by such an appellation applied to a mortal creature. He told me, that
sometimes, though very rarely, a child happened to be
born in a family with a red circular spot in the forehead,
directly over the left eyebrow, which was an infallible
mark that it should never die. The spot, as he described
it, was about the compass of a silver threepence, but in
the course of time grew larger, and changed its colour;
for at twelve years old it became green, so continued till

five and twenty, then turned to a deep blue; at five and forty it grew coal black, and as large as an English shilling, but never admitted any further alteration. He said these births were so rare, that he did not believe they could be above eleven hundred *struldbrugs* of both sexes in the whole kingdom, of which he computed about fifty in the metropolis, and among the rest a young girl born about three years ago. That these productions were not peculiar to any family, but a mere effect of chance; and the children of the *struldbrugs* themselves, were equally mortal with the rest of the people.

I freely own myself to have been struck with inexpressible delight upon hearing this account: and the person who gave it me happening to understand the Balnibarbian language, which I spoke very well, I could not forbear breaking out into expressions perhaps a little too extravagant. I cried out as in a rapture; Happy nation where every child hath at least a chance of being immortal! Happy people who enjoy so many living examples of ancient virtue, and have masters ready to instruct them in the wisdom of all former ages! but, happiest beyond all comparison are those excellent *struldbrugs*, who being born exempt from that universal calamity of human nature, have their minds free and disengaged, without the weight and depression of spirits caused by the continual apprehension of death. I discovered my admiration that I had not observed any of these illustrious persons at court; the black spot on the forehead being so remarkable a distinction, that I could not have easily overlooked it: and it was impossible that his Majesty, a most judicious prince, should not provide himself with a good number of such wise and able counsellors. Yet perhaps the virtue of those reverend sages was too strict for the corrupt and libertine manners of a court. And we often find by experience that young men are too opinionative and volatile to be guided by the sober dictates of their seniors. However, since the King was pleased to allow me access to his royal person, I was resolved upon the very first occasion to deliver my opinion to him on this matter freely, and at large by the help of my interpreter; and whether he would please to take my advice or no, yet in one thing I was determined, that his Majesty having frequently offered me an establishment in this country, I would with great thankfulness accept the favour, and pass my life here in the conversation of those superior beings the *struldbrugs*, if they would please to admit me.

The gentleman to whom I addressed my discourse, because (as I have already observed) he spoke the language of Balnibarbi, said to me with sort of a smile, which usually ariseth from pity to the ignorant, that he was glad of any occasion to keep me among them, and desired my permission to explain to the company what I had spoke. He did so, and they talked together for some time in their own language, whereof I understood not a syllable, neither could I observe by their countenances what impression my discourse had made on them. After a short silence, the same person told me, that his friends and mine (so he thought fit to express himself) were very much pleased with the judicious remarks I had made on the great happiness and advantages of immortal life; and they were desirous to know in a particular manner, what scheme of living I should have formed to myself, if it had fallen to my lot to have been born a *struldbrug*.

I answered, it was easy to be eloquent on so copious and delightful a subject, especially to me who have been often apt to amuse myself with visions of what I should do if I were a king, or a great lord: and upon this very case I had frequently run over the whole system how I should employ myself, and pass the time if I were sure to live for ever.

That, if it had been my good fortune to come into the world a *struldbrug*, as soon as I could discover my own happiness by understanding the difference between life and death, I would first resolve by all arts and methods whatsoever to procure myself riches. In the pursuit of which by thrift and management, I might reasonably expect in about two hundred years, to be the wealthiest man in the kingdom. In the second place, I would from my earliest youth apply myself to the study of arts and sciences, by which I should arrive in time to excel all others in learning. Lastly, I would carefully record every action and event of consequence that happened in the public, impartially draw the characters of the several successions of princes and great ministers of state, with my own observations on every point. I would exactly set down the several changes in customs, language, fashions of dress, diet, and diversions. By all which acquirements, I should be a living treasury of knowledge and wisdom, and certainly become the oracle of the nation.

I would never marry after threescore, but live in an hospitable manner, yet still on the saving side. I would entertain myself in forming and directing the minds of hopeful young men, by convincing them from my own remembrance, experience, and observation, fortified by numerous examples, of the usefulness of virtue in public and private life. But my choice and constant companions should be a set of my own immortal brotherhood, among whom I would elect a dozen from the most ancient down to my own contemporaries. Where any of these wanted fortunes, I would provide them with convenient lodges round my own estate, and have some of them always at my table, only mingling a few of the most valuable among you mortals, whom length of time would harden me to lose with little or no reluctance, and treat your posterity after the same manner; just as a man diverts himself with the annual succession of pinks and tulips in his garden, without regretting the loss of those which withered the preceding year.

These *struldbrugs* and I would mutually communicate our observations and memorials through the course of time, remark the several gradations by which corruption steals into the world, and oppose it in every step, by giving perpetual warning and instruction to mankind; which, added to the strong influence of our own example, would probably prevent that continual degeneracy of human nature so justly complained of in all ages.

Add to all this, the pleasure of seeing the various revolutions of states and empires, the changes in the lower and upper world, ancient cities in ruins, and obscure villages become the seats of kings. Famous rivers lessening into shallow brooks, the ocean leaving one coast dry, and overwhelming another: the discovery of many countries yet unknown. Barbarity over-running the politest nations, and the most barbarous become civilized. I should then see the discovery of the longitude, the perpetual motion, the universal medicine, and many other great inventions brought to the utmost perfection.

What wonderful discoveries should we make in astronomy, by outliving and confirming our own predictions, by observing the progress and returns of comets, with the changes of motion in the sun, moon, and stars.

I enlarged upon many other topics, which the natural desire of endless life and sublunary happiness could easily furnish me with. When I had ended, and the sum of my discourse had been interpreted as before, to the rest of the company, there was a good deal of talk among them in the language of the country, not without some laughter at my expense. At last the same gentleman who had been my interpreter said, he was desired by the rest to set me right in a few mistakes, which I had fallen into through the common imbecility of human nature, and upon that allowance was less answerable for them. That this breed of *struldbrugs* was peculiar to their country, for there were no such people either in Balnibarbi or Japan, where he had the honour to be ambassador from his Majesty, and found the natives in both those kingdoms very hard to believe that the fact was possible; and it appeared from my astonishment when he first mentioned the matter to me, that I received it as a thing wholly new, and scarcely to be credited. That in the two kingdoms above mentioned, where during his residence he had conversed very much, he observed long life to be the universal desire and wish of mankind. That whoever had one foot in the grave, was sure to hold back the other as strongly as he could. That the oldest had still hopes of living one day longer, and looked on death as the greatest evil, from which nature always prompted him to retreat; only in this island of Luggnagg the appetite for living was not so eager, from the continual example of the *struldbrugs* before their eyes.

That the system of living contrived by me was unreasonable and unjust, because it supposed a perpetuity of youth, health, and vigour, which no man could be so foolish to hope, however extravagant he may be in his wishes. That the question therefore was not whether a man would chose to be always in the prime of youth, attended with prosperity and health, but how he would pass a perpetual life under all the usual disadvantages which old age brings along with it. For although few men will avow their desires of being immortal upon such hard conditions, yet in the two kingdoms before mentioned of Balnibarbi and Japan, he observed that every man desired to put off death for some time longer, let it approach ever so late; and he rarely heard of any man who died willingly, except he were incited by the extremity of grief or torture. And he appealed to me whether in those countries I had travelled as well as my own, I had not observed the same general disposition.

After this preface, he gave me a particular account of the *struldbrugs* among them. He said they commonly acted like mortals, till about thirty years old, after which by degrees they grew melancholy and dejected, increasing in both till they came to fourscore. This he learned from their own confession: for otherwise there not being above two or three of that species born in an age, they were too few to form a general observation by. When they came to fourscore years, which is reckoned the extremity of living in this country, they had not only all the follies and infirmities of other old men, but many more which arose from the dreadful prospect of never dying. They were not only opinionative, peevish, covetous, morose, vain, talkative, but uncapable of friendship, and dead to all natural affection, which never descended below their grandchildren. Envy and impotent desires are their prevailing passions. But those objects against which their envy seems principally directed, are the vices of the younger sort, and the deaths of the old. By reflecting on the former, they find themselves cut off from all possibility of pleasure; and whenever they see a funeral, they lament and repine that others have gone to a harbour of rest, to which they themselves never can hope to arrive. They have no remembrance of anything but what they learned and observed in their youth and middle age, and even that is very imperfect. And for the truth or particulars of any fact, it is safer to depend on common traditions than upon their best recollections. The least miserable among them appear to be those who turn to dotage, and entirely lose their memories; these meet with more pity and assistance, because they want many bad qualities which abound in others.

If a *struldbrug* happen to marry one of his own kind, the marriage is dissolved of course by the courtesy of the kingdom, as soon as the younger of the two comes to be fourscore. For the law thinks it a reasonable indulgence, that those who are condemned without any fault of their own to a perpetual continuance in the world, should not have their misery doubled by the load of a wife.

As soon as they have completed the term of eighty years, they are looked on as dead in law; their heirs immediately succeed to their estates, only a small pittance is reserved for their support, and the poor ones are maintained at the public charge. After that period they are held incapable of any employment of trust or profit, they cannot purchase lands or take leases, neither are they allowed to be witnesses in any cause, either civil or criminal, not even for the decision of meers and bounds.

At ninety they lose their teeth and hair, they have at that age no distinction of taste, but eat and drink whatever they can get, without relish or appetite. The diseases they were subject to still continue without increasing or diminishing. In talking they forget the common appellation of things, and the names of persons, even of those who are their nearest friends and relations. For the same reason, they never can amuse themselves with reading, because their memory will not serve to carry them from the beginning of a sentence to the end; and by this defect they are deprived of the only entertainment whereof they might otherwise be capable.

The language of this country being always upon the flux, the *struldbrugs* of one age do not understand those of another, neither are they able after two hundred years to hold any conversation (farther than by a few general words) with their neighbours the mortals; and thus they lie under the disadvantage of living like foreigners in their own country.

This was the account given me of the *struldbrugs,* as near as I can remember. I afterwards saw five or six of different ages, the youngest not above two hundred years old, who were brought to me at several times by some of my friends; but although they were told that I was a great traveller, and had seen all the world, they had not the least curiosity to ask me a question; only desired I would give them *slumskudask,* or a token of remembrance, which is a modest way of begging, to avoid the law that strictly forbids it, because they are provided for by the public, although indeed with a very scanty allowance.

They are despised and hated by all sorts of people; when one of them is born, it is reckoned ominous, and their birth is recorded very particularly: so that you may know their age by consulting the registry, which however hath not been kept above a thousand years past, or at least hath been destroyed by time or public disturbances. But the usual way of computing how old they are, is by asking them what kings or great persons they can remember, and then consulting history, for infallibly the last prince in their mind did not begin his reign after they were fourscore years old.

They were the most mortifying sight I ever beheld, and the women more horrible than the men. Besides the usual deformities in extreme old age, they acquired an additional ghastliness in proportion to their number of years, which is not to be described; and among half a dozen, I soon distinguished which was the eldest, although there was not above a century or two between them.

The reader will easily believe, that from what I had heard and seen, my keen appetite for perpetuity of life was much abated. I grew heartily ashamed of the pleasing visions I had formed, and thought no tyrant could invent a death into which I would not run with pleasure from such a life. The King heard of all that had passed between me and my friends upon this occasion, and rallied me very pleasantly, wishing I would send a couple of *struldbrugs* to my own country, to arm our people against the fear of death; but this it seems is forbidden by the fundamental laws of the kingdom, or else I should have been well content with the trouble and expense of transporting them.

I could not but agree that the laws of this kingdom, relating to the *struldbrugs*, were founded upon the strongest reasons, and such as any other country would be under the necessity of enacting in the like circumstances. Otherwise, as avarice is the necessary consequent of old age, those immortals would in time become proprietors of the whole nation, and engross the civil power, which, for want of abilities to manage, must end in the ruin of the public.

CHAP. XI

The Author leaves Luggnagg, *and sails to* Japan. *From thence he returns in a* Dutch *ship to* Amsterdam, *and from* Amsterdam *to* England.

I thought this account of the *struldbrugs* might be some entertainment to the reader, because it seems to be a little out of the common way; at least, I do not remember to have met the like in any book of travels that hath come to my hands: and if I am deceived, my excuse must be that it is necessary for travellers, who describe the same country, very often to agree in dwelling on the same particulars, without deserving the censure of having borrowed or transcribed from those who wrote before them.

There is indeed a perpetual commerce between this kingdom and the great empire of Japan, and it is very probable that the Japanese authors may have given some account of the *struldbrugs;* but my stay in Japan was so short, and I was so entirely a stranger to that language, that I was not qualified to make any enquiries. But I hope the Dutch, upon this notice, will be curious and able enough to supply my defects.

His Majesty having often pressed me to accept some employment in his court, and finding me absolutely determined to return to my native country, was pleased to give me his licence to depart, and honoured me with a letter of recommendation under his own hand to the Emperor of Japan. He likewise presented me with four hundred forty-four large pieces of gold (this nation delighting in even numbers), and a red diamond which I sold in England for eleven hundred pounds.

On the 6th day of May, 1709, I took a solemn leave

of his Majesty, and all my friends. This prince was so gracious as to order a guard to conduct me to Glanguenstald, which is a royal port to the south-west part of the island. In six days I found a vessel ready to carry me to Japan, and spent fifteen days in the voyage. We landed at a small port-town called Xamoschi, situated on the south-east part of Japan; the town lies on the western point, where there is a narrow strait, leading northward into a long arm of the sea, upon the north-west part of which, Yedo the metropolis stands. At landing, I showed the custom-house officers my letter from the King of Luggnagg to his Imperial Majesty. They knew the seal perfectly well; it was as broad as the palm of my hand. The impression was, *a King lifting up a lame beggar from the earth.* The magistrates of the town hearing of my letter, received me as a public minister. They provided me with carriages and servants, and bore my charges to Yedo, where I was admitted to an audience, and delivered my letter, which was opened with great ceremony, and explained to the Emperor by an interpreter, who then gave me notice by his Majesty's order, that I should signify my request, and, whatever it were, it should be granted for the sake of his royal brother of Luggnagg. This interpreter was a person employed to transact affairs with the Hollanders; he soon conjectured by my countenance that I was an European, and therefore repeated his Majesty's commands in Low Dutch, which he spoke perfectly well. I answered (as I had before determined), that I was a Dutch merchant, shipwrecked in a very remote country, from whence I had travelled by sea and land to Luggnagg, and then took shipping for Japan, where I knew my countrymen often traded, and with some of these I hoped to get an opportunity of returning into Europe: I therefore most humbly entreated his royal favour, to give order, that I

should be conducted in safety to Nangasac. To this
I added another petition, that for the sake of my patron
the King of Luggnagg, his Majesty would condescend
to excuse my performing the ceremony imposed on my
countrymen, of trampling upon the crucifix, because I
had been thrown into his kingdom by my misfortunes,
without any intention of trading. When this latter petition was interpreted to the Emperor, he seemed a little
surprised, and said, he believed I was the first of my
countrymen who ever made any scruple in this point,
and that he began to doubt whether I was a real Hollander, or no, but rather suspected I must be a Christian. However, for the reasons I had offered, but chiefly
to gratify the King of Luggnagg by an uncommon mark
of his favour, he would comply with the singularity of
my humour; but the affair must be managed with dexterity, and his officers should be commanded to let me
pass as it were by forgetfulness. For he assured me, that
if the secret should be discovered by my countrymen,
the Dutch, they would cut my throat in the voyage. I
returned my thanks by the interpreter for so unusual a
favour, and some troops being at that time on their
march to Nangasac, the commanding officer had orders
to convey me safe thither, with particular instructions
about the business of the crucifix.

On the 9th day of June, 1709, I arrived at Nangasac,
after a very long and troublesome journey. I soon fell
into the company of some Dutch sailors belonging to the
Amboyna, of Amsterdam, a stout ship of 450 tons. I
had lived long in Holland, pursuing my studies at Leyden, and I spoke Dutch well. The seamen soon knew
from whence I came last: they were curious to enquire
into my voyages and course of life. I made up a story as
short and probable as I could, but concealed the greatest
part. I knew many persons in Holland; I was able to

invent names for my parents, whom I pretended to be
obscure people in the province of Guelderland. I would
have given the captain (one Theodorus Vangrult) what
he pleased to ask for my voyage to Holland; but understanding I was a surgeon, he was contented to take half
the usual rate, on condition that I would serve him in
the way of my calling. Before we took shipping, I was
often asked by some of the crew, whether I had performed the ceremony above-mentioned. I evaded the
question by general answers, that I had satisfied the Emperor and court in all particulars. However, a malicious
rogue of a skipper went to an officer, and pointing to
me, told him I had not yet trampled on the crucifix: but
the other, who had received instructions to let me pass,
gave the rascal twenty strokes on the shoulders with a
bamboo, after which I was no more troubled with such
questions.

Nothing happened worth mentioning in this voyage.
We sailed with a fair wind to the Cape of Good Hope,
where we stayed only to take in fresh water. On the 10th
of April, 1710, we arrived safe at Amsterdam, having
lost only three men by sickness in the voyage, and a
fourth who fell from the foremast into the sea, not far
from the coast of Guinea. From Amsterdam I soon after
set sail for England in a small vessel belonging to that
city.

On the 16th of April we put in at the Downs. I landed
the next morning, and saw once more my native country after an absence of five years and six months complete. I went straight to Redriff, where I arrived the
same day at two in the afternoon, and found my wife
and family in good health.

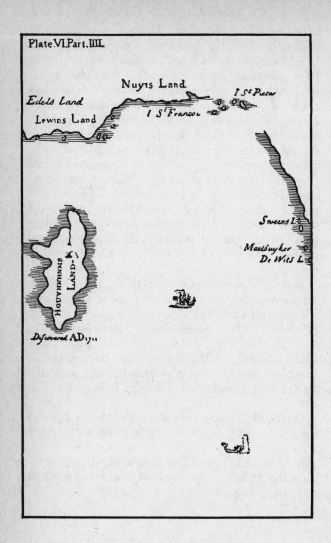

Plate.VI.Part.IIII.

Nuyts Land

Edels Land

Lewins Land

I St Francou

I St Pieter

Sweers I.

Maetsuyker

De Wits L.

HOUTMANS LAND.

Discovered A.D.1,..

440

PART IV

A Voyage to the Country of the Houyhnhnms

CHAP. I

The Author sets out as Captain of a ship. His men conspire against him, confine him a long time to his cabin, set him on shore in an unknown land. He travels up into the country. The Yahoos, a strange sort of animal, described. The Author meets two Houyhnhnms.

I CONTINUED at home with my wife and children about five months in a very happy condition, if I could have learned the lesson of knowing when I was well. I left my poor wife big with child, and accepted an advantageous offer made me to be Captain of the *Adventurer,* a stout merchantman of 350 tons: for I understood navigation well, and being grown weary of a surgeon's employment at sea, which however I could exercise upon occasion, I took a skilful young man of that calling, one Robert Purefoy, into my ship. We set sail from Portsmouth upon the seventh day of September, 1710; on the fourteenth we met with Captain Pocock of Bristol, at Teneriffe, who was going to the bay of Campechy, to cut logwood. On the sixteenth, he was parted from us by a storm; I heard since my return, that his ship foundered, and none escaped but one cabin boy. He was an honest man, and a good sailor, but a little too positive in his own opinions, which was the cause of his destruction, as it hath been of several others. For if he had followed my advice, he might have been safe at home with his family at this time, as well as myself.

I had several men died in my ship of calentures, so that I was forced to get recruits out of Barbadoes, and the Leeward Islands, where I touched by the direction of the merchants who employed me, which I had soon too much cause to repent: for I found afterwards that most of them had been buccaneers. I had fifty hands on board, and my orders were, that I should trade with the Indians in the South-Sea, and make what discoveries I could. These rogues whom I had picked up debauched my other men, and they all formed a conspiracy to seize the ship and secure me; which they did one morning, rushing into my cabin, and binding me hand and foot, threatening to throw me overboard, if I offered to stir. I told them, I was their prisoner, and would submit. This they made me swear to do, and then they unbound me, only fastening one of my legs with a chain near my bed, and placed a sentry at my door with his piece charged, who was commanded to shoot me dead, if I attempted my liberty. They sent me down victuals and drink, and took the government of the ship to themselves. Their design was to turn pirates, and plunder the Spaniards, which they could not do, till they got more men. But first they resolved to sell the goods in the ship, and then go to Madagascar for recruits, several among them having died since my confinement. They sailed many weeks, and traded with the Indians, but I knew not what course they took, being kept a close prisoner in my cabin, and expecting nothing less than to be murdered, as they often threatened me.

Upon the ninth day of May, 1711, one James Welch

came down to my cabin; and said he had orders from
the Captain to get me ashore. I expostulated with him,
but in vain; neither would he so much as tell me who
their new Captain was. They forced me into the long-
boat, letting me put on my best suit of clothes, which
were as good as new, and a small bundle of linen, but
no arms except my hanger; and they were so civil as
not to search my pockets, into which I conveyed what
money I had, with some other little necessaries. They
rowed about a league, and then set me down on a
strand. I desired them to tell me what country it was.
They all swore, they knew no more than myself, but
said, that the Captain (as they called him) was resolved,
after they had sold the lading, to get rid of me in the
first place where they could discover land. They pushed
off immediately, advising me to make haste, for fear of
being overtaken by the tide, and so bade me farewell.

In this desolate condition I advanced forward, and
soon got upon firm ground, where I sat down on a bank
to rest myself, and consider what I had best to do. When
I was a little refreshed, I went up into the country, resolving to deliver myself to the first savages I should
meet, and purchase my life from them by some bracelets, glass rings, and other toys which sailors usually provide themselves with in those voyages, and whereof I
had some about me. The land was divided by long rows
of trees, not regularly planted, but naturally growing;
there was great plenty of grass, and several fields of
oats. I walked very circumspectly for fear of being surprised, or suddenly shot with an arrow from behind or
on either side. I fell into a beaten road, where I saw
many tracks of human feet, and some of cows, but most
of horses. At last I beheld several animals in a field,
and one or two of the same kind sitting in trees. Their
shape was very singular, and deformed, which a little

discomposed me, so that I lay down behind a thicket to observe them better. Some of them coming forward near the place where I lay, gave me an opportunity of distinctly marking their form. Their heads and breasts were covered with a thick hair, some frizzled and others lank; they had beards like goats, and a long ridge of hair down their backs and the fore parts of their legs and feet, but the rest of their bodies were bare, so that I might see their skins, which were of a brown buff colour. They had no tails, nor any hair at all on their buttocks, except about the anus; which, I presume, nature had placed there to defend them as they sat on the ground; for this posture they used, as well as lying down, and often stood on their hind feet. They climbed high trees, as nimbly as a squirrel, for they had strong extended claws before and behind, terminating in sharp points, and hooked. They would often spring, and bound, and leap with prodigious agility. The females were not so large as the males; they had long lank hair on their heads, but none on their faces, nor any thing more than a sort of down on the rest of their bodies, except about the anus, and pudenda. Their dugs hung between their fore-feet, and often reached almost to the ground as they walked. The hair of both sexes was of several colours, brown, red, black, and yellow. Upon the whole, I never beheld in all my travels so disagreeable an animal, nor one against which I naturally conceived so strong an antipathy. So that thinking I had seen enough, full of contempt and aversion, I got up and pursued the beaten road, hoping it might direct me to the cabin of some Indian. I had not got far when I met one of these creatures full in my way, and coming up directly to me. The ugly monster, when he saw me, distorted several ways every feature of his visage, and stared as at an object he had never seen before; then approaching nearer, lifted up his fore-paw, whether out of curiosity or mischief, I could not tell. But I drew my hanger, and gave him a good blow with the flat side of it, for I durst not strike with the edge, fearing the inhabitants might be provoked against me, if they should come to know, that I had killed or maimed any of their cattle. When the beast felt the smart, he drew back, and roared so loud, that a herd of at least forty came flocking about me from the next field, howling and making odious faces; but I ran to the body of a tree, and leaning my back against it, kept them off by waving my hanger. Several of this cursed brood getting hold of the branches behind, leapt up into the tree, from whence they began to discharge their excrements on my head; however, I escaped pretty well, by sticking close to the stem of the tree, but was almost stifled with the filth, which fell about me on every side.

In the midst of this distress, I observed them all to run away on a sudden as fast as they could, at which I ventured to leave the tree, and pursue the road, wondering what it was that could put them into this fright. But looking on my left hand, I saw a horse walking softly in the field; which my persecutors having sooner discovered, was the cause of their flight. The horse started a little when he came near me, but soon recovering himself, looked full in my face with manifest tokens of wonder: he viewed my hands and feet, walking round me several times. I would have pursued my journey, but he placed himself directly in the way, yet looking with a very mild aspect, never offering the least violence. We stood gazing at each other for some time; at last I took the boldness to reach my hand towards his neck, with a design to stroke it, using the common style and whistle of jockeys when they are going to handle a strange horse. But this animal seeming to receive my civilities with disdain, shook his head, and bent his brows, softly raising up his right fore-foot to remove my hand. Then he neighed three or four times, but in so different a cadence, that I almost began to think he was speaking to himself in some language of his own.

While he and I were thus employed, another horse came up; who applying himself to the first in a very formal manner, they gently struck each other's right hoof before, neighing several times by turns, and varying the sound, which seemed to be almost articulate. They went some paces off, as if it were to confer together, walking side by side, backward and forward, like persons deliberating upon some affair of weight, but often turning their eyes towards me, as it were to watch that I might not escape. I was amazed to see such actions and behaviour in brute beasts, and concluded with myself, that if the inhabitants of this country were endued with a proportionable degree of reason, they must needs be the wisest people upon earth. This thought gave me so much comfort, that I resolved to go forward until I could discover some house or village, or meet with any of the natives, leaving the two horses to discourse together as they pleased. But the first, who was a dapple gray, observing me to steal off, neighed after me in so expressive a tone, that I fancied myself to understand what he meant; whereupon I turned back, and came near him, to expect his farther commands: but concealing my fear as much as I could, for I began to be in some pain, how this adventure might terminate; and the reader will easily believe I did not much like my present situation.

The two horses came up close to me, looking with great earnestness upon my face and hands. The gray steed rubbed my hat all round with his right fore-hoof, and discomposed it so much that I was forced to adjust it better, by taking it off, and settling it again; whereat both he and his companion (who was a brown bay) appeared to be much surprised: the latter felt the lappet of my coat, and finding it to hang loose about me, they both looked with new signs of wonder. He stroked my right hand, seeming to admire the softness and colour; but he squeezed it so hard between his hoof and his pastern, that I was forced to roar; after which they both touched me with all possible tenderness. They were under great perplexity about my shoes and stockings, which they felt very often, neighing to each other, and using various gestures, not unlike those of a philosopher, when he would attempt to solve some new and difficult phenomenon.

Upon the whole, the behaviour of these animals was so orderly and rational, so acute and judicious, that I at last concluded, they must needs be magicians, who had thus metamorphosed themselves upon some design, and seeing a stranger in the way, were resolved to divert themselves with him; or perhaps were really amazed at the sight of a man so very different in habit, feature, and complexion from those who might probably live in so remote a climate. Upon the strength of this reasoning, I ventured to address them in the following manner: Gentlemen, if you be conjurers, as I have good cause to believe, you can understand any language; therefore I make bold to let your worships know, that I am a poor distressed English man, driven by his misfortunes upon your coast, and I entreat one of you, to let me ride upon his back, as if he were a real horse, to some house or village, where I can be relieved. In return of which favour, I will make you a present of this knife and bracelet (taking them out of my pocket). The two creatures stood silent while I spoke, seeming to listen with great attention; and when I had ended, they neighed frequently towards each other, as if they were engaged in serious conversation. I plainly observed, that their language expressed the passions very well, and the words might with little pains be resolved into an alphabet more easily than the Chinese.

I could frequently distinguish the word *Yahoo*, which was repeated by each of them several times; and although it was impossible for me to conjecture what it meant, yet while the two horses were busy in conversation, I endeavoured to practise this word upon my tongue; and as soon as they were silent, I boldly pronounced *Yahoo* in a loud voice, imitating, at the same time, as near as I could, the neighing of a horse; at which they were both visibly surprised, and the gray repeated the same word twice, as if he meant to teach me the right accent, wherein I spoke after him as well as I could, and found myself perceivably to improve every time, though very far from any degree of perfection. Then the bay tried me with a second word, much harder to be pronounced; but reducing it to the English orthography, may be spelt thus, *Houyhnhnm*. I did not succeed in this so well as the former, but after two or three farther trials, I had better fortune; and they both appeared amazed at my capacity.

After some further discourse, which I then conjectured might relate to me, the two friends took their leaves, with the same compliment of striking each other's hoof; and the gray made me signs that I should walk before him, wherein I thought it prudent to comply, till I could find a better director. When I offered to slacken my pace, he would cry *Hhuun, Hhuun;* I guessed his meaning, and gave him to understand, as well as I could, that I was weary, and not able to walk faster; upon which, he would stand a while to let me rest.

CHAP. II

The Author conducted by a Houyhnhnm *to his house. The house described. The Author's reception. The food of the* Houyhnhnms. *The Author in distress for want of meat, is at last relieved. His manner of feeding in this country.*

Having travelled about three miles, we came to a long kind of building, made of timber, stuck in the ground, and wattled across; the roof was low, and covered with straw. I now began to be a little comforted, and took out some toys, which travellers usually carry for presents to the savage Indians of America and other parts, in hopes the people of the house would be thereby encouraged to receive me kindly. The horse made me a sign to go in first; it was a large room with a smooth clay floor, and a rack and manger extending the whole length on one side. There were three nags, and two mares, not eating, but some of them sitting down upon their hams, which I very much wondered at; but wondered more to see the rest employed in domestic business. These seemed but ordinary cattle; however, this confirmed my first opinion, that a people who could so far civilise brute animals, must needs excel in wisdom all the nations of the world. The gray came in just after, and thereby prevented any ill treatment, which the others might have given me. He neighed to them several times in a style of authority, and received answers.

Beyond this room there were three others, reaching the length of the house, to which you passed through three doors, opposite to each other, in the manner of a vista; we went through the second room towards the third; here the gray walked in first, beckoning me to attend: I waited in the second room, and got ready my presents for the master and mistress of the house: they were two knives, three bracelets of false pearl, a small looking-glass, and a bead necklace. The horse neighed three or four times, and I waited to hear some answers in a human voice, but I heard no other returns, than in the same dialect, only one or two a little shriller than his. I began to think that this house must belong to some person of great note among them, because there appeared so much ceremony before I could gain admittance. But, that a man of quality should be served all by horses, was beyond my comprehension. I feared my brain was disturbed by my sufferings and misfortunes: I roused myself, and looked about me in the room where I was left alone; this was furnished like the first, only after a more elegant manner. I rubbed my eyes often, but the same objects still occurred. I pinched my arms and sides, to awake myself, hoping I might be in a dream. I then absolutely concluded, that all these appearances could be nothing else but necromancy and magic. But I had no time to pursue these reflections; for the gray horse came to the door, and made me a sign to follow him into the third room, where I saw a very comely mare, together with a colt and foal, sitting on their haunches, upon mats of straw, not unartfully made, and perfectly neat and clean.

The mare soon after my entrance, rose from her mat, and coming up close, after having nicely observed my hands and face, gave me a most contemptuous look; then turning to the horse, I heard the word *Yahoo* often repeated betwixt them; the meaning of which word I could not then comprehend, although it were the first I had learned to pronounce; but I was soon better informed, to my everlasting mortification: for the horse beckoning to me with his head, and repeating the word

Hhuun, Hhuun, as he did upon the road, which I understood was to attend him, led me out into a kind of court, where was another building at some distance from the house. Here we entered, and I saw three of those detestable creatures, whom I first met after my landing, feeding upon roots, and the flesh of some animals, which I afterwards found to be that of asses and dogs, and now and then a cow dead by accident or disease. They were all tied by the neck with strong withes, fastened to a beam; they held their food between the claws of their fore-feet, and tore it with their teeth.

The master horse ordered a sorrel nag, one of his servants, to untie the largest of these animals, and take him into the yard. The beast and I were brought close together, and our countenances diligently compared, both by master and servant, who thereupon repeated several times the word *Yahoo.* My horror and astonishment are not to be described, when I observed, in this abominable animal, a perfect human figure: the face of it indeed was flat and broad, the nose depressed, the lips large, and the mouth wide. But these differences are common to all savage nations, where the lineaments of the countenance are distorted by the natives suffering their infants to lie grovelling on the earth, or by carrying them on their backs, nuzzling with their face against the mother's shoulders. The fore-feet of the *Yahoo* differed from my hands in nothing else but the length of the nails, the coarseness and brownness of the palms, and the hairiness on the backs. There was the same resemblance between our feet, with the same differences, which I knew very well, though the horses did not, because of my shoes and stockings; the same in every part of our bodies, except as to hairiness and colour, which I have already described.

The great difficulty that seemed to stick with the two

horses, was, to see the rest of my body so very different
from that of a *Yahoo*, for which I was obliged to my
clothes, whereof they had no conception. The sorrel nag
offered me a root, which he held (after their manner, as
we shall describe in its proper place) between his hoof
and pastern; I took it in my hand, and having smelt it,
returned it to him again as civilly as I could. He brought
out of the *Yahoo's* kennel a piece of ass's flesh, but it
smelt so offensively that I turned from it with loathing:
he then threw it to the *Yahoo*, by whom it was greedily
devoured. He afterwards showed me a wisp of hay, and
a fetlock full of oats; but I shook my head, to signify,
that neither of these were food for me. And indeed, I
now apprehended that I must absolutely starve, if I
did not get to some of my own species; for as to those
filthy *Yahoos*, although there were few greater lovers
of mankind, at that time, than myself, yet I confess I
never saw any sensitive being so detestable on all accounts; and the more I came near them, the more hateful they grew, while I stayed in that country. This the
master horse observed by my behaviour, and therefore
sent the *Yahoo* back to his kennel. He then put his fore-
hoof to his mouth, at which I was much surprised, although he did it with ease, and with a motion that
appeared perfectly natural, and made other signs to
know what I would eat; but I could not return him such
an answer as he was able to apprehend; and if he had
understood me, I did not see how it was possible to contrive any way for finding myself nourishment. While
we were thus engaged, I observed a cow passing by,
whereupon I pointed to her, and expressed a desire to
let me go and milk her. This had its effect; for he led me
back into the house, and ordered a mare-servant to open
a room, where a good store of milk lay in earthen and
wooden vessels, after a very orderly and cleanly manner.

She gave me a large bowl full, of which I drank very heartily, and found myself well refreshed.

About noon I saw coming towards the house a kind of vehicle, drawn like a sledge by four *Yahoos*. There was in it an old steed, who seemed to be of quality; he alighted with his hind-feet forward, having by accident got a hurt in his left fore-foot. He came to dine with our horse, who received him with great civility. They dined in the best room, and had oats boiled in milk for the second course, which the old horse eat warm, but the rest cold. Their mangers were placed circular in the middle of the room, and divided into several partitions, round which they sat on their haunches upon bosses of straw. In the middle was a large rack with angles answering to every partition of the manger; so that each horse and mare eat their own hay, and their own mash of oats and milk, with much decency and regularity. The behaviour of the young colt and foal appeared very modest, and that of the master and mistress extremely cheerful and complaisant to their guest. The gray ordered me to stand by him, and much discourse passed between him and his friend concerning me, as I found by the stranger's often looking on me, and the frequent repetition of the word *Yahoo*.

I happened to wear my gloves, which the master gray observing, seemed perplexed, discovering signs of wonder what I had done to my fore-feet; he put his hoof three or four times to them, as if he would signify, that I should reduce them to their former shape, which I presently did, pulling off both my gloves, and putting them into my pocket. This occasioned farther talk, and I saw the company was pleased with my behaviour, whereof I soon found the good effects. I was ordered to speak the few words I understood, and while they were at dinner, the master taught me the names for oats, milk,

fire, water, and some others; which I could readily pronounce after him, having from my youth a great facility
in learning languages.

When dinner was done, the master horse took me
aside, and by signs and words made me understand the
concern that he was in, that I had nothing to eat. Oats
in their tongue are called *hlunnh*. This word I pronounced two or three times; for although I had refused
them at first, yet upon second thoughts, I considered
that I could contrive to make of them a kind of bread,
which might be sufficient with milk to keep me alive, till
I could make my escape to some other country, and to
creatures of my own species. The horse immediately
ordered a white mare-servant of his family to bring me
a good quantity of oats in a sort of wooden tray. These
I heated before the fire as well as I could, and rubbed
them till the husks came off, which I made a shift to
winnow from the grain; I ground and beat them between two stones, then took water, and made them into
a paste or cake, which I toasted at the fire, and ate warm
with milk. It was at first a very insipid diet, though common enough in many parts of Europe, but grew tolerable by time; and having been often reduced to hard
fare in my life, this was not the first experiment I had
made how easily nature is satisfied. And I cannot but
observe, that I never had one hour's sickness, while I
stayed in this island. 'Tis true, I sometimes made a shift
to catch a rabbit, or bird, by springs made of *Yahoos'*
hairs, and I often gathered wholesome herbs, which I
boiled, and eat as salads with my bread, and now and
then, for a rarity, I made a little butter, and drank the
whey. I was at first at a great loss for salt; but custom
soon reconciled the want of it; and I am confident that
the frequent use of salt among us is an effect of luxury,
and was first introduced only as a provocative to drink;

except where it is necessary for preserving of flesh in long voyages, or in places remote from great markets. For we observe no animal to be fond of it but man: and as to myself, when I left this country, it was a great while before I could endure the taste of it in anything that I eat.

This is enough to say upon the subject of my diet, wherewith other travellers fill their books, as if the readers were personally concerned whether we fared well or ill. However, it was necessary to mention this matter, lest the world should think it impossible that I could find sustenance for three years in such a country, and among such inhabitants.

When it grew towards evening, the master horse ordered a place for me to lodge in; it was but six yards from the house, and separated from the stable of the *Yahoos*. Here I got some straw, and covering myself with my own clothes, slept very sound. But I was in a short time better accommodated, as the reader shall know hereafter, when I come to treat more particularly about my way of living.

CHAP. III

The Author studious to learn the language, the Houyhnhnm *his master assists in teaching him. The language described. Several* Houyhnhnms *of quality come out of curiosity to see the Author. He gives his master a short account of his voyage.*

My principal endeavour was to learn the language, which my master (for so I shall henceforth call him), and his children, and every servant of his house, were desirous to teach me. For they looked upon it as a prodigy that a brute animal should discover such marks of a rational creature. I pointed to every thing, and enquired the name of it, which I wrote down in my journal-book when I was alone, and corrected my bad accent by desiring those of the family to pronounce it often. In this employment, a sorrel nag, one of the under servants, was very ready to assist me.

In speaking, they pronounce through the nose and throat, and their language approaches nearest to the High-Dutch, or German, of any I know in Europe; but is much more graceful and significant. The Emperor Charles V. made almost the same observation, when he said, that if he were to speak to his horse, it should be in High-Dutch.

The curiosity and impatience of my master were so great, that he spent many hours of his leisure to instruct me. He was convinced (as he afterwards told me) that I must be a *Yahoo*, but my teachableness, civility, and cleanliness, astonished him; which were qualities altogether so opposite to those animals. He was most perplexed about my clothes, reasoning sometimes with himself, whether they were a part of my body: for I never pulled them off till the family were asleep, and got them on before they waked in the morning. My master was eager to learn from whence I came, how I acquired those appearances of reason, which I discovered in all my actions, and to know my story from my own mouth, which he hoped he should soon do by the great proficiency I made in learning and pronouncing their words and sentences. To help my memory, I formed all I learned into the English alphabet, and writ the words down with the translations. This last, after some time, I ventured to do in my master's presence. It cost me much trouble to explain to him what I was doing; for the inhabitants have not the least idea of books or literature.

In about ten weeks time I was able to understand most of his questions, and in three months could give him some tolerable answers. He was extremely curious to know from what part of the country I came, and how I was taught to imitate a rational creature, because the *Yahoos* (whom he saw I exactly resembled in my head, hands, and face, that were only visible), with some appearance of cunning, and the strongest disposition to mischief, were observed to be the most unteachable of all brutes. I answered, that I came over the sea from a far place, with many others of my own kind, in a great hollow vessel made of the bodies of trees. That my companions forced me to land on this coast, and then left me to shift for myself. It was with some difficulty, and by the help of many signs, that I brought him to understand me. He replied, that I must needs be mistaken, or that I *said the thing which was not.* (For they have no word in their language to express lying or falsehood.) He knew it was impossible that there could be a country beyond the sea, or that a parcel of brutes could move a wooden vessel whither they pleased upon water. He was sure no *Houyhnhnm* alive could make such a vessel, nor would trust *Yahoos* to manage it.

The word *Houyhnhnm,* in their tongue, signifies a *horse,* and in its etymology, *the perfection of nature.* I told my master, that I was at a loss for expression, but would improve as fast as I could; and hoped in a short time I should be able to tell him wonders: he was pleased to direct his own mare, his colt and foal, and the servants of the family, to take all opportunities of instructing me, and every day for two or three hours, he was at the same pains himself. Several horses and mares of quality in the neighbourhood came often to our house upon the report spread of a wonderful *Yahoo,* that could speak like a *Houyhnhnm,* and seemed in his words and actions to discover some glimmerings of reason. These delighted to converse with me: they put many questions, and received such answers as I was able to return. By all these advantages, I made so great a progress, that in five months from my arrival I understood whatever was spoke, and could express myself tolerably well.

The *Houyhnhnms* who came to visit my master, out of a design of seeing and talking with me, could hardly believe me to be a right *Yahoo,* because my body had a different covering from others of my kind. They were astonished to observe me without the usual hair or skin, except on my head, face, and hands; but I discovered that secret to my master, upon an accident, which happened about a fortnight before.

I have already told the reader, that every night when the family were gone to bed, it was my custom to strip and cover myself with my clothes: it happened one morning early, that my master sent for me, by the sorrel nag, who was his valet; when he came, I was fast asleep, my clothes fallen off on one side, and my shirt above my waist. I awaked at the noise he made, and observed him to deliver his message in some disorder; after which he went to my master, and in a great fright gave him a very confused account of what he had seen. This I presently discovered; for going as soon as I was dressed, to pay my attendance upon his Honour, he asked me the meaning of what his servant had reported, that I was not the same thing when I slept as I appeared to be at other times; that his valet assured him, some part of me was white, some yellow, at least not so white, and some brown.

I had hitherto concealed the secret of my dress, in order to distinguish myself, as much as possible, from that cursed race of *Yahoos;* but now I found it in vain to do so any longer. Besides, I considered that my clothes and shoes would soon wear out, which already were in a declining condition, and must be supplied by some contrivance from the hides of *Yahoos* or other brutes; whereby the whole secret would be known. I therefore told my master, that in the country from whence I came, those of my kind always covered their bodies with the hairs of certain animals prepared by art, as well for decency as to avoid the inclemencies of air, both hot and cold; of which, as to my own person, I would give him immediate conviction, if he pleased to command me: only desiring his excuse, if I did not expose those parts that nature taught us to conceal. He said my discourse was all very strange, but especially the last part; for he could not understand why nature should teach us to conceal what nature had given. That neither himself nor family were ashamed of any parts of their bodies; but however I might do as I pleased. Whereupon, I first unbuttoned my coat, and pulled it off. I did the same with my waistcoat; I drew off my shoes, stockings, and breeches. I let my shirt down to my waist, and drew up the bottom, fastening it like a girdle about my middle to hide my nakedness.

My master observed the whole performance with great signs of curiosity and admiration. He took up all my clothes in his pastern, one piece after another, and examined them diligently; he then stroked my body very gently, and looked round me several times, after which he said, it was plain I must be a perfect *Yahoo;* but that I differed very much from the rest of my species, in the softness, and whiteness, and smoothness of my skin, my want of hair in several parts of my body, the shape and shortness of my claws behind and before, and my affectation of walking continually on my two hinder feet. He desired to see no more, and gave me leave to put on my clothes again, for I was shuddering with cold.

I expressed my uneasiness at his giving me so often the appellation of *Yahoo*, an odious animal, for which I had so utter a hatred and contempt. I begged he would forbear applying that word to me, and take the same order in his family, and among his friends whom he suffered to see me. I requested likewise, that the secret of my having a false covering to my body might be known to none but himself, at least as long as my present clothing should last; for as to what the sorrel nag his valet had observed, his Honour might command him to conceal it.

All this my master very graciously consented to, and thus the secret was kept till my clothes began to wear out, which I was forced to supply by several contrivances, that shall hereafter be mentioned. In the meantime, he desired I would go on with my utmost diligence to learn their language, because he was more astonished at my capacity for speech and reason, than at the figure of my body, whether it were covered or no; adding, that he waited with some impatience to hear the wonders which I promised to tell him.

From thenceforward he doubled the pains he had been at to instruct me; he brought me into all company, and made them treat me with civility, because, as he told them, privately, this would put me into good humour, and make me more diverting.

Every day when I waited on him, beside the trouble he was at in teaching, he would ask me several questions concerning myself, which I answered as well as I could; and by these means he had already received some general ideas, though very imperfect. It would be tedious to relate the several steps by which I advanced to a more regular conversation: but the first account I gave of myself in any order and length, was to this purpose:

That I came from a very far country, as I already had

attempted to tell him, with about fifty more of my own
species; that we travelled upon the seas, in a great hollow vessel made of wood, and larger than his Honour's
house. I described the ship to him in the best terms
I could, and explained by the help of my handkerchief displayed, how it was driven forward by the wind.
That upon a quarrel among us, I was set on shore on
this coast, where I walked forward without knowing
whither, till he delivered me from the persecution of
those execrable *Yahoos*. He asked me, who made the
ship, and how it was possible that the *Houyhnhnms* of
my country would leave it to the management of brutes?
My answer was, that I durst proceed no further in my
relation, unless he would give me his word and honour
that he would not be offended, and then I would tell
him the wonders I had so often promised. He agreed;
and I went on by assuring him, that the ship was made
by creatures like myself, who in all the countries I had
travelled, as well as in my own, were the only governing,
rational animals; and that upon my arrival hither, I was
as much astonished to see the *Houyhnhnms* act like rational beings, as he or his friends could be in finding
some marks of reason in a creature he was pleased to
call a *Yahoo*, to which I owned my resemblance in every
part, but could not account for their degenerate and
brutal nature. I said farther, that if good fortune ever
restored me to my native country, to relate my travels
hither, as I resolved to do, every body would believe
that I *said the thing which was not;* that I invented the
story out of my own head; and with all possible respect
to himself, his family and friends, and under his promise
of not being offended, our countrymen would hardly
think it probable, that a *Houyhnhnm* should be the pre-
siding creature of a nation, and a *Yahoo* the brute.

CHAP. IV

The Houyhnhnm's *notion of truth and falsehood. The Author's discourse disapproved by his master. The Author gives a more particular account of himself, and the accidents of his voyage.*

My master heard me with great appearances of uneasiness in his countenance, because *doubting,* or *not believing,* are so little known in this country, that the inhabitants cannot tell how to behave themselves under such circumstances. And I remember in frequent discourses with my master concerning the nature of manhood, in other parts of the world, having occasion to talk of *lying* and *false representation,* it was with much difficulty that he comprehended what I meant, although he had otherwise a most acute judgment. For he argued thus: that the use of speech was to make us understand one another, and to receive information of facts; now if any one *said the thing which was not,* these ends were defeated; because I cannot properly be said to understand him; and I am so far from receiving information, that he leaves me worse than in ignorance, for I am led to believe a thing black when it is white, and short when it is long. And these were all the notions he had concerning that faculty of *lying,* so perfectly well understood, and so universally practised, among human creatures.

To return from this digression; when I asserted that the *Yahoos* were the only governing animals in my country, which my master said was altogether past his conception, he desired to know, whether we had *Houyhnhnms* among us, and what was their employment: I told him, we had great numbers, that in summer they grazed in the fields, and in winter were kept in houses, with hay

and oats, where *Yahoo* servants were employed to rub
their skins smooth, comb their manes, pick their feet,
serve them with food, and make their beds. I understand you well, said my master, it is now very plain,
from all you have spoken, that whatever share of reason
the *Yahoos* pretend to, the *Houyhnhnms* are your masters; I heartily wish our *Yahoos* would be so tractable.
I begged his Honour would please to excuse me from
proceeding any farther, because I was very certain that
the account he expected from me would be highly displeasing. But he insisted in commanding me to let him
know the best and the worst: I told him, he should be
obeyed. I owned, that the *Houyhnhnms* among us, whom
we called horses, were the most generous and comely
animals we had, that they excelled in strength and
swiftness; and when they belonged to persons of quality,
employed in travelling, racing, or drawing chariots, they
were treated with much kindness and care, till they fell
into diseases, or became foundered in the feet; and then
they were sold, and used to all kind of drudgery till they
died; after which their skins were stripped and sold for
what they were worth, and their bodies left to be devoured by dogs and birds of prey. But the common race
of horses had not so good fortune, being kept by farmers
and carriers, and other mean people, who put them to
greater labour, and fed them worse. I described, as well
as I could, our way of riding, the shape and use of a
bridle, a saddle, a spur, and a whip, of harness and
wheels. I added, that we fastened plates of a certain
hard substance called iron at the bottom of their feet,
to preserve their hoofs from being broken by the stony
ways on which we often travelled.

My master, after some expressions of great indignation, wondered how we dared to venture upon a *Houyhnhnm's* back, for he was sure, that the weakest serv-

ant in his house would be able to shake off the strongest *Yahoo*, or by lying down, and rolling on his back, squeeze the brute to death. I answered, that our horses were trained up from three or four years old to the several uses we intended them for; that if any of them proved intolerably vicious, they were employed for carriages; that they were severely beaten while they were young for any mischievous tricks; that the males, designed for common use of riding or draught, were generally castrated about two years after their birth, to take down their spirits, and make them more tame and gentle; that they were indeed sensible of rewards and punishments; but his Honour would please to consider, that they had not the least tincture of reason any more than the *Yahoos* in this country.

It put me to the pains of many circumlocutions to give my master a right idea of what I spoke; for their language doth not abound in variety of words, because their wants and passions are fewer than among us. But it is impossible to express his noble resentment at our savage treatment of the *Houyhnhnm* race, particularly after I had explained the manner and use of castrating horses among us, to hinder them from propagating their kind, and to render them more servile. He said, if it were possible there could be any country where *Yahoos* alone were endued with reason, they certainly must be the governing animal, because reason will in time always prevail against brutal strength. But, considering the frame of our bodies, and especially of mine, he thought no creature of equal bulk was so ill contrived, for employing that reason in the common offices of life; whereupon he desired to know whether those among whom I lived resembled me or the *Yahoos* of his country. I assured him, that I was as well shaped as most of my age; but the younger and the females were much more soft and tender, and the skins of the latter generally as white as milk. He said, I differed indeed from other *Yahoos*, being much more cleanly, and not altogether so deformed, but, in point of real advantage, he thought I differed for the worse. That my nails were of no use either to my fore or hinder-feet; as to my fore-feet, he could not properly call them by that name, for he never observed me to walk upon them; that they were too soft to bear the ground; that I generally went with them uncovered, neither was the covering I sometimes wore on them, of the same shape, or so strong as that on my feet behind. That I could not walk with any security, for if either of my hinder-feet slipped, I must inevitably fall. He then began to find fault with other parts of my body, the flatness of my face, the prominence of my nose, my eyes placed directly in front, so that I could not look on either side without turning my head: that I was not able to feed myself, without lifting one of my fore-feet to my mouth: and therefore nature had placed those joints to answer that necessity. He knew not what could be the use of those several clefts and divisions in my feet behind; these were too soft to bear the hardness and sharpness of stones without a covering made from the skin of some other brute; that my whole body wanted a fence against heat and cold, which I was forced to put on and off every day with tediousness and trouble. And lastly, that he observed every animal in this country naturally to abhor the *Yahoos*, whom the weaker avoided, and the stronger drove from them. So that supposing us to have the gift of reason, he could not see how it were possible to cure that natural antipathy which every creature discovered against us; nor consequently, how we could tame and render them serviceable. However, he would (as he said) debate the matter no farther, because he was more desirous to know my own story, the country where I was born, and the several actions and events of my life before I came hither.

I assured him, how extremely desirous I was that he should be satisfied on every point; but I doubted much, whether it would be possible for me to explain myself on several subjects whereof his Honour could have no conception, because I saw nothing in his country to which I could resemble them. That, however, I would do my best, and strive to express myself by similitudes, humbly desiring his assistance when I wanted proper words; which he was pleased to promise me.

I said, my birth was of honest parents in an island called England, which was remote from this country, as many days' journey as the strongest of his Honour's servants could travel in the annual course of the sun. That I was bred a surgeon, whose trade it is to cure wounds and hurts in the body, got by accident or violence; that my country was governed by a female man, whom we called a Queen. That I left it to get riches, whereby I might maintain myself and family when I should return. That, in my last voyage, I was commander of the ship, and had about fifty *Yahoos* under me, many of which died at sea, and I was forced to supply them by others picked out from several nations. That our ship was twice in danger of being sunk; the first time by a great storm, and the second, by striking against a rock. Here my master interposed, by asking me, how I could persuade strangers out of different countries to venture with me, after the losses I had sustained, and the hazards I had run. I said, they were fellows of desperate fortunes, forced to fly from the places of their birth, on account of their poverty or their crimes. Some were undone by lawsuits; others spent all they had in drinking, whoring, and gaming; others fled for treason; many for murder, theft, poisoning, robbery,

perjury, forgery, coining false money, for committing
rapes or sodomy, for flying from their colours, or desert-
ing to the enemy, and most of them had broken prison;
none of these durst return to their native countries for
fear of being hanged, or of starving in a jail; and therefore were under the necessity of seeking a livelihood in
other places.

During this discourse, my master was pleased to interrupt me several times; I had made use of many circumlocutions in describing to him the nature of the several
crimes for which most of our crew had been forced to
fly their country. This labour took up several days' conversation, before he was able to comprehend me. He
was wholly at a loss to know what could be the use or
necessity of practising those vices. To clear up which I
endeavoured to give some ideas of the desire of power
and riches, of the terrible effects of lust, intemperance,
malice, and envy. All this I was forced to define and
describe by putting of cases, and making of supposi-
tions. After which, like one whose imagination was
struck with something never seen or heard of before, he
would lift up his eyes with amazement and indignation.
Power, government, war, law, punishment, and a thousand other things had no terms, wherein that language
could express them, which made the difficulty almost
insuperable to give my master any conception of what
I meant. But being of an excellent understanding, much
improved by contemplation and converse, he at last
arrived at a competent knowledge of what human nature in our parts of the world is capable to perform, and
desired I would give him some particular account of that
land which we call Europe, but especially of my own
country.

CHAP. V

The Author, at his master's commands, informs him of the state of England. *The causes of war among the princes of* Europe. *The Author begins to explain the* English *constitution.*

The reader may please to observe, that the following extract of many conversations I had with my master, contains a summary of the most material points, which were discoursed at several times for above two years; his Honour often desiring fuller satisfaction as I farther improved in the *Houyhnhnm* tongue. I laid before him, as well as I could, the whole state of Europe; I discoursed of trade and manufactures, of arts and sciences; and the answers I gave to all the questions he made, as they arose upon several subjects, were a fund of conversation not to be exhausted. But I shall here only set down the substance of what passed between us concerning my own country, reducing it into order as well as I can, without any regard to time or other circumstances, while I strictly adhere to truth. My only concern is, that I shall hardly be able to do justice to my master's arguments and expressions, which must needs suffer by my want of capacity, as well as by a translation into our barbarous English.

In obedience, therefore, to his Honour's commands, I related to him the Revolution under the Prince of Orange; the long war with France entered into by the said prince, and renewed by his successor, the present Queen, wherein the greatest powers of Christendom were engaged, and which still continued: I computed at his request, that about a million of *Yahoos* might have been killed in the whole progress of it; and perhaps a hundred or more cities taken, and thrice as many ships burnt or sunk.

He asked me what were the usual causes or motives that made one country go to war with another. I answered they were innumerable; but I should only mention a few of the chief. Sometimes the ambition of princes, who never think they have land or people enough to govern; sometimes the corruption of ministers, who engage their master in a war in order to stifle or divert the clamour of the subjects against their evil administration. Difference in opinions hath cost many millions of lives: for instance, whether flesh be bread, or bread be flesh; whether the juice of a certain berry be blood or wine; whether whistling be a vice or a virtue; whether it be better to kiss a post, or throw it into the fire; what is the best colour for a coat, whether black, white, red, or gray; and whether it should be long or short, narrow or wide, dirty or clean; with many more. Neither are any wars so furious and bloody, or of so long continuance, as those occasioned by difference in opinion, especially if it be in things indifferent.

Sometimes the quarrel between two princes is to decide which of them shall dispossess a third of his dominions, where neither of them pretend to any right. Sometimes one prince quarrelleth with another, for fear the other should quarrel with him. Sometimes a war is entered upon, because the enemy is too strong, and sometimes because he is too weak. Sometimes our neighbours want the things which we have, or have the things which we want; and we both fight, till they take ours or give us theirs. It is a very justifiable cause of a war to invade a country after the people have been wasted by famine, destroyed by pestilence, or embroiled by factions among themselves. It is justifiable to enter into war against our nearest ally, when one of his towns lies convenient for us, or a territory of land, that would render our dominions round and complete. If a prince sends forces into a nation, where the people are poor and ignorant, he may lawfully put half of them to death, and make slaves of the rest, in order to civilize and reduce them from their barbarous way of living. It is a very kingly, honourable, and frequent practice, when one prince desires the assistance of another to secure him against an invasion, that the assistant, when he hath driven out the invader, should seize on the dominions himself, and kill, imprison, or banish the prince he came to relieve. Alliance by blood or marriage is a frequent cause of war between princes; and the nearer the kindred is, the greater is their disposition to quarrel: poor nations are hungry, and rich nations are proud; and pride and hunger will ever be at variance. For these reasons, the trade of a soldier is held the most honourable of all others; because a soldier is a *Yahoo* hired to kill in cold blood as many of his own species, who have never offended him, as possibly he can.

There is likewise a kind of beggarly princes in Europe, not able to make war by themselves, who hire out their troops to richer nations, for so much a day to each man; of which they keep three fourths to themselves, and it is the best part of their maintenance; such are those in Germany and other northern parts of Europe.

What you have told me (said my master), upon the subject of war, does indeed discover most admirably the effects of that reason you pretend to: however, it is happy that the shame is greater than the danger; and that nature hath left you utterly uncapable of doing much mischief.

For your mouths lying flat with your faces, you can hardly bite each other to any purpose, unless by consent. Then as to the claws upon your feet before and behind, they are so short and tender, that one of our *Yahoos* would drive a dozen of yours before him. And therefore in recounting the numbers of those who have been killed in battle, I cannot but think that you have *said the thing which is not.*

I could not forbear shaking my head, and smiling a little at his ignorance. And being no stranger to the art of war, I gave him a description of cannons, culverins, muskets, carabines, pistols, bullets, powder, swords, bayonets, battles, sieges, retreats, attacks, undermines, countermines, bombardments, sea fights; ships sunk with a thousand men, twenty thousand killed on each side; dying groans, limbs flying in the air, smoke, noise, confusion, trampling to death under horses' feet; flight, pursuit, victory; fields strewed with carcases left for food to dogs, and wolves, and birds of prey; plundering, stripping, ravishing, burning and destroying. And to set forth the valour of my own dear countrymen, I assured him, that I had seen them blow up a hundred enemies at once in a siege, and as many in a ship, and beheld the dead bodies come down in pieces from the clouds, to the great diversion of the spectators.

I was going on to more particulars, when my master commanded me silence. He said, whoever understood the nature of *Yahoos* might easily believe it possible for so vile an animal to be capable of every action I had named, if their strength and cunning equalled their malice. But as my discourse had increased his abhorrence of the whole species, so he found it gave him a disturbance in his mind, to which he was wholly a stranger before. He thought his ears being used to such abominable words, might by degrees admit them with less detestation. That although he hated the *Yahoos* of this country, yet he no more blamed them for their odious qualities, than he did a *gnnayh* (a bird of prey) for its cruelty, or a sharp stone for cutting his hoof. But when a creature pretending to reason could be capable of such enormities, he dreaded lest the corruption of that faculty might be worse than brutality itself. He seemed therefore confident, that instead of reason, we were only possessed of some quality fitted to increase our natural vices; as the reflection from a troubled stream returns the image of an ill-shapen body, not only larger, but more distorted.

He added, that he had heard too much upon the subject of war, both in this, and some former discourses. There was another point which a little perplexed him at present. I had informed him, that some of our crew left their country on account of being ruined by *Law;* that I had already explained the meaning of the word; but he was at a loss how it should come to pass, that the law which was intended for every man's preservation, should be any man's ruin. Therefore he desired to be farther satisfied what I meant by law, and the dispensers thereof, according to the present practice in my own country; because he thought nature and reason were sufficient guides for a reasonable animal, as we pretended to be, in showing us what we ought to do, and what to avoid.

I assured his Honour, that law was a science wherein I had not much conversed, further than by employing advocates, in vain, upon some injustices that had been done me: however, I would give him all the satisfaction I was able.

I said, there was a society of men among us, bred up from their youth in the art of proving by words multiplied for the purpose, that white is black, and black is white, according as they are paid. To this society all the rest of the people are slaves. For example, if my neighbour hath a mind to my cow, he hires a lawyer to prove that he ought to have my cow from me. I must then hire another to defend my right, it being against all rules of law that any man should be allowed to speak for himself. Now in this case, I, who am the right owner, lie under two great disadvantages. First, my lawyer, being practised almost from his cradle in defending falsehood, is quite out of his element when he would be an advocate for justice, which as an office unnatural, he always attempts with great awkwardness, if not with ill-will. The second disadvantage is, that my lawyer must proceed with great caution, or else he will be reprimanded by the judges, and abhorred by his brethren, as one that would lessen the practice of the law. And therefore I have but two methods to preserve my cow. The first is, to gain over my adversary's lawyer with a double fee; who will then betray his client, by insinuating that he hath justice on his side. The second way is for my lawyer to make my cause appear as unjust as he can, by allowing the cow to belong to my adversary: and this, if it be skilfully done, will certainly bespeak the favour of the bench.

Now, your Honour is to know, that these judges are persons appointed to decide all controversies of property, as well as for the trial of criminals, and picked out from the most dexterous lawyers, who are grown old or lazy, and having been biassed all their lives against truth and equity, are under such a fatal necessity of favouring fraud, perjury, and oppression, that I have known several of them refuse a large bribe from the side where justice lay, rather than injure the faculty, by doing any thing unbecoming their nature or their office.

It is a maxim among these lawyers, that whatever hath been done before, may legally be done again: and therefore they take special care to record all the decisions formerly made against common justice, and the general reason of mankind. These, under the name of *precedents,* they produce as authorities, to justify the most iniquitous opinions; and the judges never fail of directing accordingly.

In pleading, they studiously avoid entering into the merits of the cause; but are loud, violent, and tedious in dwelling upon all circumstances which are not to the purpose. For instance, in the case already mentioned: they never desire to know what claim or title my adversary hath to my cow; but whether the said cow were red or black; her horns long or short; whether the field I graze her in be round or square; whether she was milked at home or abroad; what diseases she is subject to, and the like; after which they consult precedents, adjourn the cause from time to time, and in ten, twenty, or thirty years, come to an issue.

It is likewise to be observed, that this society hath a peculiar cant and jargon of their own, that no other mortal can understand, and wherein all their laws are written, which they take special care to multiply; whereby they have wholly confounded the very essence of truth and falsehood, of right and wrong; so that it will take thirty years to decide whether the field left me by my ancestors for six generations belongs to me, or to a stranger three hundred miles off.

In the trial of persons accused for crimes against the state, the method is much more short and commendable: the judge first sends to sound the disposition of those in power, after which he can easily hang or save the criminal, strictly preserving all due forms of law.

Here my master interposing, said it was a pity, that creatures endowed with such prodigious abilities of mind as these lawyers, by the description I gave of them, must certainly be, were not rather encouraged to be instructors of others in wisdom and knowledge. In answer to which, I assured his Honour, that in all points out of their own trade, they were usually the most ignorant and stupid generation among us, the most despicable in common conversation, avowed enemies to all knowledge and learning, and equally disposed to pervert the general reason of mankind in every other subject of discourse, as in that of their own profession.

CHAP. VI

A continuation of the state of England. *The character of a first or chief minister of state in* European *courts.*

My master was yet wholly at a loss to understand what motives could incite this race of lawyers to perplex, disquiet, and weary themselves, and engage in a confederacy of injustice, merely for the sake of injuring their fellow-animals; neither could he comprehend what I meant in saying they did it for hire. Whereupon I was at much pains to describe to him the use of money, the materials it was made of, and the value of the metals; that when a *Yahoo* had got a great store of this precious substance, he was able to purchase whatever he had a mind to; the finest clothing, the noblest houses, great tracts of land, the most costly meats and drinks, and have his choice of the most beautiful females. Therefore since money alone was able to perform all these feats, our *Yahoos* thought they could never have enough of it to spend or to save, as they found themselves inclined from their natural bent either to profusion or avarice. That the rich man enjoyed the fruit of the poor man's labour, and the latter were a thousand to one in proportion to the former. That the bulk of our people were forced to live miserably, by labouring every day for small wages to make a few live plentifully. I enlarged myself much on these and many other particulars to the same purpose; but his Honour was still to seek; for he went upon a supposition that all animals had a title to their share in the productions of the earth, and especially those who presided over the rest. Therefore he desired I would let him know, what these costly meats were, and how any of us happened to want them. Whereupon I enumerated as many sorts as came into my head, with the various methods of dressing them, which could not be done without sending vessels by sea to every part of the world, as well for liquors to drink, as for sauces, and innumerable other conveniences. I assured him, that this whole globe of earth must be at least three times gone round, before one of our better female *Yahoos* could get her breakfast, or a cup to put it in. He said, that must needs be a miserable country which cannot furnish food for its own inhabitants. But what he chiefly wondered at, was how such vast tracts of ground as I described should be wholly without fresh water, and the people put to the necessity of sending over the sea for drink. I replied, that England (the dear place of my nativity) was computed to produce three times the quantity of food, more than its inhabitants are able to consume, as well as liquors extracted from grain, or pressed out of the fruit of certain trees, which made excellent drink, and the same proportion in every other convenience of life. But, in order to feed the luxury and intemperance of the males, and the vanity of the females, we sent away the greatest part of our necessary things to other countries, from whence in return we brought the materials of diseases, folly, and vice, to spend among ourselves. Hence it follows of necessity, that vast numbers of our people are compelled to seek their livelihood by begging, robbing, stealing, cheating, pimping, forswearing, flattering, suborning, forging, gaming, lying, fawning, hectoring, voting, scribbling, star-gazing, poisoning, whoring, canting, libelling, free-thinking, and the like occupations: every one of which terms, I was at much pains to make him understand.

That wine was not imported among us from foreign countries, to supply the want of water or other drinks, but because it was a sort of liquid which made us merry, by putting us out of our senses; diverted all melancholy thoughts, begat wild extravagant imaginations in the brain, raised our hopes, and banished our fears, sus-pended every office of reason for a time, and deprived us of the use of our limbs, till we fell into a profound sleep; although it must be confessed, that we always awaked sick and dispirited, and that the use of this liq-uor filled us with diseases, which made our lives uncom-fortable and short.

But beside all this, the bulk of our people supported themselves by furnishing the necessities or conveniences of life to the rich, and to each other. For instance, when I am at home and dressed as I ought to be, I carry on my body the workmanship of an hundred tradesmen; the building and furniture of my house employ as many more, and five times the number to adorn my wife.

I was going on to tell him of another sort of people, who get their livelihood by attending the sick, having upon some occasions informed his Honour that many of my crew had died of diseases. But here it was with the utmost difficulty, that I brought him to apprehend what I meant. He could easily conceive, that a *Houyhnhnm* grew weak and heavy a few days before his death, or by some accident might hurt a limb. But that nature, who works all things to perfection, should suffer any pains to breed in our bodies, he thought impossible, and desired to know the reason of so unaccountable an evil. I told him, we fed on a thousand things which operated contrary to each other; that we eat when we were not hungry, and drank without the provocation of thirst; that we sat whole nights drinking strong liquors without eating a bit, which disposed us to sloth, inflamed our bodies, and precipitated or prevented digestion. That prostitute female *Yahoos* acquired a certain malady, which bred rottenness in the bones of those who fell into their embraces; that this and many other diseases were propagated from father to son, so that great numbers came into the world with complicated maladies upon them; that it would be endless to give him a catalogue of all diseases incident to human bodies; for they would not be fewer than five or six hundred, spread over every limb and joint; in short, every part, external and intestine, having diseases appropriated to each. To remedy which, there was a sort of people bred up among us, in the profession or pretence of curing the sick. And because I had some skill in the faculty, I would in gratitude to his Honour, let him know the whole mystery and method by which they proceed.

Their fundamental is, that all diseases arise from repletion, from whence they conclude, that a great evacuation of the body is necessary, either through the natural passage, or upwards at the mouth. Their next business is, from herbs, minerals, gums, oils, shells, salts, juices, seaweed, excrements, barks of trees, serpents, toads, frogs, spiders, dead men's flesh and bones, birds, beasts, and fishes, to form a composition for smell and taste the most abominable, nauseous, and detestable, they can possibly contrive, which the stomach immediately rejects with loathing; and this they call a vomit; or else from the same store-house, with some other poisonous additions, they command us to take in at the orifice above or below (just as the physician then happens to be disposed) a medicine equally annoying and disgustful to the bowels; which relaxing the belly, drives down all before it, and this they call a purge, or a clyster. For nature (as the physicians allege) having intended the superior anterior orifice only for the intromission of solids and liquids, and the inferior posterior for ejection, these artists ingeniously considering that in all diseases nature is forced out of her seat, therefore to replace her in it, the body must be treated in a manner directly contrary, by interchanging the use of each orifice; forcing solids and liquids in at the anus, and making evacuations at the mouth.

But, besides real diseases, we are subject to many that are only imaginary, for which the physicians have invented imaginary cures; these have their several names, and so have the drugs that are proper for them, and with these our female *Yahoos* are always infested.

One great excellency in this tribe is their skill at prognostics, wherein they seldom fail; their predictions in real diseases, when they rise to any degree of malignity, generally portending death, which is always in their power, when recovery is not: and therefore, upon any unexpected signs of amendment, after they have pronounced their sentence, rather than be accused as false prophets, they know how to approve their sagacity to the world by a seasonable dose.

They are likewise of special use to husbands and wives, who are grown weary of their mates; to eldest sons, to great ministers of state, and often to princes.

I had formerly upon occasion discoursed with my master upon the nature of government in general, and particularly of our own excellent constitution, deservedly the wonder and envy of the whole world. But having here accidentally mentioned a minister of state, he commanded me some time after to inform him, what species of *Yahoo* I particularly meant by that appellation.

I told him, that a First or Chief Minister of State, who was the person I intended to describe, was a creature wholly exempt from joy and grief, love and hatred, pity and anger; at least made use of no other passions but a violent desire of wealth, power, and titles; that he applies his words to all uses, except to the indication of his mind; that he never tells a truth, but with an intent that you should take it for a lie; nor a lie, but with a design that you should take it for a truth; that those he speaks worst of behind their backs, are in the surest way of preferment; and whenever he begins to praise you to others or to yourself, you are from that day forlorn. The worst mark you can receive is a promise, especially when it is confirmed with an oath; after which every wise man retires, and gives over all hopes.

There are three methods by which a man may rise to be chief minister: the first is, by knowing how with prudence to dispose of a wife, a daughter, or a sister: the second, by betraying or undermining his predecessor: and the third is, by a furious zeal in public assemblies against the corruptions of the court. But a wise prince would rather choose to employ those who practise the last of these methods; because such zealots prove always the most obsequious and subservient to the will and passions of their master. That these ministers having all employments at their disposal, preserve themselves in power, by bribing the majority of a senate or great council; and at last, by an expedient called an Act of Indemnity (whereof I described the nature to him) they secure themselves from after-reckonings, and retire from the public, laden with the spoils of the nation.

The palace of a chief minister is a seminary to breed up others in his own trade: the pages, lackeys, and porters, by imitating their master, become ministers of state in their several districts, and learn to excel in the three principal ingredients, of insolence, lying, and bribery. Accordingly, they have a subaltern court paid to them by persons of the best rank, and sometimes by the force of dexterity and impudence, arrive through several gradations to be successors to their lord.

He is usually governed by a decayed wench, or favourite footman, who are the tunnels through which all graces are conveyed, and may properly be called, in the last resort, the governors of the kingdom.

One day in discourse my master, having heard me mention the nobility of my country, was pleased to make me a compliment which I could not pretend to deserve: that he was sure I must have been born of some noble family, because I far exceeded in shape, colour, and cleanliness, all the *Yahoos* of his nation, although I seemed to fail in strength and agility, which must be imputed to my different way of living from those other brutes; and besides, I was not only endowed with the faculty of speech, but likewise with some rudiments of reason, to a degree, that with all his acquaintance I passed for a prodigy.

He made me observe, that among the *Houyhnhnms,* the white, the sorrel, and the iron-gray, were not so exactly shaped as the bay, the dapple-gray, and the black; nor born with equal talents of the mind, or a capacity to improve them; and therefore continued always in the condition of servants, without ever aspiring to match out of their own race, which in that country would be reckoned monstrous and unnatural.

I made his Honour my most humble acknowledgments for the good opinion he was pleased to conceive of me; but assured him at the same time, that my birth was of the lower sort, having been born of plain honest parents, who were just able to give me a tolerable education; that nobility among us was altogether a different thing from the idea he had of it; that our young noblemen are bred from their childhood in idleness and luxury; that as soon as years will permit, they consume their vigour, and contract odious diseases among lewd females; and when their fortunes are almost ruined, they marry some woman of mean birth, disagreeable person, and unsound constitution, merely for the sake of money, whom they hate and despise. That the productions of such marriages are generally scrofulous, ricketty, or deformed children; by which means the family seldom continues above three generations, unless the wife takes care to provide a healthy father among her neighbours or domestics, in order to improve and continue the breed. That a weak diseased body, a meagre countenance, and sallow complexion, are the true marks of noble blood; and a healthy robust appearance is so disgraceful in a man of quality, that the world concludes his real father to have been a groom or a coachman. The imperfections of his mind run parallel with those of his body, being a composition of spleen, dullness, ignorance, caprice, sensuality, and pride.

Without the consent of this illustrious body, no law can be enacted, repealed, or altered; and these have the decision of all our possessions without appeal.

CHAP. VII

*The Author's great love of his native country. His master's
observations upon the constitution and administration of
England, as described by the Author, with parallel cases
and comparisons. His master's observations upon human
nature.*

The reader may be disposed to wonder how I could prevail on myself to give so free a representation of my
own species, among a race of mortals who are already
too apt to conceive the vilest opinion of human kind,
from that entire congruity betwixt me and their *Yahoos*.
But I must freely confess, that the many virtues of those
excellent quadrupeds placed in opposite view to human
corruptions, had so far opened my eyes and enlarged
my understanding, that I began to view the actions and
passions of man in a very different light, and to think
the honour of my own kind not worth managing; which,
besides, it was impossible for me to do before a person
of so acute a judgment as my master, who daily convinced me of a thousand faults in myself, whereof I had
not the least perception before, and which with us would
never be numbered even among human infirmities. I
had likewise learned from his example an utter detestation of all falsehood or disguise; and truth appeared so
amiable to me, that I determined upon sacrificing every
thing to it.

Let me deal so candidly with the reader, as to confess,
that there was yet a much stronger motive for the freedom I took in my representation of things. I had not
been a year in this country, before I contracted such a
love and veneration for the inhabitants, that I entered
on a firm resolution never to return to human kind, but to

pass the rest of my life among these admirable *Houyhn-nhms* in the contemplation and practice of every virtue; where I could have no example or incitement to vice. But it was decreed by fortune, my perpetual enemy, that so great a felicity should not fall to my share. However, it is now some comfort to reflect, that in what I said of my countrymen, I extenuated their faults as much as I durst before so strict an examiner, and upon every article gave as favourable a turn as the matter would bear. For, indeed, who is there alive that will not be swayed by his bias and partiality to the place of his birth?

I have related the substance of several conversations I had with my master, during the greatest part of the time I had the honour to be in his service, but have indeed for brevity sake omitted much more than is here set down.

When I had answered all his questions, and his curiosity seemed to be fully satisfied; he sent for me one morning early, and commanding me to sit down at some distance (an honour which he had never before conferred upon me), he said, he had been very seriously considering my whole story, as far as it related both to myself and my country; that he looked upon us as a sort of animals to whose share, by what accident he could not conjecture, some small pittance of reason had fallen, whereof we made no other use than by its assistance to aggravate our natural corruptions, and to acquire new ones, which nature had not given us. That we disarmed ourselves of the few abilities she had bestowed, had been very successful in multiplying our original wants, and seemed to spend our whole lives in vain endeavours to supply them by our own inventions. That as to myself, was manifest I had neither the strength or agility of a common *Yahoo;* that I walked infirmly on my hinder feet; had found out a contrivance to make my claws of no use or defence, and to remove the hair from my chin, which was intended as a shelter from the sun and the weather. Lastly, that I could neither run with speed, nor climb trees like my brethren (as he called them) the *Yahoos* in this country.

That our institutions of government and law were plainly owing to our gross defects in reason, and by consequence, in virtue; because reason alone is sufficient to govern a rational creature; which was therefore a character we had no pretence to challenge, even from the account I had given of my own people; although he manifestly perceived, that in order to favour them, I had concealed many particulars, and often *said the thing which was not.*

He was the more confirmed in this opinion, because he observed, that as I agreed in every feature of my body with other *Yahoos,* except where it was to my real disadvantage in point of strength, speed and activity, the shortness of my claws, and some other particulars where nature had no part; so from the representation I had given him of our lives, our manners, and our actions, he found as near a resemblance in the disposition of our minds. He said the *Yahoos* were known to hate one another more than they did any different species of animals; and the reason usually assigned was the odiousness of their own shapes, which all could see in the rest, but not in themselves. He had therefore begun to think it not unwise in us to cover our bodies, and by that invention conceal many of our own deformities from each other, which would else be hardly supportable. But he now found he had been mistaken, and that the dissensions of those brutes in his country were owing to the same cause with ours, as I had described them. For if (said he), you throw among five *Yahoos* as much food as would be sufficient for fifty, they will, instead of eating peaceably, fall together by the ears, each single one impatient to have all to itself; and therefore a servant was usually employed to stand by while they were feeding abroad, and those kept at home were tied at a distance from each other: that if a cow died of age or accident, before a *Houyhnhnm* could secure it for his own *Yahoos*, those in the neighbourhood would come in herds to seize it, and then would ensue such a battle as I had described, with terrible wounds made by their claws on both sides, although they seldom were able to kill one another, for want of such convenient instruments of death as we had invented. At other times the like battles have been fought between the *Yahoos* of several neighbourhoods without any visible cause; those of one district watching all opportunities to surprise the next before they are prepared. But if they find their project hath miscarried, they return home, and, for want of enemies, engage in what I call a civil war among themselves.

That in some fields of his country, there are certain shining stones of several colours, whereof the *Yahoos* are violently fond, and when part of these stones is fixed in the earth, as it sometimes happeneth, they will dig with their claws for whole days to get them out, then carry them away, and hide them by heaps in their kennels; but still looking round with great caution, for fear their comrades should find out their treasure. My master said, he could never discover the reason of this unnatural appetite, or how these stones could be of any use to a *Yahoo;* but now he believed it might proceed from the same principle of avarice which I had ascribed to mankind: that he had once, by way of experiment, privately removed a heap of these stones from the place where one of his *Yahoos* had buried it: whereupon, the sordid animal missing his treasure, by his loud lamenting brought the whole herd to the place, there miserably howled, then fell to biting and tearing the rest, began to pine away, would neither eat, nor sleep, nor work, till he ordered a servant privately to convey the stones into the same hole, and hide them as before; which when his *Yahoo* had found, he presently recovered his spirits and good humour, but took good care to remove them to a better hiding place, and hath ever since been a very serviceable brute.

My master farther assured me, which I also observed myself, that in the fields where the shining stones abound, the fiercest and most frequent battles are fought, occasioned by perpetual inroads of the neighbouring *Yahoos*.

He said, it was common when two *Yahoos* discovered such a stone in a field, and were contending which of them should be the proprietor, a third would take the advantage, and carry it away from them both; which my master would needs contend to have some kind of resemblance with our suits at law; wherein I thought it for our credit not to undeceive him; since the decision he mentioned was much more equitable than many decrees among us; because the plaintiff and defendant there lost nothing beside the stone they contended for, whereas our courts of equity would never have dismissed the cause while either of them had any thing left.

My master continuing his discourse, said, there was nothing that rendered the *Yahoos* more odious than their undistinguishing appetite to devour every thing that came in their way, whether herbs, roots, berries, the corrupted flesh of animals, or all mingled together: and it was peculiar in their temper, that they were fonder of what they could get by rapine or stealth at a greater distance, than much better food provided for them at home.

If their prey held out, they would eat till they were ready to burst, after which nature had pointed out to them a certain root that gave them a general evacuation.

There was also another kind of root very juicy, but somewhat rare and difficult to be found, which the *Yahoos* sought for with much eagerness, and would suck it with great delight; and it produced in them the same effects that wine hath upon us. It would make them sometimes hug, and sometimes tear one another; they would howl and grin, and chatter, and reel, and tumble, and then fall asleep in the mud.

I did indeed observe, that the *Yahoos* were the only animals in this country subject to any diseases; which, however, were much fewer than horses have among us, and contracted not by any ill treatment they meet with, but by the nastiness and greediness of that sordid brute. Neither has their language any more than a general appellation for those maladies, which is borrowed from the name of the beast, and called *Hnea-Yahoo,* or *Yahoo's evil,* and the cure prescribed is a mixture of their own dung and urine forcibly put down the *Yahoo's* throat. This I have since often known to have been taken with success, and do freely recommend it to my countrymen, for the public good, as an admirable specific against all diseases produced by repletion.

As to learning, government, arts, manufactures, and the like, my master confessed he could find little or no resemblance between the *Yahoos* of that country and those in ours. For he only meant to observe what parity there was in our natures. He had heard indeed some curious *Houyhnhnms* observe, that in most herds there was a sort of ruling *Yahoo* (as among us there is generally some leading or principal stag in a park), who was always more deformed in body, and mischievous in disposition, than any of the rest. That this leader had usually a favourite as like himself as he could get, whose employment was to lick his master's feet and posteriors, and drive the female *Yahoos* to his kennel; for which he was now and then rewarded with a piece of ass's flesh. This favourite is hated by the whole herd, and therefore to protect himself, keeps always near the person of his leader. He usually continues in office till a worse can be found; but the very moment he is discarded, his successor, at the head of all the *Yahoos* in that district, young and old, male and female, come in a body, and discharge their excrements upon him from head to foot. But how far this might be applicable to our courts and favourites, and ministers of state, my master said I could best determine.

I durst make no return to this malicious insinuation, which debased human understanding below the sagacity of a common hound, who has judgment enough to distinguish and follow the cry of the ablest dog in the pack, without being ever mistaken.

My master told me, there were some qualities remarkable in the *Yahoos,* which he had not observed me to mention, or at least very slightly, in the accounts I had given him of human kind. He said, those animals, like other brutes, had their females in common; but in this they differed, that the she-*Yahoo* would admit the male while she was pregnant; and that the hees would quarrel and fight with the females as fiercely as with each other. Both which practices were such degrees of infamous brutality, that no other sensitive creature ever arrived at.

Another thing he wondered at in the *Yahoos,* was their strange disposition to nastiness and dirt, whereas there appears to be a natural love of cleanliness in all other animals. As to the two former accusations, I was glad to let them pass without any reply, because I had not a word to offer upon them in defence of my species, which otherwise I certainly had done from my own inclinations. But I could have easily vindicated human kind from the imputation of singularity upon the last article, if there had been any swine in that country (as unluckily for me there were not), which although it may be a sweeter quadruped than a *Yahoo*, cannot I humbly conceive in justice pretend to more cleanliness; and so his Honour himself must have owned, if he had seen their filthy way of feeding, and their custom of wallowing and sleeping in the mud.

My master likewise mentioned another quality which his servants had discovered in several *Yahoos*, and to him was wholly unaccountable. He said, a fancy would sometimes take a *Yahoo* to retire into a corner, to lie down and howl, and groan, and spurn away all that came near him, although he were young and fat, wanted neither food nor water; nor did the servants imagine what could possibly ail him. And the only remedy they found was to set him to hard work, after which he would infallibly come to himself. To this I was silent out of partiality to my own kind; yet here I could plainly discover the true seeds of spleen, which only seizeth on the lazy, the luxurious, and the rich; who, if they were forced to undergo the same regimen, I would undertake for the cure.

His Honour had further observed, that a female *Yahoo* would often stand behind a bank or a bush, to gaze on the young males passing by, and then appear, and hide, using many antic gestures and grimaces, at which time it was observed, that she had a most offensive smell; and when any of the males advanced, would slowly retire, looking often back, and with a counterfeit show of fear, run off into some convenient place where she knew the male would follow her.

At other times if a female stranger came among them, three or four of her own sex would get about her, and stare and chatter, and grin, and smell her all over; and then turn off with gestures that seemed to express contempt and disdain.

Perhaps my master might refine a little in these speculations, which he had drawn from what he observed himself, or had been told him by others; however, I could not reflect without some amazement, and much sorrow, that the rudiments of lewdness, coquetry, censure, and scandal, should have place by instinct in womankind.

I expected every moment, that my master would accuse the *Yahoos* of those unnatural appetites in both sexes, so common among us. But nature, it seems, hath not been so expert a school-mistress; and these politer pleasures are entirely the productions of art and reason, on our side of the globe.

CHAP. VIII

The Author relates several particulars of the Yahoos. *The great virtues of the* Houyhnhnms. *The education and exercise of their youth. Their general assembly.*

As I ought to have understood human nature much better than I supposed it possible for my master to do, so it was easy to apply the character he gave of the *Yahoos* to myself and my countrymen; and I believed I could yet make farther discoveries from my own observation. I therefore often begged his favour to let me go among the herds of *Yahoos* in the neighbourhood, to which he always very graciously consented, being perfectly convinced that the hatred I bore those brutes would never suffer me to be corrupted by them; and his

Honour ordered one of his servants, a strong sorrel nag,
very honest and good-natured, to be my guard, without
whose protection I durst not undertake such adventures.
For I have already told the reader how much I was
pestered by those odious animals upon my first arrival.
And I afterwards failed very narrowly three or four
times of falling into their clutches, when I happened to
stray at any distance without my hanger. And I have
reason to believe they had some imagination that I was
of their own species, which I often assisted myself, by
stripping up my sleeves, and showing my naked arms
and breast in their sight, when my protector was with
me. At which times they would approach as near as they
durst, and imitate my actions after the manner of monkeys, but ever with great signs of hatred; as a tame jack-
daw with cap and stockings is always persecuted by the
wild ones, when he happens to be got among them.

They are prodigiously nimble from their infancy;
however, I once caught a young male of three years old,
and endeavoured by all marks of tenderness to make it
quiet; but the little imp fell a squalling, and scratching,
and biting with such violence, that I was forced to let
it go; and it was high time, for a whole troop of old ones
came about us at the noise, but finding the cub was safe
(for away it ran), and my sorrel nag being by, they
durst not venture near us. I observed the young animal's
flesh to smell very rank, and the stink was somewhat between a weasel and a fox, but much more disagreeable.
I forgot another circumstance (and perhaps I might have
the reader's pardon if it were wholly omitted), that
while I held the odious vermin in my hands, it voided
its filthy excrements of a yellow liquid substance, all
over my clothes; but by good fortune there was a small
brook hard by, where I washed myself as clean as I

could; although I durst not come into my master's presence, until I were sufficiently aired.

By what I could discover, the *Yahoos* appear to be the most unteachable of all animals, their capacities never reaching higher than to draw or carry burdens. Yet I am of opinion, this defect ariseth chiefly from a perverse, restive disposition. For they are cunning, malicious, treacherous, and revengeful. They are strong and hardy, but of a cowardly spirit, and by consequence, insolent, abject, and cruel. It is observed, that the red-haired of both sexes are more libidinous and mischievous than the rest, whom yet they much exceed in strength and activity.

The *Houyhnhnms* keep the *Yahoos* for present use in huts not far from the house; but the rest are sent abroad to certain fields, where they dig up roots, eat several kinds of herbs, and search about for carrion, or sometimes catch weasels and *luhimuhs* (a sort of wild rat), which they greedily devour. Nature hath taught them to dig deep holes with their nails on the side of a rising ground, wherein they lie by themselves; only the kennels of the females are larger, sufficient to hold two or three cubs.

They swim from their infancy like frogs, and are able to continue long under water, where they often take fish, which the females carry home to their young. And upon this occasion, I hope the reader will pardon my relating an odd adventure.

Being one day abroad with my protector the sorrel nag, and the weather exceeding hot, I entreated him to let me bathe in a river that was near. He consented, and I immediately stripped myself stark naked, and went down softly into the stream. It happened that a young female *Yahoo*, standing behind a bank, saw the whole proceeding, and inflamed by desire, as the nag and I conjectured, came running with all speed, and leaped into the water, within five yards of the place where I bathed. I was never in my life so terribly frighted; the nag was grazing at some distance, not suspecting any harm. She embraced me after a most fulsome manner; I roared as loud as I could, and the nag came galloping towards me, whereupon she quitted her grasp, with the utmost reluctancy, and leaped upon the opposite bank, where she stood gazing and howling all the time I was putting on my clothes.

This was matter of diversion to my master and his family, as well as of mortification to myself. For now I could no longer deny that I was a real *Yahoo* in every limb and feature, since the females had a natural propensity to me, as one of their own species. Neither was the hair of this brute of a red colour (which might have been some excuse for an appetite a little irregular), but black as a sloe, and her countenance did not make an appearance altogether so hideous as the rest of the kind; for, I think, she could not be above eleven years old.

Having lived three years in this country, the reader I suppose will expect, that I should, like other travellers, give him some account of the manners and customs of its inhabitants, which it was indeed my principal study to learn.

As these noble *Houyhnhnms* are endowed by nature with a general disposition to all virtues, and have no conceptions or ideas of what is evil in a rational creature, so their grand maxim is, to cultivate reason, and to be wholly governed by it. Neither is reason among them a point problematical as with us, where men can argue with plausibility on both sides of the question; but strikes you with immediate conviction; as it must needs do where it is not mingled, obscured, or discoloured by passion and interest. I remember it was with extreme difficulty that I could bring my master to understand the meaning of the word *opinion,* or how a point could be disputable; because reason taught us to affirm or deny only where we are certain; and beyond our knowledge we cannot do either. So that controversies, wranglings, disputes, and positiveness in false or dubious propositions, are evils unknown among the *Houyhnhnms.* In the like manner when I used to explain to him our several systems of natural philosophy, he would laugh that a creature pretending to reason, should value itself upon the knowledge of other people's conjectures, and in things, where that knowledge, if it were certain, could be of no use. Wherein he agreed entirely with the sentiments of Socrates, as Plato delivers them; which I mention as the highest honour I can do that prince of philosophers. I have often since reflected what destruction such a doctrine would make in the libraries of Europe; and how many paths to fame would be then shut up in the learned world.

Friendship and benevolence are the two principal virtues among the *Houyhnhnms;* and these not confined to particular objects, but universal to the whole race. For a stranger from the remotest part is equally treated with the nearest neighbour, and wherever he goes, looks upon himself as at home. They preserve decency and civility in the highest degrees, but are altogether ignorant of ceremony. They have no fondness for their colts or foals, but the care they take in educating them proceeds entirely from the dictates of reason. And I observed my master to show the same affection to his neighbour's issue that he had for his own. They will have it that nature teaches them to love the whole species, and it is reason only that maketh a distinction of persons, where there is a superior degree of virtue.

When the matron *Houyhnhnms* have produced one of each sex, they no longer accompany with their consorts, except they lose one of their issue by some casualty, which very seldom happens; but in such a case they meet again, or when the like accident befalls a person whose wife is past bearing, some other couple bestow him one of their own colts, and then go together again till the mother is pregnant. This caution is necessary to prevent the country from being overburthened with numbers. But the race of inferior *Houyhnhnms* bred up to be servants is not so strictly limited upon this article; these are allowed to produce three of each sex, to be domestics in the noble families.

In their marriages they are exactly careful to choose such colours as will not make any disagreeable mixture in the breed. Strength is chiefly valued in the male, and comeliness in the female; not upon the account of love, but to preserve the race from degenerating; for where a female happens to excel in strength, a consort is chosen with regard to comeliness. Courtship, love, presents, jointures, settlements, have no place in their thoughts; or terms whereby to express them in their language. The young couple meet and are joined, merely because it is the determination of their parents and friends: it is what they see done every day, and they look upon it as one of the necessary actions of a reasonable being. But the violation of marriage, or any other unchastity, was never heard of: and the married pair pass their lives with the same friendship, and mutual benevolence that they bear to all others of the same species, who come in their way; without jealousy, fondness, quarrelling, or discontent.

In educating the youth of both sexes, their method is admirable, and highly deserves our imitation. These are not suffered to taste a grain of oats, except upon certain days, till eighteen years old; nor milk, but very rarely;

and in summer they graze two hours in the morning, and as many in the evening, which their parents likewise observe; but the servants are not allowed above half that time, and a great part of their grass is brought home, which they eat at the most convenient hours, when they can be best spared from work.

Temperance, industry, exercise, and cleanliness, are the lessons equally enjoined to the young ones of both sexes: and my master thought it monstrous in us to give the females a different kind of education from the males, except in some articles of domestic management; whereby as he truly observed, one half of our natives were good for nothing but bringing children into the world: and to trust the care of our children to such useless animals, he said, was yet a greater instance of brutality.

But the *Houyhnhnms* train up their youth to strength, speed, and hardiness, by exercising them in running races up and down steep hills, and over hard stony grounds; and when they are all in a sweat, they are ordered to leap over head and ears into a pond or a river. Four times a year the youth of a certain district meet to show their proficiency in running and leaping, and other feats of strength and agility; where the victor is rewarded with a song made in his or her praise. On this festival the servants drive a herd of *Yahoos* into the field, laden with hay, and oats, and milk, for a repast to the *Houyhnhnms;* after which, these brutes are immediately driven back again, for fear of being noisome to the assembly.

Every fourth year, at the vernal equinox, there is a representative council of the whole nation, which meets in a plain about twenty miles from our house, and continues about five or six days. Here they enquire into the state and condition of the several districts; whether they

abound or be deficient in hay or oats, or cows or *Yahoos.*
And wherever there is any want (which is but seldom),
it is immediately supplied by unanimous consent and
contribution. Here likewise the regulation of children is
settled: as for instance, if a *Houyhnhnm* hath two males,
he changeth one of them with another that hath two
females; and when a child hath been lost by any casualty, where the mother is past breeding, it is determined
what family in the district shall breed another to supply
the loss.

CHAP. IX

A grand debate at the general assembly of the Houyhnhnms,
and how it was determined. The learning of the Houyhnhnms. *Their buildings. Their manner of burials. The defectiveness of their language.*

One of these grand assemblies was held in my time,
about three months before my departure, whither my
master went as the representative of our district. In this
council was resumed their old debate, and indeed, the
only debate which ever happened in that country;
whereof my master after his return gave me a very particular account.

The question to be debated was, whether the *Yahoos*
should be exterminated from the face of the earth. One
of the members for the affirmative offered several arguments of great strength and weight, alleging, that as the
Yahoos were the most filthy, noisome, and deformed
animal which nature ever produced, so they were the
most restive and indocible, mischievous and malicious:
they would privately suck the teats of the *Houyhnhnms'*
cows, kill and devour their cats, trample down their oats

and grass, if they were not continually watched, and commit a thousand other extravagancies. He took notice of a general tradition, that *Yahoos* had not been always in that country; but, that many ages ago, two of these brutes appeared together upon a mountain; whether produced by the heat of the sun upon corrupted mud and slime, or from the ooze and froth of the sea, was never known. That these *Yahoos* engendered, and their brood in a short time grew so numerous as to over-run and infest the whole nation. That the *Houyhnhnms* to get rid of this evil, made a general hunting, and at last enclosed the whole herd; and destroying the elder, every *Houyhnhnm* kept two young ones in a kennel, and brought them to such a degree of tameness, as an animal so savage by nature can be capable of acquiring; using them for draught and carriage. That there seemed to be much truth in this tradition, and that those creatures could not be *Ylnhniamshy* (or *aborigines* of the land), because of the violent hatred the *Houyhnhnms*, as well as all other animals, bore them; which although their evil disposition sufficiently deserved, could never have arrived at so high a degree, if they had been aborigines, or else they would have long since been rooted out. That the inhabitants taking a fancy to use the service of the *Yahoos*, had very imprudently neglected to cultivate the breed of asses, which were a comely animal, easily kept, more tame and orderly, without any offensive smell, strong enough for labour, although they yield to the other in agility of body; and if their braying be no agreeable sound, it is far preferable to the horrible howlings of the *Yahoos*.

Several others declared their sentiments to the same purpose, when my master proposed an expedient to the assembly, whereof he had indeed borrowed the hint from me. He approved of the tradition mentioned by the honourable member, who spoke before, and affirmed, that the two *Yahoos* said to be first seen among them, had been driven thither over the sea; that coming to land, and being forsaken by their companions, they retired to the mountains, and degenerating by degrees, became in process of time, much more savage than those of their own species in the country from whence these two originals came. The reason of this assertion was, that he had now in his possession a certain wonderful *Yahoo* (meaning myself), which most of them had heard of, and many of them had seen. He then related to them, how he first found me; that my body was all covered with an artificial composure of the skins and hairs of other animals; that I spoke in a language of my own, and had thoroughly learned theirs: that I had related to him the accidents which brought me thither: that when he saw me without my covering, I was an exact *Yahoo* in every part, only of a whiter colour, less hairy, and with shorter claws. He added, how I had endeavoured to persuade him, that in my own and other countries the *Yahoos* acted as the governing, rational animal, and held the *Houyhnhnms* in servitude: that he observed in me all the qualities of a *Yahoo,* only a little more civilized by some tincture of reason, which however was in a degree as far inferior to the *Houyhnhnm* race, as the *Yahoos* of their country were to me: that, among other things, I mentioned a custom we had of castrating *Houyhnhnms* when they were young, in order to render them tame; that the operation was easy and safe; that it was no shame to learn wisdom from brutes, as industry is taught by the ant, and building by the swallow. (For so I translate the word *lyhannh,* although it be a much larger fowl.) That this invention might be practised upon the younger *Yahoos* here, which, besides rendering them tractable and fitter for use, would in an age put an end to the whole species without destroying life. That in the mean time the *Houyhnhnms* should be exhorted to cultivate the breed of asses, which, as they are in all respects more valuable brutes, so they have this advantage, to be fit for service at five years old, which the others are not till twelve.

This was all my master thought fit to tell me at that time, of what passed in the grand council. But he was pleased to conceal one particular, which related personally to myself, whereof I soon felt the unhappy effect, as the reader will know in its proper place, and from whence I date all the succeeding misfortunes of my life.

The *Houyhnhnms* have no letters, and consequently their knowledge is all traditional. But there happening few events of any moment among a people so well united, naturally disposed to every virtue, wholly governed by reason, and cut off from all commerce with other nations, the historical part is easily preserved without burthening their memories. I have already observed, that they are subject to no diseases, and therefore can have no need of physicians. However, they have excellent medicines composed of herbs, to cure accidental bruises and cuts in the pastern or frog of the foot by sharp stones, as well as other maims and hurts in the several parts of the body.

They calculate the year by the revolution of the sun and moon, but use no subdivision into weeks. They are well enough acquainted with the motions of those two luminaries, and understand the nature of eclipses; and this is the utmost progress of their astronomy.

In poetry they must be allowed to excel all other mortals; wherein the justness of their similes, and the minuteness, as well as exactness of their descriptions, are indeed inimitable. Their verses abound very much in both of these, and usually contain either some exalted notions of friendship and benevolence, or the praises of those who were victors in races, and other bodily exercises. Their buildings, although very rude and simple, are not inconvenient, but well contrived to defend them from all injuries of cold and heat. They have a kind of tree, which at forty years old loosens in the root, and falls with the first storm: it grows very straight, and being pointed like stakes with a sharp stone (for the *Houyhnhnms* know not the use of iron), they stick them erect in the ground about ten inches asunder, and then weave in oat-straw, or sometimes wattles betwixt them. The roof is made after the same manner, and so are the doors.

The *Houyhnhnms* use the hollow part between the pastern and the hoof of their fore-feet, as we do our hands, and this with greater dexterity than I could at first imagine. I have seen a white mare of our family thread a needle (which I lent her on purpose) with that joint. They milk their cows, reap their oats, and do all the work which requires hands, in the same manner. They have a kind of hard flints, which by grinding against other stones, they form into instruments, that serve instead of wedges, axes, and hammers. With tools made of these flints, they likewise cut their hay, and reap their oats, which there groweth naturally in several fields: the *Yahoos* draw home the sheaves in carriages, and the servants tread them in certain covered huts, to get out the grain, which is kept in stores. They make a rude kind of earthen and wooden vessels, and bake the former in the sun.

If they can avoid casualties, they die only of old age, and are buried in the obscurest places that can be found, their friends and relations expressing neither joy nor grief at their departure; nor does the dying person discover the least regret that he is leaving the world, any

more than if he were upon returning home from a visit
to one of his neighbours. I remember my master having
once made an appointment with a friend and his family
to come to his house upon some affair of importance;
on the day fixed, the mistress and her two children came
very late; she made two excuses, first for her husband, who, as she said, happened that very morning to
shnuwnh. The word is strongly expressive in their language, but not easily rendered into English; it signifies,
to retire to his first mother. Her excuse for not coming
sooner was, that her husband dying late in the morning,
she was a good while consulting her servants about a
convenient place where his body should be laid; and I
observed she behaved herself at our house as cheerfully
as the rest. She died about three months after.

They live generally to seventy or seventy-five years,
very seldom to fourscore: some weeks before their death
they feel a gradual decay, but without pain. During this
time they are much visited by their friends, because
they cannot go abroad with their usual ease and satisfaction. However, about ten days before their death,
which they seldom fail in computing, they return the
visits that have been made them by those who are nearest in the neighbourhood, being carried in a convenient
sledge drawn by *Yahoos;* which vehicle they use, not
only upon this occasion, but when they grow old, upon
long journeys, or when they are lamed by any accident.
And therefore when the dying *Houyhnhnms* return those
visits, they take a solemn leave of their friends, as if they
were going to some remote part of the country, where
they designed to pass the rest of their lives.

I know not whether it may be worth observing, that
the *Houyhnhnms* have no word in their language to express any thing that is evil, except what they borrow
from the deformities or ill qualities of the *Yahoos*. Thus

they denote the folly of a servant, an omission of a child, a stone that cuts their feet, a continuance of foul or unseasonable weather, and the like, by adding to each the epithet of *Yahoo*. For instance, *Hhnm Yahoo, Whnaholm Yahoo, Ynlhmndwihlma Yahoo,* and an ill-contrived house *Ynholmhnmrohlnw Yahoo.*

I could with great pleasure enlarge further upon the manners and virtues of this excellent people; but intending in a short time to publish a volume by itself expressly upon that subject, I refer the reader thither. And in the mean time, proceed to relate my own sad catastrophe.

CHAP. X

The Author's economy, and happy life among the Houyhnhnms. *His great improvement in virtue, by conversing with them. Their conversations. The Author has notice given him by his master that he must depart from the country. He falls into a swoon for grief, but submits. He contrives and finishes a canoe, by the help of a fellow-servant, and puts to sea at a venture.*

I had settled my little economy to my own heart's content. My master had ordered a room to be made for me after their manner, about six yards from the house; the sides and floors of which I plastered with clay, and covered with rush-mats of my own contriving; I had beaten hemp, which there grows wild, and made of it a sort of ticking: this I filled with the feathers of several birds I had taken with springs made of *Yahoos'* hairs, and were excellent food. I had worked two chairs with my knife, the sorrel nag helping me in the grosser and more laborious part. When my clothes were worn to rags, I made myself others with the skins of rabbits, and of a certain beautiful animal about the same size, called *nnuhnoh*, the skin of which is covered with a fine down. Of these I likewise made very tolerable stockings. I soled my shoes with wood which I cut from a tree, and fitted to the upper leather, and when this was worn out, I supplied it with the skins of *Yahoos* dried in the sun. I often got honey out of hollow trees, which I mingled with water, or eat with my bread. No man could more verify the truth of these two maxims, *That nature is very easily satisfied;* and *That necessity is the mother of invention.* I enjoyed perfect health of body, and tranquillity of mind; I did not feel the treachery of inconstancy of a friend, nor the injuries of a secret or open enemy. I had no occasion of bribing, flattering or pimping, to procure the favour of any great man or of his minion. I wanted no fence against fraud or oppression; here was neither physician to destroy my body, nor lawyer to ruin my fortune; no informer to watch my words and actions, or forge accusations against me for hire: here were no gibers, censurers, backbiters, pickpockets, highwaymen, house-breakers, attorneys, bawds, buffoons, gamesters, politicians, wits, splenetics, tedious talkers, controvertists, ravishers, murderers, robbers, virtuosos; no leaders or followers of party and faction; no encouragers to vice, by seducement or examples; no dungeon, axes, gibbets, whipping-posts, or pillories; no cheating shopkeepers or mechanics; no pride, vanity, or affectation; no fops, bullies, drunkards, strolling whores, or poxes; no ranting, lewd, expensive wives; no stupid, proud pedants; no importunate, overbearing, quarrelsome, noisy, roaring, empty, conceited, swearing companions; no scoundrels, raised from the dust for the sake of their vices, or nobility thrown into it on account of their virtues; no lords, fiddlers, judges, or dancing-masters.

I had the favour of being admitted to several *Houyhn-hnms,* who came to visit or dine with my master; where his Honour graciously suffered me to wait in the room, and listen to their discourse. Both he and his company would often descend to ask me questions, and receive my answers. I had also sometimes the honour of attending my master in his visits to others. I never presumed to speak, except in answer to a question; and then I did it with inward regret, because it was a loss of so much time for improving myself: but I was infinitely delighted with the station of an humble auditor in such conversations, where nothing passed but what was useful, expressed in the fewest and most significant words; where (as I have already said) the greatest decency was observed, without the least degree of ceremony; where no person spoke without being pleased himself, and pleasing his companions; where there was no interruption, tediousness, heat, or difference of sentiments. They have a notion, that when people are met together, a short silence doth much improve conversation: this I found to be true; for during those little intermissions of talk, new ideas would arise in their thoughts, which very much enlivened the discourse. Their subjects are generally on friendship and benevolence, or order and economy; sometimes upon the visible operations of nature, or ancient traditions; upon the bounds and limits of virtue; upon the unerring rules of reason, or upon some determinations to be taken at the next great assembly; and often upon the various excellencies of poetry. I may add, without vanity, that my presence often gave them sufficient matter for discourse, because it afforded my master an occasion of letting his friends into the history of me and my country, upon which they were all pleased to descant in a manner not very advantageous to human kind; and for that reason I shall not repeat what they said: only I may be allowed to observe, that his Honour, to my great admiration, appeared to understand the nature of *Yahoos* much better than myself. He went through all our vices and follies, and discovered many which I had never mentioned to him, by only supposing what qualities a *Yahoo* of their country, with a small proportion of reason, might be capable of exerting; and concluded, with too much probability, how vile as well as miserable such a creature must be.

I freely confess, that all the little knowledge I have of any value, was acquired by the lectures I received from my master, and from hearing the discourses of him and his friends; to which I should be prouder to listen, than to dictate to the greatest and wisest assembly in Europe. I admired the strength, comeliness, and speed of the inhabitants; and such a constellation of virtues in such amiable persons produced in me the highest veneration. At first, indeed, I did not feel that natural awe which the *Yahoos* and all other animals bear towards them; but it grew upon me by degrees, much sooner than I imagined, and was mingled with a respectful love and gratitude, that they would condescend to distinguish me from the rest of my species.

When I thought of my family, my friends, my countrymen, or human race in general, I considered them as they really were, *Yahoos* in shape and disposition, perhaps a little more civilized, and qualified with the gift of speech, but making no other use of reason, than to improve and multiply those vices, whereof their brethren in this country had only the share that nature allotted them. When I happened to behold the reflection of my own form in a lake or fountain, I turned away my face in horror and detestation of myself, and could better endure the sight of a common *Yahoo*, than of my own person. By conversing with the *Houyhnhnms,* and looking upon them with delight, I fell to imitate their gait and gesture, which is now grown into a habit, and my friends often tell me in a blunt way, that *I trot like a horse;* which, however, I take for a great compliment. Neither shall I disown, that in speaking I am apt to fall into the voice and manner of the *Houyhnhnms,* and hear myself ridiculed on that account without the least mortification.

In the midst of all this happiness, and when I looked upon myself to be fully settled for life, my master sent for me one morning a little earlier than his usual hour. I observed by his countenance that he was in some perplexity, and at a loss how to begin what he had to speak. After a short silence, he told me, he did not know how I would take what he was going to say; that in the last general assembly, when the affair of the *Yahoos* was entered upon, the representatives had taken offence at his keeping a *Yahoo* (meaning myself) in his family more like a *Houyhnhnm* than a brute animal. That he was known frequently to converse with me, as if he could receive some advantage or pleasure in my company; that such a practice was not agreeable to reason or nature, or a thing ever heard of before among them. The assembly did therefore exhort him, either to employ me like the rest of my species, or command me to swim back to the place from whence I came. That the first of these expedients was utterly rejected by all the *Houyhnhnms* who had ever seen me at his house or their own: for they alleged, that because I had some rudiments of reason, added to the natural pravity of those animals, it was to be feared, I might be able to seduce them into the woody and mountainous parts of the country, and bring them in troops by night to destroy the *Houyhnhnms*' cattle, as being naturally of the ravenous kind, and averse from labour.

My master added, that he was daily pressed by the *Houyhnhnms* of the neighbourhood to have the assembly's exhortation executed, which he could not put off much longer. He doubted it would be impossible for me to swim to another country, and therefore wished I would contrive some sort of vehicle resembling those I had described to him, that might carry me on the sea; in which work I should have the assistance of his own servants, as well as those of his neighbours. He concluded, that for his own part, he could have been content to keep me in his service as long as I lived; because he found I had cured myself of some bad habits and dispositions, by endeavouring, as far as my inferior nature was capable, to imitate the *Houyhnhnms*.

I should here observe to the reader, that a decree of the general assembly in this country is expressed by the word *hnheoayn,* which signifies an exhortation, as near as I can render it; for they have no conception how a rational creature can be compelled, but only advised, or exhorted; because no person can disobey reason, without giving up his claim to be a rational creature.

I was struck with the utmost grief and despair at my master's discourse; and being unable to support the agonies I was under, I fell into a swoon at his feet; when I came to myself, he told me, that he concluded I had been dead (for these people are subject to no such imbecilities of nature). I answered, in a faint voice, that death would have been too great an happiness; that although I could not blame the assembly's exhortation, of the urgency of his friends; yet, in my weak and corrupt judgment, I thought it might consist with reason to have been less rigorous. That I could not swim a league, and probably the nearest land to theirs might be distant above an hundred: that many materials, necessary for making a small vessel to carry me off, were wholly wanting in this country, which, however, I would attempt in obedience and gratitude to his Honour, although I concluded the thing to be impossible, and therefore looked on myself as already devoted to destruction. That the certain prospect of an unnatural death was the least of my evils: for, supposing I should escape with life by some strange adventure, how could I think with temper of passing my days among *Yahoos*, and relapsing into my old corruptions, for want of examples to lead and keep me within the paths of virtue. That I knew too well upon what solid reasons all the determinations of the wise *Houyhnhnms* were founded, not to be shaken by arguments of mine, a miserable *Yahoo*; and therefore, after presenting him with my humble thanks for the offer of his servants' assistance in making a vessel, and desiring a reasonable time for so difficult a work, I told him I would endeavour to preserve a wretched being; and, if ever I returned to England, was not without hopes of being useful to my own species, by celebrating the praises of the renowned *Houyhnhnms*, and proposing their virtues to the imitation of mankind.

My master in a few words made me a very gracious reply, allowed me the space of two months to finish my boat; and ordered the sorrel nag, my fellow-servant (for so at this distance I may presume to call him) to follow my instructions, because I told my master, that his help would be sufficient, and I knew he had a tenderness for me.

In his company my first business was to go to that part of the coast where my rebellious crew had ordered me to be set on shore. I got upon a height, and looking on every side into the sea, fancied I saw a small island, towards the north-east: I took out my pocket-glass, and could then clearly distinguish it about five leagues off, as I computed; but it appeared to the sorrel nag to be only a blue cloud: for, as he had no conception of any country beside his own, so he could not be as expert in distinguishing remote objects at sea, as we who so much converse in that element.

After I had discovered this island, I considered no farther; but resolved it should, if possible, be the first place of my banishment, leaving the consequence to fortune.

I returned home, and consulting with the sorrel nag, we went into a copse at some distance, where I with my knife, and he with a sharp flint fastened very artificially, after their manner, to a wooden handle, cut down several oak wattles about the thickness of a walking-staff, and some larger pieces. But I shall not trouble the reader with a particular description of my own mechanics; let it suffice to say, that in six weeks time, with the help of the sorrel nag, who performed the parts that required most labour, I finished a sort of Indian canoe, but much larger, covering it with the skins of *Yahoos* well stitched together, with hempen threads of my own making. My sail was likewise composed of the skins of the same animal; but I made use of the youngest I could get, the older being too tough and thick; and I likewise provided myself with four paddles. I laid in a stock of boiled flesh, of rabbits and fowls, and took with me two vessels, one filled with milk, and the other with water.

I tried my canoe in a large pond near my master's house, and then corrected in it what was amiss; stopping all the chinks with *Yahoos*' tallow, till I found it staunch, and able to bear me, and my freight. And when it was as complete as I could possibly make it, I had it drawn on a carriage very gently by *Yahoos* to the seaside, under the conduct of the sorrel nag, and another servant.

When all was ready, and the day came for my departure, I took leave of my master and lady, and the whole family, my eyes flowing with tears, and my heart quite sunk with grief. But his Honour, out of curiosity, and, perhaps (if I may speak it without vanity) partly out of kindness, was determined to see me in my canoe, and got several of his neighbouring friends to accompany him. I was forced to wait above an hour for the tide, and then observing the wind very fortunately bearing towards the island, to which I intended to steer my course, I took a second leave of my master: but as I was going to prostrate myself to kiss his hoof, he did me the honour to raise it gently to my mouth. I am not ignorant how much I have been censured for mentioning this last particular. For my detractors are pleased to think it improbable, that so illustrious a person should descend to give so great a mark of distinction to a creature so inferior as I. Neither have I forgot, how apt some travellers are to boast of extraordinary favours they have received. But if these censurers were better acquainted with the noble and courteous disposition of the *Houyhnhnms*, they would soon change their opinion.

I paid my respects to the rest of the *Houyhnhnms* in his Honour's company; then getting into my canoe, I pushed off from shore.

CHAP. XI

The Author's dangerous voyage. He arrives at New Holland, *hoping to settle there. Is wounded with an arrow by one of the natives. Is seized and carried by force into a* Portuguese *ship. The great civilities of the Captain. The Author arrives at* England.

I began this desperate voyage on February 15, 1714–15, at 9 o'clock in the morning. The wind was very favourable; however, I made use at first only of my paddles; but considering I should soon be weary, and that the wind might chop about, I ventured to set up my little sail; and thus, with the help of the tide, I went at the rate of a league and a half an hour, as near as I could guess. My master and his friends continued on the shore, till I was almost out of sight; and I often heard the sorrel nag (who always loved me) crying out, *Hnuy illa nyha majah Yahoo,* Take care of thyself, gentle *Yahoo.*

My design was, if possible, to discover some small island uninhabited, yet sufficient by my labour to furnish me with the necessaries of life, which I would have thought a greater happiness than to be first minister in the politest court of Europe; so horrible was the idea I conceived of returning to live in the society and under the government of *Yahoos.* For in such a solitude as I desired, I could at least enjoy my own thoughts, and reflect with delight on the virtues of those inimitable *Houyhnhnms,* without any opportunity of degenerating into the vices and corruptions of my own species.

The reader may remember what I related when my crew conspired against me, and confined me to my cabin. How I continued there several weeks, without knowing what course we took; and when I was put ashore in the long boat, how the sailors told me with oaths, whether true or false, that they knew not in what part of the world we were. However, I did then believe us to be about ten degrees southward of the Cape of Good Hope, or about forty-five degrees southern latitude, as I gathered from some general words I overheard among them, being I supposed to the south-east in their intended voyage to Madagascar. And although this were little better than conjecture, yet I resolved to steer my course eastward, hoping to reach the southwest coast of New Holland, and perhaps some such island as I desired, lying westward of it. The wind was full west, and by six in the evening I computed I had gone eastward at least eighteen leagues, when I spied a very small island about half a league off, which I soon reached. It was nothing but a rock with one creek, naturally arched by the force of tempests. Here I put in my canoe, and climbing up a part of the rock, I could plainly discover land to the east, extending from south to north. I lay all night in my canoe; and repeating my voyage early in the morning, I arrived in seven hours to the south-east point of New Holland. This confirmed me in the opinion I have long entertained, that the maps and charts place this country at least three degrees more to the east than it really is; which thought I communicated many years ago to my worthy friend Mr. Herman Moll, and gave him my reasons for it, although he hath rather chosen to follow other authors.

I saw no inhabitants in the place where I landed, and being unarmed, I was afraid of venturing far into the country. I found some shellfish on the shore, and eat them raw, not daring to kindle a fire, for fear of being discovered by the natives. I continued three days feeding on oysters and limpets, to save my own provisions;

and I fortunately found a brook of excellent water, which gave me great relief.

On the fourth day, venturing out early a little too far, I saw twenty or thirty natives upon a height, not above five hundred yards from me. They were stark naked, men, women, and children round a fire, as I could discover by the smoke. One of them spied me, and gave notice to the rest; five of them advanced towards me, leaving the women and children at the fire. I made what haste I could to the shore, and getting into my canoe, shoved off: the savages observing me retreat, ran after me; and before I could get far enough into the sea, discharged an arrow, which wounded me deeply on the inside of my left knee (I shall carry the mark to my grave). I apprehended the arrow might be poisoned, and paddling out of the reach of their darts (being a calm day), I made a shift to suck the wound, and dress it as well as I could.

I was at a loss what to do, for I durst not return to the same landing-place, but stood to the north, and was forced to paddle; for the wind, though very gentle, was against me, blowing north-west. As I was looking about for a secure landing-place, I saw a sail to the north-north-east, which appearing every minute more visible, I was in some doubt whether I should wait for them or no; but at last my detestation of the *Yahoo* race prevailed, and turning my canoe, I sailed and paddled together to the south, and got into the same creek from whence I set out in the morning, choosing rather to trust myself among these barbarians, than live with European *Yahoos*. I drew up my canoe as close as I could to the shore, and hid myself behind a stone by the little brook, which, as I have already said, was excellent water.

The ship came within half a league of this creek, and sent her long boat with vessels to take in fresh water (for the place it seems was very well known), but I did not observe it till the boat was almost on shore, and it was too late to seek another hiding-place. The seamen at their landing observed my canoe, and rummaging it all over, easily conjectured that the owner could not be far off. Four of them well armed searched every cranny and lurking-hole, till at last they found me flat on my face behind the stone. They gazed awhile in admiration at my strange uncouth dress; my coat made of skins, my wooden-soled shoes, and my furred stockings; from whence, however, they concluded I was not a native of the place, who all go naked. One of the seamen in Portuguese bid me rise, and asked who I was. I understood that language very well, and getting upon my feet, said, I was a poor *Yahoo*, banished from the *Houyhnhnms*, and desired they would please to let me depart. They admired to hear me answer them in their own tongue, and saw by my complexion I must be an European; but were at a loss to know what I meant by *Yahoos* and *Houyhnhnms*, and at the same time fell a laughing at my strange tone in speaking, which resembled the neighing of a horse. I trembled all the while betwixt fear and hatred. I again desired leave to depart, and was gently moving to my canoe; but they laid hold of me, desiring to know, what country I was of? whence I came? with many other questions. I told them, I was born in England, from whence I came about five years ago, and then their country and ours were at peace. I therefore hoped they would not treat me as an enemy, since I meant them no harm, but was a poor *Yahoo*, seeking some desolate place where to pass the remainder of his unfortunate life.

When they began to talk, I thought I never heard or saw any thing so unnatural; for it appeared to me as monstrous as if a dog or a cow should speak in England, or a *Yahoo* in *Houyhnhnm-land*. The honest Portuguese were equally amazed at my strange dress, and the odd manner of delivering my words, which however they understood very well. They spoke to me with great humanity, and said they were sure their Captain would carry me *gratis* to Lisbon, from whence I might return to my own country; that two of the seamen would go back to the ship, inform the Captain of what they had seen, and receive his orders; in the mean time, unless I would give my solemn oath not to fly, they would secure me by force. I thought it best to comply with their proposal. They were very curious to know my story, but I gave them very little satisfaction; and they all conjectured that my misfortunes had impaired my reason. In two hours the boat, which went loaden with vessels of water, returned with the Captain's command to fetch me on board. I fell on my knees to preserve my liberty; but all was in vain, and the men having tied me with cords, heaved me into the boat, from whence I was taken into the ship, and from thence into the Captain's cabin.

His name was Pedro de Mendez; he was a very courteous and generous person; he entreated me to give some account of myself, and desired to know what I would eat or drink; said, I should be used as well as himself, and spoke so many obliging things, that I wondered to find such civilities from a *Yahoo*. However, I remained silent and sullen; I was ready to faint at the very smell of him and his men. At last I desired something to eat out of my own canoe; but he ordered me a chicken and some excellent wine, and then directed that I should be put to bed in a very clean cabin. I would not undress myself, but lay on the bed-clothes, and in half an hour stole out, when I thought the crew was at dinner, and getting to the side of the ship was going to leap into the sea, and swim for my life, rather than continue among *Yahoos*. But one of the seamen prevented me, and having informed the Captain, I was chained to my cabin.

After dinner Don Pedro came to me, and desired to know my reason for so desperate an attempt; assured me he only meant to do me all the service he was able; and spoke so very movingly, that at last I descended to treat him like an animal which had some little portion of reason. I gave him a very short relation of my voyage; of the conspiracy against me by my own men; of the country where they set me on shore, and of my three years' residence there. All which he looked upon as if it were a dream or a vision; whereat I took great offence; for I had quite forgot the faculty of lying, so peculiar to *Yahoos* in all countries where they preside, and, consequently the disposition of suspecting truth in others of their own species. I asked him, whether it were the custom in his country to *say the thing that was not?* I assured him I had almost forgot what he meant by falsehood, and if I had lived a thousand years in *Houyhnhnmland,* I should never have heard a lie from the meanest servant; that I was altogether indifferent whether he believed me or no; but however, in return for his favours, I would give so much allowance to the corruption of his nature, as to answer any objection he would please to make, and then he might easily discover the truth.

The Captain, a wise man, after many endeavours to catch me tripping in some part of my story, at last began to have a better opinion of my veracity. But he added, that since I professed so inviolable an attachment to truth, I must give him my word of honour to bear him company in this voyage, without attempting any thing against my life, or else he would continue me a prisoner till we arrived at Lisbon. I gave him the promise he required; but at the same time protested that I would suffer the greatest hardships rather than return to live among *Yahoos*.

Our voyage passed without any considerable accident. In gratitude to the Captain I sometimes sat with him at his earnest request, and strove to conceal my antipathy to human kind, although it often broke out, which he suffered to pass without observation. But the greatest part of the day, I confined myself to my cabin, to avoid seeing any of the crew. The Captain had often entreated me to strip myself of my savage dress, and offered to lend me the best suit of clothes he had. This I would not be prevailed on to accept, abhorring to cover myself with any thing that had been on the back of a *Yahoo*. I only desired he would lend me two clean shirts, which having been washed since he wore them, I believed would not so much defile me. These I changed every second day, and washed them myself.

We arrived at Lisbon, Nov. 5, 1715. At our landing the Captain forced me to cover myself with his cloak, to prevent the rabble from crowding about me. I was conveyed to his own house, and at my earnest request, he led me up to the highest room backwards. I conjured him to conceal from all persons what I had told him of the *Houyhnhnms*, because the least hint of such a story would not only draw numbers of people to see me, but probably put me in danger of being imprisoned, or burnt by the Inquisition. The Captain persuaded me to accept a suit of clothes newly made; but I would not suffer the tailor to take my measure; however, Don Pedro being almost my size, they fitted me well enough. He accoutred me with other necessaries all new, which I aired for twenty-four hours before I would use them.

The Captain had no wife, nor above three servants,

none of which were suffered to attend at meals, and his whole deportment was so obliging, added to very good *human* understanding, that I really began to tolerate his company. He gained so far upon me, that I ventured to look out of the back window. By degrees I was brought into another room, from whence I peeped into the street, but drew my head back in a fright. In a week's time he seduced me down to the door. I found my terror gradually lessened, but my hatred and contempt seemed to increase. I was at last bold enough to walk the street in his company, but kept my nose well stopped with rue, or sometimes with tobacco.

In ten days, Don Pedro, to whom I had given some account of my domestic affairs, put it upon me as a matter of honour and conscience, that I ought to return to my native country, and live at home with my wife and children. He told me, there was an English ship in the port just ready to sail, and he would furnish me with all things necessary. It would be tedious to repeat his arguments, and my contradictions. He said it was altogether impossible to find such a solitary island as I desired to live in; but I might command in my own house, and pass my time in a manner as recluse as I pleased.

I complied at last, finding I could not do better. I left Lisbon the 24th day of November, in an English merchantman, but who was the master I never inquired. Don Pedro accompanied me to the ship, and lent me twenty pounds. He took kind leave of me, and embraced me at parting, which I bore as well as I could. During this last voyage I had no commerce with the master or any of his men; but pretending I was sick, kept close in my cabin. On the fifth of December, 1715, we cast anchor in the Downs about nine in the morning, and at three in the afternoon I got safe to my house at Rotherhith.

My wife and family received me with great surprise and joy, because they concluded me certainly dead; but I must freely confess the sight of them filled me only with hatred, disgust, and contempt, and the more by reflecting on the near alliance I had to them. For, although since my unfortunate exile from the *Houyhnhnm* country, I had compelled myself to tolerate the sight of *Yahoos*, and to converse with Don Pedro de Mendez; yet my memory and imagination were perpetually filled with the virtues and ideas of those exalted *Houyhnhnms*. And when I began to consider, that by copulating with one of the *Yahoo* species I had become a parent of more, it struck me with the utmost shame, confusion, and horror.

As soon as I entered the house, my wife took me in her arms, and kissed me; at which, having not been used to the touch of that odious animal for so many years, I fell in a swoon for almost an hour. At the time I am writing it is five years since my last return to England: during the first year, I could not endure my wife or children in my presence, the very smell of them was intolerable; much less could I suffer them to eat in the same room. To this hour they dare not presume to touch my bread, or drink out of the same cup, neither was I ever able to let one of them take me by the hand. The first money I laid out was to buy two young stone-horses, which I keep in a good stable, and next to them the groom is my greatest favourite; for I feel my spirits revived by the smell he contracts in the stable. My horses understand me tolerably well; I converse with them at least four hours every day. They are strangers to bridle or saddle; they live in great amity with me, and friendship to each other.

CHAP. XII

*The Author's veracity. His design in publishing this work.
His censure of those travellers who swerve from the truth.
The Author clears himself from any sinister ends in writing.
An objection answered. The method of planting colonies.
His native country commended. The right of the Crown to
those countries described by the Author, is justified. The
difficulty of conquering them. The Author takes his last
leave of the reader; proposeth his manner of living for the
future, gives good advice, and concludes.*

Thus, gentle reader, I have given thee a faithful history
of my travels for sixteen years and above seven months;
wherein I have not been so studious of ornament as
truth. I could perhaps like others have astonished thee
with strange improbable tales; but I rather chose to relate plain matter of fact in the simplest manner and
style; because my principal design was to inform, and
not to amuse thee.

It is easy for us who travel into remote countries,
which are seldom visited by Englishmen or other Europeans, to form descriptions of wonderful animals both at
sea and land. Whereas a traveller's chief aim should be
to make men wiser and better, and to improve their
minds by the bad as well as good example of what they
deliver concerning foreign places.

I could heartily wish a law was enacted, that every
traveller, before he were permitted to publish his voyages, should be obliged to make oath before the Lord
High Chancellor that all he intended to print was absolutely true to the best of his knowledge; for then the
world would no longer be deceived as it usually is, while
some writers, to make their works pass the better upon

the public, impose the grossest falsities on the unwary
reader. I have perused several books of travels with
great delight in my younger days; but having since gone
over most parts of the globe, and been able to contradict
many fabulous accounts from my own observation, it
hath given me a great disgust against this part of reading, and some indignation to see the credulity of mankind so impudently abused. Therefore since my acquaintance were pleased to think my poor endeavours
might not be unacceptable to my country, I imposed on
myself as a maxim, never to be swerved from, that I
would *strictly adhere to truth;* neither indeed can I be
ever under the least temptation to vary from it, while
I retain in my mind the lectures and example of my
noble master, and the other illustrious *Houyhnhnms,* of
whom I had so long the honour to be an humble hearer.

> *Nec si miserum Fortuna Sinonem*
> *Finxit, vanum etiam, mendacemque improba finget.*

I know very well how little reputation is to be got by
writings which require neither genius nor learning, nor
indeed any other talent, except a good memory, or an
exact journal. I know likewise, that writers of travels,
like dictionary-makers, are sunk into oblivion by the
weight and bulk of those who come after, and therefore
lie uppermost. And it is highly probable, that such
travellers who shall hereafter visit the countries described in this work of mine, may, by detecting my
errors (if there be any), and adding many new discoveries of their own, justle me out of vogue, and stand
in my place, making the world forget that I was ever an
author. This indeed would be too great a mortification
if I wrote for fame: but, as my sole intention was the
PUBLIC GOOD, I cannot be altogether disappointed. For
who can read of the virtues I have mentioned in the

glorious *Houyhnhnms,* without being ashamed of his own vices, when he considers himself as the reasoning, governing animal of his country? I shall say nothing of those remote nations where *Yahoos* preside; amongst which the least corrupted are the *Brobdingnagians,* whose wise maxims in morality and government it would be our happinesss to observe. But I forbear descanting farther, and rather leave the judicious reader to his own remarks and applications.

I am not a little pleased that this work of mine can possibly meet with no censurers: for what objections can be made against a writer who relates only plain facts that happened in such distant countries, where we have not the least interest with respect either to trade or negotiations? I have carefully avoided every fault with which common writers of travels are often too justly charged. Besides, I meddle not the least with any party, but write without passion, prejudice, or ill-will against any man or number of men whatsoever. I write for the noblest end, to inform and instruct mankind, over whom I may, without breach of modesty, pretend to some superiority, from the advantages I received by conversing so long among the most accomplished *Houyhnhnms.* I write without any view towards profit or praise. I never suffer a word to pass that may look like reflection, or possibly give the least offence even to those who are most ready to take it. So that I hope I may with justice pronounce myself an author perfectly blameless, against whom the tribes of answerers, considerers, observers, reflecters, detecters, remarkers, will never be able to find matter for exercising their talents.

I confess, it was whispered to me, that I was bound in duty as a subject of England, to have given in a memorial to a Secretary of State, at my first coming over; because, whatever lands are discovered by a subject, belong to the Crown. But I doubt whether our conquests in the countries I treat of, would be as easy as those of Ferdinando Cortez over the naked Americans. The *Lilliputians* I think, are hardly worth the charge of a fleet and army to reduce them; and I question whether it might be prudent or safe to attempt the *Brobdingnagians;* or whether an English army would be much at their ease with the Flying Island over their heads. The *Houyhnhnms,* indeed, appear not to be so well prepared for war, a science to which they are perfect strangers, and especially against missive weapons. However, supposing myself to be a minister of state, I could never give my advice for invading them. Their prudence, unanimity, unacquaintedness with fear, and their love of their country, would amply supply all defects in the military art. Imagine twenty thousand of them breaking into the midst of an European army, confounding the ranks, overturning the carriages, battering the warriors' faces into mummy by terrible yerks from their hinder hoofs; for they would well deserve the character given to Augustus: *Recalcitrat undique tutus.* But instead of proposals for conquering that magnanimous nation, I rather wish they were in a capacity or disposition to send a sufficient number of their inhabitants for civilizing Europe, by teaching us the first principles of honour, justice, truth, temperance, public spirit, fortitude, chastity, friendship, benevolence, and fidelity. The names of all which virtues are still retained among us in most languages and are to be met with in modern as well as ancient authors; which I am able to assert from my own small reading.

But I had another reason which made me less forward to enlarge his Majesty's dominions by my discoveries. To say the truth, I had conceived a few scruples with relation to the distributive justice of princes upon these occasions. For instance, a crew of pirates are driven by a storm they know not whither; at length a boy discovers land from the topmast; they go on shore to rob and plunder; they see an harmless people, are entertained with kindness, they give the country a new name, they take formal possession of it for their king, they set up a rotten plank or a stone for a memorial, they murder two or three dozen of the natives, bring away a couple more by force for a sample, return home, and get their pardon. Here commences a new dominion acquired with a title by *divine right*. Ships are sent with the first opportunity; the natives driven out or destroyed, their princes tortured to discover their gold; a free licence given to all acts of inhumanity and lust, the earth reeking with the blood of its inhabitants: and this execrable crew of butchers employed in so pious an expedition, is a *modern colony* sent to convert and civilize an idolatrous and barbarous people.

But this description, I confess, doth by no means affect the British nation, who may be an example to the whole world for their wisdom, care, and justice in planting colonies; their liberal endowments for the advancement of religion and learning; their choice of devout and able pastors to propagate Christianity; their caution in stocking their provinces with people of sober lives and conversations from this the mother kingdom; their strict regard to the distribution of justice, in supplying the civil administration through all their colonies with officers of the greatest abilities, utter strangers to corruption; and to crown all, by sending the most vigilant and virtuous governors, who have no other views than the happiness of the people over whom they preside, and the honour of the King their master.

But, as those countries which I have described do not appear to have any desire of being conquered, and enslaved, murdered or driven out by colonies; nor abound either in gold, silver, sugar, or tobacco; I did humbly conceive, they were by no means proper objects of our zeal, our valour, or our interest. However, if those whom it more concerns think fit to be of another opinion, I am ready to depose, when I shall be lawfully called, that no European did ever visit these countries before me. I mean, if the inhabitants ought to be believed; unless a dispute may arise about the two *Yahoos,* said to have been seen many ages ago on a mountain in *Houyhnhnm-land.*

But, as to the formality of taking possession in my Sovereign's name, it never came once into my thoughts; and if it had, yet as my affairs then stood, I should perhaps in point of prudence and self-preservation, have put it off to a better opportunity.

Having thus answered the only objection that can ever be raised against me as a traveller, I here take a final leave of all my courteous readers, and return to enjoy my own speculations in my little garden at Redriff, to apply those excellent lessons of virtue which I learned among the *Houyhnhnms;* to instruct the *Yahoos* of my own family as far as I shall find them docible animals; to behold my figure often in a glass, and thus if possible habituate myself by time to tolerate the sight of a human creature: to lament the brutality of *Houyhnhnms* in my own country, but always treat their persons with respect, for the sake of my noble master, his family, his friends, and the whole *Houyhnhnm* race, whom these of ours have the honour to resemble in all their lineaments, however their intellectuals came to degenerate.

I began last week to permit my wife to sit at dinner with me, at the farthest end of a long table; and to answer (but with the utmost brevity) the few questions I asked her. Yet the smell of a *Yahoo* continuing very offensive, I always keep my nose well stopped with rue, lavender, or tobacco leaves. And although it be hard for a man late in life to remove old habits, I am not altogether out of hopes in some time to suffer a neighbour *Yahoo* in my company, without the apprehensions I am yet under of his teeth or his claws.

My reconcilement to the *Yahoo*-kind in general might not be so difficult, if they would be content with those vices and follies only which nature hath entitled them to. I am not in the least provoked at the sight of a lawyer, a pickpocket, a colonel, a fool, a lord, a gamester, a politician, a whore-master, a physician, an evidence, a suborner, an attorney, a traitor, or the like; this is all according to the due course of things: but when I behold a lump of deformity, and diseases both in body and mind, smitten with *pride*, it immediately breaks all the measures of my patience; neither shall I be ever able to comprehend how such an animal and such a vice could tally together. The wise and virtuous *Houyhnhnms,* who abound in all excellencies that can adorn a rational creature, have no name for this vice in their language, which hath no terms to express any thing that is evil, except those whereby they describe the detestable qualities of their *Yahoos,* among which they were not able to distinguish this of pride, for want of thoroughly understanding human nature, as it showeth itself in other countries, where that animal presides. But I, who had more experience, could plainly observe some rudiments of it among the wild *Yahoos*.

But the *Houyhnhnms,* who live under the government of reason, are no more proud of the good qualities they possess, than I should be for not wanting a leg or an arm, which no man in his wits would boast of, although he must be miserable without them. I dwell the longer upon this subject from the desire I have to make the society of an English *Yahoo* by any means not insupportable; and therefore I here entreat those who have any tincture of this absurd vice, that they will not presume to come in my sight.

Finis.

On the Death of Mrs. Johnson
[Stella]

THIS day, being Sunday, January 28, 1727–8,
about eight o'clock at night, a servant brought me
a note, with an account of the death of the truest, most
virtuous, and valuable friend that I, or perhaps any
other person, ever was blessed with. She expired about
six in the evening of this day; and as soon as I am left
alone, which is about eleven at night, I resolve, for my
own satisfaction, to say something of her life and character.

She was born at Richmond, in Surrey, on the thir-
teenth day of March, in the year 1681. Her father was
a younger brother of a good family in Nottinghamshire,
her mother of a lower degree; and indeed she had little
to boast of her birth. I knew her from six years old, and
had some share in her education, by directing what
books she should read, and perpetually instructing her
in the principles of honour and virtue; from which she
never swerved in any one action or moment of her life.
She was sickly from her childhood until about the age
of fifteen; but then grew into perfect health, and was
looked upon as one of the most beautiful, graceful, and
agreeable young women in London, only a little too fat.
Her hair was blacker than a raven, and every feature of
her face in perfection. She lived generally in the country, with a family, where she contracted an intimate
friendship with another lady of more advanced years. I

was then (to my mortification) settled in Ireland; and about a year after, going to visit my friends in England, I found she was a little uneasy upon the death of a person on whom she had some dependance. Her fortune, at that time, was in all not above fifteen hundred pounds, the interest of which was but a scanty maintenance, in so dear a country, for one of her spirit. Upon this consideration, and indeed very much for my own satisfaction, who had few friends or acquaintance in Ireland, I prevailed with her and her dear friend and companion, the other lady, to draw what money they had into Ireland, a great part of their fortune being in annuities upon funds. Money was then ten *per cent.* in Ireland, besides the advantage of turning it, and all necessaries of life at half the price. They complied with my advice, and soon after came over; but, I happening to continue some time longer in England, they were much discouraged to live in Dublin, where they were wholly strangers. She was at that time about nineteen years old, and her person was soon distinguished. But the adventure looked so like a frolic, the censure held for some time, as if there were a secret history in such a removal; which, however, soon blew off by her excellent conduct. She came over with her friend on the —— in the year 170–; and they both lived together until this day, when death removed her from us. For some years past, she had been visited with continual ill health; and several times, within these two years, her life was despaired of. But for this twelvemonth past, she never had a day's health; and, properly speaking, she hath been dying six months, but kept alive, almost against nature, by the generous kindness of two physicians, and the care of her friends. Thus far I writ the same night between eleven and twelve.

Never was any of her sex born with better gifts of the

mind, or more improved them by reading and conversation. Yet her memory was not of the best, and was impaired in the latter years of her life. But I cannot call to mind that I ever once heard her make a wrong judgment of persons, books, or affairs. Her advice was always the best, and with the greatest freedom, mixed with the greatest decency. She had a gracefulness, somewhat more than human, in every motion, word, and action. Never was so happy a conjunction of civility, freedom, easiness, and sincerity. There seemed to be a combination among all that knew her, to treat her with a dignity much beyond her rank; yet people of all sorts were never more easy than in her company. Mr. Addison, when he was in Ireland, being introduced to her, immediately found her out; and, if he had not soon after left the kingdom, assured me he would have used all endeavours to cultivate her friendship. A rude or conceited coxcomb passed his time very ill, upon the least breach of respect; for in such a case she had no mercy, but was sure to expose him to the contempt of the standers-by; yet in such a manner as he was ashamed to complain, and durst not resent. All of us who had the happiness of her friendship, agreed unanimously that, in an afternoon or evening's conversation, she never failed, before we parted, of delivering the best thing that was said in the company. Some of us have written down several of her sayings, or what the French call *bons mots*, wherein she excelled almost beyond belief. She never mistook the understanding of others; nor ever said a severe word, but where a much severer was deserved.

Her servants loved, and almost adored her at the same time. She would, upon occasions, treat them with freedom; yet her demeanour was so awful, that they durst not fail in the least point of respect. She chid them seldom, but it was with severity, which had an effect upon them for a long time after.

January 29. My head aches, and I can write no more.

January 30. Tuesday.

This is the night of the funeral, which my sickness will not suffer me to attend. It is now nine at night, and I am removed into another apartment, that I may not see the light in the church, which is just over against the window of my bed-chamber.

With all the softness of temper that became a lady, she had the personal courage of a hero. She and her friend having removed their lodgings to a new house, which stood solitary, a parcel of rogues, armed, attempted the house, where there was only one boy. She was then about four-and-twenty; and having been warned to apprehend some such attempt, she learned the management of a pistol; and the other women and servants being half dead with fear, she stole softly to her dining-room window, put on a black hood to prevent being seen, primed the pistol fresh, gently lifted up the sash, and taking her aim with the utmost presence of mind, discharged the pistol, loaden with the bullets, into the body of one villain, who stood the fairest mark. The fellow, mortally wounded, was carried off by the rest, and died the next morning; but his companions could not be found. The Duke of Ormond hath often drank her health to me upon that account, and had always an high esteem of her. She was indeed under some apprehensions of going in a boat, after some danger she had narrowly escaped by water, but she was reasoned thoroughly out of it. She was never known to cry out, or discover any fear, in a coach or on horseback; or any uneasiness by those sudden accidents with which most of her sex, either by weakness or affectation, appear so much disordered.

She never had the least absence of mind in conversation, nor given to interruption, or appeared eager to put in her word, by waiting impatiently until another had done. She spoke in a most agreeable voice, in the plainest words, never hesitating, except out of modesty before new faces, where she was somewhat reserved: nor, among her nearest friends, ever spoke much at a time. She was but little versed in the common topics of female chat; scandal, censure, and detraction, never came out of her mouth; yet, among a few friends, in private conversation, she made little ceremony in discovering her contempt of a coxcomb, and describing all his follies to the life; but the follies of her own sex she was rather inclined to extenuate or to pity.

When she was once convinced, by open facts, of any breach of truth or honour in a person of high station, especially in the Church, she could not conceal her indignation, nor hear them named without shewing her displeasure in her countenance; particularly one or two of the latter sort, whom she had known and esteemed, but detested above all mankind when it was manifest that they had sacrificed those two precious virtues to their ambition, and would much sooner have forgiven them the common immoralities of the laity.

Her frequent fits of sickness, in most parts of her life, had prevented her from making that progress in reading which she would otherwise have done. She was well versed in the Greek and Roman story, and was not unskilled in that of France and England. She spoke French perfectly, but forgot much of it by neglect and sickness. She had read carefully all the best books of travels, which serve to open and enlarge the mind. She understood the Platonic and Epicurean philosophy, and judged very well of the defects of the latter. She made very judicious abstracts of the best books she had read.

She understood the nature of government, and could point out all the errors of Hobbes, both in that and religion. She had a good insight into physic, and knew somewhat of anatomy; in both which she was instructed in her younger days by an eminent physician, who had her long under his care, and bore the highest esteem for her person and understanding. She had a true taste of wit and good sense, both in poetry and prose, and was a perfect good critic of style; neither was it easy to find a more proper or impartial judge, whose advice an author might better rely on, if he intended to send a thing into the world, provided it was on a subject that came within the compass of her knowledge. Yet, perhaps, she was sometimes too severe, which is a safe and pardonable error. She preserved her wit, judgment, and vivacity to the last, but often used to complain of her memory.

Her fortune, with some accession, could not, as I have heard say, amount to much more than two thousand pounds, whereof a great part fell with her life, having been placed upon annuities in England, and one in Ireland.

In a person so extraordinary, perhaps it may be pardonable to mention some particulars, although of little moment, further than to set forth her character. Some presents of gold pieces being often made to her while she was a girl, by her mother and other friends, on promise to keep them, she grew into such a spirit of thrift that in about three years they amounted to above two hundred pounds. She used to shew them with boasting; but her mother, apprehending she would be cheated of them, prevailed, in some months, and with great importunities, to have them put out to interest: when the girl lost the pleasure of seeing and counting her gold, which she never failed of doing many times

in a day, and despaired of heaping up such another
treasure, her humour took the quite contrary turn; she
grew careless and squandering of every new acquisition,
and so continued till about two-and-twenty; when, by
advice of some friends, and the fright of paying large
bills of tradesmen, who enticed her into their debt, she
began to reflect upon her own folly, and was never at
rest until she had discharged all her shop-bills, and re-
funded herself a considerable sum she had run out. After
which, by the addition of a few years, and a superior understanding, she became, and continued all her life, a
most prudent economist; yet still with a strong bent to
the liberal side, wherein she gratified herself by avoiding
all expense in clothes (which she ever despised) beyond
what was merely decent. And, although her frequent returns of sickness were very chargeable, except fees to
physicians, of which she met with several so generous
that she could force nothing on them (and indeed she
must otherwise have been undone), yet she never was
without a considerable sum of ready money. Insomuch
that, upon her death, when her nearest friends thought
her very bare, her executors found in her strong box
about a hundred and fifty pounds in gold. She lamented
the narrowness of her fortune in nothing so much as that
it did not enable her to entertain her friends so often,
and in so hospitable a manner, as she desired. Yet they
were always welcome; and while she was in health to
direct, were treated with neatness and elegance, so that
the revenues of her and her companion passed for much
more considerable than they really were. They lived
always in lodgings, their domestics consisted of two
maids and one man. She kept an account of all the
family expenses, from her arrival in Ireland to some
months before her death; and she would often repine,
when looking back upon the annals of her household

bills, that every thing necessary for life was double the price, while interest of money was sunk almost to one half; so that the addition made to her fortune was indeed grown absolutely necessary.

[I since writ as I found time.]

But her charity to the poor was a duty not to be diminished, and therefore became a tax upon those tradesmen who furnish the fopperies of other ladies. She bought clothes as seldom as possible, and those as plain and cheap as consisted with the situation she was in; and wore no lace for many years. Either her judgment or fortune was extraordinary, in the choice of those on whom she bestowed her charity; for it went further in doing good than double the sum from any other hand. And I have heard her say, she always met with gratitude from the poor; which must be owing to her skill in distinguishing proper objects, as well as her gracious manner in relieving them.

But she had another quality that much delighted her, although it may be thought a kind of check upon her bounty; however, it was a pleasure she could not resist: I mean that of making agreeable presents; wherein I never knew her equal, although it be an affair of as delicate a nature as most in the course of life. She used to define a present, That it was a gift to a friend of something he wanted, or was fond of, and which could not be easily gotten for money. I am confident, during my acquaintance with her, she hath, in these and some other kinds of liberality, disposed of to the value of several hundred pounds. As to presents made to herself, she received them with great unwillingness, but especially from those to whom she had ever given any; being on all occasions the most disinterested mortal I ever knew or heard of.

From her own disposition, at least as much as from

the frequent want of health, she seldom made any visits;
but her own lodgings, from before twenty years old,
were frequented by many persons of the graver sort,
who all respected her highly, upon her good sense, good
manners, and conversation. Among these were the late
Primate Lindsay, Bishop Lloyd, Bishop Ashe, Bishop
Brown, Bishop Stearne, Bishop Pulleyn, with some
others of later date; and indeed the greatest number of
her acquaintance was among the clergy. Honour, truth,
liberality, good nature, and modesty, were the virtues
she chiefly possessed, and most valued in her acquaintance: and where she found them, would be ready to
allow for some defects; nor valued them less, although
they did not shine in learning or in wit: but would
never give the least allowance for any failures in the
former, even to those who made the greatest figure in
either of the two latter. She had no use of any person's
liberality, yet her detestation of covetous people made
her uneasy if such a one was in her company; upon
which occasion she would say many things very entertaining and humorous.

She never interrupted any person who spoke; she
laughed at no mistakes they made, but helped them out
with modesty; and if a good thing were spoken, but
neglected, she would not let it fall, but set it in the best
light to those who were present. She listened to all that
was said, and had never the least distraction or absence
of thought.

It was not safe, nor prudent, in her absence, to offend
in the least word against modesty; for she then gave full
employment to her wit, her contempt, and resentment,
under which even stupidity and brutality were forced
to sink into confusion; and the guilty person, by her
future avoiding him like a bear or a satyr, was never in
a way to transgress a second time.

It happened one single coxcomb, of the pert kind, was in her company, among several other ladies; and in his flippant way began to deliver some double meanings; the rest flapped their fans, and used the other common expedients practised in such cases, of appearing not to mind or comprehend what was said. Her behaviour was very different, and perhaps may be censured. She said thus to the man: "Sir, all these ladies and I understand your meaning very well, having, in spite of our care, too often met with those of your sex who wanted manners and good sense. But, believe me, neither virtuous nor even vicious women love such kind of conversation. However, I will leave you, and report your behaviour: and whatever visit I make, I shall first enquire at the door whether you are in the house, that I may be sure to avoid you." I know not whether a majority of ladies would approve of such a proceeding; but I believe the practice of it would soon put an end to that corrupt conversation, the worst effect of dullness, ignorance, impudence, and vulgarity, and the highest affront to the modesty and understanding of the female sex.

By returning very few visits, she had not much company of her own sex, except those whom she most loved for their easiness, or esteemed for their good sense: and those, not insisting on ceremony, came often to her. But she rather chose men for her companions, the usual topics of ladies' discourse being such as she had little knowledge of, and less relish. Yet no man was upon the rack to entertain her, for she easily descended to any thing that was innocent and diverting. News, politics, censure, family management, or town-talk, she always diverted to something else; but these indeed seldom happened, for she chose her company better: and therefore many, who mistook her and themselves, having solicited her acquaintance, and finding themselves disappointed, after a few visits dropped off; and she was never known to enquire into the reason, or ask what was become of them.

She was never positive in arguing; and she usually treated those who were so in a manner which well enough gratified that unhappy disposition; yet in such a sort as made it very contemptible, and at the same time did some hurt to the owners. Whether this proceeded from her easiness in general, or from her indifference to persons, or from her despair of mending them, or from the same practice which she much liked in Mr. Addison, I cannot determine; but when she saw any of the company very warm in a wrong opinion, she was more inclined to confirm them in it than oppose them. The excuse she commonly gave, when her friends asked the reason, was that it prevented noise, and saved time. Yet I have known her very angry with some, whom she much esteemed, for sometimes falling into that infirmity.

She loved Ireland much better than the generality of those who owe both their birth and riches to it; and having brought over all the fortune she had in money, left the reversion of the best part of it, one thousand pounds, to Dr. Stephens's Hospital. She detested the tyranny and injustice of England in their treatment of this kingdom. She had indeed reason to love a country, where she had the esteem and friendship of all who knew her, and the universal good report of all who ever heard of her, without one exception, if I am told the truth by those who keep general conversation. Which character is the more extraordinary, in falling to a person of so much knowledge, wit, and vivacity, qualities that are used to create envy, and consequently censure; and must be rather imputed to her great modesty, gentle behaviour, and inoffensiveness, than to her superior virtues.

Although her knowledge, from books and company, was much more extensive than usually falls to the share of her sex; yet she was so far from making a parade of it, that her female visitants, on their first acquaintance, who expected to discover it by what they call hard words and deep discourse, would be sometimes disappointed, and say they found she was like other women. But wise men, through all her modesty, whatever they discoursed on, could easily observe that she understood them very well, by the judgment shewn in her observations as well as in her questions.

A Vindication of Mr. Gay, and the *Beggar's Opera*

Contributed to *The Intelligencer*, No. 3, May 25, 1728, published in Dublin. Swift is credited with suggesting to Gay that he might lay the scene of a burlesque pastoral in Newgate prison. At any rate, in August 1716 Swift in a letter to Pope mentioned various forms of pastoral ridicule which Gay might choose, and asked: "Or what think you of a Newgate pastoral, among the whores and thieves there?"   c.v.d.

> *Ipse per omnes*
> *Ibit personas, et turbam reddet in unam.*

THE players having now almost done with the comedy called the *Beggar's Opera*, for this season, it may be no unpleasant speculation to reflect a little upon this dramatic piece, so singular in the subject, and the manner, so much an original, and which hath frequently given so very agreeable an entertainment.

Although an evil taste be very apt to prevail, both here and in London, yet there is a point which whoever can rightly touch, will never fail of pleasing a very great majority; so great that the dislikers, out of dullness or affectation will be silent, and forced to fall in with the herd; the point I mean is what we call humour, which in its perfection is allowed to be much preferable to wit, if it be not rather the most useful and agreeable species of it.

I agree with Sir William Temple that the word is peculiar to our English tongue, but I differ from him in the opinion that the thing itself is peculiar to the English nation, because the contrary may be found in many Spanish, Italian, and French productions, and particularly, whoever hath a taste for true humour, will find a hundred instances of it in those volumes printed in France, under the name of *Le Théâtre Italien,* to say nothing of Rabelais, Cervantes, and many others.

Now I take the comedy or farce (or whatever name the critics will allow it) called the *Beggar's Opera* to excel in this article of humour; and, upon that merit, to have met with such prodigious success both here and in England.

As to poetry, eloquence, and music, which are said to have most power over the minds of men, it is certain that very few have a taste of judgment of the excellencies of the two former, and if a man succeeds in either, it is upon the authority of those few judges that lend their taste to the bulk of readers, who have none of their own. I am told there are as few good judges in music, and that among those who crowd the operas, nine in ten go thither merely out of curiosity, fashion, or affectation.

But a taste for humour is in some manner fixed to the very nature of man, and generally obvious to the vulgar, except upon subjects too refined, and superior to their understanding.

And as this taste of humour is purely natural, so is humour itself; neither is it a talent confined to men of wit or learning; for we observe it sometimes among common servants, and the meanest of the people, while the very owners are often ignorant of the gift they possess.

I know very well that this happy talent is contemptibly treated by critics, under the name of low humour, or low comedy; but I know likewise that the Spaniards and Italians, who are allowed to have the most wit of any nation in Europe, do most excel in it, and do most esteem it.

By what disposition of the mind, what influence of the stars, or what situation of the climate this endowment is bestowed upon mankind, may be a question fit for philosophers to discuss. It is certainly the best ingredient towards that kind of satire which is most useful and gives the least offence; which instead of lashing, laughs men out of their follies and vices, and is the character which gives Horace the preference to Juvenal.

And although some things are too serious, solemn, or sacred to be turned into ridicule, yet the abuses of them are certainly not, since it is allowed that corruption in religion, politics, and law, may be proper topics for this kind of satire.

There are two ends that men propose in writing satire, one of them less noble than the other, as regarding nothing further than personal satisfaction and pleasure of the writer; but without any view towards personal malice; the other is a public spirit, prompting men of genius and virtue, to mend the world as far as they are able. And as both these ends are innocent, so the latter is highly commendable. With regard to the former, I demand whether I have not as good a title to laugh, as men have to be ridiculous, and to expose vice, as another hath to be vicious. If I ridicule the follies and corruptions of a court, a ministry, or a senate; are they not amply paid by pensions, titles, and power, while I expect and desire no other reward than that of laughing with a few friends in a corner. Yet if those who take offence, think me in the wrong, I am ready to change the scene with them, whenever they please.

But if my design be to make mankind better, then I think it is my duty, at least I am sure it is the interest of those very courts and ministers, whose follies or vices I ridicule, to reward me for my good intentions; for, if it be reckoned a high point of wisdom to get the laughers on our side, it is much more easy, as well as wise, to get those on our side who can make millions laugh when they please.

My reason for mentioning courts and ministers (whom I never think on, but with the most profound veneration) is because an opinion obtains that in the *Beggar's Opera* there appears to be some reflection upon courtiers and statesmen, whereof I am by no means a judge.

It is true indeed that Mr. Gay, the author of this piece, hath been somewhat singular in the course of his fortunes, for it hath happened, that after fourteen years attending the court, with a large stock of real merit, a modest and agreeable conversation, a hundred promises, and five hundred friends, [he] hath failed of preferment, and upon a very weighty reason. He lay under the suspicion of having written a libel, or lampoon, against a great m[inister]. It is true that great m[inister] was demonstratively convinced, and publicly owned his conviction, that Mr. Gay was not the author; but having lain under the suspicion, it seemed very just that he should suffer the punishment; because in this most reformed age, the virtues of a great m[inister] are no more to be suspected than the chastity of Cæsar's wife.

It must be allowed that the *Beggar's Opera* is not the first of Mr. Gay's works wherein he hath been faulty, with regard to courtiers and statesmen. For, to omit his other pieces even in his Fables, published within two years past, and dedicated to the Duke of Cumberland, for which he was promised a reward; he hath been thought somewhat too bold upon courtiers. And although it is highly probable he meant only the courtiers

of former times, yet he acted unwarily, by not considering that the malignity of some people might misinterpret
what he said to the disadvantage of present persons and
affairs.

But I have now done with Mr. Gay as a politician,
and shall consider him henceforward only as author of
the *Beggar's Opera*, wherein he hath by a turn of humour, entirely new, placed vices of all kinds in the
strongest and most odious light; and thereby done eminent service, both to religion and morality. This appears
from the unparalleled success he hath met with. All
ranks, parties, and denominations of men, either crowding to see his opera, or reading it with delight in their
closets, even ministers of state, whom he is thought
to have most offended (next to those whom the actors
more immediately represent), appearing frequently at
the theatre, from a consciousness of their own innocence, and to convince the world how unjust a parallel,
malice, envy, and disaffection to the government have
made.

I am assured that several worthy clergymen in this
city went privately to see the *Beggar's Opera* represented; and that the fleering coxcombs in the pit amused
themselves with making discoveries, and spreading the
names of those gentlemen round the audience.

I shall not pretend to vindicate a clergyman, who
would appear openly in his habit at a theatre, among
such a vicious crew as would probably stand round him,
and at such lewd comedies and profane tragedies as are
often represented. Besides I know very well that persons
of their function are bound to avoid the appearance of
evil, or of giving cause of offence. But when the lords
chancellors, who are keepers of the king's conscience,
when the judges of the land, whose title is *reverend*,
when ladies, who are bound by the rules of their sex

to the strictest decency, appear in the theatre without censure, I cannot understand why a young clergyman who goes concealed out of curiosity to see an innocent and moral play should be so highly condemned; nor do I much approve the rigour of a great p[rela]te, who said, "He hoped none of his clergy were there." I am glad to hear there are no weightier objections against that reverend body, planted in this city, and I wish there never may. But I should be very sorry that any of them should be so weak as to imitate a court chaplain in England who preached against the *Beggar's Opera*, which will probably do more good than a thousand sermons of so stupid, so injudicious, and so prostitute a divine.

In this happy performance of Mr. Gay, all the characters are just, and none of them carried beyond nature, or hardly beyond practice. It discovers the whole system of that commonwealth, or that *imperium in imperio* of iniquity, established among us, by which neither our lives, nor our properties are secure, either in the highways, or in public assemblies, or even in our own houses. It shews the miserable lives and the constant fate of those abandoned wretches; for how little they sell their lives and souls; betrayed by their whores, their comrades, and the receivers and purchasers of these thefts and robberies. This comedy contains likewise a satire which, although it doth by no means affect the present age, yet might have been useful in the former, and may possibly be so in ages to come. I mean where the author takes occasion of comparing those common robbers to robbers of the public; and their several stratagems of betraying, undermining, and hanging each other, to the several arts of politicians in times of corruption.

This comedy likewise exposeth with great justice that unnatural taste for Italian music among us, which is wholly unsuitable to our northern climate and the genius of the people, whereby we are over-run with Italian effeminacy and Italian nonsense. An old gentleman said to me that many years ago, when the practice of an unnatural vice grew so frequent in London that many were prosecuted for it, he was sure it would be a forerunner of Italian operas and singers; and then we should want nothing but stabbing or poisoning to make us perfect Italians.

Upon the whole, I deliver my judgment, that nothing but servile attachment to a party, affection of singularity, lamentable dullness, mistaken zeal, or studied hypocrisy, can have the least reasonable objection against this excellent moral performance of the celebrated Mr. Gay.

A Modest Proposal

FOR PREVENTING THE CHILDREN OF POOR PEO-
PLE FROM BEING A BURTHEN TO THEIR PAR-
ENTS OR COUNTRY, AND FOR MAKING THEM
BENEFICIAL TO THE PUBLIC.

IT IS a melancholy object to those who walk through
this great town, or travel in the country, when they
see the streets, the roads, and cabin-doors crowded with
beggars of the female sex, followed by three, four, or
six children, *all in rags*, and importuning every passen-
ger for an alms. These mothers, instead of being able to
work for their honest livelihood, are forced to employ
all their time in strolling, to beg sustenance for their
helpless infants, who, as they grow up, either turn
thieves for want of work, or leave their dear Native
Country to fight for the Pretender in Spain, or sell themselves to the Barbadoes.

I think it is agreed by all parties that this prodigious
number of children, in the arms, or on the backs, or at
the heels of their mothers, and frequently of their fathers, is in the present deplorable state of the kingdom
a very great additional grievance; and therefore whoever could find out a fair, cheap, and easy method of
making these children sound useful members of the
commonwealth would deserve so well of the public as
to have his statue set up for a preserver of the nation.

But my intention is very far from being confined to
provide only for the children of professed beggars; it is

of a much greater extent, and shall take in the whole number of infants at a certain age who are born of parents in effect as little able to support them as those who demand our charity in the streets.

As to my own part, having turned my thoughts, for many years, upon this important subject, and maturely weighed the several schemes of other projectors, I have always found them grossly mistaken in their computation. It is true a child, just dropped from its dam, may be supported by her milk for a solar year with little other nourishment, at most not above the value of two shillings, which the mother may certainly get, or the value in scraps, by her lawful occupation of begging, and it is exactly at one year old that I propose to provide for them, in such a manner as, instead of being a charge upon their parents, or the parish, or wanting food and raiment for the rest of their lives, they shall, on the contrary, contribute to the feeding and partly to the clothing of many thousands.

There is likewise another great advantage in my scheme, that it will prevent those voluntary abortions, and that horrid practice of women murdering their bastard children, alas, too frequent among us, sacrificing the poor innocent babes, I doubt, more to avoid the expense than the shame, which would move tears and pity in the most savage and inhuman breast.

The number of souls in this kingdom being usually reckoned one million and a half, of these I calculate there may be about two hundred thousand couple whose wives are breeders, from which number I subtract thirty thousand couples who are able to maintain their own children, although I apprehend there cannot be so many under the present distresses of the kingdom, but this being granted, there will remain an hundred and sev-

enty thousand breeders. I again subtract fifty thousand
for those women who miscarry, or whose children die by
accident or disease within the year. There only remain
an hundred and twenty thousand children of poor parents annually born: The question therefore is, how this
number shall be reared, and provided for, which, as I
have already said, under the present situation of affairs,
is utterly impossible by all the methods hitherto proposed, for we can neither employ them in handicraft,
or agriculture; we neither build houses (I mean in the
country), nor cultivate land: they can very seldom pick
up a livelihood by stealing till they arrive at six years
old, except where they are of towardly parts, although,
I confess they learn the rudiments much earlier, during
which time they can however be properly looked upon
only as *probationers,* as I have been informed by a principal gentleman in the County of Cavan, who protested
to me that he never knew above one or two .instances
under the age of six, even in a part of the kingdom so
renowned for the quickest proficiency in that art.

I am assured by our merchants that a boy or a girl,
before twelve years old, is no saleable commodity, and
even when they come to this age, they will not yield
above three pounds, or three pounds and half-a-crown
at most on the Exchange, which cannot turn to account
either to the parents or the kingdom, the charge of
nutriment and rags having been at least four times that
value.

I shall now therefore humbly propose my own
thoughts, which I hope will not be liable to the least objection.

I have been assured by a very knowing American of
my acquaintance in London, that a young healthy child
well nursed is at a year old a most delicious, nourishing,

and wholesome food, whether stewed, roasted, baked, or boiled, and I make no doubt that it will equally serve in a fricassee, or a ragout.

I do therefore humbly offer it to public consideration, that of the hundred and twenty thousand children already computed, twenty thousand may be reserved for breed, whereof only one fourth part to be males, which is more than we allow to sheep, black-cattle, or swine, and my reason is that these children are seldom the fruits of marriage, a circumstance not much regarded by our savages, therefore one male will be sufficient to serve four females. That the remaining hundred thousand may at a year old be offered in sale to the persons of quality, and fortune, through the kingdom, always advising the mother to let them suck plentifully in the last month, so as to render them plump, and fat for a good table. A child will make two dishes at an entertainment for friends, and when the family dines alone, the fore or hind quarter will make a reasonable dish, and seasoned with a little pepper or salt will be very good boiled on the fourth day, especially in winter.

I have reckoned upon a medium, that a child just born will weigh 12 pounds, and in a solar year if tolerably nursed increaseth to 28 pounds.

I grant this food will be somewhat dear, and therefore very proper for landlords, who, as they have already devoured most of the parents, seem to have the best title to the children.

Infants' flesh will be in season throughout the year, but more plentiful in March, and a little before and after, for we are told by a grave author, an eminent French physician, that fish being a prolific diet, there are more children born in Roman Catholic countries about nine months after Lent than at any other season; therefore reckoning a year after Lent, the markets will be more glutted than usual, because the number of Popish infants is at least three to one in this kingdom, and therefore it will have one other collateral advantage by lessening the number of Papists among us.

I have already computed the charge of nursing a beggar's child (in which list I reckon all cottagers, labourers, and four-fifths of the farmers) to be about two shillings *per annum,* rags included, and I believe no gentleman would repine to give ten shillings for the carcass of a good fat child, which, as I have said, will make four dishes of excellent nutritive meat, when he hath only some particular friend or his own family to dine with him. Thus the Squire will learn to be a good landlord, and grow popular among his tenants, the mother will have eight shillings net profit, and be fit for work till she produces another child.

Those who are more thrifty (as I must confess the times require) may flay the carcass; the skin of which, artificially dressed, will make admirable gloves for ladies, and summer boots for fine gentlemen.

As to our City of Dublin, shambles may be appointed for this purpose, in the most convenient parts of it, and butchers we may be assured will not be wanting, although I rather recommend buying the children alive, and dressing them hot from the knife, as we do roasting pigs.

A very worthy person, a true lover of this country, and whose virtues I highly esteem, was lately pleased, in discoursing on this matter, to offer a refinement upon my scheme. He said that many gentlemen of this kingdom, having of late destroyed their deer, he conceived that the want of venison might be well supplied by the bodies of young lads and maidens, not exceeding fourteen years of age, nor under twelve, so great a number of both sexes in every country being now ready to starve, for want of work and service: and these to be disposed of by their parents if alive, or otherwise by their nearest relations. But with due deference to so excellent a friend, and so deserving a patriot, I cannot be altogether in his sentiments; for as to the males, my American acquaintance assured me from frequent experience that their flesh was generally tough and lean, like that of our schoolboys, by continual exercise, and their taste disagreeable, and to fatten them would not answer the charge. Then as to the females, it would, I think with humble submission, be a loss to the public, because they soon would become breeders themselves: And besides, it is not improbable that some scrupulous people might be apt to censure such a practice (although indeed very unjustly) as a little bordering upon cruelty,, which, I confess, hath always been with me the strongest objection against any project, however so well intended.

But in order to justify my friend, he confessed that this expedient was put into his head by the famous Psalmanazar, a native of the island Formosa, who came from thence to London, above twenty years ago, and in conversation told my friend that in his country when any young person happened to be put to death, the executioner sold the carcass to persons of quality, as a prime dainty, and that, in his time, the body of a plump girl of fifteen, who was crucified for an attempt to poison the emperor, was sold to his Imperial Majesty's Prime Minister of State, and other great Mandarins of the Court, in joints from the gibbet, at four hundred crowns. Neither indeed can I deny that if the same use were made of several plump young girls in this town, who, without one single groat to their fortunes, cannot stir abroad without a chair, and appear at the playhouse, and assemblies in foreign fineries, which they never will pay for, the kingdom would not be the worse.

Some persons of a desponding spirit are in great concern about that vast number of poor people, who are aged, diseased, or maimed, and I have been desired to employ my thoughts what course may be taken to ease the nation of so grievous an encumbrance. But I am not in the least pain upon that matter, because it is very well known that they are every day dying, and rotting, by cold, and famine, and filth, and vermin, as fast as can be reasonably expected. And as to the younger labourers they are now in almost as hopeful a condition. They cannot get work, and consequently pine away for want of nourishment, to a degree, that if at any time they are accidentally hired to common labour, they have not strength to perform it; and thus the country and themselves are happily delivered from the evils to come.

I have too long digressed, and therefore shall return to my subject. I think the advantages by the proposal which I have made are obvious and many, as well as of the highest importance.

For first, as I have already observed, it would greatly lessen the number of Papists, with whom we are yearly over-run, being the principal breeders of the nation, as well as our most dangerous enemies, and who stay at home on purpose with a design to deliver the kingdom to the Pretender, hoping to take their advantage by the absence of so many good Protestants, who have chosen rather to leave their country than stay at home, and pay tithes against their conscience to an Episcopal curate.

Secondly, The poorer tenants will have something valuable of their own, which by law be made liable to distress, and help to pay their landlord's rent, their corn and cattle being already seized, and *money a thing unknown*.

Thirdly, Whereas the maintenance of an hundred thousand children, from two years old, and upwards, cannot be computed at less than ten shillings a piece *per annum*, the nation's stock will be thereby increased fifty thousand pounds *per annum*, besides the profit of a new dish, introduced to the tables of all gentlemen of fortune in the kingdom, who have any refinement in taste, and the money will circulate among ourselves, the goods being entirely of our own growth and manufacture.

Fourthly, The constant breeders, besides the gain of eight shillings sterling *per annum*, by the sale of their children, will be rid of the charge of maintaining them after the first year.

Fifthly, This food would likewise bring great custom to taverns, where the vintners will certainly be so prudent as to procure the best receipts for dressing it to perfection, and consequently have their houses frequented by all the fine gentlemen, who justly value themselves upon their knowledge in good eating; and a skilful cook, who understands how to oblige his guests, will contrive to make it as expensive as they please.

Sixthly, This would be a great inducement to marriage, which all wise nations have either encouraged by rewards, or enforced by laws and penalties. It would increase the care and tenderness of mothers toward their children, when they were sure of a settlement for life, to the poor babes, provided in some sort by the public to their annual profit instead of expense. We should see an honest emulation among the married women, which of them could bring the fattest child to the market, men would become as fond of their wives, during the time of their pregnancy, as they are now of their mares in foal, their cows in calf, or sows when they are ready to farrow, nor offer to beat or kick them (as it is too frequent a practice) for fear of a miscarriage.

Many other advantages might be enumerated: For instance, the addition of some thousand carcasses in our exportation of barrelled beef; the propagation of swine's flesh, and improvement in the art of making good bacon, so much wanted among us by the great destruction of pigs, too frequent at our tables, which are no way comparable in taste or magnificence to a well-grown, fat yearling child, which roasted whole will make a considerable figure at a Lord Mayor's feast, or any other public entertainment. But this and many others I omit, being studious of brevity.

Supposing that one thousand families in this city would be constant customers for infants' flesh, besides others who might have it at merry-meetings, particularly weddings and christenings, I compute that Dublin would take off annually about twenty thousand carcasses, and the rest of the kingdom (where probably they will be sold somewhat cheaper) the remaining eighty thousand.

I can think of no one objection that will possibly be raised against this proposal, unless it should be urged that the number of people will be thereby much lessened in the kingdom. This I freely own, and was indeed one principal design in offering it to the world. I desire the reader will observe, that I calculate my remedy for this one individual *Kingdom of Ireland, and for no other that ever was, is, or, I think, ever can be upon earth.* Therefore let no man talk to me of other expedients: *Of taxing our absentees at five shillings a pound: Of using neither clothes, nor household furniture, except what is of our own growth and manufacture: Of utterly rejecting the materials and instruments that promote foreign luxury: Of curing the expensiveness of pride, vanity, idleness, and gaming in our women: Of introducing a vein of parsimony, prudence, and temperance: Of learning to love our Country, wherein we differ even from* LAPLANDERS, *and the inhabitants of* TOPINAMBOO:

Of quitting our animosities and factions, nor act any longer like the Jews, who were murdering one another at the very moment their city was taken: Of being a little cautious not to sell our country and consciences for nothing: Of teaching landlords to have at least one degree of mercy toward their tenants. Lastly, of putting a spirit of honesty, industry, and skill into our shopkeepers, who, if a resolution could now be taken to buy only our native goods, would immediately unite to cheat and exact upon us in the price, the measure, and the goodness, nor could ever yet be brought to make one fair proposal of just dealing, though often and earnestly invited to it.

Therefore I repeat, let no man talk to me of these and the like expedients, till he hath at least some glimpse of hope that there will ever be some hearty and sincere attempt to put them in practice.

But as to myself, having been wearied out for many years with offering vain, idle, visionary thoughts, and at length utterly despairing of success, I fortunately fell upon this proposal, which as it is wholly new, so it hath something solid and real, of no expense and little trouble, full in our own power, and whereby we can incur no danger in *disobliging* ENGLAND. For this kind of commodity will not bear exportation, the flesh being of too tender a consistence to admit a long continuance in salt, *although perhaps I could name a country which would be glad to eat up our whole nation without it.*

After all I am not so violently bent upon my own opinion as to reject any offer, proposed by wise men, which shall be found equally innocent, cheap, easy, and effectual. But before something of that kind shall be advanced in contradiction to my scheme, and offering a better, I desire the author, or authors, will be pleased maturely to consider two points. First, as things now stand, how they will be able to find food and raiment for an hundred thousand useless mouths and backs. And secondly, there being a round million of creatures in human figure, throughout this kingdom, whose whole subsistence put into a common stock would leave them in debt two millions of pounds sterling; adding those, who are beggars by profession, to the bulk of farmers, cottagers, and labourers with their wives and children, who are beggars in effect. I desire those politicians, who dislike my overture, and may perhaps be so bold to attempt an answer, that they will first ask the parents of these mortals whether they would not at this day think it a great happiness to have been sold for food at a year old, in the manner I prescribe, and thereby have avoided such a perpetual scene of misfortunes as they have since gone through, by the oppression of landlords, the impossibility of paying rent without money or trade, the want of common sustenance, with neither house nor clothes to cover them from the inclemencies of the weather, and the most inevitable prospect of entailing the like, or greater miseries upon their breed for ever.

I profess in the sincerity of my heart that I have not the least personal interest in endeavouring to promote this necessary work, having no other motive than the *public good of my country, by advancing our trade, providing for infants, relieving the poor, and giving some pleasure to the rich.* I have no children by which I can propose to get a single penny; the youngest being nine years old, and my wife past child-bearing.

To Viscount Bolingbroke

YOU tell me you have not quitted the design of collecting, writing, &c. This is the answer of every sinner who defers his repentance. I wish Mr. Pope were as great an urger as I, who long for nothing more than to see truth, under your hands, laying all detraction in the dust. I find myself disposed every year, or rather every month, to be more angry and revengeful; and my rage is so ignoble, that it descends even to resent the folly and baseness of the enslaved people among whom I live. I knew an old Lord in Leicestershire, who amused himself with mending pitchforks and spades for his tenants gratis. Yet I have higher ideas left, if I were nearer to objects on which I might employ them; and contemning my private fortune, would gladly cross the channel and stand by while my betters were driving the boars out of the garden, if there be any probable expectation of such an endeavour. When I was of your age I often thought of death, but now, after a dozen years more, it is never out of my mind, and terrifies me less. I conclude that Providence has ordered our fears to decrease with our spirits; and yet I love *la bagatelle* better than ever, for, finding it troublesome to read at night, and the company here growing tasteless, I am always writing bad prose, or worse verses, either of rage or raillery, whereof some few escape to give offence, or mirth, and the rest are burnt. They print some Irish trash in London, and charge it on me, which you will clear me

560

of to my friends, for all are spurious except one paper, for which Mr. Pope very lately chid me.

I remember your Lordship used to say, that a few good speakers would in time carry any point that was right; and that the common method of a majority, by calling to the question, would never hold long when reason was on the other side. Whether politics do not change like gaming, by the invention of new tricks, I am ignorant; but I believe in your time you would never, as a Minister, have suffered an Act to pass through the House of Commons, only because you were sure of a majority in the House of Lords to throw it out, because it would be unpopular, and consequently a loss of reputation. Yet this, we are told, has been the case in the Qualification Bill relating to Pensioners. It would seem to me that corruption, like avarice, has no bounds. I had opportunities to know the proceedings of your Ministry better than any man of my rank; and having not much to do, I have often compared it with these last sixteen years of a profound peace all over Europe, and we running seven millions in debt. I am forced to play at small game, to set the beasts here a-madding merely for want of better game. *Tentanda via est qua me quoque possim,* &c. The d— take those politics, where a dunce might govern for a dozen years together. I will come in person to England if I am provoked, and send for the dictator from the plough. I disdain to say, *O mihi praeteritos,* but *cruda deo viridisque senectus.*

Pray, my Lord, how are the gardens? Have you taken down the mount, and removed the yew hedges? Have you not bad weather for the spring corn? Has Mr. Pope gone farther in his ethic poems? And is the headland sown with wheat? And what says Polybius? And how does my Lord St. John, which last question is very material to me, because I love Burgundy, and riding between Twickenham and Dawley? I built a wall five years ago, and when the masons played the knaves, nothing delighted me so much as to stand by while my servants threw down what was amiss. I have likewise seen a monkey overthrow all the dishes and plates in a kitchen, merely for the pleasure of seeing them tumble, and hearing the clatter they made in their fall. I wish you would invite me to such another entertainment; but you think, as I ought to think, that it is time for me to have done with the world, and so I would if I could get into a better before I was called into the best, and not die here in a rage, like a poisoned rat in a hole. I wonder you are not ashamed to let me pine away in this kingdom, while you are out of power.

I come from looking over the *mélange* above-written, and declare it to be a true copy of my present disposition, which must needs please you, since nothing was ever more displeasing to myself. I desire you to present my most humble respects to my Lady.

To John Arbuthnot

MY DEAR FRIEND,
I never once suspected your forgetfulness or
want of friendship, but very often dreaded your want of
health, to which alone I imputed every delay longer
than ordinary in hearing from you. I should be very ungrateful, indeed, if I acted otherwise to you, who are
pleased to take such generous constant care of my health,
my interests, and my reputation, who represented me so
favourably to that blessed Queen your mistress, as well
as to her Ministers, and to all your friends. The letters
you mention, which I did not answer, I cannot find, and
yet I have all that ever came from you, for I constantly
endorse yours and those of a few other friends, and date
them; only if there be anything particular, though of no
consequence, when I go to the country I send them to
some friends among other papers for fear of accidents
in my absence. I thank you kindly for your favour to the
young man who was bred in my choir. The people of
skill in music represent him to me as a lad of virtue, and
hopeful and endeavouring in his way. It is your own
fault if I give you trouble, because you never refused
me anything in your life.

You tear my heart with the ill account of your health;
yet if it should please God to call you away before me,
I should not pity you in the least, except on the account
of what pains you might feel before you passed into a
better life. I should pity none but your friends, and

among them chiefly myself, although I never can hope
to have health enough to leave this country till I leave
the world. I do not know among mankind any person
more prepared to depart from us than yourself, not even
the Bishop of Marseilles, if he be still alive; for among
all your qualities that have procured you the love and
esteem of the world, I ever most valued your moral and
Christian virtues, which were not the product of years
or sickness, but of reason and religion, as I can witness
after above five-and-twenty years' acquaintance. I except only the too little care of your fortune; upon which
I have been so free as sometimes to examine and to
chide you, and the consequence of which hath been to
confine you to London, when you are under a disorder
for which I am told, and know, that the clear air of the
country is necessary.

The great reason that hinders my journey to England,
is the same that drives you from Highgate. I am not in
circumstances to keep horses and servants in London.
My revenues by the miserable oppressions of this kingdom are sunk three hundred pounds a year, for tithes
are become a drug, and I have but little rents from the
deanery lands, which are my only sure payments. I have
here a large convenient house; I live at two-thirds
cheaper here than I could there; I drink a bottle of
French wine myself every day, though I love it not, but
it is the only thing that keeps me out of pain; I ride
every fair day a dozen miles, on a large strand or turn-
pike roads. You in London have no such advantages. I
can buy a chicken for a groat, and entertain three or
four friends, with as many dishes, and two or three
bottles of French wine, for ten shillings. When I dine
alone, my pint and chicken with the appendixes cost me
about fifteen pence. I am thrifty in everything but wine,
of which though I be not a constant housekeeper, I

spend between five and six hogshead a year. When I ride to a friend a few miles off, if he be not richer than I, I carry my bottle, my bread and chicken, that he may be no loser.

I talk thus foolishly to let you know the reasons which, joined to my ill health, make it impossible for me to see you and my other friends; and perhaps this domestic tattle may excuse me and amuse you. I could not live with my Lord Bolingbroke or Mr. Pope: they are both too temperate and too wise for me, and too profound and too poor. And how could I afford horses? And how could I ride over their cursed roads in winter, and be turned into a ditch by every carter or hackney-coach? Every parish minister of this city is governor of all carriages, and so are the two Deans, and every carrier should make way for us at their peril. Therefore, like Cæsar, I will be one of the first here rather than the last among you. I forget that I am so near the bottom. I am now with one of my Prebendaries, five miles in the country, for five days. I brought with me eight bottles of wine, with bread and meat for three days, which is my club; he is a bachelor, with three hundred pounds a year. May God preserve you, my dear friend.

Entirely yours,

J. Swift.

‾On Poetry: A Rhapsody

This poem is here printed as it stands in the first edition (London, 1733) except that a few words there left blank are now supplied in square brackets. Even with those discreet omissions the poem's bold comments on King and Court led to the imprisonment for more than a year of not only Motte, the London printer, but also Mary Barber, Swift's friend who carried the manuscript over from Dublin. C.V.D.

ALL Human Race wou'd fain be *Wits*,
    And Millions miss, for one that hits.
Young's universal Passion, *Pride*,
Was never known to spread so wide.
Say *Britain,* cou'd you ever boast,—
Three *Poets* in an Age at most?
Our chilling Climate hardly bears
A *Sprig* of Bays in Fifty Years:
While ev'ry Fool his Claim alledges,
As if it grew in common Hedges.
What Reason can there be assign'd
For this Perverseness in the Mind?
Brutes find out where their Talents lie:
A *Bear* will not attempt to fly:
A founder'd *Horse* will oft debate,
Before he tries a five-barr'd Gate:
A *Dog* by Instinct turns aside,
Who sees the Ditch too deep and wide.
But *Man* we find the only Creature,
Who, led by *Folly,* fights with *Nature;*

Who, when *she* loudly cries, *Forbear,*
With Obstinacy fixes there;
And, where his *Genius* least inclines,
Absurdly bends his whole Designs.

Not *Empire* to the Rising-Sun,
By Valour, Conduct, Fortune won;
Nor highest *Wisdom* in Debates
For framing Laws to govern States;
Nor Skill in Sciences profound,
So large to grasp the Circle round;
Such heavenly Influence require,
As how to strike the *Muses Lyre.*

Not Beggar's Brat, on Bulk begot;
Nor Bastard of a Pedlar *Scot;*
Nor Boy brought up to cleaning Shoes,
The Spawn of *Bridewell,* or the Stews;
Nor Infants dropt, the spurious Pledges
Of *Gipsies* littering under Hedges,
Are so disqualified by Fate
To rise in *Church,* or *Law,* or *State,*
As he, whom *Phebus* in his Ire
Hath *blasted* with poetick Fire.

What hope of Custom in the *Fair,*
While not a Soul demands your Ware?
Where you have nothing to produce
For private Life, or publick Use?
Court, City, Country want you not;
You cannot bribe, betray, or plot.
For Poets, Law makes no Provision:
The Wealthy have you in Derision.
Of State-Affairs you cannot smatter,
Are awkward when you try to flatter.

Your Portion, taking *Britain* round,
Was just one annual Hundred Pound.[1]
Now not so much as in Remainder
Since *Cibber* brought in an Attainder;
For ever fixt by Right Divine,
(A Monarch's Right) on *Grubstreet* Line.
Poor starv'ling Bard, how small thy Gains!
How unproportion'd to thy Pains!

And here a *Simile* comes Pat in:
Tho' *Chickens* take a Month to fatten,
The Guests in less than half an Hour
Will more than half a Score devour.
So, after toiling twenty Days,
To earn a Stock of Pence and Praise,
Thy Labours, grown the Critick's Prey,
Are swallow'd o'er a Dish of Tea;
Gone, to be never heard of more,
Gone, where the *Chickens* went before.

How shall a new Attempter learn
Of diff'rent Spirits to discern,
And how distinguish, which is which,
The Poet's Vein, or scribling Itch?
Then hear an old experienc'd Sinner
Instructing thus a young Beginner.

Consult yourself, and if you find
A powerful Impulse urge your Mind,
Impartial judge within your Breast
What Subject you can manage best;
Whether your Genius most inclines
To Satire, Praise, or hum'rous Lines;

---

[1] Paid to the Poet Laureat, which place was given to one *Cibber*,
a Player.

To Elegies in mournful Tone,
Or Prologue sent from Hand unknown.
Then rising with *Aurora's* Light,
The Muse invok'd, sit down to write;
Blot out, correct, insert, refine,
Enlarge, diminish, interline;
Be mindful, when Invention fails,
To scratch your Head, and bite your Nails.

Your Poem finish'd, next your Care
Is needful, to transcribe it fair.
In modern Wit all printed Trash, is
Set off with num'rous *Breaks*— and *Dashes*—

To Statesman wou'd you give a Wipe,
You print it in *Italick Type*.
When Letters are in vulgar Shapes,
'Tis ten to one the Wit escapes;
But when in *Capitals* exprest,
The dullest Reader smoaks the Jest:
Or else perhaps he may invent
A better than the Poet meant,
As learned Commentators view
In *Homer* more than *Homer* knew.

Your Poem in its modish Dress,
Correctly fitted for the Press,
Convey by Penny-Post to *Lintot*,
But let no Friend alive look into't.
If *Lintot* thinks 'twill quit the Cost,
You need not fear your Labour lost:
And, how agreeably surpriz'd
Are you to see it advertiz'd!
The Hawker shews you one in Print,
As fresh as Farthings from the Mint:

The Product of your Toil and Sweating;
A Bastard of your own begetting.

Be sure at *Will's* the following Day,
Lie Snug, and hear what Criticks say.
And if you find the general Vogue
Pronounces you a stupid Rogue;
Damns all your Thoughts as low and little,
Sit still, and swallow down your Spittle.
Be silent as a Politician,
For talking may beget Suspicion:
Or praise the Judgment of the Town,
And help yourself to run it down.
Give up your fond paternal Pride,
Nor argue on the weaker Side;
For Poems read without a Name
We justly praise, or justly blame:
And Criticks have no partial Views,
Except they know whom they abuse.
And since you ne'er provok'd their Spight,
Depend upon't their Judgment's right:
But if you blab, you are undone;
Consider what a Risk you run.
You lose your Credit all at once;
The Town will mark you for a Dunce:
The vilest Doggrel *Grubstreet* sends,
Will pass for yours with Foes and Friends.
And you must bear the whole Disgrace,
'Till some fresh Blockhead takes your Place.

Your Secret kept, your Poem sunk,
And sent in Quires to line a Trunk;
If still you be dispos'd to rhime,
Go try your Hand a second Time.

Again you fail, yet Safe's the Word,
Take Courage, and attempt a Third.
But first with Care imploy your Thoughts,
Where Criticks mark'd your former Faults.
The trivial Turns, the borrow'd Wit,
The *Similes* that nothing fit;
The *Cant* which ev'ry Fool repeats,
Town-Jests, and Coffee-house Conceits;
Descriptions tedious, flat and dry,
And introduc'd the Lord knows why;
Or where we find your Fury set
Against the harmless Alphabet;
On A's and B's your Malice vent,
While Readers wonder whom you meant.
A publick, or a private *Robber;*
A *Statesman,* or a South-Sea *Jobber.*
A *Prelate* who no God believes;
A [Parliament], or a Den of Thieves.
A Pick-purse at the Bar, or Bench;
A Duchess, or a Suburb-Wench.
Or oft when Epithets you link,
In gaping Lines to fill a Chink;
Like stepping Stones to save a Stride,
In Streets where Kennels are too wide:
Or like a Heel-piece to support
A Cripple with one Foot too short:
Or like a Bridge that joins a Marish
To Moorlands of a diff'rent Parish.
So have I seen ill-coupled Hounds,
Drag diff'rent Ways in miry Grounds.
So Geographers in *Afric*-Maps
With Savage-Pictures fill their Gaps;
And o'er unhabitable Downs
Place Elephants for want of Towns.

But tho' you miss your third Essay,
You need not throw your Pen away.
Lay now aside all Thoughts of Fame,
To spring more profitable Game.
From Party-Merit seek Support;
The vilest Verse thrives best at Court.
A Pamphlet in Sir *Rob's* Defence
Will never fail to bring in Pence;
Nor be concern'd about the Sale,
He pays his Workmen on the Nail.

A Prince the Moment he is crown'd,
Inherits ev'ry Virtue round,
As Emblems of the sov'reign Pow'r,
Like other Bawbles of the Tow'r.
Is gen'rous, valiant, just and wise,
And so continues 'till he dies.
His humble *Senate* this professes,
In all their *Speeches, Votes, Addresses.*
But once you fix him in a Tomb,
His Virtues fade, his Vices bloom;
And each Perfection wrong imputed
Is fully at his Death confuted.
The Loads of Poems in his Praise,
Ascending make one Funeral-Blaze.
As soon as you can hear his Knell,
This God on Earth turns *Devil* in Hell.
And, lo, his Ministers of State,
Transform'd to Imps, his Levee wait:
Where, in this Scene of endless Woe,
They ply their former Arts below:
And as they sail in *Charon's* Boat,
Contrive to bribe the Judge's Vote.
To *Cerberus* they give a Sop,
His triple-barking Mouth to stop:

Or in the Iv'ry Gate of Dreams,
Project [Excise] and [*South-Sea* Schemes]:
Or hire their Party-Pamphleteers,
To set *Elysium* by the Ears.

   Then *Poet,* if you mean to thrive,
Employ your Muse on Kings alive;
With Prudence gath'ring up a Cluster
Of all the Virtues you can muster:
Which form'd into a Garland sweet,
Lay humbly at your Monarch's Feet;
Who, as the Odours reach his Throne,
Will smile, and think 'em all his own:
For *Law* and *Gospel* both determine
All Virtues lodge in royal Ermine.
(I mean the Oracles of Both,
Who shall depose it upon Oath.)
Your Garland in the following Reign,
Change but their Names, will do again.

   But if you think this Trade too base,
(Which seldom is the Dunce's Case)
Put on the Critick's Brow, and sit
At *Wills* the puny Judge of Wit.
A Nod, a Shrug, a scornful Smile,
With Caution us'd, may serve a-while.
Proceed no further in your Part,
Before you learn the Terms of Art:
(For you may easy be too far gone,
In all our Modern Criticks Jargon.)
Then talk with more authentick Face,
Of *Unities, in Time and Place.*
Get Scraps of *Horace* from your Friends,
And have them at your Fingers' Ends.
Learn *Aristotle's* Rules by Rote,

And at all Hazards boldly quote:
Judicious *Rymer* oft review:
Wise *Dennis,* and profound *Bossu.*
Read all the *Prefaces* of *Dryden,*
For these our Criticks much confide in,
(Tho' meerly writ at first for filling
To raise the Volume's Price, a Shilling.)

A forward Critick often dupes us
With sham Quotations *Peri Hupsous*[2]:
And if we have not read *Longinus,*
Will magisterially out-shine us.
Then, lest with *Greek* he over-run ye,
Procure the Book for Love or Money,
Translated from *Boileau's* Translation,[3]
And quote *Quotation* on *Quotation.*

At *Wills* you hear a Poem read,
Where *Battus* from the Table-head,
Reclining on his Elbow-chair,
Gives Judgment with decisive Air.
To whom the Tribe of circling Wits,
As to an Oracle submits.
He gives Directions to the Town,
To cry it up, or run it down.
(Like *Courtiers,* when they send a Note,
Instructing *Members* how to Vote.)
He sets the Stamp of Bad and Good,
Tho' not a Word be understood.
Your Lesson learnt, you'll be secure
To get the Name of *Connoisseur.*
And when your Merits once are known,
Procure Disciples of your own.

---

[2] A famous Treatise of *Longinus.*
[3] By Mr. *Welsted.*

Our Poets (you can never want 'em,
Spread thro' *Augusta Trinobantum*)
Computing by their Pecks of Coals,
Amount to just Nine thousand Souls.
These o'er their proper Districts govern,
Of Wit and Humour, Judges sov'reign.
In ev'ry Street a City-bard
Rules, like an Alderman his Ward.
His indisputed Rights extend
Thro' all the Lane, from End to End.
The Neighbours round admire his *Shrewdness*,
For Songs of *Loyalty* and *Lewdness*.
Out-done by none in Rhyming well,
Altho' he never learnt to spell.

Two bordering Wits contend for Glory;
And one is *Whig* and one is *Tory*.
And this, for Epicks claims the Bays,
And that, for Elegiack Lays.
Some famed for Numbers soft and smooth,
By Lovers spoke in *Punch's* Booth.
And some as justly Fame extols
For lofty Lines in *Smithfield* Drols.
Bavius in *Wapping* gains Renown,
And *Mævius* reigns o'er *Kentish-Town:*
Tigellius plac'd in *Phœbus'* Car,
From *Ludgate* shines to *Temple-bar*.
Harmonius *Cibber* entertains
The Court with annual Birth-day Strains;
Whence *Gay* was banish'd in Disgrace,
Where *Pope* will never show his Face;
Where Y[*oung*] must torture his Invention,
To flatter *Knaves*, or lose his *Pension*.

But these are not a thousandth **Part**
Of Jobbers in the Poets Art,
Attending each his proper **Station,**
And all in due Subordination;
Thro' ev'ry Alley to be found,
In Garrets high, or under Ground:
And when they join their *Pericranies,*
Out skips a *Book of Miscellanies.*
Hobbes clearly proves that ev'ry Creature
Lives in a State of War by Nature.
The Greater for the Smaller watch,
But meddle seldom with their Match.
A Whale of moderate Size will draw
A Shole of Herrings down his Maw.
A Fox with Geese his Belly crams;
A Wolf destroys a thousand Lambs.
But search among the rhiming Race,
The Brave are worried by the Base.
If, on *Parnassus'* Top you sit,
You rarely bite, are always bit:
Each Poet of inferior Size
On you shall rail and criticize;
And strive to tear you Limb from **Limb,**
While others do as much for him.

The Vermin only teaze and pinch
Their Foes superior by an Inch.
So, Nat'ralists observe, a Flea
Hath smaller Fleas that on him prey,
And these have smaller Fleas to bite 'em,
And so proceed *ad infinitum:*
Thus ev'ry Poet in his Kind,
Is bit by him that comes behind;
Who, tho' too little to be seen,
Can teaze, and gall, and give the Spleen;

Call Dunces, Fools, and Sons of Whores,
Lay *Grubstreet* at each others Doors:
Extol the *Greek* and *Roman* Masters,
And curse our modern Poetasters.
Complain, as many an ancient Bard did,
How Genius is no more rewarded;
How wrong a Taste prevails among us;
How much our Ancestors out-sung us;
Can personate an awkward Scorn
For those who are not Poets born:
And all their Brother Dunces lash,
Who crowd the Press with hourly Trash.

O, *Grubstreet!* how do I bemoan thee,
Whose graceless Children scorn to own thee!
Their filial Piety forgot,
Deny their Country like a Scot:
Tho' by their Idiom and Grimace
They soon betray their native Place:
Yet *thou* hast greater Cause to be
Asham'd of them, than they of thee.
Degenerate from their ancient Brood,
Since first the Court allow'd them Food.

Remains a Difficulty still,
To purchase Fame by writing ill:
From *Flecknoe* down to *Howard's* Time,
How few have reach'd the *low Sublime?*
For when our high-born *Howard* dy'd,
Blackmore alone his Place supply'd:
And least a Chasm should intervene,
When Death had finish'd *Blackmore's* Reign,
The *leaden Crown* devolv'd to thee,
Great Poet [4] of the *Hollow-Tree.*

---

[4] Lord G[rimston].

But, oh, how unsecure thy Throne!
A thousand Bards thy Right disown:
They plot to turn in factious Zeal,
Duncenia to a Common-weal;
And with rebellious Arms pretend
An equal Priv'lege to *descend*.

In Bulk there are not more Degrees,
From *Elephants* to *Mites* in Cheese,
Than what a curious Eye may trace
In Creatures of the rhiming Race.
From bad to worse, and worse they fall,
But, who can reach the Worst of all?
For, tho' in Nature Depth and Height
Are equally held infinite,
In Poetry the Height we know;
'Tis only infinite below.
For Instance: When you rashly think,[5]
No Rhymer can like *Welsted* sink.
His Merits ballanc'd you shall find,
The Laureat leaves him far behind.
Concannen, more aspiring Bard,
Climbs downwards, deeper, by a Yard:
Smart JEMMY· MOOR with Vigor drops,
The Rest pursue as thick as Hops:
With Heads to Points the Gulph they enter,
Linkt perpendicular to the Centre:
And as their Heels elated rise,
Their Heads attempt the nether Skies.

O, what Indignity and Shame
To prostitute the Muse's Name,
By flatt'ring Kings whom Heaven design'd
The Plagues and Scourges of Mankind.

---

[5] Vide The Treatise on the *Profound*, and Mr. *Pope's Dunciad*.

Bred up in Ignorance and Sloth,
And ev'ry Vice that nurses both.

Fair *Britain* in thy Monarch blest,
Whose Virtues bear the strictest Test;
Whom never *Faction* cou'd bespatter,
Nor *Minister,* nor *Poet* flatter.
What Justice in rewarding Merit?
What Magnanimity of Spirit?
What Lineaments divine we trace
Thro' all the Features of his Face;
Tho' Peace with Olive bind his Hands,
Confest the conqu'ring Hero stands.
Hydaspes, Indus, and the *Ganges,*
Dread from his Hand impending Changes.
From him the *Tartar,* and *Chinese,*
Short by the Knees intreat for Peace.
The *Consort* of his Throne and Bed,
A perfect Goddess born and bred.
Appointed sov'reign Judge to sit
On Learning, Eloquence and Wit.
Our eldest Hope, divine *Iülus,*
(Late, very late, O, may he rule us.)
What early Manhood has he shown,
Before his downy Beard was grown!
Then think, what Wonders will be done
By going on as he begun;
An Heir for *Britain* to secure
As long as Sun and Moon endure.

The Remnant of the royal Blood,
Comes pouring on me like a Flood.
Bright Goddesses, in Number five;
Duke *William,* sweetest Prince alive.

Now sing the *Minister* of *State*,
Who shines alone, without a Mate.
Observe with what majestick Port
This *Atlas* stands to prop the Court:
Intent the Publick Debts to pay,
Like prudent *Fabius*[6] by *Delay*.
Thou great Vicegerent of the King,
Thy Praises ev'ry Muse shall sing.
In all Affairs thou sole Director,
Of Wit and Learning chief Protector;
Tho' small the Time thou hast to spare,
The Church is thy peculiar Care.
Of pious Prelates what a Stock
You chuse to rule the Sable-flock.
You raise the Honour of the Peerage,
Proud to attend you at the Steerage.
You dignify the noble Race,
Content yourself with humbler Place.
Now Learning, Valour, Virtue, Sense,
To Titles give the sole Pretence.
St. George beheld thee with Delight,
Vouchsafe to be an azure Knight,
When on thy Breast and Sides *Herculean,*
He fixt the *Star* and *String Cerulean*.

Say, Poet, in what other Nation,
Shone ever such a Constellation.
Attend ye *Popes,* and *Youngs,* and *Gays,*
And tune your Harps, and strow your Bays.
Your Panegyricks here provide,
You cannot err on Flatt'ry's Side.
Above the Stars exalt your Stile,
You still are low ten thousand Mile.
On *Lewis* all his Bards bestow'd,

---

[6] *Unus Homo nobis Cunctando restituit rem.*

Of Incense many a thousand Load;
But *Europe* mortify'd his Pride,
And swore the fawning Rascals ly'd:
Yet what the World refus'd to *Lewis,*
Apply'd to *George* exactly true is:
Exactly true! Invidious Poet!
'Tis fifty thousand Times below it.

    Translate me now some Lines, if you can,
From *Virgil, Martial, Ovid, Lucan;*
They could all Pow'r in Heaven divide,
And do no Wrong to either Side:
They'll teach you how to split a Hair,
Give *George* and *Jove* an equal Share.[7]
Yet, why should we be lac'd so straight;
I'll give my Monarch Butter-weight.
And Reason good; for many a Year
Jove never intermeddl'd here:
Nor, tho' his Priests be duly paid,
Did ever we *desire* his Aid:
We now can better do without him,
Since *Woolston* gave us Arms to rout him.

        Cætera desiderantur

---

[7] *Divisum Imperium cum* Jove Cæsar *habet.*

Verses on the Death of
Dr. Swift

Occasioned by reading a Maxim in *Rochefoucault*

*Dans l'adversité de nos meilleurs amis nous trouvons quelque
chose, qui ne nous deplaist pas.*
In the Adversity of our best Friends, we find something that
doth not displease us.

This text is that of the Dublin edition of 1739, which
was printed with Swift's permission and more or less
under his supervision. The notes, certainly Swift's and
certainly characteristic, are here included as an essential
part of the total work. Several words and passages both
in poem and notes in the printed text of 1739 are now
supplied from trustworthy manuscript additions in contemporary copies.   C.V.D.

A S *Rochefoucault* his Maxims drew
    From Nature, I believe 'em true:
They argue no corrupted Mind
In him; the Fault is in Mankind.

    This Maxim more than all the rest
Is thought too base for human Breast;
"In all Distresses of our Friends
"We first consult our private Ends,
"While Nature kindly bent to ease us,
"Points out some Circumstance to please us."

If this perhaps your Patience move
Let Reason and Experience prove.

We all behold with envious Eyes,
Our *Equal* rais'd above our *Size;*
Who wou'd not at a crowded Show,
Stand high himself, keep others low?
I love my Friend as well as you,
But would not have him stop my View;
Then let me have the higher Post;
I ask but for an Inch at most.

If in a Battle you should find,
One, whom you love of all Mankind,
Had some heroick Action done,
A Champion kill'd, or Trophy won;
Rather than thus be over-topt,
Would you not wish his Lawrels cropt?

Dear honest *Ned* is in the Gout,
Lies rackt with Pain, and you without:
How patiently you hear him groan!
How glad the Case is not your own!

What Poet would not grieve to see,
His Brethren write as well as he?
But rather than they should excel,
He'd wish his Rivals all in Hell.

Her End when Emulation misses,
She turns to Envy, Stings and Hisses:
The strongest Friendship yields to Pride,
Unless the Odds be on our Side.

Vain human Kind! Fantastick Race!
Thy various Follies, who can trace?

Self-love, Ambition, Envy, Pride,
Their Empire in our Hearts divide:
Give others Riches, Power, and Station,
'Tis all on me an Usurpation.
I have no Title to aspire;
Yet, when you sink, I seem the higher.
In POPE, I cannot read a Line,
But with a Sigh, I wish it mine:
When he can in one Couplet fix
More Sense than I can do in Six:
It gives me such a jealous Fit,
I cry, Pox take him, and his Wit.

Why must I be outdone by GAY,
In my own hum'rous biting Way?

ARBUTHNOT is no more my Friend,
Who dares to Irony pretend;
Which I was born to introduce,
Refin'd it first, and shew'd its Use.

ST. JOHN, as well as PULTNEY knows,
That I had some Repute for Prose;
And till they drove me out of Date,
Could maul a Minister of State:
If they have mortify'd my Pride,
And made me throw my Pen aside;
If with such Talents Heav'n hath blest 'em
Have I not Reason to detest 'em?

To all my Foes, dear Fortune, send
Thy Gifts, but never to my Friend:
I tamely can endure the first,
But, this with Envy makes me burst.

Thus much may serve by way of Proem,
Proceed we therefore to our Poem.

The Time is not remote, when I
Must by the Course of Nature dye:
When I foresee my special Friends,
Will try to find their private Ends:
Tho' it is hardly understood,
Which way my Death can do them good,
Yet, thus methinks, I hear 'em speak;
See, how the Dean begins to break:
Poor Gentleman, he droops apace,
You plainly find it in his Face:
That old Vertigo in his Head,
Will never leave him, till he's dead:
Besides, his Memory decays,
He recollects not what he says;
He cannot call his Friends to Mind;
Forgets the Place where last he din'd:
Plyes you with Stories o'er and o'er,
He told them fifty Times before.
How does he fancy we can sit,
To hear his out-of-fashion'd Wit?
But he takes up with younger Fokes,
Who for his Wine will bear his Jokes:
Faith, he must make his Stories shorter,
Or change his Comrades once a Quarter:
In half the Time, he talks them round;
There must another Sett be found.

For Poetry, he's past his Prime,
He takes an Hour to find a Rhime:
His Fire is out, his Wit decay'd,
His Fancy sunk, his Muse a Jade.

I'd have him throw away his Pen;
But there's no talking to some Men.

And, then their Tenderness appears
By adding largely to my Years:
"He's older than he would be reckon'd,
"And well remembers *Charles* the Second.

"He hardly drinks a Pint of Wine;
"And that, I doubt, is no good Sign.
"His Stomach too begins to fail:
"Last year we thought him strong and hale;
"But now, he's quite another Thing;
"I wish he may hold out till Spring."

Then hug themselves, and reason thus;
"It's not yet so bad with us."

In such a Case they talk in Tropes,
And, by their Fears express their Hopes,
Some great Misfortune to portend,
No Enemy can match a Friend.
With all the Kindness they profess,
The Merit of a lucky Guess
(When daily Howd'y's come of Course,
And Servants answer; *Worse and Worse*)
Wou'd please 'em better than to tell,
That, GOD prais'd, the Dean is well.
Then he who prophecy'd the best,
Approves his Foresight to the rest:
"You know, I always fear'd the worst,
"And often told you so at first":
He'd rather chuse, that I should dye,
Than his Prediction prove a Lye.

Not one foretels I shall recover;
But, all agree, to give me over.

Yet shou'd some Neighbour feel a Pain,
Just in the Parts, where I complain;
How many a Message would he send?
What hearty Prayers that I should mend?
Enquire what Regimen I kept;
What gave me Ease, and how I slept?
And more lament, when I was dead,
Than all the Sniv'llers round my Bed.

My good Companions, never fear,
For though you may mistake a Year;
Though your Prognosticks run too fast,
They must be verify'd at last.

"Behold the fatal Day arrive!
"How is the Dean? He's just alive.
"Now the departing Prayer is read:
"He hardly breathes. The Dean is dead.
"Before the Passing-Bell begun,
"The News thro' half the Town has run.
"O, may we all for Death prepare!
"What has he left? And who's his Heir?
"I know no more than what the News is,
" 'Tis all bequeath'd to publick Uses.
"To publick Use! A perfect Whim!
"What had the Publick done for him!
"Meer Envy, Avarice, and Pride!
"He gave it all:—But first he dy'd.
"And had the Dean, in all the Nation,
"No worthy Friend, no poor Relation?
"So ready to do Strangers good,
"Forgetting his own Flesh and Blood?"

Now Grub-street Wits are all employ'd,
With Elegies, the Town is cloy'd:
Some Paragraph in ev'ry Paper,
To *curse* the *Dean,* or *bless* the *Drapier.*[1]

The Doctors tender of their Fame,
Wisely on me lay all the Blame:
"We must confess his Case was nice;
"But he would never take Advice:
"Had he been rul'd, for ought appears,
"He might have liv'd these Twenty Years:
"For when we open'd him we found,
"That all his vital Parts were sound."

From *Dublin* soon to *London* spread,
'Tis told at Court, the Dean is dead.[2]

Kind Lady *Suffolk* [3] in the Spleen,
Runs laughing up to tell the [Queen],
The [Queen] so Gracious, Mild, and Good,
Cries, "Is he gone? 'Tis time he shou'd.
"He's dead you say; [Why, let him] rot;

---

[1] The Author supposes, that the Scriblers of the prevailing Party, which he always opposed, will libel him after his Death; but that others, who remember the Service he had done to Ireland, under the Name of M. B. Drapier, by utterly defeating the destructive Project of Wood's Half-pence, in five Letters to the People of Ireland, at that Time read universally, and convincing every Reader, will remember him with Gratitude.

[2] The Dean supposeth himself to dye in Ireland.

[3] Mrs Howard, afterwards Countess of Suffolk, then of the Bed-chamber to the Queen, professed much Favour for the Dean. The Queen then Princess, sent a dozen times to the Dean (then in London) with her Command to attend her; which at last he did, by Advice of all his Friends. She often sent for him afterwards, and always treated him very Graciously. He taxed her with a Present worth Ten Pounds, which she promised before he should return to Ireland, but on his taking Leave, the Medals were not ready.

"I'm glad [the medals were] forgot.[4]

"I promis'd [him, I own, but] when?

"I only [was a Princess] then;

"But now as Consort of [a King]

"You know 'tis quite a different Thing."

Now, *Chartres* [5] at Sir *R[obert]'s* Levee,

Tells, with a Sneer, the Tidings heavy:

"Why, is he dead without his Shoes?

(Cries *B[ob]*[6]) "I'm sorry for the News;

"Oh, were the Wretch but living still,

"And, in his Place my good Friend *Will* [7];

---

[4] *The Medals were to be sent to the Dean in four Months, but [She forgot, or thought them too dear. The Dean being in Ireland sent Mrs Howard a piece of plad made in that Kingdom, which the Queen seeing took it from her and wore it herself, and sent to the Dean for as much as would clothe herself and Children—desiring he would send the charge of it. He did the former: it cost 35l. but he said he would have nothing except the medals: he went next summer to England and was treated as usual, and she being then Queen, Ye Dean was promised a settlement in England but return'd as he went, and instead of receiving of her intended favours or ye medals hath been ever since under her Majesty's displeasure.]*

[5] *Chartres is a most infamous, vile Scoundrel, grown from a Foot-Boy, or worse, to a prodigious Fortune both in England and Scotland: He had a Way of insinuating himself into all Ministers under every Change, either as Pimp, Flatterer, or Informer. He was Tryed at Seventy for a Rape, and came off by sacrificing a great Part of his Fortune (he is since dead, but this Poem still preserves the Scene and Time it was writ in.)*

[6] *Sir Robert Walpole, Chief Minister of State, treated the Dean in 1726, with great Distinction, invited him to Dinner at Chelsea, with the Dean's Friends chosen on Purpose; appointed an Hour to talk with him of Ireland, to which Kingdom and People the Dean found him no great Friend; for he defended Wood's Project of Half-pence, &c. The Dean would see him no more; and upon his next Year's return to England, Sir Robert on an accidental Meeting, only made a civil Compliment, and never invited him again.*

[7] *Mr. William Pultney, from being Mr. [Walpole]'s intimate Friend, detesting his Administration, became his mortal Enemy, and joyned with my Lord Bolingbroke, to expose him in an excellent Paper, called the Craftsman, which is still continued.*

"Or, had a Mitre on his Head
"Provided *Bolingbroke*[8] were dead."
Now, *Curl* [9] his Shop from Rubbish drains;
Three genuine Tomes of *Swift's* Remains.
And then, to make them pass the glibber,
Revis'd by *Tibbalds, Moore,* and *Cibber.*[10]
He'll treat me as he does my Betters.
Publish my Will, my Life, my Letters.[11]
Revive the Libels born to dye;
Which POPE must bear, as well as I.

Here shift the Scene, to represent
How those I love, my Death lament.
Poor POPE will grieve a Month; and GAY
A Week; and ARBUTHNOTT a Day.

---

[8] Henry St. John, Lord Viscount Bolingbroke, Secretary of State
to Queen Anne of blessed Memory. *He is reckoned the most Universal Genius in Europe;* [Walpole] *dreading his Abilities, treated
him most injuriously, working with* [King George] *who forgot his
Promise of restoring the said Lord, upon the restless Importunity of*
[Sir Robert Walpole].

[9] Curl, *hath been the most infamous Bookseller of any Age or
Country: His Character in Part may be found in Mr.* POPE's *Dunciad. He published three Volumes all charged on the Dean, who
never writ three Pages of them: He hath used many of the Dean's
Friends in almost as vile a Manner.*

[10] *Three stupid Verse Writers in London, the last to the Shame
of the Court, and the highest Disgrace to Wit and Learning, was
made Laureat. Moore, commonly called Jemmy Moore, Son of
Arthur Moore, whose Father was Jaylor of Monaghan in Ireland. See
the Character of Jemmy Moore, and Tibbalds, Theobald in the Dunciad.*

[11] Curl *is notoriously infamous for publishing the Lives, Letters,
and last Wills and Testaments of the Nobility and Ministers of
State, as well as of all the Rogues, who are hanged at Tyburn. He
hath been in Custody of the House of Lords for publishing or forging
the Letters of many Peers; which made the Lords enter a Resolution
in their Journal Book, that no Life or Writings of any Lord should
be published without the Consent of the next Heir at Law, or
Licence from their House.*

St. John himself will scarce forbear,
To bite his Pen, and drop a Tear.
The rest will give a Shrug, and cry,
I'm sorry; but we all must dye.
Indifference Clad in Wisdom's Guise,
All Fortitude of Mind supplies:
For how can stony Bowels melt,
In those who never Pity felt;
When *We* are lash'd, *They* kiss the Rod;
Resigning to the Will of God.

The Fools, my Juniors by a Year,
Are tortur'd with Suspence and Fear.
Who wisely thought my Age a Screen,
When death approach'd, to stand between:
The Screen remov'd, their Hearts are trembling,
They mourn for me without dissembling.

My female Friends, whose tender Hearts,
Have better learn'd to Act their Parts,
Receive the News in *doleful Dumps*,
"The Dean is Dead, (*and what is Trumps?*)
"Then Lord have Mercy on his Soul.
"(Ladies I'll venture for the *Vole.*)
"Six Dean's they say must bear the Pall.
"(I wish I knew what *King* to call.)
"Madam, your Husband will attend
"The Funeral of so good a Friend.
"No Madam, 'tis a shocking Sight,
"And he's engag'd To-morrow Night!
"My Lady *Club* wou'd take it ill,
"If he shou'd fail her at *Quadrill.*
"He lov'd the Dean. (*I led a Heart.*)
"But dearest Friends, they say, must part.

"His Time was come, he ran his Race;
"We hope he's in a better Place."

Why do we grieve that Friends should dye?
No Loss more easy to supply.
One Year is past; a different Scene;
No further mention of the Dean;
Who now, alas, no more is mist,
Than, if he never did exist.
Where's now this Fav'rite of *Apollo?*
Departed; *and his Works must follow:*
Must undergo the common Fate;
His Kind of Wit is out of Date.
Some Country Squire to *Lintot* [12] goes,
Enquires for SWIFT in Verse and Prose:
Says *Lintot,* "I have heard the Name:
"He dy'd a Year ago." The same.
He searches all his Shop in vain;
"Sir you may find them in *Duck-lane*[13]:
"I sent them with a Load of Books,
"Last *Monday,* to the Pastry-cooks.
"To fancy they cou'd live a Year!
"I find you're but a Stranger here.
"The Dean was famous in his Time;
"And had a Kind of Knack at Rhyme:
"His way of Writing now is past;
"The Town hath got a better Taste:
"I keep no antiquated Stuff;
"But, spick and span I have enough.
"Pray, do but give me leave to shew 'em,
"Here's *Colley Cibber's* Birth-day Poem.
"This Ode you never yet have seen,

---

[12] Bernard Lintot, *a Bookseller in* London, Vide *Mr.* Pope's Dunciad.
[13] *A Place where old Books are sold in* London.

"By [*Stephen Duck*], upon the Queen.
"Then, here's a Letter finely penn'd
"Against the *Craftsman* and his Friend;
"It clearly shews that all Reflection
"On Ministers, is Disaffection.
"Next, here's Sir *R[obert]'s Vindication*,[14]
"And Mr. *Henly's* last Oration[15]:
"The Hawkers have not got 'em yet,
"Your Honour please to buy a Set?
"Here's *Wolston's*[16] Tracts, the twelfth Edition;
" 'Tis read by ev'ry Politician:
"The Country Members, when in Town,
"To all their Boroughs send them down:
"You never met a Thing so smart;
"The Courtiers have them all by Heart:
"Those Maids of Honour (who can read)
"Are taught to use them for their Creed.
'The rev'rend Author's good Intention,
"Hath been rewarded with a Pension:
"He doth an Honour to his Gown,
"By bravely running *Priest-craft* down:
"He shews, as sure as GOD's in *Gloc'ster*,
"That [*Jesus*] was a Grand Impostor:
"That all his Miracles were Cheats,

---

[14] [Walpole] *hath a Set of Party Scriblers, who do nothing else but write in his Defence.*

[15] Henly *is a Clergyman who wanting both Merit and Luck to get Preferment, or even to keep his Curacy in the Established Church, formed a new Conventicle, which he calls an Oratory. There, at set Times, he delivereth strange Speeches compiled by himself and his Associates, who share the Profit with him: Every Hearer pays a Shilling each Day for Admittance. He is an absolute Dunce, but generally reputed crazy.*

[16] Wolston *was a Clergyman, but for want of Bread, hath in several Treatises, in the most blasphemous Manner, attempted to turn Our Saviour and his Miracles into Ridicule. He is much caressed by many great Courtiers, and by all the Infidels, and his Books read generally by the Court Ladies.*

"Perform'd as Juglers do their Feats:
"The Church had never such a Writer:
"A Shame, he hath not got a Mitre!"

Suppose me dead; and then suppose
A Club assembled at the *Rose;*
Where from Discourse of this and that,
I grow the Subject of their Chat:
And, while they toss my Name about,
With Favour some, and some without;
One quite indiff'rent in the Cause,
My Character impartial draws.

"The Dean, if we believe Report,
"Was never ill receiv'd at Court.
"As for his Works in Verse and Prose,
"I own my self no Judge of those:
"Nor, can I tell what Criticks thought 'em;
"But, this I know, all People bought 'em;
"As with a moral View design'd
"To cure the Vices of Mankind:
"His Vein, ironically grave,
"Expos'd the Fool, and lash'd the Knave:
"To steal a Hint was never known,
"But what he writ, was all his own.

"He never thought an Honour done him,
"Because a Duke was proud to own him:
"Would rather slip aside, and chuse
"To talk with Wits in dirty Shoes:
"Despis'd the Fools with Stars and Garters,
"So often seen caressing *Chartres*[17]:
"He never courted Men in Station,
"*Nor Persons had in Admiration;*

---

[17] *See the Notes before on Chartres.*

"Of no Man's Greatness was afraid,
"Because he sought for no Man's Aid.
"Though trusted long in great Affairs,
"He gave himself no haughty Airs:
"Without regarding private Ends,
"Spent all his Credit for his Friends:
"And, only chose the Wise and Good;
"No Flatt'rers; no Allies in Blood;
"But succour'd Virtue in Distress,
"And seldom fail'd of good Success;
"As Numbers in their Hearts must own,
"Who, but for him, had been unknown.

"With Princes Kept a due Decorum,
"But never stood in Awe before 'em:
"He follow'd *David's* Lesson just,
"*In Princes never put thy Trust.*
"And, would you make him truly sower;
"Provoke him with *a Slave in Power:*
"The [Irish] S[enate], if you nam'd,
"With what Impatience he declaim'd!
"Fair LIBERTY was all his Cry;
"For her he stood prepar'd to die;
"For her he boldly stood alone;
"For her he oft expos'd his own.
"Two Kingdoms,[18] just as Faction led,

---

[18] In the Year 1713, the late Queen was prevailed with by an Address of the House of Lords in England, to publish a Proclamation, promising Three Hundred Pounds to whatever Person would discover the Author of a Pamphlet called, The Publick Spirit of the Whiggs; and in Ireland, in the Year 1724, my Lord Carteret at his first coming into the Government, was prevailed on to issue a Proclamation for promising the like reward of Three Hundred Pounds, to any Person who could discover the Author of a Pamphlet called, The Drapier's Fourth Letter, &c. writ against that destructive Project of coining Half-pence for Ireland; but in neither Kingdoms was the Dean discovered.

"Had set a Price upon his Head;
"But, not a Traytor cou'd be found,
"To sell him for Six Hundred Pound.

"Had he but spar'd his Tongue and Pen,
"He might have rose like other Men:
"But, Power was never in his Thought;
"And, Wealth he valu'd not a Groat:
"Ingratitude he often found,
"And pity'd those who meant the Wound:
"But, kept the Tenor of his Mind,
"To merit well of human Kind:
"Nor made a Sacrifice of those
"Who still were true, to please his Foes.
"He labour'd many a fruitless Hour
"To reconcile his Friends in Power[19];
"Saw Mischief by a Faction brewing,
"While they pursu'd each others Ruin.
"But, finding vain was all his Care,
"He left the Court in meer Despair.

"And, oh! how short are human Schemes!
"Here ended all our golden Dreams.
"What St. John's Skill in State Affairs,
"What Ormond's *Valour*, Oxford's Cares,
"To save their sinking Country lent,
"Was all destroy'd by one Event.

---

[19] Queen Anne's Ministry fell to Variance from the first Year after their Ministry began: Harcourt the Chancellor, and Lord Bolingbroke the Secretary, were discontented with the Treasurer Oxford, for his too much Mildness to the Whig Party; this Quarrel grew higher every Day till the Queen's Death: The Dean, who was the only Person that endeavoured to reconcile them, found it impossible; and thereupon retired to the Country about ten Weeks before that fatal Event: Upon which he returned to his Deanry in Dublin, where for many Years he was worryed by the new People in Power, and had Hundreds of Libels writ against him in England.

"Too soon that precious Life was ended,[20]
"On which alone, our Weal depended.

"When up a dangerous faction starts,[21]
"With Wrath and Vengeance in their Hearts;
"*By solemn League and Cov'nant bound,*
"To ruin, slaughter, and confound;
"To turn Religion to a Fable,
"And make the Government a *Babel:*
"Pervert the Law, disgrace the Gown,
"Corrupt the [Senate], rob the [Crown];
"To sacrifice old [England's] Glory,
"And make her infamous in Story.
"When such a Tempest shook the Land,
"How could unguarded Virtue stand?

"With Horror, Grief, Despair the Dean
"Beheld the dire destructive Scene:
"His Friends in Exile, or the Tower,
"Himself within the Frown of Power[22];
"Pursu'd by base envenom'd Pens,
"Far to the Land of [Slaves] and Fens[23];

---

[20] *In the Height of the Quarrel between the Ministers, the Queen died.*

[21] *Upon Queen* ANNE's *Death the Whig Faction was restored to Power, which they exercised with the utmost Rage and Revenge; impeached and banished the Chief Leaders of the Church Party, and stripped all their Adherents of what Employments they had [after which England was never known to make so mean a figure in Europe: The greatest preferments in the Church in both Kingdoms were given to the most ignorant men. Fanaticks were publickly caressed; Ireland utterly ruined and enslaved; only great Ministers heaping up Millions; and so affairs continue to this 3d. of May 1732, and are likely to remain so].*

[22] *Upon the Queen's Death, the Dean returned to live in Dublin, at his Deanry-House: Numberless Libels were writ against him in England, as a Jacobite; he was insulted in the Street, and at Nights he was forced to be attended by his Servants armed.*

[23] *The Land of* [Slaves] *and Fens, is Ireland.*

"A servile Race in Folly nurs'd,
"Who truckle most, when treated worst.

   "By Innocence and Resolution,
"He bore continual Persecution;
"While Numbers to Preferment rose;
"Whose Merits were, to be his Foes.
"When, *ev'n his own familiar Friends*
"Intent upon their private Ends;
"Like Renegadoes now he feels,
"*Against him lifting up their Heels.*

   "The Dean did by his Pen defeat
"An infamous destructive Cheat.[24]
"Taught Fools their Int'rest how to know;
"And gave them Arms to ward the Blow.
"Envy hath own'd it was his doing,
"To save that helpless Land from Ruin;
"While they who at the Steerage stood,
"And reapt the Profit, sought his Blood.

   "To save them from their evil Fate,
"In him was held a Crime of State.
"A wicked Monster on the Bench,[25]

---

[24] One Wood, a *Hardware-man from England, had a Patent for coining Copper Half-pence in Ireland, to the Sum of* 108,000l. *which in the Consequence, must leave that Kingdom without Gold or Silver (See Drapier's Letters.)*

[25] One W[hitshed] *was then Chief Justice: He had some Years before prosecuted a Printer for a Pamphlet writ by the Dean, to persuade the People of Ireland to wear their own Manufactures. Whitshed sent the Jury down eleven Times, and kept them nine Hours, until they were forced to bring in a special Virdict. He sat as Judge afterwards on the Tryal of the Printer of the Drapier's Fourth Letter; but the Jury, against all he could say or swear, threw out the Bill: All the Kingdom took the Drapier's Part, except the Courtiers, or those who expected Places. The Drapier was celebrated in many Poems and Pamphlets: His Sign was set up in most Streets of Dublin (where many of them still continue) and in several Country Towns.*

"Whose Fury Blood could never quench;
"As vile and profligate a Villain,
"As modern *Scroggs,* or old *Tressilian*[26];
"Who long all Justice.had discarded,
"Nor fear'd he GOD, nor Man regarded;
"Vow'd on the Dean his Rage to vent,
"And make him of his Zeal repent;
"But Heav'n his Innocence defends,
"The grateful People stand his Friends:
"Not Strains of Law, nor Judges Frown,
"Nor Topicks brought to please the [Crown],
"Nor Witness hir'd, nor Jury pick'd,
"Prevail to bring him in convict.

"In Exile[27] with a steady Heart,
"He spent his Life's declining Part;
"Where, Folly, Pride, and Faction sway,
"Remote from ST. JOHN,[28] POPE, and GAY.
"His Friendship there to few confin'd,[29]
"Were always of the midling Kind:
"No Fools of Rank, a mungril Breed,
"Who fain would pass for [Lords] indeed;
"Where Titles give no Right or Power,
"And [Peerage] is a wither'd Flower,[30]

[26] Scroggs was *Chief Justice under King* Charles *the Second: His Judgment always varied in State Tryals, according to Directions from Court.* Tressilian *was a wicked Judge, hanged above three Hundred Years ago.*

[27] *In* Ireland, *which he had Reason to call a Place of Exile; to which Country nothing could have driven him, but the Queen's Death, who had determined to fix him in England, in Spight of the Dutchess of Somerset, &c.*

[28] Henry St. John, *Lord Viscount Bolingbroke, mentioned before.*

[29] *In* Ireland *the Dean was not acquainted with one single Lord Spiritual or Temporal. He only conversed with private Gentlemen of the Clergy or Laity, and but a small Number of either.*

[30] *The Peers of* Ireland *lost their Jurisdiction by one single Act,* [and tamely submitted to the infamous mark of slavery without the least resentment or remonstrance.]

"He would have held it a Disgrace,
"If such a Wretch had known his Face.
"On Rural Squires, that Kingdoms Bane,
"He vented oft his Wrath in vain:
"[Biennial] Squires, to Market brought[31];
"Who sell their Souls and [Votes] for Naught;
"The [Nation stripp'd] go joyful back,
"To [rob] the Church, their Tenants rack,
"Go Snacks with [Rogues and Rapparees[32]]
"And, keep the Peace, to pick up Fees:
"In every Jobb to have a Share,
"A Jayl or [Barrack] to repair[33];
"And turn the [Tax] for publick Roads
"Commodious to their own Abodes.

"Perhaps I may allow, the Dean
"Had too much Satyr in his Vein;
"And seem'd determin'd not to starve it,
"Because no Age could more deserve it.
"Yet, Malice never was his Aim;
"He lash'd the Vice, but spar'd the Name.
"No Individual could resent,
"Where Thousands equally were meant.
"His Satyr points at no Defect,
"But what all Mortals may correct:
"For he abhorr'd that senseless Tribe,
"Who call it Humour when they jibe:

---

[31] The [Parliament, as they call it, in Ireland meet but once in two years, and after having given five times more than they can afford return home to reimburse themselves by all country jobs and oppressions of which some few only are mentioned.]

[32] [The Highwaymen in Ireland, are, since the late wars there, usually called Rapparees, which was a name given to those Irish soldiers who in small parties used at that time to plunder Protestants.]

[33] [The army in Ireland are lodged in Barracks, the building and repairing whereof and other charges have cost a prodigious sum to that unhappy Kingdom.]

"He spar'd a Hump, or crooked Nose,
"Whose Owners set not up for Beaux.
"True genuine Dullness mov'd his Pity,
"Unless it offer'd to be witty.
"Those, who their Ignorance confess'd,
"He ne'er offended with a Jest;
"But laugh'd to hear an Idiot quote,
"A Verse from *Horace*, learn'd by Rote.

"He knew an hundred pleasant Stories,
"With all the Turns of *Whigs* and *Tories*:
"Was chearful to his dying Day,
"And Friends would let him have his Way.

"He gave the little Wealth he had,
"To build a House for Fools and Mad:
"And shew'd by one satyric Touch,
"No Nation wanted it so much:
"That Kingdom[34] he hath left his Debtor,
"I wish it soon may have a Better."

---

[34] Meaning Ireland, where he now lives, and probably may dye.